Katy Colins learned there is always a second chance in life.

Jilted before her wedding, she sold all she owned, filled a backpack and booked a one-way ticket to the other side of the world.

Her solo travels inspired her to pen 'The Lonely Hearts Travel Club' series and saw her dubbed the 'Backpacking Bridget Jones' by the global media. And, in a stunning twist of fate, Katy found her happy-ever-after by marrying the journalist who shared her story with the world.

She now lives in the middle of England with her husband, John, and two young children.

You can find out more about Katy, her writing and her travels at www.katycolins.com or @notwedordead on social media platforms.

Also by Katy Colins
Chasing the Sun

The Lonely Heart Travel Club series:
Destination: Thailand
Destination: India
Destination: Chile

How to Say Goodbye

Katy Colins

ONE PLACE. MANY STORIES

HQ
An imprint of HarperCollinsPublishers Ltd.
1 London Bridge Street
London SE1 9GF

This edition 2019

1
First published in Great Britain by
HQ, an imprint of HarperCollinsPublishers Ltd. 2019

ISBN PB: 978-0-00-820222-4

MIX
Paper from
responsible sources
FSC™ C007454

This book is produced from independently certified FSC paper
to ensure responsible forest management.

For more information visit: www.harpercollins.co.uk/green

This book is set in 11.85/15.5 pt. Sabon

Printed and bound by
CPI Group, Croydon CR0 4YY

Dad, I think you'd like this one.

'That it will never come again is
what makes life so sweet'
- EMILY DICKINSON

Prologue

I straightened my chiffon scarf so the small forget-me-nots lay flat against my crisp, white shirt. A quick tug of my sleeves, brushing off imaginary fluff, a pat of my hair, tied back in a neat ponytail, and I was as ready as I would ever be. My rubber-soled shoes allowed me to silently do the last check of the small room. Every seat was presentable – the flowers arranged just so – and the windows and mirrors were spotless. Not a fingerprint or smudge in sight. The lights were set to the correct level, the gaudy air freshener that had been here when I'd arrived was where it belonged – in the bin – the synthetic lily of the valley scent no longer catching at the back of your throat. I smiled at the calming space. It looked perfect.

It had been another late night, preparing for today and the other services I had this week. I could hear my boss Frank's voice warning me that I was going to end up burnt out if I wasn't careful. I'd already had niggles with my neck and shoulders that he was convinced were stress-related, despite my insistences that I was fine. I'd catch up on sleep this weekend, I promised myself.

The sound of car tyres pulled me away from giving

one of the red ribbons I'd looped though the end of the pews a final flourish. The family hadn't specified a colour scheme but, as Mr Oakes had been a lifelong Liverpool FC fan, I thought they'd appreciate the gesture.

I straightened up and nodded to Leon, who was giving the sound system a once-over. He was my favourite of the team. He understood what I was trying to achieve without too much questioning, usually a slight raising of his bushy grey eyebrows or pressing his thin lips together would be all he'd say about some of my more 'out there' ideas. I ran a finger over the lectern. Clean as a whistle.

'Leon, before I forget, did you get my message about next Wednesday? The Rivers family want to change their dove release from before to after the memorial slot.'

Leon nodded. 'Don't you worry. When would I ever let you down?'

'Thank you.' I was about to mention something else when a soft tinkle of an alarm began playing.

'That's our two-minute warning,' I said, fishing my phone from my pocket, switching it to silent and double-checking the time.

Earlier I'd received a call that the cars had left precisely on time. I'd asked the drivers to take a slight detour that I hoped would bring some comfort to the family, if it went to plan. I had already checked the online route map for any last-minute traffic jams, diversions or roadworks, and had breathed a sigh of relief – everything looked clear.

I'd also made sure to check the weather app in case we needed to provide more umbrellas – Spring had been all over the place. I'd learnt quickly that small things like bottles of water in the cars and even sunscreen could make a huge difference. People didn't remember to take things like that with them on days like these.

'Seriously, Grace.' Leon nodded at my phone, unable to hide a smile. 'An alarm?'

'You get on with your job and I'll get on with mine,' I replied politely.

'I forgot, *organisation is liberation*,' he parroted. I think it was meant to mimic me. A flourish of blush spread across his cheeks at the look I gave him.

I let it go and cleared my throat.

'It's time.'

He composed himself, gave a solemn nod, then pressed play. The room was suddenly filled with the sound of Gerry and the Pacemakers' 'You'll Never Walk Alone'. It played at just the right volume from the hidden speakers that had recently been installed at my suggestion, the sound optimised so that the acoustics were the same for all the guests.

'Show time,' Leon whispered and pulled open the doors.

We took our positions. We were mere background players from then on. There to observe, supervise and, above all, ensure everything went to plan. The family slowly walked in, steely determination etched on their pale faces.

A light oak-veneered coffin was carried over the threshold. Heads bowed, feet shuffled, the odd gasp of breath was just audible over packets of tissues rustling.

As the service got underway, I scanned my eyes around the congregation. Mr Oakes had clearly been a popular man. I'd gone to the liberty of printing off extra orders of service just in case the numbers given by his family were off slightly, and I appeared to be proven right. Nearly every seat was taken.

I sensed Leon smiling at me.

'You're miming the words again,' he whispered. I looked away to hide any sign of blushing. I had a habit of doing that.

Mr Oakes's son, Edward, made his way to the lectern. Each slow step was painful to watch. He tugged at his shirt collar and fidgeted in his black suit. Clearly a trip to the dentist or a gruelling job interview would be a walk in the park compared to this. Some people revelled in being centre stage, no matter what the occasion. Edward Oakes was not one of those people.

He took two deep breaths to compose himself. The microphone whined that he was too close, a jolting sound that clearly didn't help with his nervous state. He jerked back and wiped his glistening forehead.

'I've been asked to give a reading and then introduce the piece of music Dad loved so much.' He swallowed and tried to focus his red-rimmed eyes on the card in his trembling hands. I ran through the short, concise speech in my head. His mother had chosen the text and the song was one they'd danced to on their wedding night.

He cleared his throat once more and began to read.

Before long, guests exited the room, blinking back the bright spring sunlight and exclaiming what a good service it had been.

'He would have been proud.'

'It summed him up perfectly. He'd have been sorry to have missed it.'

I bowed my head as they filed past.

'Grace? Thank you.' Mrs Oakes had come up to me and was now gripping my elbow. Her mascara had smudged and her voice trembled with emotion but she was doing a remarkable job of holding herself together. I wondered how long she would cope, keeping up this pretence.

'You're more than welcome. I hope everything went well?'

She let out a loud sniff. I subconsciously patted in my back pocket for the packet of tissues I always kept with me. She kept in the threat of tears and gave my arm a rub.

'He would have been delighted. I noticed the red ribbons. A lovely touch. I didn't know we'd mentioned him being a Liverpool fan – he was mad for them.' She flicked her eyes heavenward and smiled sadly. 'We were driven past his favourite pub on the way here, where he used to go and watch the games on the big screen. The landlord and the staff all lined up as we went past. It was very touching. I didn't even know they'd been told the news.'

I'd go and thank the team for pulling that off. I'd had a long chat with the landlord, who'd insisted he do something to mark the passing of one of his locals.

'I'm so pleased it all went to plan. You had quite the turn-out too. Your husband was clearly a much-loved gentleman.'

Mrs Oakes blinked at the guests still making their way out from the ceremony room. For a second it seemed like she'd forgotten why she was here. 'He was.'

'I won't keep you, but if there is anything else you need then please don't hesitate to give me a call.'

She smiled and sniffed again. Her game face going on. 'Oh and thank you for your lovely note, it was very thoughtful.'

I had popped it through her letterbox yesterday evening, wanting to let her know that I was thinking of her. The night before you bury your husband was never going to be a pleasant one.

'You're welcome. My phone number is on there if you ever can't get me at work. Take care of yourself, Mrs Oakes.'

I left her surrounded by her family and friends and allowed myself a slight rush of pride as I walked over to my car. Another success. Mrs Oakes and the other families that I helped would never know the lengths I went to in order to deliver on the day. I was proud of the unseen ways in which I ensured a personal and heartfelt tribute to the people in my care. I took it upon myself to see the side of people that others *don't* see. I knew how important this was. It made the late nights, extra work and long shifts worth it – knowing I had done as much as I possibly could.

This was not a dress rehearsal, after all. You only get one chance at the perfect goodbye.

Chapter 1

'Morning, Mrs Craig. Can you believe it's Friday already?' I sang, opening the door.

Mrs Craig stayed silent.

'It's set to be another cold one this weekend. I just hope we don't get the snow that they're predicting. Can you believe it, snow in March? I wouldn't want that to ruin your big day.'

There was still no sound from Mrs Craig.

'Right, I'm going to put the kettle on.'

Leaving Mrs Craig to it, I settled at my desk to have my breakfast, first making sure to pop out the tiny white pills that must be taken on an empty stomach, just as Doctor Ahmed prescribed. I opened the newspaper and allowed myself ten minutes before the day properly began. Flipping straight to page thirty-four, I checked that all the names had been spelled correctly and the text was free from grammatical errors. I still remembered the waves of nausea when I'd noticed they had printed a colon instead of a semi-colon for Mrs Briars back in 2015. I glanced at the clock. I had ten minutes before the rest of the team would be in, so I decided to quickly do a last-minute check of Facebook and Instagram before any interruptions. I tried my hardest not to use those sites at work, but I'd been so busy that I was finding it tough to stay on top of things.

When the doorbell went, I didn't need to check the video monitor to know who was waiting on the doorstep. There she was, a vision in beige. Ms Norris's visits were like clockwork: every Friday morning, the same for the past nine months.

'What is *with* this weather?'

The plump woman tutted, readjusting the flowery chiffon neck scarf that had twisted in the howling gale. It was severely tangled around her saggy, powdered jowls like some sort of butterfly-patterned noose.

'I'm sure I never heard that nice weather man with the funny accent say anything about a hurricane this week. I just don't know if I'm coming or going. One moment they're saying it's warmer than average and the next it's like living in the North Pole. Bring on summer, I say!'

I stood up and hurried to help close the door behind her, crunching on leaves that had blown in like fallen confetti around her sensible black shoes. I'd have to get the Hoover out the minute she left. Tan-coloured tights bagged at her swollen ankles.

'Morning, Ms Norris,' I smiled.

Her normally sleek porcelain grey bob now resembled tousled candy floss.

'I wasn't expecting you to brave it out in this weather.'

'It'll take a bit more than Storm Elmo or whatever ridiculous name they've given this one to keep me indoors. Purdy doesn't watch the weather report, so it doesn't matter one jot to her if it's glacial or a heatwave. When she needs a walk, she needs a walk.'

I peered past Ms Norris, now taking off her thick beige pea coat, to see Purdy tied up to the railings outside. The flat-faced pug, also beige, was shivering dramatically.

'Er… will she be OK out there?'

Ms Norris wafted a liver-spotted hand, red-lacquered nails flashing in front of my face. 'She's the ultimate drama queen, that one.'

I nodded uncertainly. The pug had, thankfully, stopped shaking and was now more interested in the leaves skittering across the small drive.

'Linda not in yet?' She glanced over at the empty chair and blank screen of Linda's computer. The first day Ms Norris had come in to the office she had originally been booked in with Linda, but after a series of 'creative differences', i.e. a bit of a personality clash, she was placed with me and we'd been working together ever since.

'Not yet.'

'Hmph. I should have a word with Frank about her timekeeping… Shall I just go through, dear?' Ms Norris asked, already on her way down the corridor to the only meeting room. 'I'll have a cuppa, if you're making one.'

I snapped back to attention. 'Oh, of course, the kettle has just boiled actually.'

'So, I've been thinking about songs.' Ms Norris cleared her throat before I had the chance to put down her well-thumbed file and sit down opposite her.

'Songs?'

'Yes. Songs.'

I flicked a thumb through the many papers, frowning. 'I thought we'd covered music?'

Ms Norris adjusted herself in the teal-coloured armchair. 'Well, we had, but I've been thinking about my song choices and, well, I've changed my mind.'

I forced myself to stay impassive. This was the third time Ms Norris had been 'thinking about her song choices' in the last month. Not that it was a problem to amend the details, it just worried me that she would change her mind yet again before her big day.

'Sinatra.'

'Sinatra?'

'I know it has been done to death but I think we should go back to "My Way" and stick with it. I don't know what I was thinking with Vera.'

'Right.' I marked a thick line through 'We'll Meet Again'. 'Any other thoughts whilst I have your notes here?'

'Yes. You can take Blythe Summers off your list too. Her kids have moved her to Brighton to be near them, and spend her numbered days in some council-run nursing home being served cold soup and looking at the sea through grubby windows. Outrageous if you ask me, just so they can relieve some guilt on their part by pretending it's what she wants. I know for a fact that she doesn't even like the seaside that much, and I can't say I blame her!'

I turned to the list of invitees that Ms Norris had given me a while ago. She liked to keep this up to date so that, when the time came, her friend and point of contact, Alma Dawes, would take charge of the plans, knowing the guest list was set to her requirements. 'This is rather fun!' she'd said when we'd first met. 'I've never had a wedding so it feels exciting to be planning a big party!'

But since she'd first visited, we'd scored so many names off – people who had passed away, moved on or, perhaps most often, those she'd had a falling out with, that the guest list was looking a bit thin. But, as Ms Norris said, 'It's my day so I can invite who I want. The rest of them can like it or lump it.'

'Anything else?'

Ms Norris shook her head. 'Nope, that's it for now. Oh! I remembered your Tupperware this week,' she said, struggling to bend down to pick a carrier bag off the floor. She placed the empty box on the table between us with a flourish. 'You excelled yourself this time, Grace.'

I blushed. 'I'm glad you enjoyed them. I'll swap you for a batch of raspberry macarons on your way out. I have to say this was your trickiest one yet.'

Our mini bake-off had started out as an innocent request from Ms Norris for a decent Victoria sponge. She was adamant that none of the coffee shops in town appeared to be able to get this simple recipe right. She proudly told me how, back in the day, she had been a bit of a star baker, but arthritis had limited her repertoire. I was at a loose end so had offered to give it a go; she insisted I used one of her recipes, and it was such a hit that I included a baking session into my weekly routine. I actually looked forward to the challenges she set me and the constructive criticism she liked to spoon out afterwards.

'Did you use caster sugar and not granulated, like I told you?' Her lips set in a thin line.

I nodded.

A warm smile broke out. 'Wonderful. I'll report back next week.' She swallowed a mouthful of tea before continuing. 'So, how are things with you, dear?'

'I'm fine, thank you. Same old, same old.'

'You got anything fun planned for the weekend?'

Same questions week in, week out.

'The usual.'

Same answers week in, week out.

She kept her eyes on me. 'I do wish you'd surprise me one time and tell me that you were sky diving, speed dating or getting a tattoo.' She chuckled at the face I pulled. 'What? It's good to mix things up a little, Grace.'

'Hmm.'

'I know you can't escape death but you can choose to live, and it's a lot more fun with a nice man by your side.' She paused. 'My neighbour was telling me about her niece who's found a lovely chap on this other dating website, Tindem or something. Apparently there are tons of them for single people, all looking for the same thing.'

She probably meant love, but I couldn't help being cynical about the other thing many people on dating sites were looking for. I tried to ignore her pointed stare and burrowed my eyes into the dove leaflet in front of me. It costs £30 more to release a white dove at a wedding than at a funeral. Same company, same dove and same service.

I looked up from the leaflet. The colour of the font and the irregularity of the pricing irritated me. Anyway, I'd sworn off dating since my ex. Henry had well and truly broken my heart, and I didn't much fancy putting it back out there to be broken further.

'Grace? What do you think?'

I forced a smile. 'Yep, I'll look into it.'

'You must. If I was a little younger, then I'd be on there too. You've got youth on your side, Grace, you need to use it before it fades. Right, I'd better be off. Got a lot to do.' She rose to her feet with a struggle. Her joints cracked as she stood.

I handed her the macarons and helped her with her coat. Purdy's ears pricked to attention the second the door opened.

'Bye, Grace. Hope I don't see you soon!'

I laughed politely. Same joke every week. I couldn't take any offence. In my job, no one ever wanted to see me again. *I* wouldn't want to see me again. I watched her carefully waddle down the steps and unfasten Purdy's lead from the railing.

With a final wave, I went to check on Mrs Craig. My regular visits might not make any difference to her day, but they mattered to me.

Chapter 2

A gust of icy wind cut through my winter coat as I waited for the temporary traffic lights to change. Amber pools of light from passing cars lit up the non-stop drizzle that fell from the heavy grey clouds. Darkness curled around me. Last week it had been bright sunshine; the row of forlorn daffodils at the roadside were presumably regretting their optimistic decision to pop open. I awkwardly used my elbow to press the button at the crossing. I'd been trapped there that morning on my way to work, forced to ignore two stocky men wearing grubby hi-viz vests who'd hollered to me from the scaffolding opposite. The workmen had long downed tools and gone home.

I'd stayed much later than I'd planned, working on the final prep for Mr Stuart's big day next week. I hadn't even realised what time it was. Finally, the traffic stopped and the beeps rang out. I still made sure to turn my head two, three times to check the coast was clear before I put a foot in the road. You couldn't be too careful. I'd read recently that the number of road deaths had hit a five-year high.

'Ah, here she is, our saving Grace,' Raj bellowed as I walked into his shop.

'Evening,' I smiled.

'Oh, wait!' He held up a chubby hand and reached the other under the counter, which was covered in neat displays of chewing gum, reams of scratch cards and a plastic cabinet containing e-cigarette liquid. He pulled out a pocket-sized notebook and flicked through it.

'OK, here we go.' He cleared his throat and lowered his voice slightly. 'Hello, Grace. How's life?'

'Fine, thanks.'

'No!'

He made me jump. 'What?'

He sighed loudly and ran a hand across his sweating brow. 'Ah, wait. I've got it wrong. *You're* meant to say how's life and then I reply with, fine, pause, and how's death! Geddit?' He chuckled.

This was Raj's thing. Since I'd bought the flat upstairs and he'd realised who his neighbour was and what she did for a living, he'd decided to use me as some sort of muse for his fledgling stand-up routine. A way to test out naff jokes and build up his material. It had been going on for years. If you asked him what he did he'd tell you he was a comedian, despite never performing for a paying audience in his life. His proper job was running the Minimart-post-office-deli. Every time a witty, or not so witty, one-liner came to him he'd immediately pull out his joke notebook and jot it down. Often I would ask him when he was going to actually perform this material at a stand-up night, but he'd always insist he wasn't ready yet. I could understand why he was reluctant.

'Good one,' I smiled awkwardly. It was marginally better than when he insisted on saying 'Good Mourning' to me, heavily emphasising the mouuuurrning part, then doing a funny thing with his index fingers as if banging an imaginary drum in the air.

'Oh, I've got another too. It came to me when I was helping Rani with the latest stocktake.' He licked his lips and changed his stance as if standing under an imaginary spotlight. 'Every year we get sent birthday cards, but how about a deathiversary card? They would really put the *fun* into funerals.' He waited for my reaction.

Inside I cringed but, not wanting to hurt his feelings, I forced myself to clap weakly. 'Ha, yeah, that would be, er, interesting.'

'It needs a bit extra work that one. Oh, guess what!'

'What?'

'No, you need to guess!'

I pretended to look like I was deep in thought, clearly taking too long to come up with a suitable suggestion for this slightly tedious game.

'Ok, I'll tell you. You won't get it anyway. Peter Kay messaged me back!' He did this funny jazz hands thing and had his mouth so wide open I could see the fillings on his bottom row of teeth.

'That's, er, nice. Do I know him?'

'He's a famous comedian, Grace. He did that whole thing about garlic bread...'

I was still lost.

'Never mind. He's just, like, a *big deal* on the circuit.

And now I guess I am too!' He paused, the smile faltering slightly at my lukewarm reaction.

'So how do you know this Peter King?'

'Kay. I follow him on Twitter.'

I knew he was expecting me to match his levels of excitement.

He paused then scrunched up his face, thinking. 'Well, he didn't *exactly* message me. He liked a tweet. That joke I told you last week, how thinking about burial plots is the last thing you need.'

Twitter had never been my thing. From the looks of his timeline it was just him spamming comedians with some of his material. Also, I knew for a fact that Raj used a younger – and much more handsome – Bollywood actor as his profile picture. He'd shown me one time, when he'd tried to explain about likes and retweets.

'But hey, when I do go on tour I can now say *as liked by Peter Kay*!' He spread his hands across the counter as if presenting a banner.

'Isn't that a lie though?'

'Nah, a bit of celebrity endorsement will do wonders for my career. Trust me.'

'But won't this Peter Kay find out?'

Raj shook his head. 'He's a busy man, Grace. Far too busy to be worrying about the likes of me. Well, for the moment at least!' He chuckled. 'Anyway, what can I get for you? The usual?' He had thankfully put his joke book away.

I didn't mind that he found my job such an amusing source of entertainment. I was used to people's extreme reactions when they found out what I did. Being a funeral arranger is either a serious conversation starter or an awkward conversation killer. It was also one reason why I wouldn't play the dating game, despite Ms Norris's kind encouragement. The one and only time that I'd reluctantly agreed to go for a coffee date, just to get my mum off my back, it had ended in complete disaster. It was bad enough that it wasn't Henry sitting across the table from me. Instead it was a slightly anaemic man named Ian whose eyebrows were so well groomed I struggled to lower my eyes to the rest of his face. When I did, it wasn't worth it.

I'd been dreading him asking me, 'So, what do you do?'

Explaining that I work with death on a daily basis is hard for others to get their heads around. I'm sure other people don't go on dates and discuss the last funeral they went to, but Ian felt he needed to tell me, in detail, all about his grandad, Ron, who'd died in July 2007. I could almost taste the egg vol-au-vents served at his wake. Not exactly pillow talk. I shuddered as Ian and his overpreened eyebrows swam in my head.

'Yes, thanks, just these.'

I watched Raj place a pint of milk and a small granary loaf into the Bag for Life I always carried.

*

Back in my flat, my coat neatly hanging on the coat stand that Mum had bought me as a moving-in present

– slightly excessive to have a whole stand for just me but it passed my practicability test so it stayed. I took my notebook out of my bag and sat down at my small kitchen table to see what I needed to tick off that weekend. It was one of those compact space-saver ones with sides that could flip up if I needed to create room for more people. I wasn't even sure it worked but it was nice to have the option.

- Check smoke alarms and change battery if required
- Sanitise sponges
- Clean inside the microwave (I made my own all-purpose cleaner using a plant spray bottle, baking soda and water)
- Wash the skirting boards

See! I didn't have time to be larking about and bungee jumping or whatever silly things Ms Norris expected me to do. I filled my free time adequately, and before I knew it Monday would roll around again. I was very good at keeping on top of clutter in my flat, something that I was extremely proud of. Last year, Linda, my not-so-secret secret Santa, had bought me a book on cleaning that apparently *everyone* was reading – for what reason I have no idea. I'd flicked through it so as not to offend her, and made some exclamations on the 'useful tips' inside, but Linda had never been to my house, so could hardly know that I didn't need this. Linda's book had ended up in the charity shop bag.

Before starting anything else, I had something I needed to do. I flipped open my laptop. As I waited for the page to load I thought back to the first time I'd done this, which in turn reminded me of the first time I saw a dead body. It was during my extensive training. The female corpse was lying under a white sheet in a sterile room, with glazed eyes and a gaping mouth. She looked so... well, dead. We weren't told her name, just that the woman had died of lung cancer in her early eighties. Routine. I vowed then to find out as much about the people in my care as I could. That woman lying stiffly on the cold steel table had a name, an identity and a back story. This desire to discover more about my clients became the motivation behind my quest to provide the perfect funerals for them, and my secret weapon had arrived in the form of Facebook.

I had been working with the family of a nineteen-year-old, Mollie Stevenson, who'd died after being hit by a car whilst crossing the road. Like many nineteen-year-olds she had been obsessed with social media, and her family proudly told me that her Facebook account had been memorialised by one of her friends. Intrigued, I'd created a Facebook profile, never having had much need for one before, and had then searched for this memorial page after work one night. It was like being given an invitation into the private life of this bubbly, happy and sociable teenage girl.

Her whole world was available for anyone to see. There were recent statuses at pop concerts, nights out and pictures of hipster meals she'd tried; endless snaps and pouting selfies with the same group of friends; numerous check-ins at places around town where she liked to go.

I made sure to stay as discreet as possible, only looking and never commenting, amazed at the picture I could build up of someone's life, even once they were dead.

I suddenly had a wealth of information about Mollie and her habits, hobbies and likes, allowing me to get creative with ways we could incorporate this into her funeral. Her mum and dad were understandably inconsolable and, although eager to give her the best send-off, you could clearly see that they were too lost in the tunnel of grief, shock and pain to think of ways to honour their daughter.

Which is where I stepped in.

Over a couple of evenings after work, I trawled through her page, and those of her friends, and was able to imagine the life Mollie had led. Her family were delighted with my suggestions of ways we could make the funeral more personal for their wonderful daughter. Obviously, I never admitted where I'd learnt this information. When Frank asked, I'd told a white lie, saying that my own (fictional) nineteen-year-old cousin loved the same sort of things that Mollie did – the trendy milkshake bar she liked to hang out at, the hula-themed nightclub in town, Arianna Grande. I knew I was stretching the definition of honesty by doing this research, but I was sure it was the right thing to do. It was as if Mollie herself was helping to plan her own funeral.

All the subterfuge was worth it when Mollie's parents came up to me after the packed-out service, thanking me for going the extra mile. I hadn't felt a high like it. Guests wore bright floral leis, had 'One Last Time' playing as they entered, and drank freakshakes at the wake. We'd managed to turn the desperately sad occasion into a unique tribute to this young woman who'd been taken way too soon.

*

Thanks to Mollie, I had learned that most people lived their lives online, leaving a trail of breadcrumbs for others to discover even after they've died. For every funeral after Mollie's, I scheduled in time to do my own research into the lives of the people I was lucky enough to be taking care of. After all, you can't take this day back and repeat it. We all only get one shot at a goodbye. I took it upon myself to make sure that, for my clients, it was the closest thing to perfect it could be.

Of course, this wasn't without its obstacles. Some people's Facebook accounts were set to 'private', although it was sometimes still possible to view the biographical information they'd listed, as well as their lists of friends – many of whom had public accounts, which made it possible to glean information second-hand. Another hiccup was that many people simply didn't *have* Facebook accounts. For my older clients – those who hadn't become 'silver-surfers' – it was a little trickier to track them down online and build up a picture of their full lives. However, they were often in the albums of their family members, mentioned in a status celebrating a birthday or anniversary, or snapped along with their grandchildren.

Aside from Facebook and the other social media sites, there were other online avenues to explore. Google searches yielded newspaper articles, profiles on business websites, features in local community forums. Everyone, it seems, has some kind of digital footprint, and anything I could find about my clients would help to inform how their funeral would play out. This is our last moment in the spotlight, after all, and it's the personal touches that people remember, even years later. I've had families come to me because of the funerals I'd arranged for people they knew, telling me that the extra details had meant so much, and had made sure it was memorable for the right reasons.

I sometimes struggled with encouraging Frank to think outside the box – not that he knew where I was getting these bolts of creativity from. He was a traditionalist at heart. He was fine with families requesting mourners wear Hawaiian shirts, matching colours, or even a quirky memento of the deceased's hobby, as long as it wasn't too garish. But he wasn't as quick to get on board with the extras, like the time we had a unicorn leading the funeral procession. This was something I'd organised for a young girl, Ava Harper, aged just seven, who I'd learned had been obsessed with them. Her recent birthday party had been unicorn-themed, and I managed to find a pure white horse whose owner dressed her up as a unicorn for regular visits to the children's hospital. Casting her red-rimmed, exhausted eyes on the tastefully decorated horse, I saw her mother smile for the first time since meeting her.

Linda and Frank didn't know that I used social media to create my personal goodbyes. It probably wasn't against the rules, but I'd decided it wasn't something I needed to shout about. It was another reason I tended to do my digging at home, in the evenings or weekends. I had three services coming up that I was struggling to find details for. I was soon lost in the timelines and news feeds of people I would never get to properly meet in real life.

It was only when my stomach rumbled that I checked my watch and realised I should probably think about starting dinner.

There was a game I liked to play, which was to open the cupboard with my eyes shut and pull out a tin, and whatever I landed on was my supper. When I'd told Ms Norris about the game a few months ago she'd burst into such a fit of laughter I was worried I'd have to call an ambulance. It wasn't right, a woman her age having such a reaction like that. I worried about her health at the best of times. When she'd finally composed herself and realised that I wasn't laughing along too, she'd tilted her head to one side and gently patted my hand and given me a strange, desperate sort of look. I busied about and made her another cup of tea. She's not mentioned it again and neither have I.

But I still carried on playing my game.

Chapter 3

It was my birthday. I was grateful that so far that morning neither Linda nor Frank had made a fuss. Or even acknowledged it. I'd had a text from my mum telling me she'd give me my present when she saw me next. She was busy travelling around Latvia with a new boyfriend in his retro campervan, so I wasn't holding my breath. I'd not heard from anyone else, but then I wasn't sure who I expected to get in touch. The one person I foolishly still wanted to hear from had long forgotten about me.

The first birthday after Henry had left me was the worst. By the end of the day I felt wrung out from all the adrenalin that had coursed through me every time my emails pinged or my phone rang, imagining it was him ringing, him emailing. Of course he hadn't sent me a card in the post, he hadn't sent me anything at all, not even a text message. That evening I cried and cried. He was the only person I wanted to hear from on my special day, and I got nothing. These days I didn't raise any hope of hearing from him, and the acceptance did make the hurt a little easier to bear.

'Ah, Grace, there you are.' Frank wandered out of the employee bathroom wiping his hands on his pale grey suit trousers, breaking my thoughts. 'Team meeting in five, guys!'

He wasn't going to sing Happy Birthday like last year, was he? I wasn't sure I could stand that level of embarrassment.

Luckily, as we took our seats around his messy oval table, there wasn't a cake or candles or streamers to be seen. I was safe.

'Hope you've all had good weekends?' he asked Linda and I.

'Oh yes, excellent.' Linda slurped her tea. She would only ever drink out of the colour-changing unicorn mug that wasn't dishwasher-friendly. 'Ladies' night at the Swan.' She gave a knowing smile. 'You should come along one of these days, Grace. Us single gals need to stick together.'

I laughed awkwardly. Linda was at least ten years older than me and fancied herself as a bit of a man-eater since her bitter divorce four years ago.

'Maybe…'

'Grace?' Frank asked. 'Good weekend?'

'Yep, just a quiet one for me…' I coughed as my voice crackled, reminding me that this was the first time I'd spoken to anyone since Raj in his shop on Friday evening.

'Good. Right then.' Frank clapped his large hands together. 'Let's get down to business. Linda, an update from Coffin Club please?'

Her eyes lit up. 'I think this was the best one yet! Over two hundred exhibitors from across the world; there was loads on offer. I felt so inspired. You should come along to the next one, Grace.'

'Er, no, well, I –'

'Grace wouldn't go if you paid her, isn't that right?' Frank chuckled.

I preferred to stay out of anything to do with Coffin Club, the affectionate name given to the annual Funeral Expo held in London. I'd managed to think up excuses to avoid going every year, until Frank had given up asking me. Linda liked to make a weekend of it anyway; she would meet up with some of her industry friends and gossip about changes to the profession, returning with armfuls of freebies.

Frank, along with my mum, thought they knew why I'd left my life in London behind me. I'd told them the cost of living, pollution, and sheer volume of people wasn't for me. No one knew the real reason I'd fled the capital, and that was how it was going to stay.

'Something like that.' I cleared my throat.

'As usual, there was showcasing of the most innovative products. Did you know that you can now add QR codes to gravestones?!'

Linda was always like this after the expo, returning buoyed up by ideas and ways we could be more future-thinking as a business, until Frank would have to gently bring her back down to earth. The funeral industry didn't do forward-thinking very well. The ideas she always seemed most fired up about were all high-concept, and usually came with a high price tag.

'Sorry, you know I'm not so up on my technology-speak,' Frank admitted with a self-conscious chuckle.

'A QR code. You know, those funny little black and

white squares, a bit like a barcode, that you can scan on your phone?' Still blank. 'Never mind, you'd know one if you saw it. Anyway, they're encouraging funeral homes to install this software so the families can input their loved ones' details and then anyone with a QR reader at a gravesite can just scan it and the whole history of the person comes up!'

'Next you'll be telling me they're adding phone screens and Facebook pages to tombstones,' Frank guffawed.

Linda leant forward excitedly. 'Actually there's a company in Slovenia, I think, who incorporate fourteen-inch touchscreens onto headstones. At the touch of a button they share information about the deceased's life, with videos and photos. It even has the ability to play films!'

'Can you imagine!' Frank said, half choking on the words. 'The cost would be extortionate.'

I spotted Linda's shoulders sink.

'It's a bit unusual,' I said, 'but it would be fascinating. Imagine wandering amongst graves, being able to find out the stories of the names written in the stone. Stories that we'd never get to know without some serious digging around the genealogy department of the library. It would be a great way to keep their memories alive.'

'Exactly. Surely we could add it to the maybe list?'

'I've been in this business for nearly forty years and never heard of such a thing. But I guess times have changed. People want bells and whistles and eco, vegan, plastic-free funerals nowadays...' Frank trailed off, looking miserable. 'OK, let's move on. Can we have an update on the recent services? Grace, if you could start first please?'

I flicked through my notepad, ignoring a slight huff from Linda that her idea had been rejected so quickly.

'Sure, well the Davidson family burial was well attended and went without a hitch –'

'Ah, let me stop you there. I actually have my own feedback somewhere.' Frank flicked through his folder. 'Ah, here.' He picked up a torn white envelope. 'It was addressed to me but really it should have gone to you.' I felt the rush of heat on my cheeks as I read the heartfelt thank you card from Mrs Davidson for the funeral we'd arranged for her husband, Ernest. A keen fisherman and golfer who'd lost his long battle with throat cancer. 'Another one singing your praises.'

'You're going to need to find another blank wall to fill soon, Grace,' Linda said.

'I hope that's not a hint of jealousy, Linda?' Frank let out a tinkle of a chuckle.

'Of course not! I was just pointing out how well Grace is doing. I think it's very sweet receiving a card and all,' she said, crossing her arms in front of her ample chest, belittling the heartfelt words from Mrs Davidson. 'But can we also remember that I've brought in yet another prepaid funeral plan sign-up?'

'Yes! Terribly sorry for not mentioning that. A new monthly record, actually,' Frank spluttered.

Linda sat back in her chair and smiled smugly. People like Ms Norris, who paid upfront, and got their big day all planned out and in order whilst they were still with us, made a huge difference to the company accounts.

I needed to up my game. Linda was right, the many incredible acknowledgements from families I'd helped were heartwarming, but they didn't always bring any further business – unlike the prepaid sign-ups that she was renowned for. Linda had this can-do attitude that I'd never seen in anyone before. I wanted to stay positive and trust in the word-of-mouth recommendations from my personal funeral services, but that wasn't something that could be as easily counted as numbers on a page.

'The truth is we all need to think outside the box more, without any extra budget unfortunately. Instead of pie-in-the-sky technology fads we should focus on securing more prepaid sign-ups, getting more five-star reviews, and making the effort to push what we do out there into the community – as well as continuing to provide excellent customer service.'

Simple.

'Another thing I wanted to mention is the Love of My Light service. I know it's ages away, but I want us to get a little more creative with it this year.'

The Love of My Light service was a sort of remembrance event held in the church at the top of town in November. There was something soul-nourishing about standing amongst those who were there for one reason: to remember the person or people they had lost, to light a candle in their honour, and to support one another in whatever stage of grief they were.

'Last year was great,' Frank flashed a look to Linda; it

had been her project for the past few years. 'But I'd like us to get more community-focussed. I'm not saying we should use it as a marketing opportunity, but I think it makes sense to make sure the people of Ryebrook know what we're able to offer. Great – I think that's everything. Back to it, team!'

*

'What do you think about tribute wreaths, dear, the ones that spell something out, like "Nan" or "Poppa"?' Ms Norris asked, shuffling through the pamphlets spread in front of her. 'I've never had my name in lights so maybe my name in petals is the next best thing? But, then again, perhaps they are a little on the garish side. I don't want people to go away from the day discussing the lovely service that was ruined by an in-your-face flower arrangement.'

'Hmm.'

'Or, even worse, imagine if the florist made a mistake with the spelling! Grace?'

'Sorry,' I shook my head. 'I was miles away.'

'Please tell me it was some delicious daydream about an attractive man?'

'Er, no.'

She let out a deep sigh followed by a wink. 'Shame. Well you were certainly lost in some deep thought. You need to watch you don't get wrinkles frowning away like that.'

I raised my eyebrows dramatically to iron out any

creases. 'Sorry, very rude of me. What were you saying about flowers?'

'That can wait. Come on, tell me what's on your mind. I've not seen you looking so perplexed before.'

I wafted a hand. 'It's just a work thing.'

'Linda?'

'No – listen, it doesn't matter.'

'Oh blimey, Grace, will you spit it out? A problem shared is a problem halved.'

I took a deep breath. Over the many months of Ms Norris's weekly visits we had built up an odd friendship, one I felt that I could trust enough with what was going on in my head.

'Well, I feel like I need to do something to attract more business. Linda is doing a really good job at bringing in more prepaid funeral plans, and I just feel like I'm letting the side down.'

'Ah, and how is Lovely Linda managing to go about this?'

'Cold calling mostly.'

She let out a sort of 'pfft' noise.

Linda had no fear of calling a very recent widower, or grieving parents, and making it seem like she was helping by reminding them they ought to be considering their own funeral plans. I was much happier in my comfort zone of funeral planning, and getting lost in the detail of personal preparations. I thought it best to leave the families to focus on their grief after the funeral, not to be pestering them to think about how they wanted their own big day to be.

I found it unbelievably tough to ask someone if they'd thought about their own death and, if so, what they wanted their funeral to be like. Of course, I knew how important it was to get things laid out and decisions made so you didn't burden those left behind, but it's still not something people actively choose to think about. Judging by Frank's latest team meeting, I was going to have to get over this, and quickly, whether I liked it or not. My stomach churned at the thought of it.

Ms Norris scrunched up her neat nose, thinking. 'Hmm. Well, you both have different skill sets so the key would be to maximise on yours. I read that once, in a *Bella* magazine article, I think. Anyway, what I'm saying is that you're a *people person*. You're excellent at planning and have a lovely bedside manner. So, do that.'

'Sorry? Do what?'

'Well, I imagine many people are fascinated by what you do, but don't have a clue what that actually is. Why don't you tap into that and use it as a way to break some of the negative stereotypes people must have, as well as encouraging people to get their funeral plans in place?'

I looked at her blankly.

'What I'm thinking is for you to host a sort of Ask a Funeral Arranger event. You could make it a nice and relaxed evening with a friendly, informative Q and A, to show people how warm and lovely you are so they don't feel like they'll be getting the hard sell. In fact, you don't need to sell anything. Just being you will be enough.'

I tried to hide the snort that escaped as she said that. 'I'm not sure.'

'We could pick some of your excellent bakes and serve them with tea and coffee – that would certainly bring the crowds in! I know no one can resist a slice of your apple flapjack.'

'*Your* apple flapjack,' I corrected her.

I appreciated her help, but there was no way I could stand up in a room full of strangers. The thought alone made me feel itchy and uncomfortable. My preferred position was behind the scenes; Linda was the one who took centre stage.

'You don't give yourself enough credit. I'm sure you would surprise yourself. Right, I'd best be getting on, but think about my idea. I'd make sure to come along so at least you would know one friendly face!'

'Thank you.'

I led her to the front door and helped her with her coat. Her heart was in the right place, even if her suggestions were a little off the mark.

'Oh, and Grace?' I turned to see a wide smile on her cheeks. 'Happy birthday.'

She patted a five-pound note into my hands and left.

Chapter 4

Most of my morning had been spent on the phone to the crematorium, trying to stay calm as they explained that staff shortages had meant a host of unexpected delays. They also, like everyone else, tried to blame the recent snow flurries for interfering with their schedule. I downed my second cup of strong coffee, more than my daily quota, just to get me through the nerves of passing on this bad news to the families desperate to lay their loved ones to rest. Each phone call only brought frustration that I couldn't do more. I also still had to work out a way to get some prepaid funeral plans under my belt. It had been a week since our last staff meeting and I had brought in precisely zero, to Linda's three. I'd be taking Ms Norris up on her Ask a Funeral Arranger idea at this rate.

My stomach grumbled so I decided to take a break and have some lunch. I was tucking into a tuna salad when there was a ring on the doorbell. I stopped chewing and peered at the intercom. Frank had positioned it too high, so all I could see was the dark blonde head of a tall man bobbing around the entrance. I double-checked the calendar on my desk; we didn't have anything in the diary. Swallowing too quickly, a piece of romaine lettuce lodged in my throat as I pressed the buzzer.

'I'll be right there,' I rasped, taking my finger from the button to cough louder.

I hurriedly flicked through the diary again. Usually, family visits were arranged so we could make sure they went undisturbed and – crucially – ensure that we wouldn't be talking with our mouths full of lunch. I scanned Linda's messy desk and saw a Post-it note stuck to the bottom of her laptop screen. *Callum Anderson visit, 27th @1pm.* That must be the man bobbing up and down on the doorstep. Cursing Linda and her haphazard organisation style, I stood up and straightened my skirt.

'Good afternoon, so sorry to keep you –' The apology froze in my mouth. The man in front of me was wrapped in a light grey shearling jacket and was very handsome. I wasn't good at dealing with handsome.

'I think I'm a little early. Callum Anderson? I spoke to, er, Linda, I think?'

His deep voice was strained. His bloodshot light blue eyes, behind tortoiseshell glasses, refused to meet mine, and he was wringing his hands together so vigorously I thought he'd pull the skin off.

'Hello, yes, please come in, Callum. I'm Grace, Grace Salmon,' I offered a hand that he took with a strong, firm grip.

His clean, navy trainers were planted outside, as if by stepping over the doormat it would all become real. He teetered cautiously for a few seconds longer, unsure of me and this whole terrifying process he was about to embark on.

'Salmon?' His jaw was tense but his lips curled ever so slightly.

'Yes, like the fish.' Growing up, I had hated my surname. But here, in this job, it brought light relief to those who needed to make that first step into my world, and their unknown future. If I could provoke a hint of a smile with my ridiculous name then that more than made up for the years of teasing at school. 'Would you like to come through? I've just made coffee, if you want one?'

I held the door open wider. He nodded then moved one foot over the step and into the neutrally decorated room.

'Er, yeah, coffee would be great.' He cleared his throat, glancing at the framed picture of a woodland in spring on the wall opposite.

Inoffensive, Linda had claimed as she'd roughly banged a nail into the wall when she went through the last redesign in here. It was marginally better than the daffodils in a watering can that had been there previously.

'Black, no sugar. Thank you.'

After he was seated, I went to get the necessary paperwork and made us both a drink, knowing neither would get touched but that at least it would be something to hold onto. As the coffee machine whirred to life I scanned Linda's desk again, hoping for something other than just Callum's name to inform me who he was here for. Usually the initial telephone call covered the details we needed, so I wouldn't have to go over old ground, asking people to repeat fresh, painful information that burned their tongue. But there was nothing in amongst Linda's doodled drawings, half-finished crossword puzzles and scribbled shopping lists.

I returned to the room, bracing myself to ask Callum for the details of why he was here, again. He was hurriedly tapping out a message on his phone.

'Here you go.' I placed the mug on a coaster in front of him. He put his phone on the table and sat up straight. 'So, Callum, will anyone else be joining you?'

'My sister, Mel – er, she should be here actually. She's always running late. I thought today, of all days, she'd be on time…'

He cleared his throat again.

'OK. Would you like us to wait for her?'

He shook his head. 'Let's just get on with it.'

I opened a fresh file and pressed down on a pen. 'I'm very sorry but my colleague didn't pass on the information you would have given her when you made this appointment. Are you OK to tell me who we are here for?'

Callum clenched his jaw and absentmindedly played with his silver wedding band.

'My wife. Abbie.'

'And when did Abbie die?'

'Sunday night. The twenty-fifth. Two days ago.' He shook his head as if it had felt like a lifetime, not just forty-eight hours. He sighed and rubbed his hands over his face as if forcing himself to wake up and focus. 'She died in a car accident out by Rowberry Way.'

Immediately I knew. The crash had been the talk

of the Post Office. I'd overheard the girl behind the counter complaining to her colleagues that she'd had to take the long route in, as police had blocked the road to retrieve a car from a ditch. It was the Arctic cold weather, she said, and black ice on the road, combined with rows of hazardously placed oak trees lining the winding country lane. It was a death trap waiting to happen.

People take that corner too fast all the time, someone said. *There should be speed cameras or better lighting,* someone else loudly agreed. *Probably a teenage boy racer trying to impress a girl,* an old lady said, to a collective murmur of agreement, as if a death sentence served him right for his stupidity. I'd bitten my lip, waiting for them to hurry up, wondering if I would be dealing with the arrangements. Now I was sitting opposite the man whose life had changed because of that night.

'I just need to get some details from you, if that's OK?'

He nodded.

'What's Abbie's full name?'

'Abigail Sarah Anderson. But everyone calls her Abbie.'

'Date of birth?'

'Nineteenth of March. She'd only just turned thirty-three, last week.'

A shiver trailed up my spine.

We shared the same birthday.

'Thanks.' I tried to brush the surprise of this huge coincidence away, and turned back to the matter at hand. 'Now I know this must all feel unreal, but do you have any thoughts at this stage of what sort of service you might like?'

He fixed his blank, bloodshot eyes on mine as if I'd just asked him if he could solve an algebra equation using morse code. He shook his head.

'The two options are cremation or burial. If you have an idea of which Abbie would have wanted, then we can focus on that?'

He paused for a second before nodding his head assertively. 'Cremation.'

'OK. Now, there are a few things you'll need to think about, such as the type of coffin you would like. In this brochure, you can see the caskets available, from wicker to cherry wood.' I swivelled the thick guide over to him. 'Callum, I know this is unbelievably tough. I just want you to know that whatever you want for the service – whatever Abbie would have wanted – is a possibility.'

Callum didn't speak, but scanned his tired eyes across the images, his hands repeatedly rubbing at the same patch of skin on his arm.

'Can you tell me about Abbie?'

For some families, all they wanted was to tell me every detail about their loved ones. For others, that question was the grenade that sent them hurtling out of the room, too tearful to carry on. I asked it so that I could hopefully pick up on the details they shared, to help them with some of the decisions they needed to make. So far, I knew that her birthday would make her an Aquarius, like me. My mum was into the whole star-sign thing, telling me that was why I was truthful and imaginative but could also be detached. I wondered if Abbie had similar attributes, or if it was a load of mumbo jumbo nonsense.

'She just loved life. Hurricane Abbie, I'd call her. She was this… beautiful whirlwind.' He swallowed and closed the brochure, stamping a thick hand over the front cover as if to block it out. 'She travelled the world as a model. She's gorgeous. She was, she is… Sorry, I'm getting confused with the right tense to use.' He shook his head and sniffed loudly.

'I'm here! I'm here!' An explosion of wild, poppy-red hair burst into the room. 'The door was unlocked so I just came in. Oh, Cal! I'm so sorry I'm late!'

At the sight of his sister, I presumed, Callum shot to his feet and let her wrap her arms around him. A waft of sweet perfume came in with her.

'I'll give you two a minute,' I said, getting to my feet.

'No! I've already held things up. Sorry, I'm Mel, Callum's sister.' She offered her hand. It was warm and soft, and a collection of bangles clinked together as I shook it.

'This is Grace Salmon,' Callum said, using the heel of his hand to rub at his eyes.

Mel flicked an odd look at her brother then smiled warmly at me. 'Hello, Grace Salmon, I'm so sorry for being late. Finn just wouldn't get his shoes on and then Noah needed a full nappy and outfit change. You should have seen the state of him. A proper poonami. Oh…' She abruptly stopped chatting as if realising where she was. Her voice grew low and serious. 'Oh god, sorry. Are there…' She bobbed her head to the closed door and grimaced. 'You know? In there…'

Callum was swiping through his phone, apparently unaware of what his sister was trying to ask. I nodded, confirming that, in the room next door, separated by a flimsy wall, was a dead body. Or as I preferred it: Mr Sullivan.

'Oh, right.'

This was all she needed to compose herself and take a seat next to her brother, pulling her chair closer to his and unwinding a long, bobbly, mustard-yellow scarf from her neck. She was wearing a multi-coloured jumper with pompoms dangling from the cuffs of the bell sleeves. My sombre navy suit seemed even more dour in her sunshine light. She placed a hand on Callum's and squeezed gently. His shoulders dropped a fraction at having her by his side.

'There's going to be an inquest, that's what the police said,' Mel said to me. 'At first we didn't know if we had to wait for that to happen before we planned the funeral, but then they said it could take months and that we were to go ahead.'

I nodded. 'Inquests can take a while, depending on the case or the backlog that the courts are dealing with. My advice is to try and put that to one side and focus on what you can control.'

'It was an accident,' she added. 'No one was to blame. It's not like there will be a trial or anything.' I noticed Callum hadn't moved his eyes from the carpet. 'It was just a horrific accident. You don't expect black ice at this time of year. But I guess they need to tick whatever boxes they have to tick.'

42

'Hopefully it won't take too long. Your most important job right now is to take care of each other and get through as best you can. Can I just ask, Callum, will you be the main point of contact or would a member of Abbie's family like to be involved too?'

'She didn't have any siblings and her parents won't be attending.'

Mel must have seen the look on my face. 'They weren't very close, Abbie and her parents. They live in Borneo and rarely visit, too busy with their new life as prominent members of the Borneo Primates' Committee to think about us. But they are arranging the catering for the wake, so that's something, I guess.'

Callum turned to his sister. 'We need to pick a coffin.'

'Oh, right, of course. Well…' Mel struggled not to purse her lips. 'The most expensive, knowing Abbie.' Callum flashed her a look that silenced her immediately.

'We'll go for this one.' He stamped a thumb on the image of the standard light oak coffin. I wondered if Mel had clocked that it wasn't the most expensive one.

'Do you think you'd like something to go in the local paper? An obituary notice?'

'Does anyone even read them?'

'Well, it will be online and in the actual paper. It's a good way of letting local people know, especially if you have any requests when it comes to flowers or donations.'

'Yeah, I think that's a good idea.' Mel spoke for her brother.

'No problem. Regarding timings, I will need the text sent to the paper by Wednesday – tomorrow – for it to appear in Friday's edition. If you're happy with that, then in terms of dates, I think we'll be looking at the funeral to take place about a week or so after that. Possibly the Monday or Tuesday. Do you have a preference for which day or time?' They both looked at me blankly. 'Some people like a morning slot and others prefer for later in the day so guests can arrive if they are travelling some distance.'

'Let's go for Monday. It's already the most depressing day of the week,' Mel said, as Callum nodded in agreement. 'I think morning would work best. You don't want to be waiting around all day…' *Better to get it over with*, Mel looked like she wanted to say.

'The ninth, then. I'll run it past the crematorium guys then give you a call to confirm so you can start telling people.' I cleared my throat. 'Have you been to many funerals? I just wondered if there was anything that you had experienced before that you might like to recreate?'

Mel took a breath. 'Well, our mum –'

'No.' Callum immediately cut his sister off and flashed her a warning look. 'We're not regular funeral-goers.'

The room fell silent.

Mel caught my eye and bit her lip. 'Can we leave it here for now? There's a lot to take in, we're still just getting our heads around the fact it's even happened.'

'Of course.' I closed the file softly.

'It still feels like we're all in a daze,' Mel added, getting to her feet.

'It's bound to feel that way but you've given me a lot of really helpful information already, so I can make a start.'

I watched as Mel linked an arm through Callum's and helped steer him out, chatting about going to grab a coffee before she needed to get to the childminder's. Mel flashed a look of gratitude back at me. I could see how desperately she wanted to do or say the right thing. Her broken-hearted brother looked as if he was on auto-pilot, wanting to be told where to go and what to do, in order to not have to think too deeply about how his life had changed in a split second.

Chapter 5

'"Ask A Funeral Arranger,"' read Frank. '"Everything you wanted to know but were afraid to ask." I think it has a great ring to it. I hope you get the outcome you deserve.' He smiled, looking again at the printout of the e-flyer I'd created and posted on our Facebook page. 'I have to say I was surprised that our resident wallflower would be hosting an event like this.'

You can say that again.

'It's good to try something different every now and then.' I was convinced my over-the-top laugh belied how I really felt.

Since I'd decided to throw caution to the wind and invite perfect strangers to the back room of a church hall, I had to continue with this fake bravado. I'd spent ages writing and re-writing the perfect welcome speech, succinctly summing up my job role and what we offered to those who got their affairs in order with us. As long as I had those index cards in my hands I would be OK, or so I kept telling myself. Sadly, Frank couldn't make it, and Friday nights were Linda's regular girls' night to drink one too many Malibu and cokes and watch the burly men of the Red Lion play darts. I'd seen her

Facebook statuses. To be honest, I was grateful that she wasn't able to pop down. I didn't need her judging me from the sidelines. I was already a little wound up at the way her eyes had rolled and her painted lips had curled up at the edges every time Frank had mentioned tonight.

It had seemed so simple to put the evening together but, in reality, it had taken a lot more work than I'd imagined. First, I'd had to find a suitable – and free – venue. There were fire exits, disabled access and general health and safety to think of. I had followed Ms Norris's idea of baking a selection of some of my favourite cakes, but I didn't want to isolate anyone with dietary restrictions so had spent several evenings trapped in the kitchen making sure I would please any gluten-free, dairy-intolerant vegans who might attend. Maybe Linda's approach of just cold-calling potential customers would have been easier. It certainly would have been quicker, and saved me a small fortune in ingredients. I just knew there was no way I'd have been able to pick up the phone to a stranger and encourage them to sign up to their funeral in the effortless way she did it.

'Best of luck tonight, Grace. I have to say I can't wait to hear how you get on!' Frank smiled.

I felt my stomach do a tiny flip of anticipation.

*

Maybe the clock on the wall was wrong. It looked like it had been there for some time, after all. In fact, the whole of the room could do with a bit of TLC. No wonder they'd let me hire it for free. My eyes strayed to the peeling paint chips and scuffed wooden tables. I'd tried my best to get rid of the musty smell in here with the air freshener I'd brought with me, but it hadn't managed to do the job. I re-checked my watch, which was showing the same time as the clock, and kept my gaze on the doors, waiting for them to open, shifting on an uncomfortable seat.

The circle of identical red plastic chairs that I'd painstakingly heaved into position around me were all empty. The only sound was the loud ticking of the annoyingly correct wall clock and my feet nervously tapping on the faded lino.

The trestle table I'd set up at the front of the room, under the stained glass window, was full of untouched cakes, neatly laid out biscuits and chilled cartons of orange juice, alongside fanned out forms and free pens. Two balloons with our company logo on bobbed forlornly over the floor, mocking me and this seemingly stupid idea.

I'd been sitting there for the past twenty minutes, psyching myself up whenever the flash of headlights swiped past the window. I swallowed the lump in my throat and shook away the tears threatening to prick my eyes. *Someone* had to show up, surely? Not even in my wildest nightmares about holding this event did *no one* turn up. But that was how it appeared to be.

I sighed loudly. Maybe I should have done more to get the word out? When I'd posted about it on our Facebook page it had received a couple of likes, which had foolishly buoyed my confidence. I thought the residents of

Ryebrook would be queuing up to ask me something. Maybe I should have booked a different location? Taken a stall at the library, or had a table set up in the atrium of Asda instead? Perhaps I should have chosen to hold it on a different day of the week. People clearly didn't want to think about their own funeral on a Friday night.

I told myself to give it another five minutes then call it quits. Linda's face would be painful when she heard what a disaster it had been, but not as painful as sitting in an empty church hall on my own, listening to the clock hands ticking by.

When the tediously slow five minutes were up, I wearily got to my feet and pulled out the Tupperware boxes to pack away the homemade cakes. Maybe there was a homeless shelter I could go and drop them off at. Someone should benefit at least.

Suddenly I heard faint footsteps, followed by the creak of the door opening.

'Ah, Grace! Sorry I'm late –' the familiar voice chimed, then stopped. She glanced around the room. 'Am I late? Or am I early?'

'Evening, Ms Norris!' I couldn't help but smile at her. 'You're right on time. Come on in.'

'I wasn't sure if I could make it, which is why I didn't mention it to you earlier. I had to see if Alma would watch Purdy for me, you see, and Alma is a bit of a stickler for a routine,' she babbled, taking off her coat and laying it on an empty chair. 'A bit like you, actually,' she chuckled.

'Well, it's great to see you. Help yourself to some cake

or a drink. You, er, you didn't see anyone else out there did you?'

'No dear, I'm afraid I didn't.'

My heart sank. Stay positive, Grace.

'I'll just go and have a final check.' I jogged to the creaky doors, out to an empty corridor, and peered through the main doors. Ms Norris was right; not a soul in sight.

'So, erm, thanks again for coming. Possibly it's the weather keeping others away…'

At that exact moment, the thin window frames, dripping in condensation, gave an almighty rattle.

'These are delicious,' she grinned as crumbs of chocolate brownie fell on her plum-coloured skirt.

I couldn't help but smile. 'It's your recipe. I have to say that using a dash of cayenne pepper really worked.'

'It's been my secret ingredient for many years.' She tapped a finger to the side of her nose.

I glanced at the clock. Seven thirty-five. We had this room for another twenty-five minutes. I couldn't pack away now; she'd made such an effort to brave the outdoors to attend.

'So…' I cleared my throat and rummaged in my suit jacket pocket for my index cards. I was about to launch into my pre-prepared speech, for something to fill the time, when a loud creak stopped me.

'Is this the funeral meet-up thing?' asked a wobbly, high-pitched voice.

I spun on my chair to see a young boy – he couldn't have been older than fifteen or sixteen – stick his jet-black, shaggy hair into the room. His dark eyes darted from side to side. The rest of his body remained outside, unsure whether or not to enter.

I leapt to my feet. 'Oh yes, hi, please come in!'

The lad shuffled in, dragging his feet. He refused to smile but his serious dark brown eyes lit up when he saw the cakes on offer.

'I'm Grace – I work at Ryebrook Funeral Home – and this is Ms Norris.' The old lady gave a cheerful wave, dropping more crumbs to the floor.

'I'm Marcus,' he mumbled, sloping into the room. 'Can I have some cake?'

'Sure, help yourself. There's plenty to go round.'

Hungrily, Marcus started filling his paper plate with one of everything. I glanced at the clock. Seven forty. The invite had said seven. I wasn't very good with things not running to plan, but at least people had shown up. Never mind the fact that Marcus was not exactly our target audience, being much too young to sign up to a prepaid funeral plan.

I decided that I would still stick to my original script. I should be able to get through everything before the line dancing group needed the room at eight p.m. I stood up and cleared my throat with as much authority as I could muster. I was conscious that we looked a bit ridiculous, the three of us, sat in such a large circle of empty chairs. I focussed on the pastel-coloured cards in my hands.

'Thank you for coming this evening. My name is Grace Salmon, and I'm a funeral arranger at Ryebrook Funeral Home. We are a small business who have been in the funeral trade for over fifty-five years. Our aim is for you to have your funeral *your* way, on your big day. I wanted to host this event tonight as a way to debunk some of the myths around what we do. For example, not all funeral arrangers are fans of Halloween.'

I chuckled. My awkward laugh was the only sound in the room.

'Um. Anyway – there have been a lot of misconceptions from pop culture and horror films, but the truth is that we're here to assist in one of the most rewarding and important events, in the most dignified way that we can. I'm going to run through a few of the other popular myths before passing over to the room for your questions –' I stopped abruptly and looked at the clock.

'Actually, as there's only the three of us you probably don't need to hear all of this…' I sat back down, feeling self-conscious, and placed the stack of cards on the empty seat next to me. 'We don't have much time left before we need to go, so, er, maybe it's easier if you ask me whatever you would like to know and I'll try to answer as many questions as I can?'

There was a silence, only filled with Marcus loudly chewing on a slice of Bakewell tart.

'I'll start.' Ms Norris raised a wrinkled hand. 'I wanted to ask you, Grace, what made you get into a career like this?'

'Well,' I cleared my throat. 'I always knew I wanted to work in a role that helped others.'

I parroted the well-worn answer. Tonight had already been a disaster; there was no chance I was going to dive into the truth.

Marcus slowly raised a skinny arm. 'I have a question.'

I smiled at him encouragingly. He had a smear of chocolate from one of the brownies on his chin. 'Go on.'

'My grandma died last year and I want to know...' He paused.

I expected him to ask what happened to her body, how embalming works or what temperature the incinerator reaches – a teenager fascinated with the ghoulish side of our world. I wasn't prepared for what he eventually found the words to ask.

'I want to know...' A deep intake of breath. 'When I'm going to start feeling happy again?'

A soft, gentle sound passed from Ms Norris's lips.

'I'm so sorry to hear that, Marcus.' He was blinking rapidly and refused to take his eyes from his scuffed trainers.

I paused for a moment. 'What was her name? Your grandma?'

'June. She was eighty-seven, which everyone said was "a good innings" and "her time" and other things like that. I just don't get why there's loads of old people still alive when she isn't. It's not fair.' He angrily kicked the leg of the chair next to him then flashed a wide-eyed look at Ms Norris. 'God, sorry. I didn't mean, like...'

'It's quite alright, dear. It's very normal to be angry when you lose someone you love.' Ms Norris bobbed her head in sympathy.

Marcus lowered his voice. 'She was like you, actually. She loved those mini apple pies from Aldi. She'd pick off the edges and secretly give them to my dog when my mam wasn't looking.' He pointed to the neat line of crumbs that Ms Norris had left on her paper plate. 'I just miss her so much.' His voice cracked and tightly bunched-up fists flew to stem the tears from his eyes. 'My mam thought if I came here tonight it might help…'

I'd foolishly expected questions on what options people have during a cremation, the most popular funeral songs, or whether eco-funerals were the future. Not this.

'Do you talk about June – I mean your grandma – much at home?' I asked gently.

Marcus shook his head.

'When I lost my Billy I could hardly function,' Ms Norris said, handing Marcus a tissue that he accepted. He blew his nose noisily.

'I'm so sorry to hear that.' I paused then turned to her. 'Who's Billy?'

In our regular meetings I'd never heard her mention a Billy.

'My dog. I had Billy before Purdy. A King Charles Cavalier and exceedingly handsome if I do say so myself. Anyway, it doesn't matter if it's a pet or a person.' She wafted a wrinkled hand. 'To be honest I've met nicer animals than I have people in my time. When someone or something you love dies, it can make you feel like the world has spun off its axis and you're barely holding onto the edges.'

Marcus nodded slowly in agreement.

'That's normal. But Marcus, your grandma would have known how much you loved her, and no one can ever take away that special bond you had.'

He let out a loud sniff and used the sleeve of his hoody to wipe his nose.

'Ms Norris is right,' I added. 'Also, it might help if you spoke to someone? Maybe tell your mum how you're feeling?'

I felt completely out of my comfort zone offering what I hoped was good advice. I was fine with planning funerals, arranging hearses and comparing coffins. I could comfort the recently bereaved by fixing as much of their pain as I could with a perfect send-off, but I wasn't ready to deal with the raw loss and love of a teenage boy for his grandma.

'Don't you ever get scared of… you know… dying?' Marcus asked Mrs Norris, looking a little more composed.

'Not so much that it stops me from *living*. You can't do anything to avoid it, but you can make the most of whatever time you have. It's something I wish I'd learnt a long time ago,' she said wistfully. 'I don't expect you to live every day as if it's your last, or any silly nonsense like that, but I do think we should all be more aware of how lucky we are.'

'Hashtag blessed.' Marcus nodded along.

'Um, exactly. What I'm saying is: you need light and shade.'

I could hear footsteps growing outside; the line dancing class waiting to get in. It was nearly eight o'clock.

'I'm so sorry, but we have to leave it there.'

'Is it going to be on next week?' Marcus asked, lolling to his feet and pulling the sleeves of his hoody low over his hands. 'I'll try not to cry next time.'

'Oh, well, I…' I stuttered. 'It was actually just a one-off evening… I'm not a trained bereavement counsellor to start with and –'

'Hear hear! I think it's a wonderful idea to hold it again next week. Maybe you'd get more people turning up if it was a regular thing too?' Ms Norris said, pulling on her thick coat. 'You've gone to so much effort, lovey, it would be a shame to waste it.'

A forlorn balloon bobbed past, as if on cue.

'Er.' I bit my lip. I couldn't suffer the embarrassment of sitting in an empty hall for half an hour again. I didn't want to waste anyone's time.

'Well, see ya next week then,' Marcus said, slipping a brownie into each of his low slung pockets and flashing a wave as he bobbed out of the room.

'What a lovely young man.' Ms Norris smiled after him. 'So brave of him to come here and open up.'

The sound of impatient huffing from outside made me jump into action. I began swiping up everything into two large reusable shopping bags.

'It looks like I'll see you here next week then, dear!' Ms Norris opened the door and let the moody-faced dancers file in. We'd run over by six minutes.

'Yeah, I guess so…' I trailed off, hurrying to get out before being dragged into a grapevine formation.

The thought of hosting an event again would have to wait. I had somewhere to be – somewhere I desperately did not want to go, and I was running late.

Chapter 6

'*Grace!*' my mum shrieked. 'Coo-eee! Gracie!'

Tina Salmon had always talked too loudly. She was one of those people who simply believed that the world desperately needed to hear what she had to say, whether the world liked it or not. Right then, her louder-than-average voice had to compete with the whiny strains of a saxophonist in the local band. An enthusiastic but tone-deaf singer was screeching into a microphone too close to his mouth. It was also about three hundred degrees. Bodies squeezed to get closer to the wrought-iron bar, desperate for the harassed members of staff to serve them.

Despite my protestations that I'd long given up celebrating and that my birthday had already come and gone, my mum had other ideas. It had been too long, she'd insisted, since we'd all got together, and this was the first evening all of us could make – hence my presence at a noisy bar in town. Still, I would *really* rather have been at home working on Mr Thomson's service. Coming out on a Friday night wreaked havoc with my anxiety levels. Thankfully she had at least managed to get a table. She was perched on a high stool, with absolutely no lumbar support whatsoever, at a high table tucked into the corner.

I slowly headed over to her. I was still trying to put a positive spin on the Ask A Funeral Arranger event I'd rushed here from. But I just felt embarrassed. How could I have thought I could get the people of Ryebrook to come to a draughty church hall on a Friday night to hear me chattering on about funerals? The only thing to be taken from this evening was that I should trust my instincts. I'd stepped out of my comfort zone, left the safety of my flat, and put myself out there. I was annoyed at how much time I had wasted in preparing for the event, and in sitting alone in that musty hall before anyone arrived. Time I could have spent productively planning for the services I had coming up next week. I still hadn't tracked down the perfect top hat to go as a coffin topper for Mr Deacon, a local milliner who'd recently passed away. I really wasn't convinced that running the event again next week would have a more positive outcome, but I'd agreed to it, so it didn't look like I had much choice.

'Ooh! Grace! Over here!' Mum was still waving a tanned arm in my direction, despite the fact I was heading her way. Rolls of mature skin were stuffed into the unforgiving, low-cut, shiny black vest top, and she jiggled as she beckoned me over. I sighed. Climbing into my bed seemed a long way off.

Next to her was my half-brother, Freddie, his face lit up by the blue hue of his phone screen, eyebrows knotted together, lost in some virtual world, ignoring

Mum and the man on his right. That must be her new boyfriend. Tonight we were 'being introduced'. *Brian? Barry? Bobby?*

'Grace! Isn't this brilliant!?' Mum energetically jumped from her stool. Her cherry-red patent stilettos skidded slightly on the tiles as she pulled me into an over-the-top embrace. She smelt of cigarettes and red wine and a sickly floral perfume. She'd had her nose pierced since I saw her last.

'Hi, Mum,' I said, breathing through my mouth.

Freddie looked up, nodded in my direction, then went back to his phone.

'Oh happy birthday, my darling girl!' she shouted in my ear, pulling out an empty stool for me to sit on. The metal legs scraped in resistance. 'Grace, this is Brendan.'

'Alright!' Brendan flashed a toothy, nicotine-stained grin and tilted his half-empty glass of lager in my direction. His round head nestled onto folds of stubbly flesh spilling from his tight, dark grey turtleneck. 'So, the famous Amazing Grace. Lovely to finally meet you. Happy birthday and all that.'

'Thanks, er, it was a couple of weeks ago but thanks.'

'Freddie, make room for your sister!'

'Half-sister,' he muttered, moving over half an inch to let me get past.

'Brendan got you a bottle of fizz to celebrate but you've taken so long to get here that we had to make a start,' Mum admitted, without a hint of an apology, flicking her heavily mascaraed eyes to the upturned bottle of cava in a watery ice bucket.

She knew I didn't drink. No matter how many times she'd tried to encourage me to lighten up and let my hair down, I had to continually repeat that I didn't need alcohol to have a good time.

More for me then, was always her reply, after a quiet but audible, *If I hadn't given birth to you then I'd swear you're not my daughter*.

'Ah, well, thanks. That's very, er, thoughtful,' I said politely to Brendan. He winked and made a clicking sound with his mouth, helping Mum get back up on her stool.

'What took you so long, anyway?' Mum rearranged herself with a wobble.

'Work emergency,' I lied. I couldn't bear to go into the church hall disaster.

Freddie made a strange noise between his pursed lips, flecks of spittle jumping from his mouth onto the glossy tabletop. 'What? Too many stiffs to deal with?'

Brendan smiled as if he understood the joke. Then realised he didn't. 'Stiffs?'

'Yeah, did Mum not tell you?' Freddie said.

I noticed Mum's painted red lips tighten. She picked up a tired-looking cocktail list, zoning out from this conversation.

'Our Grace here is the local Morticia Addams.'

Brendan looked at me and back to Freddie.

'She's a funeral director,' Freddie explained.

'Arranger. A funeral *arranger*,' I corrected. Frank wouldn't be happy with me stealing his job title. Not that detail mattered to someone like Freddie. He thought feminists were hairy, angry lesbians, and still called women 'birds'. I'd once overheard him explain, in depth, that it was scientifically proven you couldn't get wasted two nights in a row, something to do with the first night cancelling out the second.

'Really?! You work with dead people!' Brendan literally recoiled, a little precariously on his stool.

'I'm going to get a mojito. Anyone else want one?' Mum said loudly, pretending to be oblivious to the topic of conversation. 'Or maybe a pornstar martini?'

'It's sick, innit. *I see dead people*...' Freddie said in a little boy's voice, ignoring her.

Brendan leant forward, placing an elbow in a small puddle of lager. His eyes widened. 'Wow, Grace, you work with corpses, what's that like?'

Inwardly I sighed.

'It's just my job and I love what I do.'

'Yeah, but it's like... you know... death.'

'And?'

'I'm not in denial, don't get me wrong. I've even planned my funeral.' Brendan sat up straighter. 'I know *exactly* what I want.' Mum looked up from the cocktail list. 'I want "I Am A Cider Drinker" playing as they carry me in for a start –'

'You're joking? You want The Wurzels played at your funeral?' She blurted out an incredulous laugh.

'Why not?' Brendan winked to hide any embarrassment. 'They're only like *the* greatest band in the world, ever!' I could see his shine fading as Mum frowned at him. 'Just a little underrated, that's all.'

'But at your *funeral*? I really don't think it's appropriate. Plus, the greatest band in the world are Queen. That's who Freddie's named after.' She squashed my brother's cheeks in her hands.

'Alright, Mum.' He swatted her away.

'No. We won't be having some country hicks play at your funeral,' Mum decided for him. 'Anyway, you won't even be there so you can't complain. Right, can we *please* change the subject? We're meant to be here celebrating Grace and her birthday. You know, Grace, who is still alive!'

'I'm going for a piss.' Freddie sprang to his feet, making a comment about how my birthday was actually ages ago and that this was a load of bollocks.

'So Grace, is your boyfriend joining us later?' Brendan asked. I squirted a dollop of antibacterial hand gel in my palms and rubbed them together, hoping to avoid the question.

'She's single and ready to mingle!' Mum sang.

'Well...' I have never been ready to mingle in my life. Just the very word made me want to uncomfortably scratch my arms and hide under my duvet.

'Ah, I get it. I guess it must be tough finding someone because of what you... do.'

'I don't know why you didn't see more of that Ian. Cheryl said he's a lovely bloke, when I bumped into her last,' Mum piped up, sloshing red wine from the bottle into her empty, lipstick-stained glass. How much had she got through this evening? Cheryl was my mum's chiropodist and Ian was another of her clients.

'Cheryl isn't the best judge of character,' I said tact-fully, desperate to move the conversation on.

I'd never told my mum about Henry. We had promised each other not to tell anyone about us – it was part of the deal. A deal that felt like it suffocated me at times. But it was a promise I had stuck to, despite everything that had happened. The only living soul who knew was Maria, but, well, that was different.

'You need to get yourself on Tinder,' Freddie had returned from the bathroom, waving his lit-up phone screen in my face, the brightness blinding me for a second.

'Ah, Tinder,' Brendan said wistfully, before sticking his reddened face into his wine glass as Mum glared at him.

'Right! Present time!' Mum shrieked. 'Freddie, put your phone away now. This is family time.'

Freddie muttered but obeyed, and slid his phone into the pocket of his tight chinos.

'Grace, Brendan and I got you this.' She rummaged in the tie-dye pillowcase thing that acted as a handbag. I'd have palpitations thinking about her gallivanting off to the next country on her travels with such a badly designed bag; a pick-pocketer's dream. She pulled out a slightly crumpled gift bag that had a boiled sweet wrap-per stuck to the back and an almost perfectly spherical tea-stain ring in the top right-hand corner.

'Whoops,' she picked off the wrapper and dropped it to the floor. 'Right, well, happy birthday my little Gracie.'

'You really didn't have to…' I started to protest as I cautiously took the packet off her and peeled it open. Last year she'd got me a clunky handmade Tunisian shell necklace. It was still in its bubble wrap, sitting patiently in the half-empty Tesco Bag for Life that was destined for my next trip to Oxfam.

'Oh…'

I wrapped my fingers around a red and yellow hand-woven cotton bracelet. The type of thing you'd give your school friend when you were about thirteen. A tiny peace sign was threaded in the centre, next to a small metal disc that was engraved with my name.

'It's personalised! Do you love it? Put it on!'

I smiled tightly and let her tie it around my wrist. I could cover it up with my watch without hurting her feelings.

'There's something else in there too!'

The other gift was a yellow plastic radio in the shape of a bumblebee. Two slim silver antennas had been coated in black paint, it's bulbous behind was covered in wire mesh for the speakers, and two thick black stripes over a sunflower-yellow body were the dials. There was no kind way to put it…

It was hideous.

'It's a radio! Isn't it funky!' Mum beamed, clapping her hands together. Freddie scoffed into his pint glass. 'I picked it up at this market in Latvia and thought it would really brighten up your house. It's about time you added a touch of personality to that place. It's so very… sterile.'

'Perfect for Grace then,' Freddie said with a smirk, before Mum told him to be nice to me as it was my birthday.

Neither Mum nor Freddie visited my home very often.

In fact, Freddie had only been once for about five minutes, when he was waiting for his friend to pick him up for a football match and it was chucking it down with rain. Whenever Mum was back in England, she sporadically popped in for a cup of tea but preferred to stay at the hotel near the library as she could fill up her bag with all the miniature toiletries. A low-cut top was all she needed to get a discount on a room from the male receptionist.

'Right, wow. Thanks.' I forced a smile, running my fingers over the chubby bee radio. There was no doubt in my mind it would be destined for the Bag for Life too.

'My gift is... on its way,' Freddie muttered. Code for he'd completely forgotten.

'It's fine. My birthday was ages ago and I really didn't expect anything anyway.'

'Is there really no one on the scene?' Mum pushed. Now presents were out the way she clearly hadn't given up on the previous conversation.

'No. I've told you. I'm fine like this.'

'You not worried about, well, you know... tick-tock, tick-tock?'

This usually happened after a bottle of wine. She would grill me about my lack of a nice young man. She would be slurring about missing out on grandchildren in another few glasses, mark my words.

'Mum, please...'

'I thought you said Grace were only twenty-seven? She's got plenty of time for babies and all that.'

'She's thirty-three! And not getting any younger, may I add!'

I could see Brendan doing the maths in his head, working out Mum's real age, a fact as unknown as the location of Cleopatra's tomb. She'd been clinging onto her early fifties for the past few years.

'You're ancient, Grace,' Freddie unhelpfully joined in. 'You may as well stop being so picky and go for the next bloke that walks in here.' He never got a grilling, despite only being three years younger than me.

'Ooh yes! It could be fate, bringing them together!' Mum clapped her hands and the three of us glanced towards the door. Brendan still stared at Mum, looking utterly perplexed.

'Wait – not them.' Mum dismissed the group coming in with a wave of her hand. 'That's a bunch of women.'

'Unless… ' Freddie raised an eyebrow and gave an unsightly smirk.

'I'm not gay,' I said to my glass. No one else was listening. They all had their eyes trained to the door of the bar, like a dog waiting for its owner to return.

'Him! That one!' Mum squealed. Freddie collapsed into a fit of laughter. In walked a man who must have been there for his first legal drink. Angry red spots burst across a painful shaving rash.

'I don't think –'

'Grace! *Go and talk to him!*' Mum bellowed, yanking my elbow.

'No, I –'

'Go on. Go and talk to him, it's not going to kill you!'

'I said no.' I roughly pulled away from her grip. 'Can we leave it please?'

'Ooooh! Touchy!' Freddie's voiced raised an octave or two.

Brendan was gently rubbing Mum's hand, frowning at me as if I'd intentionally hurt her.

'Sorry, Mum, I said I didn't –'

'It's fine, Grace. I just don't want you to be alone for the rest of your life. But, whatever. I'm only doing it because I care. I'm going to the ladies'.' She scraped her stool back and wobbled off.

I was half listening to Freddie waffle on to Brendan about the outrageousness of United's Premier League position, and half wondering what possessed a man in his late fifties to wear a single silver earring, when I felt my heart stop. I blinked hard to make sure my eyes weren't deceiving me but when I opened them again he was still there.

On the other side of the bar was Henry. My Henry.

The air left my body.

What the hell was he doing here?

'Grace?'

I heard my mum's loud voice behind me, apologising to the couple of girls on the next table for spilling their drinks as I roughly knocked past them.

Henry is here! I fought my way through the dancing crowd. The band had started up again with an energetic cover of a Bob Marley song. Elbows and hips were blocking me from getting to him. I stopped still and tried to hover on my tiptoes to get a better vantage point. *Where had he gone? He was right there a second ago.*

'Grace! Where are you going?'

Mum was still calling after me but I couldn't stop. I had to get to him.

Henry is here. Henry is here.

My feet were moving without my brain thinking. What was he wearing? He didn't own a stripy polo shirt; he must have bought it recently.

Annoyingly, he looked good in it. He had always looked good in anything. Questions roared across my mind as I forged forward.

'Alright, love!' said a man with cauliflower ears and a receding hairline, smiling a toothy grin at me. 'You won't get served standing there.' He'd spilt some of his pint onto his tan loafers. He wasn't wearing socks.

'I'm not trying to get served.'

I craned my neck to see where he'd gone. He couldn't have just disappeared. He was right there, I was certain of it. I felt funny, not sure if I wanted to vomit or cry at how overwhelming the feeling was.

'You want us to hoist you up? You might have a better chance of catching the barmaid's eye then?' The man nudged me. His equally enormous friends turned round to see who he was talking to.

'He was just here…'

'Who? Who was here?' I could see him pull a face to his mates out of the corner of my eye. A booming laugh and a meaty hand slapping his back. A waft of offensive BO. 'You alright, love? You've gone a bit pale.'

I shook my head.

It wasn't him.

My eyes had deceived me. Henry's doppelgänger, who actually didn't look very much like him after all, was laughing with an older woman at the bar. The hair colour was almost the same but his face was all wrong. That cheeky smile, the cluster of freckles and the confident way he held himself were all missing.

Waves of heat rose to my cheeks. It was much too hot in there with all those writhing bodies jostling around me. Henry wasn't there, of course he wasn't. How utterly ridiculous of me to think that after all these years he'd show up in this place. As if he'd be hanging out in a dive of a bar in Ryebrook on a Friday night. What planet was I on? I blinked back the tears threatening to overcome my gritty and tired eyes. I had to get out of there immediately.

'Hey, come back darlin', I won't bite!'

'Unless you want him to!'

I ignored the looks and irritated tutting from strangers as I pushed past. Jeers of laughter followed by wolf-whistles were drowned out by the terrible music. I fought my way to the doors, inhaling lungfuls of cool air as I tumbled outside.

I scurried past the huddle of smokers flocked under one lonely heater, holding my breath so as not to be permeated by their poisonous fumes. I'd call Mum later and tell her I wasn't feeling well, apologise for not saying bye. Thanks to the drinks she was putting away, I doubted she'd even remember my dramatic disappearance by the morning. For the first time in a long time I yearned to be anaesthetised by alcohol too.

Chapter 7

When you break up with someone it's normal to ricochet between emotions; all the books told me that. Except this wasn't a clean cut break-up. He'd just disappeared, and there were still so many things left unsaid. I'd tried. I really had. I hated feeling like that, struggling to pick myself up and get back on track. Usually baking helped, but I couldn't summon up the energy to give one of Ms Norris's recipes a go. Cleaning was the next best solution, but even that didn't seem to be working.

I decided to call Maria. She was the only person who knew about Henry, and I could trust her not to judge me. Others wouldn't understand. Surely I should feel OK by now. But it was like my head and heart hadn't read the rulebook which contained the exact date you should move on after a traumatic break-up. As time had passed, I'd forced myself to see less and less of Maria, as seeing her meant being reminded of him. Every time we met, his name wasn't far from slipping into our conversation. That's just the way it was.

I dialled her number.

'Grace? Wow. Long time! How are you doing, hun?'

I let out a breath I'd been holding. Her warmth

radiating down the line immediately washed away any of the doubts I'd had at making this call out of the blue.

'Hi! I know, it's been a while…'

'Everything OK?'

I sighed deeply.

'Stupid question. Of course not. Why else would you be calling me?' Her light tinkle of a laugh softened the dig.

'Are you around for a catch-up? I could really do with seeing you… as soon as possible.'

I could hear a rustling of papers in the background. I winced. I shouldn't have been so presumptuous that she would want to see me, especially after such a long absence.

'Oh, hun, I'm so sorry but I'm really busy at the moment. Work is manic, you know how it is.'

Of course she was busy, what was I expecting?

'Maybe I can move things around and give you a call back so we can organise a get-together soon? It would be good to see you again.'

I felt dejected. There was once a time when we were so close that she would have cancelled whatever was in her diary for me. Clearly too much time had passed. I tried to stay positive that she was a woman of her word; once things calmed down for her she'd be in touch. Until then I needed to keep busy and I knew exactly what to do to fill the time.

*

I curled my feet up under me, pulling my laptop closer, and logged in to Facebook. I needed to start my prep on Abbie Anderson.

As a model, she had a significant online presence, so I imagined it would be easy to discover lots of details we could incorporate into her funeral. I typed her name in the search bar and hovered my finger for a second before clicking.

I was soon looking at the life of a dead woman. Her profile picture was a flawless selfie, and luckily her account was not set to private. The last photo she had been tagged in before she died was a group shot. Four smiling faces around a dining table, each holding their wine glass up to the camera. A woman with a selfie stick in her outstretched arm to capture them all.

Shona Fitz nee Limbrick is feeling happy with – <u>Greg Fitz</u>, <u>Abbie Anderson</u>, *Callum Anderson*. Just found this on my phone! What a great night!! Had to share!!

Callum's name didn't come up in bold blue like Abbie or the others, which meant he wasn't on Facebook. I stared at the photo, imagining their life, being a guest at one of their dinner parties. Owning a selfie stick. The men probably moaning as the women giggled at the effort of drunkenly trying to steady their hand to get everyone in the shot. It had received ninety-four likes.

There was an album from their honeymoon a few years ago. *Seychelles, baby!* I clicked on it. Abbie wearing a barely-there white one-piece with impractical holes cut out of it, posing effortlessly on a plump cream sun lounger, an idyllic white sandy beach and turquoise clear waters in the background. A shot of her drinking a martini with dramatic bug sunglasses on, looking away from the camera. Callum diving into an infinity pool, beads of water on his tanned torso as he froze mid-air. The two of them, noses pink from the sun, cuddled together, and grinning over a table full of seafood. They looked so utterly happy together. He looked so different from the man I'd met.

I couldn't help myself, clicking on the photos that she was tagged in. Abbie wearing a burgundy mini dress with what looked like a cape attached to it. Her legs up to her armpits. I tried not to compare the size of my non-existent thigh gap with hers. Abbie in blood-red spike heels and leather-look leggings. Her face painted in white powder with a drop of crimson falling from her bottom lip. Plastic fangs in her mouth. A black velvet choker around her slim neck. Sharp collarbones and jutting ribs.

> If looks could kill!! Ready for a hair-raising night to raise money for Princess Power!

Princess Power was a local charity for young women with terminal cancer.

Abbie's slim, tanned arm wrapped around two attractive men wearing hot pink Hawaiian shirts. Thick gold cuffs on her wrists, her hair slicked back against her skull and a fierce pout at the camera.

> Hula night, bitches! – With <u>Owen Driscoll</u> and @ <u>ModelsZone</u>

Her modelling agency, by the looks of it.

The same guy, Owen, the one with the sculptured cheek-bones and glossy black hair, appeared a few more times in selfies, arty black and white modelling shoots and goofy backstage candid pics. They looked great together. Abbie had checked them into different places across Europe, probably when they were working on shoots together.

Another shot: Abbie in cargo shorts and a coral vest top, cheering at the camera from the ruins of Macchu Picchu.

We made it! #Blessed #YOLO

Abbie underwater, snorkelling past a shoal of fish, the same bright colours as her bikini.

Trying to Find Nemo! #JustKeepSwimming

Abbie jumping on an enormous plush hotel bed in a cute denim playsuit.

Paris is always a good idea!

There was a short video clip of her bending her lithe body into some impressive shapes on a beach in Turkey, taken by a drone by the looks of the crazy angles. She'd tagged in a yoga retreat company.

The only way to find zen – with @yogawarriors. Can't wait to return next year!

It was like a car crash on the other side of the motorway. I couldn't look away. My fingers danced on the cursor wanting to see more and more. Within twenty minutes, I'd inhaled seven years of her life.

Right, I needed to work out ways to incorporate what I'd learnt into a perfect goodbye. I pulled out a notepad and began to jot a few ideas down. She clearly enjoyed yoga and a holistic lifestyle, so maybe we could dot incense sticks around the chapel? Having such a strong online presence, maybe we could create a photo montage as a visual memento? She clearly loved to travel, so maybe this could be something to work with?

I glanced around my bare flat, aware of a strange gnawing feeling in my chest. There wasn't a photo, personal knick-knack or random bit of clutter in sight. I bet Abbie had lots of interesting trinkets from her exotic adventures dotted around her house, each with a fascinating story. My cleaning to-do list stared back at me forlornly from the coffee table. The budget-but-practical IKEA furniture suddenly seemed impersonal and even the two duck egg cushions that came with the sofa (in the January sales) looked drab. It was as if I was seeing through someone else's eyes for the first time. I blinked rapidly and told myself to stop overthinking things. These items were chosen for their durability, not their ability to catch dust.

What I couldn't escape from was that I was the same age as Abbie – we even had the same birthday – yet it was clear to see from her Facebook page that I'd barely led a fraction of the life that she had. I shifted uncomfortably on the sofa. I couldn't compete with her glamorous job, exotic travels, handsome husband and enormous posse of good-looking male and female friends. I shook my head. Two women, the exact same age, living in the same town, but completely worlds apart.

Abbie looked like the type of woman who always had perfectly polished toenails, who wore perfume every day – not just for a special occasion. She clearly had the upper arms of a yogi, volunteered her time for charity, and had seen the world, ticking off country after country that I could only dream of visiting. I bet she could speak at least one foreign language, made fresh healthy juices each morning, and was the person you realised was absent from social events.

Her perfect smile radiated off my laptop screen, eyes crinkled in a genuine laugh at the camera lens. You could tell by looking at her that she was someone you wanted on your team. She seemed so confident with who she was and the life she led. I had to keep reminding myself of the fact that this woman was no longer alive – it seemed impossible to get my head around it, and I hadn't even known her. What must her husband and family be going through, losing such a vibrant woman with a clear zest for life?

I clicked on my own Facebook profile, using this new-found critical eye for detail to really take a good look at myself. What would someone uncover about me once I was gone? My closest friends were an eighty-three-year-old woman and a forty-something shopkeeper.

I sighed deeply.

This was Henry's fault. I'd had close friends, a fun and exciting life in London and a promising future planned, before he ruined everything. I couldn't help but pull at one of the threads on my sleeve at the thought of him, tugging it around my finger, watching it turn the tip an angry purple colour. I shouldn't go there. I needed to concentrate on myself and what I could control. That was what Doctor Ahmed always said.

I shook my head. This wasn't about Henry. This was about Abbie Anderson and giving this vivacious, inspirational woman the send-off she deserved. For the first time, I felt overwhelmed with the uncertainty of how exactly I was going to go about this.

Chapter 8

As expected, Linda had been very eager to hear about my Ask a Funeral Arranger event. I'd given a non-committal, vague answer about how it had been a little quieter than expected, omitting the fact that only two people had turned up, one who already had a funeral plan with us and the other who was much too young to sign up for one.

'Great. So you did get some sign-ups?'

'Er…'

She raised an eyebrow. I wasn't fooling her.

'Seriously. Not one bit of interest?'

I couldn't cope with the smugness radiating from her and the way she held her biro to her pursed lips, tapping at the smirk painted on them.

'Oh, yes, well, I mean there was one man who seemed keen to know more…' I lied.

'Really?'

'I'm just about to give him a call to confirm his appointment actually…' I trailed out. She refused to take her eyes off me. Why had I said that? Why not admit it had been a total waste of time? I picked up my phone and for a moment thought about calling up the talking clock and pretending, but that was even more pathetic. I scrolled through my contacts list. Who could I call? Who would be receptive to me trying to sell them their own funeral? I settled on a gentleman I'd met a few months ago at a funeral service.

Please don't pick up, please don't pick up.

'Hello?' A gruff voice answered. My stomach dropped.

'Hello, is that Mr Baxter?'

'Yes?'

'Oh hello, my name is Grace Salmon. I'm calling from Ryebrook Funeral Home and wondered if you had a moment to talk about your funeral?'

'What? You what? It's who?'

I couldn't work out where he was, but there was music and laughter in the background. He was quite an elderly gentleman. I raised my voice.

'It's Grace Salmon! Is now a good time?'

I caught Linda sniggering into her raised fist as I shouted down the line.

'Salmon? What? I can't hear a bloody thing,' he muttered. 'Are you selling me something?'

This was not going well.

'No. Well, yes. I wanted to speak to you about arrangements for your funeral, to see about making an appointment to discuss plans to lock it in at today's prices.' I winced. Linda made this seem so effortless.

'My funeral? I really can't hear a thing...'

I was losing him. To be fair I'd never had him in the first place, but I needed to keep him on the line a little longer. I thought of a different tack, one I'd seen Linda use.

'You want to take the burden of planning your funeral away from your loved ones, don't you?'

There was a pause. What sounded like the tinkle of a fruit machine and hearty male laughter.

'Mr Baxter? Are you there?'

'I don't know who this is but I'm not interested in whatever you're selling.'

'No, sir, I'm not –'

'Wait. Is this Gerald? Ah, you got me there.' He broke into a loud guffaw. 'Calling about my funeral, you cheeky git. He set you up to this, didn't he?'

'No, I don't know anyone called Gerald…'

Linda was making spluttering noises, trying to keep her suppressed giggles in. Mr Baxter wasn't listening to my protestations.

'You tell him from me that I'll get him back for this. It's a good one, though, funeral planning. I'll have to remember that.'

He'd hung up before I could convince him that I was genuine.

'OK, well, I'll see you soon then,' I said brightly into the empty phone line, and placed the receiver down. 'He's going to have a think about it,' I said to Linda, before turning round to face my screen and hide the blush on my cheeks.

'Ladies – Abbie Anderson?' Frank broke Linda's spluttering of giggles as he walked over to our desks. He was eating a satsuma, juice dribbling between his chubby fingers.

'Sorry?'

He had a tiny flake of pith trapped in his beard.

'I've just taken a call from a local rag reporter about an Abbie Anderson. A model, apparently? They wanted to know if we were dealing with her service.'

'That name rings a bell.' Linda began rooting around her messy desk.

'Yes, we are,' I said. She stopped lifting up pieces of papers and stared at me. 'Her husband and her sister-in-law visited me to start the process.'

Frank was cut off from whatever he was about to say by a loud huff.

'I'm sure *I* made that appointment,' Linda frowned.

'Oh, well, you weren't here when Mr Anderson arrived so I took it on. I didn't want to turn him away.'

Frank held up a hand. 'Just as long as we make sure to factor in that there's media interest. She was quite a famous model, apparently. And the press loves a story of a beautiful young woman taken too soon.' He shook his head sorrowfully. 'We need to make sure the family are briefed and that the business is showcased at its best.'

I nodded decisively. The pressure was on. Frank took a lot of encouraging to get on board with some of my suggestions as it was; if there were going to be journalists covering Abbie's funeral then I knew he'd want to err on the side of caution even more.

'I'm sure you'll do a great job, Grace. Just please remember to keep it simple and classic, our signature style.'

'Sure thing…' I replied, weakly.

Frank plodded off to his office. The moment his door was closed Linda angrily tapped her false nails against her keyboard.

'I should have been looking after the Anderson funeral. But, oh well.'

'We can work together on it if you like?' I offered, knowing full well what her answer would be.

'No. It's fine. You heard what Frank said. If the press are going to be there then you'll be under enough pressure to make sure everything runs smoothly, you don't need my input too.'

'Well, I –'

She cut me off by picking up the ringing phone. I suddenly felt like Abbie's funeral was going to be one of the biggest I'd ever looked after.

Chapter 9

I got changed into the thickest and comfiest pyjamas I owned, feeling exhausted, and climbed into bed. The cool sheets were like a hug. I opened my laptop and decided to keep my head focussed on things I could control: namely, Abbie Anderson's funeral.

I thought about Frank's warning to keep her service simple. But I didn't want to give anyone I cared for a traditional, impersonal send-off. I felt like I'd gotten to know Abbie during the past few evenings spent lost in her world. I didn't need proof of just how important the perfect goodbye was. The personal services mattered; I tried not to worry about what the repercussions with my boss may be.

Abbie's Facebook feed had filled up since I'd first found her page. Messages of remembrance, photos and inspirational quotes – usually involving angels – had been posted onto her timeline. As I looked at the photos, many including Callum, I felt this strange, deep ache in the pit of my stomach, thinking of their marriage cut short. Their future plans dissolved in a split second. But it was also a kind of envy; a resentment for what he and his beautiful wife had shared, and anger that Henry had robbed me of our future too. He'd cruelly promised me the world, and then left me clinging onto his empty words; a destiny that would never materialise, just like Callum and Abbie's future.

I couldn't help myself. I was soon lost in Abbie's perfect life. A place where there was only sunshine, big smiles and happiness. No drama, no painful former relationships and no angry thoughts. Maybe if I had a life more like Abbie's, I would feel happier? Things would be different. Better.

My Facebook feed brought up the local newspaper's page. I clicked to read more. Abbie's beautiful face was shown, alongside an image of a mangled car wreck. It was a short article about her death and upcoming funeral, asking for witnesses to the crash to come forward. Underneath the main picture was one hundred and seventy-two likes.

Layla Kent had written: 'Gone too soon my sweet angel.'

Someone called Tessa Haynes had commented: 'Still feels so unreal.'

Another person called Mark McKinney had typed a crying emoji then gone on to rant about how that road had always been a death trap. 'The council need to do sumfin about it.'

Below that was a comment from someone whose name looked familiar. The handsome man who'd been tagged in her modelling photos, Owen Driscoll. 'Miss you, Abbie Anderson.'

I clicked on his name, which opened up his profile

page. It was set to private so all I could see was his profile picture and very basic information. His cover photo was a hand holding a bottle of lager in front of a tropical beach. He was a model, like I'd suspected, working at the same agency as Abbie.

I found myself back on Abbie's page once more. You meet people in life who just seem to sparkle; I just happened to meet her in death. I was like a fan-girl, wanting to soak it all up. Three of Abbie's photo albums were from fashion shoots or 'Modelling lols', in her words. Her beautiful face, long slim legs and petite frame were perfectly suited to the flamboyant dresses covering her. Her body curved away from the camera slightly to maximise the cut of the gown and shape of her figure.

Abbie is feeling fabulous at – Serenity Hair. A selfie in a hairdresser's chair with freshly blow-dried blonde locks. 'Huge thanks to the talented Andre for his serious skills! Bring on girls night tonight!' Seventy-two likes. Fifteen comments, all massaging her ego.

From childhood to teens to thirty-three years old, I'd sported the same mid-length mousy brown hair. I stuck religiously to the recommended regular trim every six to eight weeks with Chatty Claire. One of my proudest moments was when Chatty Claire told me she'd been telling another client about how few split ends I had. That hollow praise seemed nothing looking at the glowing comments Abbie got. Her hair was so shiny. Her *life* was so shiny. I blew a strand of hair from my face, suddenly feeling frumpy and old. If I needed any more proof of how unadventurous I had become, it was staring back at me every time I glanced in a mirror.

Abbie had recently shared a photo of a slate spherical ball in a snowy field that linked to a page: Daniel Sterling, Artisan Artist. In amongst the many five-star reviews on his page was one from Abbie: 'Just received the most amazing piece of art from Dan. It now has pride of place in our home. So impressed with the service and already planning my next piece with him!'

Imagine being a person who could commission their own piece of art. The thought blew my mind. I kept scrolling. The minutes ticked by as I clicked through photo after photo of Abbie. There weren't that many photos or posts with Callum in; since he wasn't on Facebook, maybe there was no point in tagging him. I was quickly learning that social media only mattered if others were going to see and comment.

I hated myself for thinking it, but I wanted to have just a touch of what this woman had had. The only flaw in Abbie's perfect life seemed to be her inability to differentiate between there and their.

I'd tried my hardest to keep my ideas for personalising her service as low key as possible. Frank had been breathing down my neck, knowing that the media could now be attending, but I wanted to make sure I hadn't missed anything crucial.

I pulled open her Instagram page. I'd already skimmed through this; a lot of the filtered photographs involved food, fitness or fashion shoots. Nothing that gave me any in-depth scope into the world behind her day job.

I scrolled right back to her first-ever post from almost three years ago. No long list of hashtags, no fashion brands tagged in, instead the shot was taken of Abbie, half reclining on the floor under a lit Christmas tree. The tree was a little wonky, the decorations not matching, and her outfit of patterned leggings and bad knitted jumper with an elf on it added to the natural charm of the shot. She had her head tilted back, laughing at something, her long wavy blonde hair tumbling down her back. She looked the prettiest I'd seen her. The photo was so natural, a side to her that she'd edited out in her later posts, a side I imagined she only shared with her closest friends and husband, a side to her that I felt almost voyeuristic in seeing.

Seeing this candid shot, I couldn't help but wonder about the sort of laid-back style she and Callum had embraced at home. Their neutrally decorated bedroom, I decided, would be spacious but full of textures, with cushions and faux fur throws over their king-sized bed. Their bathroom would have a roll-top, claw-footed bath, which sat in the centre of a large, black and white tiled floor. The room included a modern waterfall shower, with shiny silver pipes running up the wall. You would feel relaxed the moment you set foot in their house, welcomed in by a stylish log burner and maybe even an AGA stove.

Their kitchen would be modern but lived in. I imagined a fridge cluttered with magnets, worn oak work surfaces where they cooked together, dancing around each other with that ease that certain couples had. In my mind Abbie was a great cook, adventurous with her dishes, inspired by the places she'd been. Callum would be a willing guinea pig, maybe even complementing the food she prepared with his knowledge of wine. He looked like a man who would prefer wine to lager. I caught myself and shook my head with a funny sort of laugh.

What was I doing? Daydreaming about the life of a couple I could never meet? I knew that things weren't always what they seemed behind closed doors, but for some reason I believed that the Andersons were different; they did lead the perfect life. A life that had been tragically snatched away from them. It certainly put my world into perspective. I sighed and closed down the laptop and headed to bed.

Chapter 10

Callum and Mel were sitting opposite me, both a little more composed than the previous time. Most of the families I worked with were like that. It was as if crossing into my world wasn't as scary the second time around, just a little more wearying. I'd made them each a cup of coffee, self-consciously checking my reflection in the stainless steel of the coffee machine.

I felt slightly ashamed at how much I had been looking forward to seeing them both again. I liked building relationships with everyone who walked in, but for some reason the Andersons had stayed on my mind. It was something about the way Callum held himself, as if bracing in fight or flight mode for a threat that would never come. This facade of being OK in the face of everything. A facade that I knew could crumble in a second.

Walking in, he had looked drained. It was probably the whirlwind of jobs he needed to do before the funeral: paperwork to be completed and all the people to keep informed of every decision. It sounded like this was going to be a well-attended service.

The best thing is to keep busy, we tell families, giving

them a helpful step-by-step list of things to tick off. Most can't even see beyond the next hour, so having small tasks to complete gives them a sense of purpose to those never-ending first few days. *It'll get better after the funeral*, other people say. I knew, though, that the day itself was just the beginning.

'So my husband Nick will do a reading,' Mel said, glancing up from a scruffy notebook in her hand. Doodles in biro at the edges. 'Then we decided to use your guys as pallbearers; we didn't want to put pressure on family and friends who might feel like they had to say yes if we asked them.'

Pallbearers: a weight not everyone could carry. I made a mental note to tell Raj that one.

'Not a problem. The guys we use are extremely professional.'

'We wondered about the eulogy. We don't feel strong enough to speak on the day...' She flicked a look at Callum who was scrolling on his phone. He had barely spoken apart from thanking me for the coffee. 'But we would like to have an involvement in what's said, if that's OK?'

I nodded. 'The celebrant you have chosen to oversee the service will be able to do that for you. I'll arrange for him to come to your house so he can go through the style and content with you. He will also ask you about a choice of songs or hymns you may like, so it might be worth having a think beforehand, so you don't feel put on the spot.'

'Well, she had a bit of a thing about Enrique Iglesias

back in the day, didn't she? When she first met Cal they constantly had his album playing whenever I went round.'

A flash of something crossed Callum's eyes.

'You certainly don't want to pick from the *Now That's What I Call Funeral* playlist,' Mel scoffed before shuddering. 'No Robbie, no Elton and certainly no James Blunt. Sorry bro, but you don't. We just want this to be tasteful and respectful, even if it does feel like we're planning a party for someone who won't even be there.'

I nodded and moved on.

'I need to let you know that because of Abbie's career and the tragedy of her passing, we've had a reporter from the local newspaper call us as they are keen to cover her funeral.'

'Oh?' Mel blinked.

'Of course you have the choice to turn down their request to attend, or you can allow them in to the service but set rules such as no photographs or no interviews, for example.'

There was silence as they both thought about this.

'What would you do?'

'I'm afraid it has to come from you. We don't often get requests like this, but then Abbie was in the public eye.'

Callum cleared his throat. 'I'd prefer to say no.'

'Sure, no problem. OK, let's move on. Did Abbie have any favourite flowers?'

'Peonies.' Callum answered in a beat.

'Oh god,' Mel laughed. 'Remember that time when she set the house up for that shoot. What was it? *Women and Home?* Anyway, she'd ordered some flowers from the florist but the order had gone wrong and instead of three large bouquets there were thirty of the bloody things!' Mel shook her head, smiling at the memory. 'Flowers everywhere! It looked stunning, but not so great when you live with someone with hay fever.' She jabbed a thumb at Callum.

I smiled along and went back to my notes. 'You told me that Abbie loved Bali?'

'Did I?' Callum frowned.

I swallowed quickly, suddenly realising that he hadn't actually told me that; it was something I'd picked up from my Facebook session the other night. There was an album of tropical photos that Abbie had tagged herself in.

'Oh, I'm sure you mentioned that she'd visited a few times?'

Oh no, was I just digging myself a hole?

There was a long, uncomfortable silence.

Finally, Callum spoke. 'Every day has been such a blur, to be honest…'

'I'm sure it has.' I remembered to breathe and hoped my cheeks hadn't flushed with colour. 'I just wondered if you might like to incorporate her love of travel into the service somehow? Maybe we could display mementos of your travelling trips for guests to see as they enter? We could wrap colourful Balinese sarongs around the pew ends as a tribute to her wanderlust?'

They were both silent for a second. I really hoped I'd read the signs right, that they were up for a less traditional and more personal service.

'I think that's a really nice idea, Cal.' Mel smiled. 'Show the guests another side to her than just the modelling, glam, party-girl Abbie?'

That was the first time I'd heard Mel give her sister-in-law a compliment of sorts. I wondered what had gone on between the two of them; there seemed to be some frostiness on Mel's part.

'Yeah... sounds good,' he mumbled. He was clearly in that *tell me where to go and what do* stage of shock. I wasn't even sure he was taking any of this in.

A while later I closed the file, the soft sound making Callum jump.

'One last thing.' I paused. 'We've got Abbie in our care now.'

'Really? Through there?' Mel nodded to the wall separating us and the viewing room.

I nodded. 'We can arrange a time before the funeral for you to be alone with her?'

'As in, see her again?' Mel visibly shivered at the thought.

'Well, no, it will be a closed casket.' They had decided not to have Abbie embalmed. She had sustained some horrific injuries in the accident that no make-up could easily cover. 'But you're more than welcome to take a seat in the chapel of rest with her. Some people find it comforting to say goodbye that way – to take your time alone, without the other funeral guests around. Some also say that seeing the coffin before the funeral may help to avoid some of the shock on the day?'

Mel looked at Callum. 'It's up to you, bro? I don't feel like I want to but... you might?'

Callum chewed on his lip.

'You don't need to decide right now. She is here, safe and in our care until the funeral, so if you do want to sit with her, as long as you give us a call before turning up, we can make sure you won't be disturbed. Have a think about it?' I stood to my feet, making the decision for them.

'Good idea. Thanks, Grace.' Mel took my lead.

Linda was standing looking highly conspicuous, adjusting a pile of leaflets near the front door. For one moment I thought she was going to pass Mel and Callum a fact sheet on signing up for their own prepaid plan, but luckily she just smiled at the pair of them and stuck out a hand.

'Linda Bates, a colleague of Grace's. I'm so sorry for your loss. I'm sure Grace has already informed you about the media interest we've had? I'm sure the piece will make a fitting tribute to your wife,' she soothed.

'Oh, well, actually –' I began.

Callum cut me off. 'We're not allowing any journalists to come.'

Linda looked taken aback.

I noticed Mel frown, clearly thinking she was missing something.

'Really? Oh, I understand that you have your reasons but... and I don't want to tread on any toes.' She dared to glance at me. 'But we usually find that if the newspaper asks to cover a funeral it's because they see it as newsworthy. That your wife's passing could be used in both a personal tribute to the woman she was, as well as to possibly highlight issues in the community, like increasing road safety awareness... for example.'

I was quietly furious. Linda didn't have the Anderson's best interests at heart, she just wanted the media to attend as it would get the business more exposure. Plus, as a bonus, she knew that it would mean I'd be under more pressure. I clenched my teeth. 'Thanks, Linda, but I think –'

'Hang on,' Callum said, pausing to look at his sister who gave a slight shrug. 'Maybe we should say yes?'

'It's really up to you,' Mel offered.

I finally found my voice. 'You don't need to decide right now; if you want to think about it and let me know?'

'Yes, do think about it,' Linda simpered. 'I wouldn't want you to regret not making the most of an opportunity that has arisen from something so tragic.'

Callum nodded forcefully. 'Let's let them in, as long as they don't speak to anyone or expect an interview. I think you're right, Lisa –'

'Linda.'

'Sorry, Linda. I think you're right that if something good can come out of this then we should act on it.'

'If you're fine with it, then so am I,' Mel said, and gently rubbed his arm.

'I think it's the right decision. Also, please remember that the whole of the team send you their wishes and thoughts at this time,' Linda said, nodding along to herself.

What was she doing? Why did she sound like she was

reading from a bad script? Her confidence really knew no bounds.

'Thanks,' Mel said warmly.

'Our door is always open,' Linda said in this strange sing-song voice as she opened the front door.

'Er, right, see you,' Callum stuttered as they finally made their way outside.

'Such a shame,' Linda shook her head, watching the siblings through the window. 'And him, all alone... I can see now why you were adamant about keeping this one all to yourself, Grace. You never said just how attractive Mr Anderson was.'

'Excuse me.'

I was not going to take her bait. Instead I hurried back into the meeting room to collect our half-empty mugs. I hated the way she always had to have the last word. I also hated how she knew exactly which buttons to press to get a reaction.

Chapter 11

Ms Norris sat on a chair in the centre of the musty room, bringing me up to speed with what she'd been up to since I saw her last, watching me set the room up. I'd decided not to waste as much time or effort on baking so many different recipes, nor blowing up balloons that, in all likelihood, were going to go unseen.

'Right. This is for next week.' She unfolded a neatly handwritten list of ingredients. 'I thought after macarons it was only right to graduate onto baklava…'

I couldn't help but smile at the cheeky wink in her eye.

'Ah, and here comes young Marcus!' Ms Norris beamed as the door creaked open.

'Sorry I'm late. My mam needed us to stay and help find Gordon. He'd escaped again.' He rolled his eyes and scooted a chair over.

'Gordon?'

'My hamster,' he clarified with a shrug. 'This is the third time in three days he's managed to get out of his cage. My mam got it off Facebook Market Place and I reckon it's got a dud door as she only paid twenty quid and in the shops they're at least forty-five. She loves a

97

deal.' He sat back and placed a large skater-style trainer on one skinny leg of his jeans.

'Did you find him?'

'Yeah, he was hiding in the back of the telly unit where we keep old copies of the TV guide. He'd made a little nest out of Phillip Schofield's face.'

'Clever boy,' Ms Norris mused.

'Well, you're here now, that's all that matters. Thanks for coming, and it's good that Gordon has been found. Again.' I cleared my throat, about to get down to business. 'So, while we're waiting for others to join us,' I said as cheerily as I could, glancing at the closed door, 'please help yourself to one of these.' I reached into my handbag and pulled out a Tupperware box of double chocolate chip cookies that I'd baked last night.

Ms Norris's eyes lit up as she took one. 'My favourites.'

'Cheers, Grace.' Marcus grabbed two. Ms Norris made a comment about him being a growing boy.

'You're too good to us, Grace.' She patted my hand gently. Her liver-spotted skin seemed alarmingly translucent against mine. 'Marcus, do you like to bake?'

He baulked at the idea and rapidly shook his head. 'Nah, but did you know you can make meringue using a tin of chickpeas?' Marcus said with his mouth full. 'My mam's new fella, Jason, told me that. He's a vegan.'

'What will they think of next?' Ms Norris shook her head in amusement. 'I bet your mum is pleased that you're coming here.'

'Yeah, she's glad of the peace and quiet, she said.' He shrugged. 'Means she can watch *Eastenders* in peace.'

There was a beat of silence.

'Right then, I guess we should make a start.'

The optimistic stack of forms explaining our prepaid plan options taunted me from the nearby table. I'd created an Ask A Funeral Arranger Facebook group, and posted daily motivational quotes, links to interesting news articles on grief, and details of that night's meet-up. It still wasn't working though. 'It looks like it might just be the three of us...'

Ms Norris patted my hand again. 'I mentioned it to my friend Barbara when I saw her last. I'm sure she said she was going to have a think about joining us, she just finds it difficult to get about, what with her dodgy hip and all. She's had them both done, but still struggles.'

'My mam said she'd share the Facebook page with people at work but then she got into a bit of bother with her boss over summat, so...' Marcus did an over-the-top stretch, flashing a pasty white torso. 'If no one turns up to your Funeral Arranger thingy then can we just, you know, talk?'

'Talk?'

'Yeah, like, I found it good last time how you asked me about my grandma. No one's bothered to do that for months,' he admitted, blush rushing to his full cheeks. 'After I left here I spoke to me mam about what my grandma was like, when she was my age. It's good to talk, that's what they say isn't it?'

'I certainly never expected to mention my Billy,' Ms Norris chimed. 'I went home and put a photograph I had of the two of us back on my mantelpiece. For so long it had been hidden in a drawer.'

I felt a funny burst of pride that despite the last meeting being such a let-down in terms of numbers and prepaid funeral plans, they'd both got something out of it.

'So, what you mean is you want to use this time to talk about your feelings?' I clarified.

Marcus nodded brusquely. 'Yeah, but not as, like, girly as that.'

I smiled. 'Anything in particular you wanted to talk about?'

Marcus scrunched his face up. 'Well...'

'Hello?' He was cut off by a loud, booming, friendly voice that I knew very well. 'Hope I'm not too late!'

'Raj? What are you doing here?'

He flashed a sheepish grin. 'Rani is at the shop covering for me. It's nice to see her do some work for a change.' He laughed and padded over the floor, his shiny white trainers squeaking as he did. 'I thought I'd come along and see what the *fun* was about!'

My stomach dropped. I really, really could do without him cracking lame jokes. If the event was going to become a sort of bereavement session, then it needed to be a safe space with no judgement or corny punchlines. I did the introductions and offered him a cookie. At least I could slip him a prepaid form when he left, and something might come of it.

'Who have you lost, dear?' Ms Norris asked him, patting the empty chair next to her. I hadn't laid them out in the wide circle formation. I didn't want to tempt fate.

Raj sat down and cleared his throat, but was cut off by a loud creak that made us all spin our heads to the door.

'Is this the funeral meet-up?' a lanky man called out, poking his head through the gap in the door. Long, stringy brown hair hung limply around a thin face. He was wearing a faded band T-shirt and ripped drainpipe jeans that had once been black. 'There ain't no sign or nothin'.'

A sign. I probably should get one. Make it look more professional, especially now we had two walk-ins! I felt a frisson of excitement. Maybe Ms Norris was right. Build it and they will come.

'Oh, yes! This is us.' I didn't want to correct him that the official title was 'Ask a Funeral Arranger'. I couldn't help but glance at the wall clock. It was now ten to eight. 'You're welcome to come in but we don't have long left. We have to be out of here by eight, I'm afraid.'

He didn't appear to have heard as he slunk in and nodded at Ms Norris and Marcus and Raj, before pulling up a chair. I turned to face the latecomer. I wondered if I should pull out my unread speech on funeral plans from last week, but we probably didn't have time for both that and questions.

'I'm Grace. I work as a funeral arranger at Ryebrook Funeral Home.'

'Deano.' The man jabbed a skinny finger in his direction. He had a silver bar through his nose that I caught Ms Norris admiring.

'Great to have you here, Deano. So, er, do either you or Raj have any specific questions about the funeral process you would like to ask me?'

Raj had just scoffed another cookie. I waited patiently

as Deano scratched the back of his head. 'Well, no, but yeah, but…'

'It's alright dear. This is a circle of trust,' Ms Norris piped up.

'Cheers. Well, yeah. I thought, you know, given you work in funerals you might be able to help me with sumfin,'

'Go on…'

'It's not about a funeral though. It's about death. A specific death.' Deano blinked rapidly and chewed on his ravaged nail beds. 'David Bowie.'

'David Bowie?' I thought he was going to say his mum or dad or maybe a grandparent, like Marcus had.

David Bowie?!

'Yeah. I'm just, like, wanting to know where he's gone. Cause it's not like his music can just end like that.' He clicked his fingers. 'He was a legend, man. I still can't believe he's not around anymore.' Deano's breath had gone a little jumpy. 'It feels like some awful nightmare.'

'Did you know him?' Marcus asked.

'Nah, man. Not like socially. But I felt like I knew him and he knew me. Right here.' Deano pounded on his skinny chest, above where his heart lay.

'I felt exactly the same when Princess Diana passed, god rest her soul,' Ms Norris said with a soothing click of her mouth. Raj nodded along. 'It was as if the whole world was mourning but they still didn't get it. No one could understand how she made *me* feel.'

'Exactly!' Deano nodded enthusiastically. 'But my question is… where does that energy go now they've gone?'

He slumped back on the chair, looking completely bewildered, waiting for an answer. Everyone turned to look at me expectantly. I could hear the shuffling of impatient feet outside; it was eight o'clock. I had a minute or two to try and answer this unanswerable question.

'Well… I guess what you need to take from this, what we can all take from this, is the legacy that people leave behind.' I tried to ignore the growing murmurs from the corridor and focus on the faces in front of me. 'What I mean by that is,' I glanced at Marcus, 'lives cut off too young or too soon can easily become iconic because people mourn for what they never became. The Jim Morrisons, James Deans, JFKs, Amy Winehouses of this world.' For some strange reason, Abbie Anderson's face flashed in front of my mind. Her glamorous and enviable lifestyle cut short. 'But you don't need to have been a celebrity to leave a lasting impression on someone. They will stay alive in your heads and hearts.'

'Like my grandma?' Marcus asked.

I nodded then winced. 'I'm so sorry everyone, but we're going to be hounded by a stampede of angry line dancers in a minute if we don't make a move.'

Ms Norris, Marcus and Raj obediently got to their feet. Deano stayed seated, contemplating what I'd said. He was going to find himself in the centre of a do-si-do if he wasn't careful.

'Same time next week?' Marcus called out, slinging a rucksack loosely over one shoulder. He was out the door before I had time to reply. A stream of denim-clad dancers huffed into the room.

'See you later alligator,' Ms Norris chimed. 'I'll tell my friends to pop along!'

'Me too. Thank you, Grace. It has been very illuminating!' Raj nodded.

'Please do. Er, glad you enjoyed it… Deano? We've really got to go.'

Deano looked like he was in another world.

'Deano?'

'Yeah, sure thing.' He lolled to his feet and plodded out of the room as I hurriedly grabbed my things, pushed the chairs to the edge of the room and mumbled an apology at the sour-faced dance teacher.

*

'Grace, right? You got a sec?' Deano was standing at the black chipped railings that lined the edge of the church building. Clearly waiting for me.

'Oh, sure. Everything OK?'

'Did you know that Queen Victoria ordered everything to be painted black after her husband died? So the whole of London had to paint their railings because she was in mourning?'

'Er, no, I'd not heard that before.'

'Well, turns out to be one of those urban legends. Actually black paint was cheaper and dried quicker, and even so most of the railings weren't painted till after the Second World War…' He trailed out. I had no idea why he'd hung around just to tell me this pub quiz fact.

'Right… so…'

He cleared his throat. 'What you said in there made sense, you know?'

'Oh, good. I think it's called collective grief, what you feel you're going through. Despite not personally knowing the person who's died, you treat their death as if it was personal. Can I ask...' I paused. I could be getting this wrong. 'When David Bowie died, did it, er, did it bring up any memories or feelings of other people you've lost?'

Deano chipped at some flaking paint, avoiding eye contact. His Adam's apple bobbed up and down as he eventually nodded.

'My cousin, Trev.' His voice was barely a whisper. 'We were in a band together when we were growing up.'

There it was.

I nodded sympathetically. 'I'm sorry.'

'He died of an asthma attack. Stupid fella never had his inhaler on him.' Deano wiped roughly at the tears beading down his pale, hollow cheeks. 'I'll tell you something though, he could play a mean riff on the guitar. Bowie himself would have been impressed!'

A small peek of a smile dared to shine through.

'Does Bowie's music bring you closer to Trev?'

Deano nodded. 'I guess so...'

'Maybe you could find some other fans of his music online who are feeling this way? There might be a forum or something you could join? I imagine his death touched a lot of people.' Was I clutching at straws, or was this decent guidance? I had no status to be handing out advice on matters like this.

'Yeah, I could do.' Deano blew out a sigh between his thin lips. 'I'll see you here next week then, Grace. Oh, and cheers.' He nodded his head to me as if touching an imaginary hat, and strode off into the night on long, thin legs.

I watched him go, wondering once more what had just happened. Had this evening been a success? I couldn't possibly say. I had been so naïve not to realise that running an event about funerals might turn into a space for guests to share their experiences of death and grief with one another. Suddenly what Deano had just said sank in: *see you here next week*. It would appear I was now running a regular bereavement club – with the most unlikely of members.

Chapter 12

On the day of Abbie Anderson's funeral, I woke up feeling a tug of restlessness. A mixture of nervous butterflies and anticipation swished around my stomach. I'd had a restless night, all the last-minute details dancing around my brain. I'd been running over the plans, flowers and timings in my head for the past few days, certain that nothing had been missed off or forgotten.

I tried to picture Callum getting ready this morning. How he would have struggled to sleep last night, maybe popped a sleeping tablet or knocked back a couple of glasses of whisky. How he would be in a state of shock that this unimaginable day was happening. I wondered if Mel had stayed over, or if he'd been alone in their house.

I pictured him surrounded by reminders of his wife everywhere. Her favourite perfume on the dressing table, possibly a collection of printed-out photographs of the two of them tacked to the wall, her smiling and very much alive face beaming down at him. Her razor on the side of the shower, a silk kimono hanging on the back of the bedroom door waiting to be worn again. I couldn't imagine what it would be like to have reminders of your lost love thrust in your face the moment you woke up.

These thoughts ran through my brain like images from a film that I'd snuck into halfway through. I brewed my morning coffee, wondering if he was able to stomach anything to eat. If friends or family members had started arriving at his house, milling around and putting the just-boiled kettle back on for something to do. Making trays of weak tea that wouldn't be drunk, rounds of buttery toast that would go cold. The hubbub of being surrounded by those who knew you the best, yet feeling the loneliest you've ever felt.

I'd cleared my schedule so I could be at the crematorium earlier than normal to ensure everything was as it should be. I had heard from the local paper that a reporter had agreed to the stipulations set by Callum, but it still made me feel uneasy. Obviously if he was happy with them being there then that was all that mattered – I just hoped they behaved themselves, acted respectfully, and that the published article was what Callum wanted.

*

I pulled up to the car park at the crematorium feeling flustered. People drove like maniacs. I couldn't understand why other drivers were so blind to the clear signs displaying the legal speed limit. It seemed others struggled to understand the concept of leaving a two-second gap between them and the car in front. For some reason other drivers liked to beep and wave aggressively as I trundled my way through town. I was used to it. I'd seen too many cases of the after-effects of shoddy driving to let their frustration affect me.

I headed inside and quickly busied myself with the final checks. The Balinese sarongs draped over the pews softened the room. The bright paper umbrellas I'd sourced online, and asked Leon to hang along the far wall, looked even better in reality. I'd ended up watering down the props that I'd hoped to put in place. I'd even had to fight for these additions, when Frank had asked me what 'look' I was going for this time. He was keen for the room to stay traditional, but I'd argued that Abbie wasn't that person. We'd reached a compromise, but the batik wall hangings draped over the windows hadn't made the final cut. Despite that I smiled; it was coming together in here, that was for sure. A taste of the exotic world that Abbie had experienced, brought to a chapel in Ryebrook.

'Thanks for your help getting those up,' I said to Leon, nodding at the umbrellas. 'They look great.'

I pulled out the typed to-do list from my suit jacket pocket at the same time as my mobile phone rang.

'Here, pass me your list. You get that and I'll get cracking with this,' Leon said.

'Thank you.'

Hurriedly excusing myself I jogged out of the back door, knowing the front would soon be filling up with mourners. I stepped out into the spring sunlight – it felt warm against my skin – and pressed answer.

'Grace Salmon speaking.'

'Ah, Grace, lovey.'

Ms Norris. What was she doing calling me?

'Sorry to bother you but I've been having some thoughts about your Ask a Funeral Arranger events.'

'Oh, OK, well, the thing is I'm kind of tied up right now –'

'Yes, well, I mentioned it to some of the ladies at bingo who were quite interested to come along.'

I heard the sounds of 'Ave Maria' start up. The doors would be opening any second, Callum and his loved ones filing in. I needed to get back in there to make sure everything was ready.

'Mmm-hmm.'

'I know you're disappointed not to get the numbers you'd hoped for by now, but I think once word gets out you'll be inundated with people. I'm certain that it could be quite beneficial, for everyone.'

'Let's discuss this on Friday, shall we? I really do have to get on –'

She spoke over me, clearly excited by the prospect.

'I just thought that it could be a talking point for the community. A way to bring people together. Like I said, I have been spreading the word. Telling my friends that they *must* come on a Friday to have a cheerful chat about death.'

'I'm glad you're finding it helpful –'

'And young Marcus could clearly do with having a supportive ear to turn to.'

'Mmm.'

'I must say that Deano is an interesting chap, although

I'm not entirely sure about those funny things in his ears, stretching them out for some unknown reason, maybe it's a medical condition. And Raj, well he is charming. He's a comedian, did you know?'

The music had ended and the collective sound of bodies taking their seats filled my ears. Two smartly dressed members of the crematorium staff walked out and began placing flowers in the section marked off for Abbie. I nodded a brief hello as they gently positioned the arrangements on the ground.

'So, I was thinking maybe we could do a flash mob? Have you heard of those, dear? We could wear matching T-shirts and parade through town handing out leaflets to encourage others to come along? It would be ever so fun!' As Ms Norris spoke, I walked along the row of blooms, straightening them here and there, making sure the cards were clearly displayed.

'That's great, I'm so sorry, Ms Norris, but I really must go now –'

The flowers were beautiful. A real mix of shapes and sizes, summing up Abbie's vivacious personality. No bog-standard carnations here. They ranged from a riot of colour with tropical and exotic wreaths that her parents had sent, to fresh springtime greens and yellow buds from her modelling agency.

'Anyway I'll let you get on. See you then, deary!'

I stared at my phone as she hung up. Her heart was in the right place, but she needed to work on her timing. As the droning melodic notes of the organ started, I realised they were already onto the hymns. I had to get a move on. I was about to jog around to the front of the building when something caught my eye. The flowers at the far end of the row stood out – not just because it was the only pure-white collection, lilies and gypsophila – but because it didn't have a card showing who had sent it. Judging by the size of the bouquet it must have been expensive. The icy coolness was a classic choice, but very much out of place compared to the warm colours of the other bouquets and wreaths.

Where was the note? I scanned my eyes around to see if it had come loose and blown off, but there was nothing. The area was pristine, swept clear of any fallen leaves. Whoever had sent such a tribute would not be pleased that they wouldn't be credited for it. This had never happened on my watch before. I tried to run through my mind who we had taken flower deliveries from, but I was too harassed to remember properly. Ms Norris's call had thrown me off kilter.

I couldn't stand around fretting any longer. I had to get inside and make sure nothing else went off plan. I jogged around to the front door, forcing myself to slow my pace down and take a breath. I would slip in the back as quietly as I could.

I gasped as I did. I'd never seen the place so packed. Grim-faced mourners all squashed in together. Each row was completely full, with extra people squeezed onto each pew. Standing room only for the rest. It was clearly a compliment to Abbie that so many people wanted to pay their respects. A cocktail of intoxicating perfumes filled my nose as I took a space on the right, huddled next to a familiar-looking man with chiselled cheekbones, jet-black glossy hair and a suit that oozed money. He smelt of expensive aftershave and cigarettes, and judging by the fact he was standing at the back with me, had arrived late too.

It was impossible to crane my neck to try and spot Callum or Mel on the front row. A sea of tailored suit jackets, impressive black-feathered headpieces and sombre shirts were laid out before me. I hoped we had enough orders of service.

The celebrant was finishing the eulogy, his voice calm and measured as he got through to the final sentence on the card placed on the oak lectern in front of him. It's such a huge and terrifying job – summing up someone's entire existence in just five minutes.

'It's so fucking unfair,' the handsome man next to me said in a low Welsh accent. Talking to me but not really. I spotted the flash of a wedding band on his hand as he gripped a packet of tissues and shook his head.

I wondered why he looked familiar. Maybe he was a model at Abbie's agency; he was certainly good-looking enough, but then half of the congregation wouldn't have looked out of place in a fashion magazine.

Another man stood up and walked slowly to the front, swapping places with the celebrant. His hands were shaking. The colour drained from his long face. This must be Nick, Mel's husband, about to do his reading. He kept his eyes fixed to the piece of paper in his hands, and spoke self-consciously about the shortness of time and how the days are long but the years are not.

Nick did an awkward bow and went to take his seat, just as Enrique Iglesias's voice started up from the speaker. The Welsh man loudly sniffed back the tears next to me. I offered him a fresh tissue to replace the one he was pulling to shreds, his head bowed and chest shaking.

*

'Grace?'

I was rummaging in my bag for my car keys when I heard someone call my name. I'd taken the longer route to the car park in order to stay out of the Anderson family's way. No doubt Callum would be feeling utterly overwhelmed with all the faces and handshakes he was battling through. I'd give him a call in a few days and offer any more help or support. Luckily the newspaper reporter had followed his wishes and slipped in and out the back without trying to grab an interview.

I was still feeling irritated about the missing flower note. How could that have escaped my notice? I would need to be ready with an apology for the family for letting it get overlooked. I just hoped it hadn't come off in the back of the hearse. I sighed and tried to let it go.

I turned round to see Mel standing by an ornate water fountain, half tucked behind a fir tree. She was crouching down watching a little boy with red wavy hair pointing at what looked like a squirming worm in the slate chippings. Flecks of dirt clung to the hem of her flowing black skirt, her chunky black cardigan had small prints of white butterflies on it. She stood up and wiped her hands on her thighs before smiling politely at me. The little boy, her son I presumed, flicked his face at me, squinting in the sunshine, then clearly decided I was much less interesting than the insects.

'Hi!' Mel ran a hand through her hair. She'd tied it back but a few tendrils had escaped. She looked exhausted. 'It's lovely to see you.'

'Hi, you too.'

Mel's attention was drawn back to the boy who had found a stick and was attempting to lift the worm up with it.

'Noah, put it down. Mr Worm doesn't want to go flying today, thank you very much.' She tutted lovingly and rolled her eyes at me. 'He's fifteen months old. I hadn't planned on bringing him but the childminder called in sick so…' She trailed off. 'Luckily my neighbour was able to come and wait with him out here, but she's had to rush off and this little man has decided he wasn't ready to say goodbye to his new friends.'

Noah giggled as the worm flicked its marshmallow-pink tail and found itself back on the ground, writhing around, trying to free itself from his pudgy starfish handprint.

'It was a good turnout,' I said, filling the silence as Mel tried to get her son's attention away from the worm and onto a large leaf. I glanced back at the chapel. The last of the mourners were chatting next to the open doors of their cars. A few were smoking.

'Yes. She was very popular.'

'How's, er, how's Callum doing?'

'Oh, well,' she sighed. 'You know…'

I nodded. I was about to leave when she cleared her throat.

'I, er, I actually wanted to speak to you. I've been thinking about how I probably came across when we first met. You know, with my views on Abbie.' I waited, wondering what she was about to say. 'You probably picked up that we were hardly the best of friends. I just didn't want you to think badly of me. Nick is always telling me off for overthinking things but, well, I just wanted to say that although Abbie was certainly no saint, she didn't deserve what happened to her.'

'Oh. Er, right…'

'Now you think I'm even more of a weirdo!' Mel clapped a hand to her mouth, making her son giggle.

'No, of course not.'

Mel flashed a brief smile.

'Thanks. Right mister. I think it's time we went back for your nap.' Noah broke into a long whine and scrunched his face up in protest. He began banging his tiny feet on the ground. 'It looks like someone is starting early with the troublesome twos,' Mel sighed, starting to pull her son to his feet, despite his protestations. 'Are you coming back to the wake, Grace?'

'Oh, well, I don't really think…' I started, but she could barely hear me over Noah's increasing wails, tears falling down his rosy cheeks.

'I need to get this one back, then Nick is thankfully

taking over. He had to rush off as our other son, Finley, has had a bump at school.' She rolled her eyes whilst pulling a rigid little arm through a small puffer jacket. 'The joys of parenthood. I'm sure Callum would love to say thank you. Well, that's if he's not drowning himself in a bottle of Jack Daniel's.' A flash of concern crossed her harassed face. 'There's going to be way too much food and I certainly can't eat it all.'

Noah appeared to be turning his small frame into a rigid plank. His mum eventually managed to successfully get his other arm in the bright yellow sleeve.

I wanted to say thanks for the kind offer, but I had to get back to work. I swear the words were on the tip of my tongue, but curiosity got the better of me. This could be my only chance at seeing what life really was like behind closed doors for the Andersons. To see if the picture I'd created in my mind was spot on or not.

'Are you sure? I don't want to be in the way.'

Mel waved a hand, dismissing my concerns. Noah had relaxed, sobs replaced by giggles at an orange rubber monkey that she had pulled out of her pocket.

'There's going to be tons of people, all of them size zero models, so the food really will go to waste. That's another reason why we've been hiding out round here; I don't have much in common with them.' She managed to zip up Noah's coat, he was too preoccupied with the new toy to notice his mum had won the battle. 'There. Right, yes, sorry Grace. The wake will be at Callum's house. It's number three, Cherry Tree Way. If you get to Waitrose then you've gone too far.'

I repeated the address in my head. Hearing the road name, and picturing that side of town, my previous vision of the Anderson's shabby-chic home life shattered. The houses on that street were for the *seriously* rich. I was even more curious.

Noah was bored of us chatting, so thrust a chubby hand in his mother's mouth to get her attention. Mel laughed. 'Yes, OK, we'll go now. Maybe see you there then, Grace?' she called out as they headed off down the path away from me.

'Yeah, maybe,' I said, knowing full well that I couldn't *not* go.

Chapter 13

I had to park halfway down the street. The gleaming cars that I'd seen in the crematorium car park were now filling the long, sweeping driveway and nearby kerbs. I tried to walk with purpose to the front door, fighting with my conscience that was telling me to turn around, to leave this family to mourn alone in peace. But the other side of my brain reminded me that Mel had asked me to come. I didn't want to let her down.

There was a man about my age standing near the entrance to the driveway. His head was bowed, lost in the screen of his mobile phone. Every so often he glanced up at the house then back down at his phone. He looked different to the other guests; in his ill-fitting suit, the drainpipe black trousers slightly too short, flashing mismatched socks. He caught my eye and I smiled politely, wondering if he was as apprehensive as I was about being there. He didn't return the smile, but looked back down at his phone screen instead.

I made my way down the impressive driveway that was surrounded by a biscuit-coloured high brick wall. Two impeccably maintained plots of grass were separated by raised flower beds. Colourful geraniums poked their fat heads up from the soil. A muted grey front door was partly hidden inside a wooden atrium between two oil lamps fixed to the walls.

My attention was drawn by the sound of chatter, laughing and low jazz music emanating from inside. I patiently waited on the doorstep after knocking three times. I was about to go back to my car, taking this as a sign that I wasn't meant to be here, when the front door was thrust open and the handsome Welsh man I'd stood next to in the service flew out, almost bashing into me.

'Sorry,' he said in the most unapologetic of ways, an unlit cigarette in his other hand, his eyes red-rimmed and jaw tense.

He strode down the path, searching in his pocket, presumably for a lighter. He seemed to be in a great hurry to get out of there. He'd left the door wide open behind him. I felt like my feet didn't belong to me as they carried me over the doorstep and into the warmth of the bright, large hall. It reminded me of the first time I'd met Callum. Crossing the threshold into another world. My wide eyes took in the impeccably dressed crowd and animated mourners, no longer confined by the formal protocol of a funeral service, and oiled by a few glasses of the fizz that was being handed out.

'Champagne, miss?' A young man dressed in a black suit with a dicky bow tight round his neck loomed over me with a silver tray. Three flutes were standing upright, bubbles fizzing in the air.

'Oh right, thanks.' I took one, just for something to do with my hands.

The hallway was lit by a bulbous chandelier hanging low on a slim chrome flex, the light from its crystals dancing on the stark white walls. A chunky wooden console table was on my right, more suited to hold house keys and unopened post, but now littered with discarded champagne bottles and half-empty flutes, an array of lipstick smudges on the rims.

I walked through a set of wood and glass double doors, into the open-plan kitchen diner, where the real heart of the gathering was beating. I was moving as if on a conveyor belt, my feet steering me forwards out of curiosity. No one gave me a second glance. The music was louder in there, voices competing to talk over one another and snatched laughter making it feel more like a surprise birthday party than a wake. Strong musky perfume filled my nostrils as I squeezed past two women brazenly taking a selfie. I tried to spot Callum or Mel, but there were too many people crammed in there. My ears picked up on snippets of conversations, dramas about school fees and tennis clubs. I kept on moving forward.

The room was enormous. There was a curved wooden staircase in the far left-hand corner – thick planks of honey-coloured wood held together by a clear sheet of glass. The kitchen was a mix of strong midnight-blue tiles and gleaming marble, full of chrome gadgets. A huge American fridge-freezer, with an ice dispenser and a touch-screen stood in the corner. The work surface was cluttered with sympathy cards, half-empty wine glasses and cut flowers in tasteful vases.

Floor-to-ceiling glass doors looked out onto a long, manicured lawn with professionally pruned flower beds. Wide sandstone steps led down from the kitchen to a muted grey decked area, a large built-in barbecue covered up. At the far end of the long lawn was a modern brick outhouse, almost out of sight. I imagined that in the full bloom of summer the leaves from nearby trees would shield it from view, creating a perfect secret spot. There wasn't a fallen leaf in sight or stone out of place. It all looked so... perfect.

Hardly anyone was looking at the buffet, let alone taking a plate and indulging. Mel hadn't been joking when she'd said it was a spread and a half. A long table stretched down one side of the room, groaning under the weight of the food. I'd never seen anything like it in my life. A gluten-free section, a sushi platter, fresh plump pastries and an impressive fruit display. If Abbie's parents were feeling guilty for missing their own daughter's funeral, then they clearly thought this feast would make up for it.

I squeezed past two men animatedly clapping each other on the back, and managed to find an empty spot next to the buffet. I would have something to eat, like I'd promised Mel, then head back to work. On the wall behind me was a large framed photograph of Callum and Abbie on their wedding day, kissing in the centre of a snow-filled patch of grass. A winter wonderland wedding. Abbie had her hair braided, small white flowers dotted down the thick plait. She was wearing a fluffy white cover-up to keep her bronzed bare shoulders warm. They both looked so happy. I couldn't imagine how Callum had been able to get through the past couple of weeks with this bearing down on him.

'I could hardly listen to what that man was saying about poor Abbie. Saffron's lips were all I could see out of the corner of my eye,' an angular woman standing next to me in a sequined dress said to her friend. I'd tried to squeeze past her to get a plate.

'Did you see them!? And she said she only had a small top-up of filler.' Her friend tried to raise an eyebrow that was frozen in place.

'Oh, please. If that's the truth, then I'm wearing Primarni.' They both dissolved into high-pitched giggles.

'Excuse me,' I piped up. 'Would you mind passing a plate, they're just behind you?'

'Oh, right.' The frozen eyebrow lady still managed to give me an impressive dressing down with her eyes, her mouth stuck in a pinched half-smile. 'Here.'

It was a look that told me, in no uncertain terms, just how out of place I was. I fidgeted in my cardigan, suddenly feeling very warm. I took the plate and nodded my thanks. The women moved away quickly, murmuring something under their breath as they went.

'It's like they'll put on weight just by standing near the food.' The man in the ill-fitting suit, that I'd seen hovering outside, was now standing beside me. He spoke through a mouthful of sausage roll. Flecks of pastry dropped onto the wide lapel of his jacket. 'Whoops, don't want to make a mess.'

He dabbed the crumbs with a linen napkin plucked from a stack that were artfully displayed on the table.

'I always eat too much when I'm nervous.' He stuffed another huge piece into his mouth, his cheeks flushing pink. 'And talk too much... apparently.'

I smiled kindly. 'It looks like there's enough food here for an army.'

'Yeah, and judging by those here,' he cast a not-so-subtle side-eye at the room full of skinny, beautiful people, 'it's going to go to waste. Please don't let me be the only one to get stuck in.'

I reached over the wasabi dip and picked up a handful of prawn crackers that were individually wrapped. I usually wasn't so keen on an open buffet, the possibilities of cross-contamination and bacteria was insanely high. More than 500 people die of food poisoning each year, after all. But looking at the impressive selection, it appeared to be top quality and as fresh as you could get. I decided to risk it.

'Good choice.' He nodded approvingly. 'I'm Daniel, by the way.'

'Grace.' I awkwardly shook his hand with my other free hand.

'It doesn't feel right to meet someone in a situation like this and not ask "Do you come here often?"' He smiled weakly.

'Like a funeral crasher?'

'You know, those sort of people are rare but they do exist.'

'You sound like you're speaking from experience.'

'All I'm saying is that if I did crash funerals then you'd find me right here filling up on the free food. The key would be to fit in without standing out.' His hazel eyes crinkled into a smile. 'If you think about it, how hard would it be to pretend you knew the person? I mean, read the newspaper, do some digging online and you could come up with enough details to pass off why you should be here.'

'True, but what if you're asked to sign the condolence book?'

'Hmm.' He took a sip of his drink.

I felt suddenly aware that I could have something stuck between my teeth. Daniel was good-looking, in an unconventional, awkward sort of way. Maybe it was the that way his suit clearly didn't come from Savile Row, like many of the other guests, but I felt oddly comfortable around him.

'I guess you'd have to politely say you would sign it later, you needed to think of exactly the right way to express yourself. Seriously though, I've heard this story of a man who was addicted to going to funerals. Some Brazilian dude. He even quit his job, just so he could go to every funeral in his home town. He's like some sort of celebrity to the funeral directors,' Daniel's eyes creased up in mirth. 'It's an interesting hobby, that's for sure.'

'But can you imagine the drama it could cause? You could easily say the wrong thing and give people the idea the deceased had lived a double life or something!'

Daniel smiled but didn't seem like he got the joke. I had taken it too far.

'So, er, did you know Abbie well?' I asked, hoping to get back to solid ground.

He knocked the rest of his glass back in one. 'Yeah, well, something like that. I designed that,' he nodded his head to the piece of art hanging on the wall to our right, before topping up his glass from an open bottle of fizz next to the satay sticks. Tiny white clay leaves appeared to be caught mid-air, blowing across the muted wall. It was incredibly detailed.

'Wow, so you're an artist?'

He shrugged, turning away from the sculpture.

'Yeah, for my sins.' He paused briefly. 'Abbie wanted a bespoke piece that no one else would have.' Judging by the look of the people inside, the flash cars outside and the over-the-top buffet, I guessed that keeping up with the Joneses was top of most of the guests' agendas.

'Here.' He passed a business card. Daniel Sterling: Artist. I suddenly remembered reading Abbie's five-star review on his Facebook page. 'I need to get through these. What do you do, Grace?'

'Oh, I'm...'

I was interrupted by the sound of a knife tinkling against a glass. Hush descended on the room, before Callum's voice rang out. I tried to wiggle around the men huddled in front of me to see him properly. I caught Daniel watching me from the corner of his eye. He had stuffed another sausage roll into his mouth.

'Hey, er, hi.' Callum cleared his throat.

The two gossiping women were beaming at him. A bald man shouted at people chatting in the hall to quieten down. I slid into a small gap at the end of the table near the stack of marbled meringues the size of fists. Callum looked shattered. His skinny tie was askew and top shirt button open. He was standing next to Mel and the man I'd seen lead him from the service.

'I'm, er, not really sure what to say.' He glanced at his sister who nodded encouragingly at him. 'Thanks for coming, I guess.' He wiped his forehead. His other hand was gripping a champagne flute so tightly I thought the stem would shatter. 'I never ever thought I'd be making a speech at my wife's funeral, so you'll have to forgive me for not having anything better prepared...'

A low murmur of sympathetic noises came from the cluster of women. Callum cleared his throat and tried to smile light-heartedly.

'Mel and I would like to thank Abbie's parents for the food. Even though they couldn't be here today they sent enough to feed the whole street so please do make sure you eat something.' He waved a hand at the buffet table, catching my eye. I tried to telepathically send him some positive thoughts through a half-smile. He flicked his eyes back to the rest of the room and carried on. 'Thanks to everyone who helped with the service, I hope we gave her a good send-off.'

'Hear, hear,' the man next to him cheered.

'I know she'd be thrilled to see all of you in this room, kicking herself at having to miss out. We all know how much of a party-girl she was.' He cleared his throat. 'Abbie was taken from us way too soon. I can't really put into words what life without this vivacious, kind and smart woman will be like. She lit up a room when she walked in, turning heads with her looks as well as her quick mind and wit.' He paused as if to compose himself. Mel rubbed the small of his back.

I wondered what Abbie would have made of it all, if the glitz and glamour of her wake was what she had wanted. It was easy to forget the purpose of why we were all in that vast room, with the music, laughter and generous buffet fooling you into believing you were at some cocktail party, just waiting for the arrival of the hostess. A hostess who would never return. The atmosphere sobered as Callum's short speech came to an end.

'If you could all raise your glasses. To Abbie.'

'To Abbie,' the room chorused.

Chapter 14

Sitting in the waiting area, I twisted my fingers round the strap of my bag. I couldn't believe I was actually going through with it.

For reasons I couldn't begin to explain, I'd booked in for a haircut with Andre, the hairdresser Abbie had raved about online. The cold woman on the phone had informed me numerous times how lucky I was to get a cancellation spot with Andre himself so soon, as usually I'd have been waiting at least three weeks for the honour.

I put down the heavy fashion magazine that I'd picked up, hoping to look like I belonged in a place like this. A place where I'd been handed a chilled glass of fruit-infused iced water when I'd arrived and been told to take a seat; Andre would be with me shortly. It had been nine and a half minutes and still no sign of him.

Eventually, an Italian drawl rang out across the salon.

'Grace Salmone?' A tall man with jet black hair slicked back into a severe side parting, like a 1930s film star, stalked across the room then sneered down at me. He was clearly a man used to looking down his roman nose at people. I was about to correct him that my name was Grace Salmon, like the fish, but I stopped myself. Maybe now was the time to be Grace Salmone? It sounded so continental. I felt so different already.

'Excellent. Follow me,' he purred then clicked his fingers at a young girl who emerged from his shadow. A large bun on the top of her head wobbled as she held out a gown, holding it so I had to contort myself to get it on. She struggled to contain a snigger.

'I'm Andre,' he said, pressing his large tanned hands onto my shoulders and firmly pushing me into the Perspex bucket chair. 'So. What are we doing today?' His fingers pulled out my elastic hairband and shook out my hair, fanning it around my face, examining it disdainfully.

'Oh, well, I'm after something different. A new style,' I stammered, repeating what I'd been rehearsing in my head since making the appointment.

He lifted a strand and let it fall in barely hidden disgust.

'Mmm-hmm. And what is your home care regime?'

Home care regime?

'Oh, well, I probably wash it every other day.'

'Hmm. I was thinking more along the lines of what products you use…'

'Shampoo and conditioner?'

'Never mind.' He shook his head. I'd clearly failed whatever test he had set me. 'So, any ideas for this *new style*?'

'I was thinking maybe blonde bits?'

Blonde bits was perhaps not the technical term for the streaks of honey-colour that had shone from Abbie's head, but that was the sort of thing I was thinking.

Andre reared back and pursed his pillowy lips. 'No, no, no, no.'

'No?'

'No.'

'Oh.'

'You are much too pale for blonde. Not enough depth for blonde. You can *never* be a blonde.' He waved a hand elaborately in front of my face – my sallow-skinned face – and winced at my misfortune with genetics.

Well, that's it then. I shifted in the uncomfortable chair. I should have stuck to Chatty Claire, she'd never judged my pasty hue before. *But*, my brain reminded me, *she's never dyed your hair before*. Same old boring brown. Same old boring Grace. I realised that Andre was still talking, and half scowling, at me.

'I've got it.' He paused, holding his large palms flat against my head, squishing my ears slightly. '*Rrrrrred* is more your colour.' He lifted up a strand of my hair and let it fall, as if to prove some point.

'Red?' I stuttered.

'Yes, darling. *Rrrrrred*. It is in this season. *Trrrrrust* me.' He didn't give me a second to doubt his creative skills as he leant his head back and roared across the sound of hairdryers. 'Verity!' The big-bunned, big-eyed girl scurried across. 'Get Miss Salmone to the preparation area. We're going *rrrrrred*!'

'Wonderful choice, Andre,' she simpered as he flamboyantly strode off. 'You are *so* lucky! He is going to make you look, like, *so* incredible. You won't recognise yourself!'

Andre was soon back with a small dish and a slim paintbrush in his hand, ferociously whisking the bright dye mixture.

I tried to find my voice. 'When you said red… did you mean like the odd strawberry-blonde strand?'

'Shhh, Andre is at work now. Verity, get Miss Salmone some literature to relax with.'

Verity dropped a stack of new fashion magazines onto my lap and went to refill my fruity water drink.

Take a deep breath, Grace. You are very lucky to be here.

Forty minutes and a magazine later, I was sure some of the people in the 'Spotted' section of the magazine had been at Abbie's funeral. There were a lot of similar-looking Chanel jackets and logoed handbags. Andre had returned and ordered Verity to wash the colour off. I'd been so engrossed in a feature on beautiful women and their beautiful handbags, I'd half forgotten where I was.

'Every woman knows the secret to happiness is hanging off her arm, or across her body, or in the clutch of her hand. Handbags are the one accessory that makes or breaks an outfit. They are an expression of who we are and where we belong. As Nora Ephron famously said: "… your purse is, in some absolutely horrible way, you… " It's where fashion meets function and a nod to personal style and social status…'

I glanced down at the bag tucked beneath my feet, my Safest Bag in The World™. I'd read a report which said that bag-slashing was sweeping the nation, so had invested in the expensive bag with a thick, inbuilt layer of cut-proof material, secret zips and a pocket for my rape alarm. I'd only just bought it but, looking at the glitzy handbags and the happy women holding them and grinning in ecstasy, maybe I was missing out? Maybe Grace Salmone deserved a shiny bag for her shiny hair?

'Follow me!' Verity beckoned, breaking my thoughts, instructing me to lie back on the reclined chair over the sink.

I was soon lost in follicle euphoria as Verity ran her nimble fingers across my scalp, massaging in lavender shampoo. Abbie had clearly trusted Andre so I needed to do the same. *What if Verity is right and I don't recognise myself?* I thought as she vigorously kneaded in candy floss-scented conditioner. *But isn't that the whole point of being here?* Verity led me back to where Andre was waiting, slim silver scissors in one hand and a hairbrush in the other.

'Ok.' Andre paused as I sat back down, fingers under the big fluffy towel-turban that was hiding the new Grace Salmone. I felt like I couldn't breathe. 'Now...' He whipped off the towel with a flourish and as he did, vibrant red locks tumbled down; thick, wet strands slapping my cheeks.

'Wow!' Verity squealed and clapped her hands together. Andre gave a slight smile then ushered his helper to stand back.

'It's really... red!' I couldn't stop gawping at my reflection. A pale-faced woman with big eyes and hair the colour of a damp letterbox was staring back at me.

Andre brandished his scissors. The soft snipping sound woke me from my stunned silence.

'Just, just a slight trim? I really think the colour alone is enough of a change…'

No one was going to recognise me. *No one was going to recognise me!* I repeated that thought with a slight smile. I tried to let Andre work his magic, telling myself that whatever style he wanted to go for – bar a Bic razor – was going to be fine. *It's only hair, it will grow back*. He swiftly turned on the hairdryer, its turbo sounds blocking out the rising anxiety in my stomach that said that there was no way I, Grace Salmon, could pull off a traffic-stopping shade of red.

But perhaps Grace Salmone could…

Ten minutes later Andre switched off the hairdryer. 'Cover your eyes for the hairspray. I tell you when it is OK to open.'

I obeyed, making sure to shut my lips from the noxious chemicals.

'OK… annnnnnd open!'

I kept one eye shut as the other nervously flickered open. I inhaled sharply. The mousy brown mid-length hair I'd walked in with, the same style I'd had for about thirty-three years, was now a deep rich shade of red, that bobbed perfectly on my shoulders. It was full of volume, a glossy shine, and looked ridiculously healthy considering the dye and ozone-layer-destroying products on it. I blinked. Nope, it was still me.

'So, Miss Salmone. Happy?' Andre purred, running his fingers through the ends. They seemed to spring back to his touch. Verity was sniffing loudly behind me – was she crying? I couldn't take my eyes off my reflection to check. My skin looked brighter, my eyes sparkled and my fingers instinctively went to stroke my new do.

'No!' Andre batted my hand away. 'You leave it like this. Like this is perfection.'

I nodded blindly and let him spin me halfway on my chair so I could stand up. Verity took my robe, shaking off tendrils of red onto the shiny floor. I numbly followed her to the tills, giving Andre a brief wave.

I must have been in a state of shock as when the pretty receptionist told me how much the experience cost, I handed over my bank card, assuming I'd misheard her. I tried to tell myself that this feeling, one I could understand Abbie getting addicted to, was priceless.

*

Back home, I knew that Andre had said not to touch it, or I'd ruin the lines or something, but I couldn't help myself. I felt elated at what I'd achieved, tinged with the tiniest edges of disgust at how much I'd spent to achieve it. But future-Grace could worry about the bank statement. Today was about Grace Salmone and her bouncy new do. I felt like this hair deserved cocktails and dancing. It didn't deserve to be sat in with a battered copy of *Jane Eyre* and thermal pyjamas.

But, who was I going to go for cocktails with? It was like painting a house; when you finished one room you realised just how grubby and unloved the rest of it was.

I still needed to do a lot of work on the rest of me. It was plain to see that I needed to get some friends – OK, a friend. I powered up my laptop. I knew where friends were ready and waiting, if I had the courage to find them.

You have a new notification, Facebook helpfully told me. *Tina Salmon wants to be friends!* I ignored my mum's request and clicked on the search bar.

I hadn't spoken to my 'best friend' since I left London. I knew that I shouldn't, nothing good could come of it, yet I did it anyway. I typed in Tasha Birtwell. There were sixteen matches that popped up, but only one of them had worked at Cooper & Co. I clicked on it. She looked different. Older, obviously, her long chestnut hair was messily piled on her head. She had also put on quite a bit of weight and was cuddling a toddler, their similar pudgy faces beaming at the camera. Tasha Birtwell was a mother? The party-girl that was always up for a laugh, now the mum of a little girl?

I'd always imagined we would have had our babies at the same sort of time. Sharing maternity leave, enjoying coffee mornings with our cherubs and swapping tales of sleepless nights. We would have done it all together, that's what best friends do – right?

Her profile wasn't set to private so I soon had access to a snapshot of her life over the past five years. I thought I'd feel more, seeing her smiling face and silly expression beaming up at me. That biting, nauseating feeling was certainly there at the pit of my stomach, but not as ferocious as I'd imagined it might be. She'd lost the title of being my best friend, snatching the promised future we'd imagined we'd share together. And all because of *him*.

I needed to close her page down. Stop haunting myself with what could have been. My old wounds were stinging. A lot of her profile page was full of baby-related spam. Blurry photos from toddler mornings she'd been to, requests for advice on potty training and the odd selfie with a glass in hand.

Yay. It's Friday! Mummy deserves a drink #Wineoclock

I clicked my mouse on the next photo but the screen didn't change. I then realised that I'd accidentally liked it. The photo was quite well hidden in the depths of one of her photo albums, one of her and her daughter at the zoo, in front of the lion enclosure. A flush of heat rose up my body as I clicked unlike. Would she see that I'd done that? Would Facebook send a message telling her that I'd been perusing her page and liking her photos? Oh my god. I was just about to close my laptop when another image stopped me in my tracks.

It was one Tasha had posted from a Timehop, captioned.

Best days of my life – pre-kids of course!

The photo was five years old. My mouth filled with saliva looking at the candid, unfiltered shot.

In an instant I could feel the weight of his arm around my shoulders. His aftershave filling my nostrils when he leant forward, laughing at something Tasha's boyfriend had said. His teeth were the most perfect shade of white I'd ever seen. He had a small dimple in his chin that I hadn't noticed until that very moment, highlighted under the disco lights of the awards ceremony after-party. It was the first time in my life that I'd felt like I belonged. My eyes flew over the faces of people I'd known, people that were now complete strangers, huddled together, champagne flutes in their raised hands. *That feeling of togetherness.*

It had been Tasha's idea to have a group photo. Herding up our colleagues so someone could capture the moment. I'd forgotten it existed. It was one of the very few photos of us together. Henry hated having his photo taken, but in that moment, lubricated by disgusting sambuca shots when we'd won Team of the Year, he'd lost those inhibitions and jumped in at the last minute.

I didn't recognise myself, even with the old dull mousy hair and awful attempt at using some of Tasha's make-up. I remembered she'd laid out all her eyeshadows and lip glosses in the ladies' loos as we'd got ready. Laughing gently at me because I didn't know how to use a pair of torturous-looking eyelash curlers. I'd desperately tried to fit in, to be as carefree as the rest of them.

Without thinking, I moved closer to the screen and gently pressed the pad of my thumb across his face. He looked so young. We all did. I had my face slightly turned away from the camera and in his direction.

I clicked on the names of the people tagged in the photo. Only Henry and I were missing. A part of me wondered if people, outsiders, would assume we were a secretive couple who preferred to keep things private. Everyone else's pages showed they were in a relationship, or married, or they had a baby in their profile picture. Even Tasha's ex from back then was smugly coupled up, and he had a face only a mother could love. Thinking about that group shot, there was still an obvious thing missing from my life. As much as I'd hoped to prove my mum and Ms Norris wrong, I was a little lonely being single.

With my new look, I needed a new life. A new attitude. Henry had controlled my head for long enough. Maybe it was time to put myself out there? I felt buoyed with the confidence that my new hair gave me, so I took a deep breath and googled.

Looking to meet singles in your area?

Links to different dating sites filled my screen. It didn't take me long to realise I'd made a huge mistake. I clicked on a couple of site and was soon scrolling down near identical pages of near identical men.

Topless pics. Illiterate men with a penchant for flexing their biceps. Heavily filtered selfies. Cheesy, pun-filled profiles. It was just too much. I closed the laptop down and took my new hair to bed.

Chapter 15

I was just laying out a tray of rock cakes when I heard the door open. Ms Norris walked into the church hall. She spotted me and stopped in her tracks, looking around uncertainly.

'Hi, Ms Norris,' I said.

'Oh hello dear! I'm sorry, lovey, I still can't get used to you as a redhead.'

I smiled. It had been over a month, and I too kept being surprised by my reflection.

'I have to say, I've been really looking forward to this evening. It's becoming a highlight of my week!' She chuckled. She'd swapped her Friday morning catch-ups for this weekly group a couple of weeks back. 'I'm sure I don't need to tell you how much these sessions are helping everyone who attends already. Just look at young Marcus.'

I glanced at the scruffy teenager who was pocketing the rock cakes I'd made.

'He's definitely got a spring in his step since the first time we met him.'

'Hmm,' I mused. 'Do you think so?'

She nodded dramatically.

'So, Grace, I've been meaning to ask: this new look isn't for a new man is it?' My cheeks flamed under her playful stare. You had to avoid Ms Norris's eyes when she looked at you like that. She had this ability to catch a whiff of a lie before it even formed around your tongue.

'You know me, I'm not really looking...'

A millisecond later I imagined Daniel Sterlings's face in my mind's eye. What was wrong with me?! After Abbie's funeral I'll admit that I had looked him up online. I'd liked his Facebook business page where he shared photos of his finished pieces, along with a pithy sentence or two.

Inspiration comes from where you least expect it #openyoureyes

A sense of satisfaction is born from the simplest of forms

Check out this month's *Home and Interiors* magazine as I feature in their list of 40 under-40 designers to watch – made up to be included in this!

I'm no art buff but I could appreciate the time and love he poured into his pieces. He had 1.2k likes. I had been half-tempted to send him a friendly message, but decided against it. He must have left the wake quite soon after Callum had finished giving his speech. I'd looked for him but he wasn't there to say goodbye to.

'You mustn't leave it too late,' continued Ms Norris. 'You need to get out there.' She finally took her eyes off me and wandered over to say hello to Raj who'd just walked in.

I put Daniel out of my mind and clapped my hands for everyone's attention. We had got a little better at starting on time. I had decided to take my role more seriously. We may not have had the huge numbers that I'd hoped for turning up every week, but Ms Norris was right, these Ask A Funeral Arranger sessions were helping those that came. Marcus did have a slight spring in his step and Deano definitely smiled a little more. If this was going to be worth everyone's time, then it made sense to treat it with more professionalism. Tonight, we had a schedule. I'd thought of some topics relating to grief and funerals to get us started. I had also had some laminated posters made that I was going to stick around town later, and a Welcome sign that I'd placed outside the front door. Ms Norris had thankfully not repeated her idea of a flash mob to encourage more people to join us.

'If you have a topic you'd like us to cover then please write it down and pop it in the box on your way out. It can be anonymous, of course.' I smiled at the familiar faces who had taken their seats, handing out pens and pieces of paper.

'Feel like I'm back at school,' Deano grinned, before jotting something down, his tongue peeking out of the right corner of his mouth.

Ms Norris smiled at me encouragingly. 'I've got one: how to give yourself permission to grieve. It's all too easy to bottle emotions up, isn't that right, Grace?'

'Er, yeah. I'll add it to the list,' I said, fixing my eyes

on the notepad on my lap. 'So, I guess I should start by asking how everyone's week went?'

'I didn't get any detentions,' Marcus said, proudly.

'Do you usually have problems with school?' Ms Norris asked.

Marcus shrugged. 'Not before, well, before my grandma... you know.' He shifted in his seat. 'But yeah, I think I have got in trouble a bit more. It's never my fault though!' he was quick to add.

'Do you feel angry about what happened?'

'Yeah. I do,' he mumbled.

'I think that's perfectly normal,' said Raj. 'Of course you're going to feel angry when someone you love has gone and is never coming back.'

'I went to town on an old guitar I had lying around,' Deano said, a proud sort of smile on his pale face. 'Proper rock star moment.'

'If you don't let it out in some way or other then it will eat you up forever,' Ms Norris said.

I shifted on my chair. 'I guess the best solution is to find a way of release that doesn't get you or anyone else into trouble.'

'Yeah, my mam said that too,' Marcus sighed.

Deano raised a hand again. 'I also took your advice, Grace, and joined some of the Bowie fan pages on Facebook. To be honest I couldn't believe how many people were on there, all like me. It's mad, really.'

'And is that helping at all?'

He grinned. 'Yeah, it's alright. And for once I'm not the biggest Bowie fan.'

I sat back in my chair listening to them swap stories with a huge smile on my face.

*

I was about to make a start when I heard a tentative knock at the door. A sallow slip of a forty-something woman nodded her head to say hello as she peeled her hand off the door handle and stepped into the room. She was wearing a mustard-yellow jacket that only magnified how pale and taut with emotion her face was. Her sunken eyes were bloodshot and marked by deep bags. She looked utterly exhausted.

'Come in!' I sang, probably a little too manically at the newcomer. 'Welcome, take a seat.' I hurried to drag a chair over and place it in the gap next to Deano. 'I'm Grace, I'm a funeral arranger and…'

The woman had barely sat down before she began to cry. Her thin, shaking hands clutched at the remnants of a tissue that she dabbed at the tip of her red, glistening nose.

'Do you need a moment?' I asked softly, aware that this poor lady was being stared at by everyone in the room. She nodded and tried to catch her breath.

'Ok, so, er, Marcus, why don't you tell us how you've been feeling this week?'

I was half listening to Marcus as well as keeping an eye on the lady.

'Like I said, school hasn't been so bad. My mam even said that I –'

A loud, painful howl of a sob emanated from the woman. My eyes darted to Ms Norris. I wasn't sure what to do. I'd only ever been in a one-on-one situation with someone this upset, and we'd been sat in a calm, relaxed office, not a draughty church hall that suddenly felt even mustier and more imposing than ever. I nodded at Marcus to get her a glass of water, which he dutifully did. I think he was grateful to have something to do. Everyone looked uncomfortable. Deano had hunched his body together and was staring fixedly at his hands, as she let out another painful howl.

'Oh, lovey. It's OK, you can talk to us. That's what we're here for.' Ms Norris was gently patting her on the shoulder and making soothing noises.

'Here, try and have some of this.' I nodded my thanks to Marcus and passed the glass to the woman who took it, spilling some on the fabric of her jeans. 'Can you tell us your name?'

'Ju-Ju-Julie.'

'Hi, Julie, I understand that you're very upset right now. I just want you to know that we're here to help,' I said.

Julie nodded. Well, I think she did, her chest was rising and falling so drastically.

'Why don't we start by doing some deep breathing? It will be easier for you to speak to us?'

I began, sounding a little like Darth Vader as I encouraged Julie to slow down her breathing. Thankfully the other group members began to participate and soon everyone was copying me.

'Great, now try and tell us what it is that's upsetting you. It's OK, take your time.'

Julie took a deep breath. 'My mum died recently and well, I'm in charge of selling her house. It's just all been a nightmare! I have no idea how to get started or what to d-d-do…'

'I'm sorry. Do you have any other relatives who could help?'

She shook her head. 'It was only me and her. And now she's gone.' She gulped at another breath that juddered through her skeletal chest.

'OK, has anyone else in the group been through something similar? It might help Julie to hear some advice on what to do next?' I asked the others hopefully.

My stomach fell, taking in their blank faces.

'When do you need to get it done by? Is there a deadline?' Raj asked softly.

'N-n-not really, I've just been p-putting it off. I tried to make a start but I found it so traumatic I just locked the door behind me and haven't been back since. I know I need to, but it's just so overwhelming. It's only a small bungalow and a lot of the stuff is very dated; she was of the generation that believed things were to be used until they were worn away.' A small flash of a smile lit up her pale face for a second. 'Of course there's the sentimental things, but nothing of great value.'

'But priceless to you.' Ms Norris bobbed her head understandingly.

'I've got a van that I could bring round? Well, where I work has one that I'm sure I can borrow for a bit,'

Deano offered. 'Happy to help you shift a few of the bigger things if you like?'

'I volunteer at a charity shop and they're always looking for donations; they can even come and collect if that helps?' Ms Norris clasped her hands together.

'I have plenty of boxes from the shop that just need taping back together,' Raj suggested.

'If you need someone to go through the legal aspect of things, I know a few contacts through work that we've directed people to before.' I felt like I wasn't offering as much as the others. It was the only thing I could think of.

'Wow. Really?' Julie was now crying but these tears were more of gratitude and joy at the kindness of strangers than of raw wounds being sliced open.

By the end of the session everyone had swapped phone numbers with Julie and made plans to help her. I said my goodbyes and grabbed the box of topic ideas that, I noticed, was filling up nicely.

Chapter 16

Before heading home I decided to pop to the few locations I had in mind to stick up my laminated posters about Ask A Funeral Arranger. I had a stack at home that I would take to the library, doctor's surgery and retirement homes over the weekend. I'd forgotten to ask Julie how she'd found out about the session. She had left with the slightest hint of colour back in her sallow cheeks. I allowed myself to feel a surge of pride at how everyone had pulled together, genuinely wanting to help her out. I really hoped she would be back to let us know how she was getting on. It had certainly spurred me on to spread the word on ways our funny little group could help others.

I stuck larger posters on a couple of lampposts, then headed to the old-fashioned wooden noticeboard on the high street. It was a little trickier than I had expected to reach the empty space at the top. I didn't want to have to move a poster for a church tea or the next gathering of the local running club, but I was too short to hold my poster in the right spot and pin it down. Beads of sweat made themselves known as I struggled on my tiptoes.

'Hey!'

My hand froze. Was it illegal to put up flyers? I must admit I hadn't done much research into the legalities. I just figured the noticeboard was for all the residents to make use of. But maybe there was some sort of committee I needed to get permission from first?

'Hey!'

The gruff voice grew louder. A wave of anxiety washed over me. Someone from the neighbouring flats must have spied me from their windows. Could I be arrested for public damage? My hand froze in mid-air. My breath was trapped in my throat. I dared not move a muscle. I could hear raspy breaths getting closer. Coming out of the darkness was a tall frame of a man, stumbling slightly as he zig-zagged over to me. He was awkwardly holding a torch, the beam dancing unsteadily on the pavement as he moved towards me.

I instinctively grabbed my Safest Bag In The World™ tighter to my chest and mentally ran through the defence steps I'd seen on *This Morning* when I'd been off with tonsillitis two years ago. A wave of adrenalin coursed up my body. All the advice from Holly and Phil dissolved from my terrified mind. Was it to knee them in the genitals and bite their arm? Or the other way round?

The footsteps were getting closer, strangled breaths growing louder, blood pulsating in my temples. A thought whizzed into my mind. I hadn't finished *my* funeral plan – I still needed to choose which charity any donations would go to. I willed my legs to move but they remained static. I let out a strangled scream, blindly karate chopping whatever was attacking me. Spots were appearing before my eyes, my legs zinged with unspent energy.

'You!... It's... It's you?'

That voice. Wait, was that... ?

I opened my tightly shut eyes to see Callum Anderson jumping back from my mad, out of control arms.

'Grace Salmon?' The bright light from his phone torch flashed my face, blinding me.

'Callum?' I dropped my arms. The stack of leaflets billowed to the concrete.

I was unable to hide my shock. He looked a mess. His facial hair had grown into patchy clumps. His eyes were bloodshot and empty, angry dark purple circles dragging them down. He was wearing a creased grey T-shirt and grubby black jeans that hung from his frame. I wondered when he'd last had a decent meal, a proper shower or a shave.

'Hi, I, er...' I stuttered. I don't know what I was expecting; the man was in mourning after all.

He frowned as if trying to place something. 'You've changed your hair.'

'Yeah,' I smiled. 'I fancied a change.'

He nodded, then confusion flashed back as he took in the scene.

'What are you doing?' An eye-watering stench of whisky hit me as he spoke. 'Are you fly posting?'

'Distributing leaflets...' I trailed out.

He picked up the posters that I'd dropped in the chaos.

'Ask A Funeral Arranger anything. Come along to

find answers to any questions you may have about your perfect goodbye. Discover support, advice and friendship every Friday at seven p.m,' he read aloud.

'And there's cake. Homemade,' I added.

He tilted his head as if thinking. 'You know Mel reckons I should do this sort of thing. Sit in a room and share my feelings.' He rolled his eyes then let out this short, sharp, shock of a laugh that seemed to echo down the quiet street. 'She wants me to join some young widowers' support group.' He shuddered. 'Found the details online. I mean, that's a club that no one wants to be part of, isn't it! They meet fortnightly in Costa Coffee on the high street. Something about how they help others cope with the early death of their partner. I told Mel I don't need to sit in a chain coffee shop, with a group of strangers, all out-trumping each other with our dead spouse stories, to feel any less shit than I do right now.'

'It might show you that you're not alone?' I said quietly, thinking about how quickly this odd bunch of Friday night friends had rounded together.

'That's what Mel said! And I said to her that I'm not alone. I've got her, and Nick, and the boys, and Rory and, well...' He trailed off and rubbed the back of his head. His hair was unkempt and greasy. The stomach-churning smell of alcohol kept coming at me in waves.

'Well, you're more than welcome to come along to our session next week.'

He looked unsteady on his feet and glanced out into the distance.

'Why are you doing this now? It's like, midnight...'

His red-rimmed eyes blinked fast as if trying to focus. 'Isn't it?' He frowned at the night sky, as if someone was playing a trick on him.

'Er,' I checked my watch. 'It's almost ten o'clock.'

I didn't need to ask him where he'd been. I coughed at the fumes emanating from his dishevelled body. I needed him to leave me alone so I could carry on. I'd be there until dawn otherwise.

'Oh.' He frowned.

'I'm trying to stick this one up here but I can't reach the space.'

He took the poster and effortlessly held it in place, and pressed a drawing pin in.

'Like that?'

'Yep. Er, thanks.'

'Any more?'

I had an optimistic stack in my bag, but I didn't want to take up any more of his time. Then again, I could use his height to my advantage.

'A couple?'

'Come on then.'

He followed me as I wandered down the inky street to the doctor's surgery. There was an outside noticeboard there too.

'Right, I'll hold this up.' He opened the large frame of glass that was on a hinge, so I could duck in and stick up another poster.

'You OK? Sorry. The pins have bent.' I winced as I pressed the point into the pad of my thumb.

'Fine.' His voice strained at how heavy the window

was to hold open. The rough wooden frame must have been there for about fifty years.

'Done.'

I stepped back, noticing a glistening of sweat on his brow. He exhaled loudly as he closed the heavy glass door and rubbed his palms together, wincing.

'You OK?'

'Fine. Where's the next one going?'

'Wait – Callum.' He turned around. 'Your hands!' He looked down. 'You're bleeding.'

His palm was smeared with crimson. He looked surprised at the cut; the alcohol must have anaesthetised any pain.

He shrugged. 'It's nothing.'

'It doesn't look like nothing. You need to get it washed out and cleaned. You don't want an infection.'

He wiped his palms against his thighs, blood smeared down his grubby jeans.

He grimaced slightly. 'It's fine.'

I don't know if it was the fact he'd helped me, but I wanted to thank him. If I let him go back to his house in this state I knew he wouldn't bother to wash the dirt from the wound, let alone dress it correctly.

'Why don't you come up to mine? I can try to bandage it up?'

He slowly lifted his face to mine.

'I only live on the next street. It won't take long.'

He eventually nodded and let me lead the way. Neither of us spoke on the short walk. I tried not to read too much into the slight shift in the atmosphere between us.

I shouldn't have invited him back. The moment it came out of my mouth I wished I could have taken it back, but it was too late. I was going to have to act like I was totally fine with a man coming up to my flat.

A man who wasn't Henry.

Chapter 17

He seemed to take up the whole space. His presence electrified the air in my small flat. What would Linda say? I was sure this was against company policy. I needed to fix him up then ship him out as quickly as possible.

'Right, let me sort that cut out!' I sang, brighter than I felt.

I busied myself with getting my first-aid box from the bathroom. I didn't know where to put myself. I felt flustered, energy coursing through my body at the fact he was here in my personal space, emitting smells of whisky and manliness. It had been so long since I'd been this close to aromas of aftershave and alcohol.

Not since Henry.

I blinked his name out of my head and tried to focus on the task in hand. I needed to get Callum fixed up and bundled into a taxi home, where he could sleep off the killer hangover waiting for him.

'Nice place you've got here.' He'd wandered into the bathroom and began running tap water over his bloodied knuckles.

'Oh, er, thanks, it's a lot smaller than your house but

it suits me,' I babbled, feeling my cheeks heat up as both of us were now crammed into my small bathroom.

I caught him silently wincing at the sting. I flicked my eyes away from his reflection and back to the box I was struggling to open.

'Bloody hell!' He laughed loudly. I looked up from rummaging for the antiseptic cream and a suitable bandage to see him staring at me. 'You've got a complete pharmacy in there!'

'Oh, yes, well, it's good to be prepared for every eventuality...' I guess I did have rather a lot of medicines, creams, tablets and dressings.

I'd picked it up when ordering the first-aid kit for work; the low-hazard workplace set (for up to twenty-five employees) was on a buy-one-get-one-free deal. I couldn't refuse. The shatterproof case had medical paraphernalia in small, clear Perspex dividers, and it even came with a wall bracket. It was compliant with the British Standard regulations and had everything from burn dressings to clothing cutters to a face shield for mouth to mouth. It had been a very worthwhile investment.

'When nuclear war breaks out, I'll have to make sure I'm somewhere near you,' he smiled.

'I'm not sure how practical that would be. We'd need a complete survival pack with enough water, a tin opener, plenty of canned goods, toilet rolls, a makeshift toilet. In fact...' I trailed off, seeing his face change to confusion.

'It was a joke, Grace.'

I smiled tightly. 'Sorry, this might sting.' I gently sprayed the antiseptic spray and wrapped a protective gauze over the wound. 'You'll need to change the dressing regularly, but I don't think you'll have to go to hospital.'

'Thank god, I bloody hate hospitals.' He inspected my handiwork. 'Nice job. Thanks, Nurse Grace.'

'You're welcome.' He wasn't showing any signs of wanting to leave, so I offered him a drink and told him to head to the lounge. He wandered through, leaving me to pack away the first-aid box, making a mental note to refresh supplies on my next shop.

'Have you got any whisky?' he called. 'Wait – silly question. You don't look like a whisky drinker to me.'

I didn't ask him what he imagined I drank. He definitely didn't need another drink, but I suddenly wished that I did have a stash I could impress him with. To feel my bones loosen with the numbing effects of alcohol, the way I'd seen my mother relax so many times, letting out a deep exhale of satisfaction as she took her first sip. It must be nice to be able to forget. I remembered people getting stoned at university, telling me they felt better when they were high, as it meant they could forget everything. They never went into detail about what it was they wanted to forget, but they continued to 'forget' on a regular basis.

'I've got tea or coffee? Or Adam's ale?'

I didn't know where to put myself. I wanted to open a window to let more air in, but I thought it might look rude.

'Ale?' His ears pricked up.

'Sorry,' I blushed. 'It's what my mum calls tap water…'

'You don't drink, at all?'

I shook my head, hoping that would be enough of a full stop.

'Coffee is fine.' He wafted an unsteady hand.

Happy to have something to do, I clicked the kettle on and clattered around, clumsily recovering the habit of making a hot drink for someone other than myself in my own kitchen. At the last minute, I put back the instant coffee and got out my best mugs, rummaged for my cafetière and opened a fresh pack of ground coffee beans. The kitchen filled with soothing smells and rumbling noises as the kettle reaching boiling point.

Callum Anderson was in my house. The first man to ever set foot in there, apart from my brother, and the plumber three years ago when my boiler broke down. No man had ever sat on that sofa, never reclined or relaxed in the way he was sprawled out. It was actually kind of nice having someone else in the house. Just being aware of another person in the space was more comforting than I'd imagined; I hadn't realised how empty it had felt. The sound of him settling in my living room was the best sound I'd heard in months, actually.

'I don't know if you were hungry, but I've got these.' I placed a pack of bourbon biscuits that I'd artfully arranged on a side plate, wanting to make a joke about not having whisky but I did have bourbon, but unable to find the right words.

He took a biscuit and dunked it into his steaming mug. He had moved onto the floor, his back resting against the sofa he'd just been sat on.

'Are you OK down there?'

'I sit on floors now. Is that weird? I never used to sit on floors but ever since... Well, ever since recently, I've been sitting on floors.'

'It's not weird. Lots of people do it after they've been through what you've been through. Something to do with grounding yourself, connecting to the earth?' I shrugged.

'Mel would love that theory. She's a bit of a hippy, if you hadn't noticed.'

I moved to sit on the floor too. It was actually quite nice.

'I feel like I should ask how you're doing but I guess...' I trailed off, nibbling the edges of a biscuit and cupping falling crumbs in my other hand.

'Good days and bad days.' He took a slow sip of his coffee. 'Well, I should say bad days and less bad days.' He sighed and massaged his temples. 'I sometimes wonder if I'll forget her. Like, I know I'll never forget her face – I mean, I have so many photos and all her modelling portfolios – but I wonder if I'll forget *her*. What made her Abbie. Like the way she held herself. The face she pulled when she wanted me to save her from some boring fart at a party without coming across as rude. We had this silly system, she would drop in the word *sunshine* and I knew that was code for *help, get me away from this person*.'

I listened and understood what he meant. You can remember someone's face in an instant but what made them *them*, a three-dimensional whole person, certainly and sadly faded with time.

'Do you have any videos of her?'

'Er, no, not really. There are probably ones taken on

shoots but that was never my Abbie. In fact,' he took a deep breath then carried on, slurring slightly, 'if I'm honest I didn't have much time for that Abbie. The one I miss, and worry I'll lose again and again, is the one who wore Christmassy pyjama-bottoms in June. Who would scrape her hair back into this ridiculous-looking pile on her head as she took her make-up off, and picked at her nail polish absentmindedly as she watched TV.' I couldn't imagine his polished wife ever acting so… well, so normal. 'It's like I want to ration these memories in case if I overthink them, they'll disappear.'

'Savouring the memory of things which will never happen again…'

'Exactly! It's like you look at people out and about living their lives, doing really mundane things without realising that these mundane fucking things are what make up life. I'd give anything to bicker over whose turn it was to empty the dishwasher, or to order her favourite coffee in Starbucks, or to hear her heels clacking over the floor in the hall. Stupid stuff like that.'

He sighed.

'I keep thinking about things I never told her. Pointless tiny things that now have nowhere to go. She used to say I had a useless memory, but since she's gone it's like the deposit box of our joint memories has been passed over to me to look after, and all these new details have been rushing back. Like the time we went to Rome and she picked off all the olives on her pizza and the waiter took offence that she was ruining the best part of the dish. It suddenly came to me that the waiter's name was

Carlos.' He shook his head at the absurdity of the tiny things our brains hold onto. 'If you'd have asked me that two months ago I'd never have been able to tell you. Stupid isn't it?' His eyes were glassy with unshed tears.

'Not stupid,' I said with a sad smile. 'I've learnt that you can't fix people like you can fix objects. There isn't enough sticky tape in the world to mend us.'

'It would be awesome if you could. Honestly, Grace, it's just exhausting feeling like this day in, day out. It's like every day is a battle. Small bullets that come at you from out of nowhere. I still get post arriving for her, her name is still in my recent call list, the book she was reading and didn't finish is still lying by the side of the bath...'

Pain lurked in the most innocent of places. It was one of the reasons why I moved to Ryebrook.

'And the inquest date still hasn't been set. Apparently they're looking for witnesses or something. I don't know why. It's not like it's going to change anything.'

'From what you've told me there's no one to blame but it might give you some sort of closure though?'

'No one to blame? Hah,' he repeated and shook his head. 'I wish that was true.'

'Oh sorry – I thought Mel said it was an accident?' I felt a wave of heat rush to my cheeks.

'Yeah – I mean, it was an accident. But that doesn't mean someone's not to blame...'

'I don't understand?'

He sighed deeply and rubbed at his face. 'I just feel like it was my fault.'

'But –'

'We had a big fight, a stupid argument, the night Abbie died. She stormed off and never came back.' His voice was breaking but he loudly cleared his throat, refusing to look me in the eyes. 'If we hadn't fought then she wouldn't have been on the road at that time. She would still be here.'

I didn't know what to say. Silence settled around us.

'I just wish I'd tried harder, been a better husband, you know.' He blinked his large, watery eyes.

I couldn't tell him that from what I'd seen online their marriage seemed to be pretty perfect. One many would envy, in fact.

He let out a deep sigh. 'It's just… I don't know. I keep thinking back to times when I should have been there for her more. I had a habit of putting work first.'

'I'm sure that wasn't the case.'

'I'd always been focussed on my career. I was the one who brought in the main bulk of our income, after all. I'm not sure if I ever told you, I'm an architect. But now I just think how pointless it all was. How I would give anything to spend one less day working away, and be with her instead.'

From Abbie's Facebook feed, her pouting perfect photographs, you would never have guessed that what was going on behind closed doors was anything less than a perfect, happy marriage. I could feel my tongue yearning to ask more questions but I bit my lip. Relationships are like a house with no windows: you could only guess at what was going on inside. I expected Callum to change the subject or even leave, but he leant his head back and swallowed deeply.

'I don't think I ever said thanks for your help with the funeral. And, well, now this,' he raised his bandaged hand.

'You're welcome, for both things.' I paused. 'I'm not sure if you picked up my answerphone messages? We have her ashes ready for when you want to collect them.' I added quickly, 'There's no rush. You can take your time.'

'Oh.' His mouth tightened. 'I haven't even thought about what I'm going to do with them. I mean, with her.'

'That's normal, like I said there's no rush.'

He'd already survived this long without his wife. A huge achievement, although he could still kid himself that she was taking an extended holiday. Lots of people did. But it had been over a month since the funeral, and the realisation that she wasn't coming back was bound to settle in soon. Then the real test of being alone would begin.

'What do other people do?'

'Well, they usually like to take them home, store them on the mantelpiece or in a display cabinet.' He winced. 'Or in a wardrobe, safe out of harm's way. Then when you feel able, you can take them and scatter them at a place she liked.'

'Er, right… I guess.'

'But, you know, some people use the ashes and turn them into fireworks or even make them into diamonds, there are no rules.' I tried to laugh lightly but it sounded shrill in the sudden silence. 'If you like I can bring them to you? Save you making the trip to the office?'

'Really? Are you sure? I mean, yeah, that would be helpful...'

'Course, not a problem,' I said a little too brightly.

He got up to use the bathroom, leaving me to mentally punch myself in the face for making such a ridiculous offer. We didn't do an ashes home delivery service. Families were asked to come to us and sign their loved ones out before leaving our care, in case anything happened to them. What I had just offered was against company policy, and I could get into trouble.

I heard the toilet flush. I'd said it; this foolish offer was out in the world. Frank didn't need to know. I was just going to have to be very careful.

Chapter 18

I was woken by the buzzing of an alarm. The incessant sound forced me to open my eyes. Strangely, I couldn't remember setting one last night. I'd slept sounder than I had for a very long time. I rubbed my face, trying to shift the grubby, deep-sleep feeling, catching sight of my discarded clothes tossed to the floor. I frowned. I never left my clothes like that. The alarm was still going off but it wasn't coming from my alarm clock. I pulled the cover around me, half asleep and puzzled at what was going on. It was only when I spotted a crumpled flyer lying on the floor that I remembered.

Callum was in my house! He'd fallen asleep when I'd gone to the toilet, and I didn't have the heart to wake him. I knew how precious sleep was when it came. The buzzing must have been coming from his phone alarm.

I leapt out of bed faster than my sleepy brain was ready for, and grabbed my dressing gown from the back of the door. How had I even managed to sleep, let alone gone into such a deep state, when there was a man in my house? I hurried to the lounge, preparing to see him snoozing where I'd left him at whatever small hour of the morning.

The stale smell hit me first. The curtains were still drawn but the room was empty. I then realised that the buzzing wasn't an alarm but the doorbell, being intermittently pressed. It had been so long since I'd heard it that I'd forgotten how it sounded. I looked around the room. The cushions which had been used as a makeshift pillow were plumped up and back in their place at either end of the sofa. I glanced into the kitchen, clocking our dirty mugs waiting near the sink – there was something uncomfortably intimate about the sight. I checked the bathroom but he was nowhere to be seen. I tried to ignore my heart sinking at his absence and rushed down the stairs to open the door. I wondered if he'd show up at the church hall on Friday, if that was when I'd see him next, or perhaps this was him now and he had forgotten something. I was just about to open the door when it came back to me what I'd offered. To hand deliver Abbie's ashes. *What had I been thinking?*

I took a deep lungful of breath. But it wasn't Callum at my doorstep.

'There you are!' Mum sang loudly, stepping inside my flat, pulling me into a hug.

My nose filled with her scent of patchouli and rose oil, the same heady smell she'd worn all her life.

'Gracie?' Mum stepped back and peered at me. 'I *love* the new hair!'

I flashed a weak smile. I would worry about Callum and what I'd offered later.

'I wasn't expecting you.' I tried to move my cheeks from under her vice grip.

'Let me look at you. I swear you're getting thinner every time I see you.' She tutted, finally letting go.

'Mum, what are you doing here?' An old woman pulling a tartan shopping caddy stared back as she trundled past. 'Brendan not with you?'

'He's long gone.' She wafted a hand before clomping up the stairs.

'Gone?' Another one bites the dust.

I rubbed my eyes and tried to wake up.

'Grace!' Mum gasped from upstairs.

'What?'

'What's going on in here? It's like a bloody morgue.' She was pulling open the curtains and shaking her head. 'Is everything OK, love?'

'Yep, fine.' I cast my eyes around the room in case there was any Callum debris left behind. All clear. 'So.' I cleared the sleep from my throat. 'What's this spontaneous visit for?'

'Can't a mother want to spend time with her daughter without the Spanish Inquisition? Anyway, it looks like you could do with a bit of company. I've never seen it so messy in here.'

I wondered if she could smell the very faint scent of whisky and aftershave.

'I was just about to start –'

'Well, forget about that, I want to take you out.'

'Out?'

'Yes. I thought we could head over to the Stables and

grab a coffee together. You jump in the shower and I'll make a start on your dishes. I don't know why you use so many cups.'

We'd never been the type of people to 'go and grab a coffee'.

'I'm alright, thanks. I've got coffee here.'

She shook her head. 'Nope. Come on, you clearly need cheering up. Something's going on. And I need to pick up some bits from the herbal healing shop. My sciatica is playing up again. Let's go, you can tell me all on the way.'

She wasn't taking no for an answer.

*

Mum made me drive since Brendan wasn't around to chauffeur her about. She acted sheepish when I asked why they'd split up, instead insisting on telling me about this new hobby she'd started, a Japanese cooking class or something. She'd clearly taken a shine to one of the teachers there.

I'd never been to The Stables Studios before, but had read about the events, mostly aimed at families, which were held there. It was a collection of workshops and studios for creative types, under one leaky roof. I'd been following Mum's directions, silently grumbling that she didn't know her left from her right.

'Grace, I meant left!'

'Then why didn't you point with your left hand!'

'Oh, it's fine, just turn around up here. I don't know why you drive like such an old lady. You don't need to be so blooming cautious all the time.'

I ignored what she was saying as my attention was caught by bunches of wilted flowers in cellophane, taped to a thick tree trunk. I hadn't realised where I was until now. The road I was driving down was where Abbie had died. I felt my throat tighten. Knotted strands of blue and white police tape flickered in the wind, tangled up in hawthorn bushes. Shivers raced up my spine. I gripped the steering wheel tighter. These trees were the last thing Abbie saw. I wondered what she had been listening to on the radio. If she'd known what was happening before it was too late? If she'd struggled to comprehend that these were her final moments, or if the speed at which it happened, stole any rational thoughts.

Callum's admission that he felt responsible for Abbie's tragic death sprang to the front of my mind. Casting my eyes around the remote lane did make me think just what a strange place it was for Abbie to find herself, alone, in the early hours of the morning. Why would a row with your husband make you head here? The newspaper report had said that the accident had happened between one and three a.m. But Callum said they'd rowed in the evening before she'd gone out. So, why had she been here at that time in the morning?

'Oh, this is it. Turn right here!' Mum made me jump, thrusting her hand in my face.

I slowed down and flicked on my indicator even though I was the only car on this stretch of road. The turning was a single track down a bumpy, pot-holed road. Gnarled trees on the other side blocked out much of the bright sunlight.

'I think I may have sent us down the back route... Anyway, so next week we're learning all about how to make teriyaki steak and wasabi mash. You'll have to come along, it's such a laugh...'

I continued to trundle down the bumpy lane, hoping no other cars were coming in my direction, nodding at Mum's story when I needed to. The tight passing places were few and far between and I didn't fancy reversing back up the narrow path.

'Ah, here we are!' she sang as I pulled into the half-empty car park.

Car park was an exaggerated term, looking at the boggy field. I locked my car and let her link arms with me as we followed painted wooden arrows on stakes in the ground, pointing to the main entrance. A cobbled courtyard spread out in front of us. Smaller 'stables' had been converted into tiny shops as part of the town's 'creative quarter'. The path led to the main barn that used to be the centre of a working farm, but was now a retro tearoom.

'I'll just go and get the bits I need. Want to meet me here in twenty minutes or so?' Mum said, hurrying off with a wave.

I reluctantly nodded and wandered down the lane past a vegan juice bar and the crystal healing shop that she'd popped into. I really wasn't in the mood for this. I plodded past 'Grandad's Clobber', a vintage clothes store, and a man upcycling old plant pots at 'Bill and Ben's'. There was a small jewellery shop, 'Jodi's Flowers', which sold pressed flowers in pieces of plastic to make garish necklaces and bracelets. I knew I was acting like a petulant teenager. And it was nice of Mum to want to do something together, and good to get out of my little flat and into the fresh air. It was warm out, the trees flush and green with fresh leaves. I'd clearly just got out of bed on the wrong side. I absentmindedly kept walking to the last studio, preparing to head back to the coffee shop to sit and wait for Mum with a weak tea, when I stopped in my tracks. In the window was a large sign:

'Daniel Sterling, artisan creator and designer of one-off pieces that your home is missing.'

Daniel, the guy who'd nervously been stuffing sausage rolls into his mouth at Abbie's wake. The guy who I may have had more than one thought about. The guy who was now waving at me through the window. *Oh god.* I waved back before I realised what I was doing. There was no way I could just hurry back to meet Mum now.

The door to his studio opened and out wafted the dulcet sounds of a female blues singer. The smell of white spirit, from a dirty rag he was rubbing his hands on, filled my nose.

'Hey, Grace, right?! How are you? Doing a bit of shopping are we?' He was so much more at ease than the last time we'd met. His sleeves were rolled up and he had paint flecked on his forearms and across the baggy, striped shirt he was wearing. His warm brown eyes creased into a smile.

'Er, yeah. Something like that…' I stuttered. 'I didn't realise you worked here?'

'Yep, this is where the magic happens.' He glanced back at the room with a wink. 'I'm just finishing off. Will you come in for a drink? I've got a kettle and can even rustle up two clean mugs.' He held the door open wider.

I took one last look behind me.

'Are you sure? I really don't want to keep you...' I couldn't finish the rest of my sentence as a stunning sculpture caught my eye as I stepped into the warm room. It literally took my breath away. 'Wow. You made this?'

It was phenomenal. A huge mass of polished copper-coloured metal that was twisted into a sort of figure of eight.

'Yeah, that's actually a new piece in my collection. It's a work in progress though; I'm missing something that I need in order to finish it.' Daniel shrugged but I could see the pride in his eyes. 'It's a special piece. I don't even know if I have a buyer lined up, I just woke up and had to get to work on it. Don't worry, I promise I didn't invite you in for the hard sell.'

'It's incredible...' I breathed. 'Perfect.'

He shook his head with a wry smile. 'Have you ever heard of a Persian flaw?'

'No?'

'There's this legend that Persian rug makers would intentionally add a flaw into their finished work, as they believe that perfection is only for God or Allah or some higher power, not humans. It would be arrogant for us mortals to even aspire to perfection.'

I tried to follow what he was saying but all I could

think about was Abbie and how close to perfection her life seemed. Ever since her funeral, I'd felt haunted by her.

'Those intricate and stunning carpets would never be perfect. They all had a flaw, probably only visible to the one who created it, but that's also what makes them unique.'

'So the key is to embrace the flaws?'

'You've got it!' He laughed lightly. 'Sugar?'

'Sorry?'

'In your tea?'

'Oh, no thanks, just milk.'

'Soya milk OK? I'm on a bit of a health kick.' He patted his flat stomach.

'Oh, fine,' I said absently, too engrossed in the incredible art around me.

'Here. Take a seat if you like?'

He indicated two bucket chairs at the back of the studio. There was a coffee table between them, with a couple of his business cards on. He placed two steaming mugs down and settled down opposite me.

'Can I please apologise for how I was at Abbie Anderson's wake? I'd had too much to drink so was spouting rubbish. A default of mine to steer away from the reality of the situation, I guess. I don't often drink so much.'

'Oh, it's fine.' I wafted my hand. 'So, how have you been since then? Crashed any more funerals?'

'Ha, not quite. God, I really was going off on one then.' He shook his head. 'I realised that I never asked you what you did. Sorry, that was very rude of me.'

I paused. There was something about his down-to-earth nature that was really attractive. For some silly reason I didn't want to go there with the truth just yet.

'I'm a counsellor,' I said. A half-truth, as *technically* I was the group facilitator for the Friday night group.

'Very impressive.' He raised an eyebrow. 'Not some sort of therapist that's going to analyse me and my sausage roll eating habits, I hope?'

I laughed awkwardly. 'No, don't worry. So –'

'*Grace*! There you are!' Mum boomed as she swung open the door. 'I've been looking all over for you! What are you doing in here – ooh.'

Daniel quickly got to his feet, sloshing coffee on the floor, a welcoming smile on his face.

'Mum, meet Daniel. Daniel meet my mum, Tina.'

'Oooh, hello, Daniel!' Could she tell the air was thick with unspoken words, or was that just me? 'Lovely to meet you!'

'You too. Can I get you a drink? I've just made us one?'

'No!' I said. They both looked at me. 'We need to be getting on, don't we, Mum?'

I was not about to sit and drink tea with the two of them, whilst she threw me knowing looks. I could tell that she was already sizing him up for son-in-law potential.

'Oh. I'm sure we can stay for one…'

'Sorry, Daniel, we'd better be going.'

'Sure, no problem, maybe I can catch up with you some other time, Grace?'

'Yeah… great,' I said, probably a little too brightly. 'Mum, you ready?'

'Hang on a second, love. I just want to have a look at some of these wonderful paintings. Grace, you could do with some colour like this in your flat. You clearly have an eye for talent, Daniel.'

She was making her way slowly around the room, stopping to admire each separate piece, telling him how she used to paint in her younger days – I willed her not to admit that she was once a nude model. Daniel had puffed his chest out with pride, and began telling her about the inspiration behind each one.

'Do you mind if I nip to the toilet?' I asked.

'Course, it's just through those doors.'

I hurried to the small cloakroom to try and catch my breath. I felt all hot and flustered. I ran cold water over my wrists to help cool me down, moving his jacket that was hanging on the back of the door to dry my hands on the towel beneath it.

'All ready to go?'

Mum had her head thrust back, laughing at something he was saying. It was all a little too cosy for my liking. 'Alright then. See you, Daniel!'

'Thanks for popping by. See you soon, Grace.'

'Well, he seemed lovely,' Mum sang, waving over her shoulder as I steered her up the cobbled lane. 'Very handsome. And he wasn't wearing a wedding ring. Did you spot that, Grace?'

'Oh, I hadn't noticed…'

She let out a dramatic sigh. 'That's the problem with

you, Grace. You're too lost in your own head. I think he's taken rather a shine to you. How do you know him? I never had you down as the type to hang around with artists?'

'We met through work,' I said, knowing that would shut her up.

Chapter 19

I'd stayed late, telling Frank I would lock up, just so I could take Abbie's ashes without anyone seeing me. I felt awfully guilty at the concerned look Frank gave me as he left, telling me not to work so hard. If only he knew. I tried to brush off the deceit; I was doing this to check Callum was OK, that his hand was healing, that was all. I was not there to feed my curiosity at what else his wife could inspire in my own life – or so I tried to tell myself. There was something about Callum Anderson that singled him out from my other clients. I just didn't know exactly what it was. I ignored just how risky and foolish taking the ashes to him actually was. They needed to remain in the safety of the locked storeroom, not be taken on day trips. But I forgot all about that within moments of arriving at Callum's house.

A stack of junkmail, wedged in the letterbox at the end of the drive, was the first indication that things had gone downhill. The front garden had been completely neglected since I'd been there last. The previously pristine flower beds were now full of weeds and cigarette stubs; the lush green grass was scruffy and overgrown. Straining black bin bags bulged from a wheelie bin that must have not been left at the kerbside for weeks. Bird poo stains dribbled down the ground-floor windows. All of the curtains were drawn, but the empty wine and beer bottles in the recycling bin proved there was life behind the closed drapes.

I rang the doorbell, its cheery sound a contrast with the reason for my visit. I peered through the frosted glass in the front door, but couldn't make out any movement from inside. My fingers hovered on the buzzer. How soon should I press again without appearing desperate? But maybe he hadn't heard me. There was a car parked on the driveway, so I guessed he must be in. He'd probably forgotten I was coming over; he had had a lot to drink when we'd discussed it. I pressed the bell once more. I was sure I could feel someone's eyes on me. Had the curtain in the upstairs room twitched slightly? If he was in, he clearly didn't want to see me. I was just about to walk away when I heard footsteps heavy on the stairs. I suddenly felt nervous.

'Oh, hi.'

He looked marginally better than he had on Friday. The creased T-shirt and jeans remained, but he had a little more colour in his cheeks. It was still a world away from the impeccable style I'd seen him wear in Abbie's Facebook albums.

'Hi, er, is this a good time?'

'Yep. Fine.' He flashed a small but welcoming smile. It was as if he'd forgotten why I was coming over, but then he appeared to suddenly twig. 'Can I help you with that?' He bent down to pick up the bag resting near my feet. The bandage I'd wrapped around his hand had gone.

He swallowed as he hoisted up the large bag and blinked rapidly.

'Callum, are you OK?' I asked gently.

'It's heavy. I mean, she's heavy,' he said, tripping on his words, his voice sounding strained.

'Do you want me to come back another time?'

'No, no. I'm fine! Come on in,' he said quickly, looking for somewhere to put the bag. 'I just didn't expect it... I mean her, to be so heavy.'

'Between six and eight pounds,' I said, following him into the kitchen. 'Like a newborn baby.'

'Wow...'

'That's minus the weight of your soul. Apparently.'

He looked at me blankly.

'What?'

Why had I just said that?

'Twenty-one grams. The weight of a soul. Although, I've seen the people who waddle into Greggs on the high street – surely their souls would weigh a little more.' I gave a tinkle of a laugh that echoed around the large kitchen, trying to lighten the horrible atmosphere.

The last time I had been there was for Abbie's wake. Without the vast number of bodies, food and a party atmosphere, the enormous room just felt cold and stark. My heels crunched on crumbs scattered over the dark floor tiles. Sticky marks spread across the work surfaces. A stack of takeaway boxes, shoved by the kettle, were surrounded by a collection of empty beer bottle lids. The counters were marked with cup rings and spillages. The floor was slightly sticky underfoot. I felt myself stiffen at the sight of the place. I was itching to get a pair of marigolds on, grab a clean scourer, and blitz the bacteria that lurked on every surface.

'Sorry? What?' He frowned.

I could feel myself growing red.

'There was this experiment in 1901, I think, where physicians weighed dying people before and after they died. They all lost weight – twenty-one grams, around the weight of a mouse – after they died, which led everyone to speculate that that was the weight of their souls leaving their bodies,' I mumbled. 'I think it's since been disproven, but, well, mud sticks.'

He thought about this for a second. 'I sold my soul to my best mate Rory when we were eleven.'

'What for?'

'A Super Soaker. Thought it was a good deal at the time.' He shrugged, finally flashing a genuine smile at my shocked reaction.

'You sold your soul for a water gun?' He nodded. 'So when does he get to take his prize?'

'We didn't get to the fine print, thankfully. I'm hoping he's forgotten about it, to be honest.'

He gently placed the carrier bag on the dining table at the back of the room. I lingered by the door, pretending not to watch, a funny silence opening up around us.

'Tea?' he offered. 'Unless you need to get on?'

'No, I'm all yours! I mean…' I blushed. 'Yep, tea sounds great. Milk, no sugar, thanks… if you don't mind?'

He shook his head. 'Be my guest.'

Callum opened a few cupboards to find two mugs

that he seemed to deem clean enough. He placed them on a menu for a pizza place and flicked the kettle on. My mind was racing with the stats on how damp and mould can affect your health, how you're more likely to develop respiratory problems living in such squalor. I felt like my breath was getting tighter just thinking of the mould spores floating around us both. I tried to distract myself whilst he was searching in the fridge for some milk; I daren't not look in there. Callum caught me staring at the large wedding photo still hanging over the dusty dining-room table.

'Mel's coming round to help make a start on Abbie's things soon.'

'How do you feel about that?'

He gave me a look.

'Stupid question. Sorry.'

'No, I'm sorry. I'm dreading it, obviously. She's hoping it might make things feel a bit more real…' He trailed off. I could imagine it was easy for him to stay in denial, and tell himself that Abbie was working away, still. A way of the head protecting the heart, I guess. 'Listen, I should apologise for when I was at yours. I can't remember much of the night…'

'It's fine.' He didn't need to apologise for anything. There was a pause where he looked like he was about to say something.

'Crap. I'm out of milk.'

'Oh well. Don't worry.'

'I should be able to make something as fucking simple as a cup of tea,' he muttered, his jaw clenched.

'It's fine, honestly.'

He shook his head. 'No, Grace. It's not fine.'

I nodded and bit my tongue. Clearly this was not just about running out of milk.

'I'll go and get some. The walk will do me good.' He flashed a tight smile that didn't meet his eyes. 'I won't be long.'

Before I had the chance to say anything he'd grabbed a jacket from the banister, shoved his feet into a pair of trainers and hurried out of the front door.

I was alone in this man's house. In Abbie's house. All the time I'd spent poring over her virtual life, and now I was alone in her private space. My eyes darted to the washing up and sticky surfaces. My head and heart were conflicted. I desperately wanted to give our mugs a good rinse and help him get on top of the mess, but I also had the opportunity to see what Abbie's life was really like, behind the social media filters.

I went for option two.

Unsure of where this risk-taking confidence was coming from, I quickly padded up the stairs and opened the first doors off from the wide, muted grey landing. It felt like I was walking into a posh hotel as I stepped into the master bedroom. The walls were a soft, calming, almost-pinkish cream colour, the thick carpet a deep grey that swallowed your feet. There was a door open to an adjoining en suite. There wasn't a bit of clutter, stray clothing or discarded rubbish to be seen. The white sheets of the king-sized bed were tightly made; it looked like it hadn't been slept in. I frowned. Why would Callum go to such effort in making his bed, but not bother to wash himself or his dishes?

Two wide, white-lacquered cupboard doors stood to my right. I'd never been inside a walk-in wardrobe before and it didn't disappoint. It felt like a luxurious boutique, rails and rails of neatly hanging dresses, jackets, suits and trousers lined the wall.

My fingers ran across the different fabrics hanging on padded hangers. A smell of clean cotton filled my nose. Cashmere jumpers in soft berry colours, camel-coloured coats and leather biker jackets. Lighter summer looks in linen and lace partitioned off by white shelves full of shoes, heels facing outwards in perfect symmetry. There must have been over fifty pairs in there and they all looked brand new. Not a scuff or mark in sight. I realised I'd been holding my breath and had forgotten to blink. Next to the two full-length mirrors was a dressing table. An assortment of expensive-looking spa salon products were lined up against the vanity mirror on the glossy white table.

I wasn't sure how long I'd been standing there, gawping. Callum would surely be back any second. I turned to leave when a mirrored jewellery cabinet caught my eye, the soft light bouncing off the lid, pulling me over to it, teasing me to open it.

I gently lifted the lid and gasped. There must have been thousands of pounds worth of jewellery in there. Gemstones glinted from deep-set rings, diamond earrings winking up at me from a velvet plinth. I fidgeted with the handmade hippy bracelet my mum had got me for my birthday, the bright cotton strands looking cheap and childish next to the brushed metals that Abbie owned. My subconscious willed me to put something on, to feel the weight of one of the rings or bangles. I knew I'd never be able to afford anything like that in real life.

My fingers hovered over a stunning, gleaming, white gold and topaz ring. I picked it up, instantly feeling its weight on my palm. It was utterly breathtaking. Not a scratch or mark in sight, it looked brand new. I wondered what the story was, whether Callum had bought it for her? Maybe it was an anniversary gift or a generous birthday present. Maybe she'd treated herself? I was about to pick it up and slip it on when Callum's concerned voice rang up the stairs.

'Everything OK, Grace? Are you up there?'

What was I doing!? I tensed up. I hadn't heard the front door go. How long had he been home for? I pulled myself together, ashamed at how easily and quickly I'd forgotten where I was, lost in the beauty spread before me like some dirty magpie. Imagine if the ring had got stuck! How would I ever explain that to Callum? I tucked the beautiful ring back where I'd found it. Tucked under a contraceptive pill packet, the days of the month marked out on one shiny side, spaces left where the packet had been puckered and the corresponding pill taken. I closed the lid of the jewellery box and quickly but softly jogged out of the wardrobe to hurry down the stairs.

'You OK?' he asked from the hallway as I descended, frowning.

'I think I took a wrong turn!' I blustered, my cheeks heating up. 'I couldn't find the loo…'

'The downstairs bathroom is here.'

He opened a door at the base of the stairs, right next to where he was standing. I made a show of how foolish I'd been.

'What! I thought that was a cupboard!' I let out a *how-silly-am-I* sort of laugh.

He nodded but didn't look convinced. Could he tell by the colour rushing to my face that I'd been snooping? 'I got us some milk.'

'Great, thanks!' I shrilled, my heart racing and beads of sweat clinging to my underarms.

I padded ahead of him into the kitchen and told myself to take a few deep breaths as he poured boiling water into the mugs from a special fancy tap. I avoided eye contact with the bag containing his wife's ashes. It was as if I could feel her judging me and my snooping ways.

'Is soya milk OK? I stupidly picked it up out of habit. Abbie hasn't drunk cow's milk for the past two years, something to do with some report she'd watched about hormones messing with our insides. I like my coffee black so never bothered with the stuff.'

'Oh, no problem…' Everyone was going dairy-free nowadays.

'Right. Here you go.' He pushed a mug over the counter to me, pulling me from my thoughts.

'Thanks.' I needed to think of something to fill the silence between us. 'So, er, how's Mel and the boys?'

'Yeah, fine. Well, I haven't actually seen them in a

while. I figured I need to stop using their house as a crash pad and get used to being here on my own.'

I nodded, taking a sip of my tea, trying to ignore the tiny white flecks floating at the top of my mug.

'I've been trying to be more self-sufficient, not constantly relying on her and Nick to get me through. It's also a way for me to drink as much as I like without being told off.'

'Oh...'

'Joke. Kind of.'

I wasn't sure if he was joking or not.

'And, er, how's your hand? I hope you've been keeping it clean?'

'Yeah, it's fine. Thanks.'

He had taken off the bandage that I'd applied. Luckily the scratch wasn't as deep as I'd first worried. The skin had already started growing over, healing. A funny sort of silence fell between us as we both drank our drinks. I needed to finish my cup, let my heart rate return to normal and get out of there.

He caught me looking out of the window to the large garden.

'It's a bit of a jungle out there.' He winced in embarrassment.

'You've had a lot going on.' I smiled awkwardly and gulped my drink, ignoring how it scalded my tongue.

He sighed. 'It used to be pretty spectacular, especially at this time of year.'

In the six weeks or so since the funeral, the lawn had become clumpy, the edges undefined. The flower beds

– like those out front – were filled with weeds, stray grass and dead leaves. An animal – a fox or a cat – had been digging in one of the raised beds, and soil was sprayed all over the patio.

'I can help you with it if you'd like?' I blurted out.

Why had I said that? Was this ridiculous offer a way of trying to clear my conscience after snooping through his wife's things? Or maybe I just saw how much TLC the place was lacking, and wanted to help him out. He could clearly do with some extra help to get anywhere near the Callum I'd seen photos of on Abbie's Facebook page. I wondered if that man would ever return.

'Really?' He raised an eyebrow.

I nodded rapidly. I couldn't take it back now. 'Sure, I mean, I like gardening. I just don't get the chance in my little flat. I'd be happy to help.'

He paused to think about this. 'You know, you're the first person who's not done the classic "if there's anything I can do, don't hesitate to call" hollow platitudes. The last thing I feel like doing is picking up a phone and actually calling these people, giving them tasks to help me out.' He peered out of the window. 'It does look a bit of a state.' He winced as if seeing it for the first time. 'Are you sure?'

I nodded. 'I mean, I'm no expert but I used to love planting things and watching them grow in our garden when I was younger. There's something satisfying about getting your hands dirty. We even had a little vegetable patch, I was so proud of my cherry tomatoes until Freddie, my half-brother, smashed a football into them and ruined them. My mum brought some from Tesco and tried to pass them off as mine, but I knew they were a substitute.' I smiled at the memory I'd forgotten about until now. 'I'd be happy to spend some time out there weeding and freshening up your beds.'

'It's a while since anyone has put it like that…'

'I meant your flower beds!' I clasped a hand to my mouth.

His eyes suddenly flicked to the carrier bag on the dining table and a deep blush coloured his cheeks.

'Yeah, I know, sorry. I shouldn't have…'

He cleared his throat and stood up straighter. 'We used to have a gardener but I've not managed to book him back in. If you're sure you don't mind, then you can knock yourself out and plant whatever you want out there. Start whenever you like.'

Chapter 20

I started the next day, popping home to change after work and then heading to Callum's place. The evenings were drawing out as we moved towards the end of May. That first day, Callum and I barely spoke – too busy ticking off the list of jobs that I'd scribbled down on two sides of A4. I thought I saw Callum's eyes widen as he read the list aloud, but he simply nodded and got to work. I'd noticed that the takeaway cartons had been removed, and the kitchen work surfaces had been wiped; a very faint smell of bleach hung in the air as I'd walked through to the garden. We both set to our respective tasks. Any attempt at conversation was drowned out by the lawnmower, the snapping of shears or loud whirring of the jet washer.

The second day we made light small talk as we worked. We mostly stuck to safe topics, like comparing our aching muscle pain and discussing possible irrigation systems. Birdsong became our background music. By the end of the week, after popping round after work each evening, I felt so comfortable around Callum it was quite alarming. We didn't need a detailed plan to follow, we'd gotten to grips with most of the unruly shrubs and weeds, our tastes in plants were very similar and any previous formalities had vanished. Conversation flowed when necessary but equally, the silences were strangely comfortable.

'It's looking good, hey?' Callum leant back on a shovel, pulling me from my thoughts.

Soil was flecked across his nose where he'd absent-mindedly wiped the sweat from his rosy cheeks. His thin T-shirt clung to his chest, giving the hint of a defined stomach under there. I tried not to stare. The weather had been kind, and had given us both a slight sheen of colour, a welcome change from the pale pallor I was used to seeing. He'd even trimmed his beard and had his hair cut. He was looking a lot more put together.

'It really is.'

I followed his proud gaze over the wooden frame he'd constructed for runner beans to flourish. The blueprints for the design had been impressive in themselves. The satisfaction was equally shared.

'Right, are you hungry? It's ready when you are.'

He went to wash his hands. I'd pre-prepared us a simple Mediterranean vegetable and chickpea salad, with a side of herb flatbread and dips. We ate on the grass, on the towel he'd laid out as a picnic blanket for us. It was the first proper chance for a conversation since we'd begun work.

'So.' He finished chewing. 'I've been meaning to ask you more about you.'

'Oh?'

'Yeah, I realised that you've only ever heard things

about me and my situation. I wondered: what's your story?' Callum asked, scooping a great glob of tzatziki onto his plate.

'My story?'

'For example, what made you get into your job? It's a little out there as career choices go.' He let out a light laugh.

'Well, I always wanted to work in a job where I could help people.' I delivered the line I'd become accustomed to parroting at the drop of a hat. It was the answer that satisfied people's curiosity. I didn't know if I'd ever get the strength to admit the truth to anyone.

'Here I was, worried you might say you were some secret goth with a penchant for vials of blood.'

'I'm actually quite squeamish!'

'That's why you've got that impressive first-aid kit?'

'Yeah, something like that…'

I busied myself with a forkful of salad.

'OK, so what about family?' he asked, thankfully moving the subject on slightly. 'You mentioned that you have a brother –'

'Half-brother.'

I picked up a cold glass of iced water, a couple of ice cubes clanged together.

'Yeah, half-brother, Freddie isn't it?'

I nodded, impressed at his memory.

'What about the rest of your family?'

I took a long sip before answering. 'Not much to tell really. My mum, Tina, she's a bit of a wild child, always has been. She met Freddie's dad, my stepdad I guess, although they were never married, a few years after I was born. He's locked up now.'

'Locked up?'

'Yeah, petty crime, repeatedly. He says he just prefers to be inside than out but really he's a waste of space loser. My mum has a bit of a type.' I rolled my eyes.

'Doesn't everyone?'

'Well, it's not like mother, like daughter, if that's what you mean.' I laughed lightly then paused. 'I don't know if I have a type… my ex, well he was one of a kind. But it didn't end well.' Was I seriously going here? I gulped the water, wincing at the icy coldness against my teeth.

'I've had exes like that.' He nodded. 'I guess everyone has to experience their share of heartbreak at some point?'

'Yeah, erm, well this was a big one. It kind of rocked everything. It was the reason I moved up here, actually.'

'A fresh start?'

'Something like that. I needed distance in order to try and move on,' I said, wanting to get back onto safer ground. 'I'm guessing you don't believe in this "type" nonsense either?'

He rolled onto his back to face the wispy clouds. 'I think people think I do, but actually I don't.'

'What do people think is your type?' I boldly asked.

'Pretty, skinny, arm candy,' he answered in a beat.

'Is this some Oedipus thing? I bet you're going to tell me that your mum was a blonde bombshell!'

He stiffened at the mention of his mother. A low cloud crossed the sun, making my bare arms bristle into goosebumps.

'Something like that.'

I rubbed my arms as a silence opened up between us. I wished I'd not been so bold.

Finally, he cleared his throat. 'Sorry, I'm not used to talking about her.' He rubbed the back of his neck then glanced up at me, squinting without his sunglasses on. The sun had turned his hair a lighter shade of blond. It suited him. 'Well, there's certainly no Oedipus thing going on.' He tried to smile but it looked forced. 'The last time I saw her was in a contact centre. She wasn't able to look after me and Mel, so she signed us over to people who could. Except they turned out to do an equally poor job.' He flashed another false smile.

'Oh, I'm sorry… What about your dad?'

He shook his head. 'It was just us two, Mel and I, and that was how we liked it. When we were put into care we were moved from place to place, trying to settle as we refused to be split. It's where I met Rory actually, he's my best mate, more of a brother really.'

'I bet it's been good to have him around recently?'

'He lives in Scotland so I don't see him as often as I'd like. I've probably not been so good at picking up the phone either…' He trailed out. 'I mean, I know I should, Mel is always going on about me cutting myself off from those that want to help, but sometimes it's easier to just get on with things, you know?'

I nodded.

'So, are you thinking of making a fresh start after everything?'

Callum let out a sigh. 'I mean, doing the garden up is

helpful, if I did come to sell. I guess this is a big house for one person to be rattling around in. Too big for me now, but...' He wrinkled his nose. 'That just all seems like a huge mountain to climb.'

'One day at a time, right?'

He smiled softly. 'Something like that.'

Chapter 21

The woman opposite stared at me, her puffy red eyes unseeing, as if she wasn't sure why she was here. I could see her brain trying to work out where it had all gone so desperately wrong for her.

'Maybe you would like to add a favourite teddy into the coffin?'

'That… that would be nice.' Her husband, Thomas, said in a whisper. He looked equally as unsure as she did.

'Yes, I don't want her to be alone.' Rachael's voice was as fragile as glass. 'How about the pink elephant from the carnival last year? Thomas won it for me. That was before I even knew I was pregnant.'

Thomas squeezed her hand.

'Good idea, love.' His voice faltered, but he needed to show his emotion. I knew just how important it was that he let his barriers down too. 'She'd like that.'

Planning a funeral for a child – today it was for Daisy, a little girl born sleeping – was, by far, the toughest part of my job. It took all my strength and reserve to focus on the task in hand and not let my mind get overwhelmed. It is unthinkable, planning to bury your own child, but I needed to focus on the fact that it becomes an opportunity to honour and celebrate them in their own special way.

You could practically see this couple dancing around the edges of each other. Neither one wanting to put a foot wrong and say something to tip the other over the edge. It looked exhausting. Despite that, I was so grateful they had each other; not every grieving mother has that support beside her. I blinked. *Concentrate, Grace.*

'Okay, so the last thing to think about is who will carry Daisy's coffin? We have a fantastic team who can look after this if you would prefer?'

'Maybe my dad, or your Uncle Richard? God. It's not fair,' Rachael wailed and began rocking back and forth on the chair, one hand over her mouth to muffle the painful cry. I moved the box of tissues to the centre of the table, not wanting her to feel she needed to stem the tears but also not wanting her to feel like she had to ask for one.

'OK, Rach, it's OK,' Thomas said, rubbing her heaving back.

I'd seen this many times, but it never got easier. Men supporting their wives; women unable to even register that their partner was next to them. Thomas tried to choke back the tears now freely spilling down his cheeks. I could almost see him mentally telling himself off for showing emotion. *Men don't cry. Men should be brave.* I wanted to reach across the table and take both their hands in mine. Clasp them hard and tell them that they would get through this together. That sharing in this tragic loss with honesty, at their own pace but as a team, would get them through it.

'I'm not ready to say goodbye!' Rachael bit her lip. Her face was devoid of colour.

I let her sobs ease off before I spoke.

'I understand. Something that may bring a little comfort – how about writing her a letter? Of all the things you'd like to say to her? We can add it into the coffin too?'

Rachael's tense face softened at the idea.

'It might be a good way for you to try and express what you're feeling?'

She nodded slowly and nibbled an already ravaged thumbnail. 'I'd like that.'

'I know there's so much to take in,' I said softly. 'But a few families I've worked with like to have something to look forward to after the service has taken place. They ask loved ones to come together for a memorial and plant a tree in a place that means a lot to you. That may be something to think about?'

Rachael bobbed her head and sniffed loudly into the shredded sodden tissue clamped under her nose.

I already knew from Rachael's Facebook page that Thomas had proposed to her in a local beauty spot overlooking a nearby waterfall. The beaming smile as she flashed an engagement ring in a photo from three years ago would take a long time to return to her drawn face.

'There's the nature reserve up in the hills. You know, near that waterfall?' Thomas suggested to his wife, then turned to me. 'We actually got engaged there.'

I smiled softly. 'That sounds wonderful. I'm more than happy to help you organise a service there after the funeral has taken place? Whenever you feel ready, of course.'

'Thanks, Grace.'

'So, any final thoughts for today? You must both be exhausted.'

'I think we'll leave it there?' Thomas clapped his hands together, wanting to take back some sort of control.

I handed them my card, and told them to call me whenever they wanted to.

'Your daughter will get the goodbye she deserves,' I promised as I let them out. It was easy to let a heavy grey mood descend upon you, choking you with emotion you had to hide after meetings like this. I sniffed and took a deep breath.

I needed to focus. I had something up my sleeve that I hoped they would appreciate. After they left I hurried to my desk and I clicked on a local garden centre website to double-check the flowers were in season, and placed my order. I was planning on lining the aisle in the church with little plant pots that I'd spray-paint white and fill with daisies. We could then offer them to the guests to take home and plant in their own garden, a way to remember this little girl. I had a few days before the funeral to get them ready. It was an out-of-work project that I certainly didn't mind doing.

*

'So are you going to spill the beans and tell me who's been keeping you so busy?' Ms Norris asked.

'Hmm?' I locked the office door and gave the handle a good pull.

'Well, you have been busy, and I'm sure there's something you're not telling me.' Ms Norris raised an eyebrow. She untied Purdy's lead and waited for me to give the handle one final tug, satisfied it was properly locked, before we headed to the church hall together. It was one of those gorgeous early summer evenings. The air smelt warm and the hazy dusk cast everything in a fuzzy apricot glow. Ms Norris had offered to meet me at the office so we could walk over together and enjoy a balmy stroll. It also meant she could use this time to dig for any gossip.

'I've been helping a widower with a spot of gardening,' I shrugged as lightly as I could under her intrigued stare.

'That sounds very noble of you, Miss Salmon.' She tried to steer Purdy in the right direction. 'Was his wife a client?' She nodded back at the funeral home.

'Sadly, yes. I noticed he was struggling so I'm just helping him stay on top of his garden, as a way to help.'

'That's very thoughtful of you. I hope he appreciates your effort. It's always good to get out in the fresh air and gardening is such a fun way to keep trim. Purdy – get away from that.' She tugged on the lead. 'Speaking of keeping trim, I might need to introduce some less calorific options into our bake-off.' She patted her stomach.

'Oh, that reminds me. I wondered if you had any good bonfire night sort of recipes up your sleeve? I know it's months away yet, but I wanted to get thinking about baking some cakes for the remembrance event in November.'

'I'll have a look in my recipe book. I'm sure I can pull something together.'

I smiled at her. I wasn't convinced such a recipe book existed. I preferred to imagine her concocting different combinations of flavours from an array of ingredients in her small kitchen. The measurements she gave were always a little hazy and written out on scraps of paper that she said she'd 'copied' from this supposed recipe book she owned.

'I wonder if we'll get any newcomers tonight,' she said as we reached the church hall, distracting me from wondering if I should bake for Callum when I popped over next. He might appreciate the gesture.

'I hope so...'

I helped her up the stone steps and waited as she tied Purdy's lead to the railings.

Inside I felt a little pessimistic that we would gain any new members, given what a lovely summer's evening it was. Who would want to sit indoors in a stuffy room with strangers discussing grief and death when they could be making the most of this balmy evening?

'Look, Marcus is already here!' she beamed at him as he got up from the floor where he had been sitting, waiting for us to open the door.

'Marcus, you're early? Everything OK?'

'Yeah. My mam's having a barbecue with some of her work mates. They're well annoying when they've had a few drinks. Thought I'd just come and wait here instead of hearing them go on about the man from number thirty-nine who they all fancy.' He rolled his eyes.

I pulled on the door, getting a waft of hot and humid air.

'Ooof. Right, let's get these windows open.'

We began trying to make it slightly cooler, propping the door open and heaving the heavy windows as far as they would go. It didn't make much of a difference, though, as the air was so still.

'My, it is rather toasty in here.' Ms Norris looked an alarming shade of pink. Beads of sweat covered Marcus's downy upper lip. I felt a little light-headed.

'More like a sauna,' I said, fanning my face with a prepaid sign-up form. 'We can't stay in here. We'll melt.'

'No!' Marcus let out a whine. 'Don't make me go back to the drunk barbecue.'

'There's a garden out the back. Let's head there.'

Within minutes we'd decamped to the crumbling walled garden, battling through weeds and wildflowers and tall clumps of grass to set up a few chairs in a shaded spot. Ms Norris had slunk to a chair under an apple tree, her swollen legs outstretched, wiping her flushed cheeks. Thankfully Raj had come prepared with cold treats from his newsagents.

'Well this is different!' Ms Norris smiled, as a blob of vanilla ice cream dripped down her hands. 'What a lovely treat. I can't remember the last time I had an ice cream!'

'The Italians know how to do ice cream. Gelato they call it,' Deano said, waving his cornet in the air to emphasise the fact.

'Have you been? To Italy, I mean?' Julie asked. She had also brought chocolates as a thank you for everyone's help with her mum's house. She seemed a lot lighter, obviously still deep in grief but able to speak without crying, and she even managed a smile at one of Raj's jokes.

'Nah,' replied Deano. 'But the guy that drives the Mr Whippy van near mine is half Italian. That's almost the same.'

Licking the stick of my own ice lolly, I realised that I couldn't remember the last time I'd sat with the sun on my face, eating ice cream either. It had been way too long. A faded memory of Henry chasing after an ice cream van was hovering at the edges of my conscience. I blinked, tucked my empty lolly stick into a makeshift bin, and forced myself to get started. We were there for a reason, not to be lazing about with ice cream, sharing summer memories. I wanted to get down to business.

'So today's topic is how others deal with our grief.'

A shuffle of feet and bottoms in chairs. Ms Norris, Marcus, Deano, Julie, Raj, and I. The six of us settled into the al fresco set-up. As predicted, we'd had no newcomers. I tried not to feel disheartened at the clear waste of effort; the flyers Callum and I had stuck up around town had obviously not had the desired effect.

I paused from my notes at the over-the-top cough, as a familiar face stepped into the garden through the wooden gate. 'Callum? You made it!'

I ignored the look of interest Ms Norris was giving me.

'Thought I'd come and see what the fuss was about,' he said, smiling bashfully, with a nod at the others.

'Of course! You're more than welcome. Here, take a seat.' I went to pull an extra chair into the circle, from the pile that Raj and I had brought outside, but stubbed my toe on one of the legs as I wasn't looking at what I was doing. I half tumbled on the tufts of grass, and just about managed not to fall.

'Whoops! We're not usually outside but it was too nice to be stuck indoors. Er, right, where were we?' I brushed a stray strand of hair from my glowing face and tried to concentrate on the notes I'd made. 'Everyone ready to continue? We were talking about other people's reactions to grief. I wondered if any of you had anything you'd like to share?'

Callum raised a hand.

I glanced at him in surprise. He was here, sober *and* getting involved. Mel would be really proud. 'Oh, er, please, go ahead... '

'Don't get me started on the people you meet after someone's died.' He sighed and began ticking things off his fingers. 'You've got the Competitive Grievers. The ones who feel sorry for you but then seem to revel in being able to top your story with something way worse that happened to them, like it's some sort of Grief Olympics. Then, you've got the Grieving Police, the ones who judge you as a terrible, terrible person for not going around dressed in black, sobbing all the time. As if by cracking a smile or making some crap joke it means you're not upset enough. Then you've got the Cliché Clowns, those who tell you that time is a healer, that it's all part of God's plan.'

A murmur of agreement passed round the group.

'They're almost as bad as the At Least-ers. Everything starts with, well, at least she didn't suffer, at least you had five years together, at least you're still young enough to try again. Doesn't matter how you try to put a spin on it... it's just... shit.' He caught himself and flashed a look at Marcus. 'Whoops. Sorry.'

''S'alright.' Marcus blushed. 'You're totally right.'

The vein in Callum's forehead was dramatically pulsing. He'd been needing to let all of this emotion out.

'I guess people don't know what to say,' I said when he'd slumped back, the fight dissipated. 'But you're right. There's nothing anyone can say to make you feel better.'

'But this is your job,' Deano said. 'You deal with sad people every single day. How do *you* know what to say?' he asked, looking genuinely interested.

I thought about this. We had rigorous training on what *not* to say, but I guess it came so naturally now, I never had to think of how to find the right words.

'I just listen.'

'You're right. You do. But how do you do that and not want to jump in and fix things or say something to make it better?' Ms Norris asked softly, wanting to bring the atmosphere down a notch or two.

'I know I can't help people feel better at that moment, but maybe in the future they'll be grateful for what I did at the time.'

'It's only when you're in the club that you realise how the most important thing is just for someone to say *something*. The worst thing is to ignore the elephant in the room,' Julie said quietly, to a nod of agreement from the others.

'You know I'm learning so much from this group,' Raj smiled.

'Hear, hear,' chimed Ms Norris.

'I think more people should come to Grief Club, then they'd understand what it feels like.'

'Grief Club? Is that what you call it?' I shook my head gently at Raj. I never expected my Ask A Funeral Arranger event to evolve like this.

'It's a little catchier…' Marcus piped up.

'I guess,' I smiled. 'What I wanted to add to Julie's point is that a lot of these people mean well, but no one gets to tell you whether you're grieving "correctly".' I glanced at Callum. 'You're allowed to have good and bad days. You're allowed not to cry when you don't feel like crying and you're allowed to sob like a baby when you do. You're allowed to be in shock. You're allowed to laugh at random stuff. You're allowed to feel everything and nothing at the same time. You're allowed to not think about death at all and take a break from grieving.'

Callum gave a weak smile. 'If only it were that simple.'

As the session broke halfway for refreshments, I smelt Ms Norris's white musk scent as she padded over to me.

'He looks familiar.' She nodded at Callum who was pouring himself a glass of water and talking to Raj.

'Really? Do you know him?'

'I'm a whizz at remembering faces, but names… well, they're trickier to hold onto.' She tapped the side of her head and gave a sad sort of smile.

'Oh, erm, well, his wife passed away recently.'

'I think I saw something about that, was it a car crash? Oh, that was just such an awful story. She was a model? Abbie something? Such a waste of a life. I saw it in the paper.'

I wanted her to keep her voice down. I was so proud of Callum for making the effort to come tonight, I didn't want him to think we were gossiping about him.

'He's very handsome. Reminds me of a young James Dean. Don't you agree, Grace?' She gave me a sort of nudge.

I let out a sort of 'mmm-hmm' sound in response.

'What? There's something you're not telling me,' Ms Norris insisted, finally lowering her voice.

'He's the man who I've been helping with his garden.'

'What! *That's* the widower?!'

'Shush!' I hissed just as Callum walked over.

'Evening.' Ms Norris nodded to him.

'Hello,' he smiled politely back. 'Oh, Grace, you left this at mine. I wasn't sure if you needed it?' Callum bashfully handed over the notebook I'd been jotting down all my gardening ideas in.

'Oh, er, thanks.' I felt my cheeks flush under Ms Norris's interested gaze.

'I also wanted to ask you something?'

'Sure.'

'Are…' His voice was hesitant. 'Are you free on the twenty-first of June?'

I closed my eyes, pointlessly running through an empty social calendar. 'I think so. Why?'

'Mel's organising her annual summer solstice event. It's a bit airy fairy, as it's the longest night of the year, but it falls on my birthday so we usually combine the two. You don't have to come. You know, if you have other plans…'

'That sounds lovely.' Ms Norris beamed at the pair of us. 'Doesn't it, Grace?'

'Yes…' I trailed out awkwardly. Despite being outside I felt like there wasn't enough air. I didn't want to ask him how he felt about celebrating his first birthday without Abbie. Another milestone in the painful year of firsts. The fact he was planning to get out of bed on that day, let alone be swept up in his sister's enforced fun, and have me tag along, was incredible and a testament to how strong he was. I felt honoured to be included.

'Great, I'll text you the details. Can I get either of you a drink?'

'I'm fine –'

'A water would be lovely,' Ms Norris smiled kindly, watching him go.

'Care to explain? Grace Salmon? When you said you'd been helping a widower I thought you meant some elderly gentleman struggling to keep on top of his weeds because of his bad back. I never expected someone so young and handsome.'

'We've just been doing some gardening together.' The words tumbled out of my mouth sounding a lot like a euphemism. 'That's all.'

Chapter 22

'Grace!' Mel waved as I walked through the house and into the garden. Looking over the empty lawn it was a much more intimate family affair than I'd expected. I swallowed and tried to stride forward with a confidence I didn't have.

'Hi, the door was open so I just...' She pulled me into a warm hug.

Callum was standing at the barbecue with two other men, intent looks on their faces as they peered at a line of sausages and hamburgers on the grill. The air smelt of charcoal, cooked meat and freshly cut grass. It smelt of summer.

'Boys! Come and say hello to Grace,' she called over to Finley and Noah who were rolling on the grass. Mel's shout caught the men's attention.

'That's my husband, Nick. I'm not sure if you two have been properly introduced before?'

I shook my head.

Nick raised a hand in the air, squinting in the sun.

'Hey, you look nice. Thanks for coming.' Callum jogged over and went to give me a kiss on the cheek. The familiarity between us came as a welcome surprise.

'And you, love the hat.'

He touched the ridiculous neon pink party hat, tilted at a jaunty angle on his head. 'Yeah, Finn insisted I had to look like a plonker on my birthday. Can I get you a drink? A soft drink?' he added quickly, leading me to a long table under a sun umbrella on the patio. He looked relaxed and, well, happy.

'I've made you a cake.' I nodded to the box I'd managed to place on a spare chair before Mel hugged me. 'It's one of Ms Norris's recipes, a chocolate one. I wasn't sure if you liked chocolate or had a sweet tooth but I thought everyone likes chocolate.' Oh dear, I was babbling. What was the matter with me? It must have been the lack of other guests that had thrown me.

'Cheers,' he looked genuinely touched. 'And yeah, I do like chocolate.'

A few bottles of non-alcoholic grown-up squash were chilling in an ice bucket. He fixed me an elderflower fizz. I'd never had it before; the floral taste was a little odd but nice. I felt relieved to have something to do with my hands. He bent down to the cool box laid at his flip-flop covered feet, pulled out a stubby beer and flipped the cap off.

'The garden looks great,' I smiled at our hard work.

'Yeah,' he said, looking at it as if seeing it for the first time.

'Cal!' A man whose face seemed familiar bounded over to us. I knew him from somewhere, but I couldn't place him. 'Mel's sliced her finger on the cheese grater. Honest to god, it's barely more than a scratch, but she wants to know where you keep plasters?'

'Er, no idea. We've got a first-aid box somewhere, probably in the bathroom.' He didn't make any reference to the incorrect pronoun. 'Grace meet Rory, Rory meet Grace.'

'Hey, how you doing?'

'Hello.'

'Rory here is my best mate. He lives in Edinburgh but we can't seem to keep him away,' Callum teased.

Abbie's funeral. That's where I'd seen him before. He'd been standing at the front with Callum. I remembered him at the house afterwards, standing in the kitchen, deep in conversation with an older man.

'And Grace is…'

She helped me bury my wife. 'His gardener,' I smiled and shook Rory's warm hand. He was shorter than Callum. He had a thick ginger beard half covering his plump features, and a kind look in his hazel eyes. Callum laughed.

'Well, it's looking great. Right, Callum, excuse me. I need to go and play nurse to your dramatic sister.'

He wandered back to the house shouting out that Doctor Rory was on his way.

'We grew up together, the three of us. He's one of the good ones.'

'So, how have you been today? It can't have been easy.'

He sighed. 'Mel was worried I'd have a massive melt-down not receiving a card or present from my wife, but honestly, it wasn't as tough as I'd expected. Yeah, I mean, I woke up feeling a little groggy after a bit of a sesh last night but, in a funny way, I've actually looked forward to this party. It's good to keep busy, especially having the boys around. Birthdays aren't such a big deal the older you get.'

'That's true.' I nodded. 'What did Mel say about me coming here? I wasn't sure if it might be a bit weird seeing me here.'

He gave a half shrug.

'I think she thinks you're helping me. Like some sort of outreach programme.' He didn't meet my eyes, just stared out over the horizon and gulped his beer. 'I may have mentioned Grief Club to her, which she was very pleased to hear about. I have to say that it wasn't half as bad as I'd prepared myself for. In fact, don't tell Mel but I actually enjoyed it…'

'I'm glad to hear it.'

'I told you she'd been insisting on me going to talk to someone. Anyway, that's when she gave me the third degree on you and me hanging out.'

'Oh.' My heart began to gallop in my chest. I wished I'd been a fly on the wall for that conversation. 'What did you, er, what did you say, about me?'

'I said that you'd become a friend. I guess. That you'd been helping me tidy up the garden and it's been good to keep busy and chat to someone who didn't know me from before.' I could feel my cheeks growing warm. 'That's it.'

'Yep.' I paused and sipped my drink. For some reason the bubbles had gone all flat and it tasted funny. 'That's it.'

*

Mel had asked in hushed tones if I could join her in the kitchen. She wanted us to quickly put up some decorations to surprise Callum. She'd already made this stark space seem more warm and inviting. A bunch of wildflowers stood in a battered yellow jug, and the Radio 2 jingle played from a retro-style radio on the windowsill. Pictures that the boys had painted were blu-tacked to the fridge and colourful streamers thrown on the work surfaces.

'Right, if you could make sure they've all got blu-tack on them?' She nodded to the pile of photographs. 'I want to stick them onto the glass doors.'

I got to work, smiling at the ones I picked up. One of Callum with Finley and Noah caught my eye. He looked so carefree. They couldn't have been taken that long ago; Noah wasn't that much older but something about Callum, the lightness and relaxed way he held himself, wasn't there anymore.

'That's one of my favourites of those two. Thick as thieves they are. He would have made such a good dad.' Mel smiled sadly.

I didn't really know what to say to that.

'It's a lovely photo.'

Mel didn't seem to hear me as she snipped at a long piece of twine that she'd attached to some balloons.

'They were trying for a baby. Him and Abbie.' She was talking more to herself than to me. 'Abbie never got stressed about how long it was taking but I know Callum worried from time to time. But, between you and me, I think she would have been too selfish to be a mother.

Children ruin your figure for one thing!' Mel laughed and patted her pudgy stomach. 'Cal never said how much he wanted them to start going down the medical route, but I could tell he would have loved to have had a baby with her. He's a natural with the boys, spoils them rotten. It just wasn't meant to be, I guess.'

I remembered seeing a photo Abbie had been tagged in on Facebook. She sat stiffly holding a wrapped up bundle in a hospital room, that must have been one of Mel's sons. The next image had been Callum cradling the same mewling newborn in his strong arms, looking so natural and at ease. The two photos were such a contrast to one another. Another memory came to me – the packet of pills in her dressing room. I was convinced they were contraceptive pills. I shook my head. I must have been wrong.

'You never fancied them? Kids, I mean,' Mel asked, pulling my attention back to the present.

'Er, well yeah,' I stuttered. 'I mean, I guess I just need to find the right man first.' I let out a light but uncomfortable laugh.

I blinked quickly and stared at another photo of Callum in a chequered shirt, sleeves rolled up and paint splattered on his cheeks. He had an arm around Mel, who was heavily pregnant in a pair of denim dungarees, waving a paint brush at the camera, standing in front of a blank wall.

'That was when we were decorating the nursery. God, you should have seen our house when we moved in. It took months to renovate it. Cal practically moved in to help us. Nick works away a lot, so Cal didn't want me to be alone with a toddler, being such a heavily pregnant whale. Seriously, Grace, I was bloody enormous!' Mel laughed at the memory.

'Did Abbie not mind Callum being away a lot?'

'She was off on exotic modelling shoots for most of it. To be honest, even when she came back and Finley came along, she barely visited. She clearly felt out of place amongst our chaos.' She stopped herself. 'Sorry, I do have a habit of letting my mouth run away with me. You must think I'm a terrible person for speaking ill of the dead.'

She'd hardly hidden her strained relationship with her sister-in-law from the first moment I'd met her. Mel tore open a packet of party rings and offered me one. She stuffed a biscuit into her mouth.

'It's like, when you die, people are expected to forget all the bad stuff you ever did or said. But you can't forget that's what made them the person they were.'

I nibbled my biscuit, a little too nervous to stop this roll she was on.

'No one is one hundred per cent good or flawless all the time. I mean, listening to that eulogy at her funeral, you'd have thought she was the reincarnation of bloody Mother Teresa or something. I can tell you now, she wasn't like that at all and everyone in that room nodding along were just kidding themselves.'

She swallowed, waiting for me to say something.

'I guess the purpose of the funeral, and the eulogy in particular, is to look back at their life and celebrate it.

It's usually better to look at the bigger picture, rather than bringing up every bad point,' I said.

'Hmm, maybe.' She sighed. 'I just think if a person was selfish and vain in life, then death isn't going to change that. I'd be a hypocrite if I suddenly gushed about what a wonderful person she was, when in actual fact she caused Cal a lot of pain. If you hurt people whilst you're alive then why the hell should we all wipe that from our memories?'

'Surely she had some admirable qualities?' My voice was definitely getting higher. The Abbie I knew from Facebook was nothing like this version I was hearing.

Mel scrunched up her nose. 'Abbie could be the life and soul of the party. Callum was right in his speech at her wake when he said she lit up a room. But then she could also be incredibly cold, distant and shut off. She lived a life that many people would die for, but she never showed any gratitude. That was what really got to me.' She leant closer. 'Without going into it all, Cal slaved away for years to get to where he is now. The sort of modelling Abbie did was never that lucrative, not enough to live the lifestyle she craved, so he provided that for her. What pissed me off was how she took it for granted, throwing teenage strops if he sometimes put his foot down with her. You know she was working as a checkout girl when they met! But Cal never showed how he felt when she changed from the woman he'd married. He always made excuses for her cancelling at the last minute, time and time again. *Oh, it's just Abbie,* as if that made it OK. But it wasn't OK.'

I didn't know what to say.

'That's what I mean about people pretending things are what they're not. Once the trust has gone, then it's pretty much over.' She pursed her lips and paused. 'There's something that has been bothering me, Grace...' She lowered her voice and peered out to the garden. Rory and Nick were huddled around the barbecue. Callum was kicking a football to Noah, cheering at his dramatic goal-scoring celebration. 'I thought you might be the person to ask.'

'Oh?'

'Yeah, it was after her funeral service, when all the flowers were laid out at the crematorium. Well, there was something that I found strange, and I haven't been able to shift it from my mind.' She took a deep breath. I focussed on the chip in the lip of the plate, where she had half laid out the pastel-coloured biscuits. 'Among the big floral displays was one that looked out of place.'

I held my breath. I knew someone would have noticed.

'Cal and I ordered the arrangement for the coffin.' She began ticking them off on her crumb-marked fingers. 'I know her parents ordered one, that was the ridiculous garish one with those ugly spiky bright flowers. Then the people she worked with at her agency sent another one. I'm sure I read a note on behalf of some friends. But there was another, a larger one, with no note on. It looked expensive too, classic, the type that would have cost a packet.' She looked at me expectantly, waiting for me to solve the case.

I couldn't admit that I'd seen it too, how unprofessional that made us look, displaying a bouquet with no note.

'Oh, I'm not sure… Maybe whoever sent it didn't want to leave one. I know some struggle finding the right words.'

She sighed and rubbed her face. 'You must think I'm mad. Obsessing over funeral flowers… But, like I said, some things don't add up. Like, her death, for example. Cal hasn't once questioned what happened to her that night. He didn't ask any more of the police, and just accepted that she'd had a car crash. But I can't help but think: why she was there? I'm not sure if you know that road but it leads to the back end of nowhere. Why was she in that spot that night? It feels like there's something we're all missing.' She wrinkled her nose. I didn't dare admit that I'd thought the same when I'd found myself driving past that spot on that day out with Mum.

'The other thing is that I've heard rumours about her… since she died.'

'Rumours?' I leant closer, frowning at the expression on Mel's face.

'Between her and some guy named Owen? A model at the same agency as her.' *Owen Driscoll.* His face flashed to the front of my mind. The handsome Welsh man who I'd stood next to at her funeral, who'd almost fallen into me at her wake, looking as if he was in a real hurry to leave before it had started. They were tagged in a lot of photos on Facebook together. 'A friend of a friend said they'd seen them out a few times, before she died, looking very close, if you know what I mean.'

I blindly nodded along, even though I'd heard enough. I felt hot, sticky, and the smell of the food cooking was making me feel nauseous.

'Maybe they were mistaken; Abbie could be very flirty when she wanted to.' Mel shrugged and let out a deep sigh. 'Nick thinks I'm making too much of it. He tells me off for going all Miss Marple, but when I saw those flowers something just stayed in my mind, and I've been meaning to ask you about it. Sorry! I hope you don't mind me blurting all of this out. I barely know you! I bet you think I'm really bitter. I'm not, honestly, I just care for Cal.'

'Of course. I understand.'

'I'm probably reading way too much into this. When you spend most of your time at home with the kids all day, your mind tends to run away with itself a little.' She laughed but it sounded hollow. 'I just hope that once the inquest takes place, which has been delayed yet again, then we can all properly move on.'

'Has Callum heard these rumours?' I felt uneasy. Imagine what that could do to him.

'No!' Mel paused. 'Anyway, let's forget about it. I wanted to say thanks for all your help checking in on Cal. Knowing he has someone he can trust and turn to has given us such peace of mind.'

'Oh, um, sure...'

'Mummmmmyyy!' A whining voice filtered through to the kitchen from the garden.

'I'm coming!' Mel rolled her eyes. 'I'd better go and sort them out. Oh, and please, don't say anything to Cal.

I'm going to do some more digging but I don't want him to hear anything unless it comes from me. Hopefully it's a load of lies.'

'Hopefully,' I said, weakly, watching her breeze out into the garden.

Chapter 23

The oblong rattan outdoor table was soon full of noise as we took our seats and plates were clattered about. Nick tried to keep a wriggling Noah in his highchair, Mel ordered Callum to sort out drinks, and Finley was singing a repetitive song about smelly poo. I tried to relax amongst the chaos. As welcoming as they had all been, it was hard not to feel like I was intruding on what should have been a family celebration. I was very conscious of the fact I was sitting in the chair Abbie would have sat in.

'Cheers!' Mel raised her glass. 'A toast. Go on, Nick. You do it. You always do them so well.'

Nick let out a fake groan. 'OK, OK. I'd like to say a toast to thank Mummy for this yummy food. Finn, I want you to stop dropping your tomatoes to the floor thinking we can't see you do it, please.' Finn let out a whine. 'A toast to Rory for not burning the sausages.'

'*Nearly* not burning them,' Rory called out, then dropped his voice. 'Dropped a few though!'

'A bit of grass never killed anyone.' Nick winked. I felt my stomach turn at the thought, and gently pushed the sausage to the side of my plate. 'A toast to Grace for not running for the hills at the sight of this madhouse, and for introducing Callum to a lawnmower. Lord knows he needed the push.'

'Oi!' Callum laughed.

I blushed under everyone's warm smiles.

'And finally, to Uncle Callum for putting up with us all –'

'You're the ones who have put up with me,' Callum smiled, tilting his beer in the air.

'So a toast to Callum. Happy birthday, may the next year be filled with a lot more of the good times than bad. Cheers!'

We raised our glasses in unison; even the boys lifted up their purple plastic beakers.

'Mel mentioned that you'd been back working again?' Nick asked Callum, passing the salad bowl.

'Yeah, I'm feeling a lot brighter actually. Well, let's say I've been having more good days than bad ones,' Callum said, casually spearing a new potato.

Mel caught my eye, forcing me to look away under her curious stare.

'Good, I'm glad to hear it.'

'You're doing brilliantly, mate. I can't imagine how tough today's been without Abbie here.'

'Hear, hear!' Rory raised a glass and winked at his best friend.

'Mummy? Where's Aunty Abbie?' Finley asked.

I saw Mel's jaw flicker with tension as she plastered on a smile. 'I told you darling, remember? She's gone to the sky to live with Mr Bruno.'

Rory leaned closer to me and whispered. 'Mr Bruno

was their pet cat who met an unfortunate end under the wheels of a Mazda last year.'

Finn thought for a moment. 'When's she coming back?'

'Well… she's not…' Mel flicked a look at Callum, waiting for him or Nick to step in. 'We talked about this, remember?'

'Daddy said Uncle Callum had lost her. Well, when are you going to find her?'

I swallowed the lump in my throat at his confused expression. Nick shifted in his seat. Callum picked up his beer and took a long slow sip.

'No darling, sometimes we say that word but what we mean is that the person has died,' said Mel.

Finn nodded along slowly.

'We need to use clear language, you know this,' Mel hissed to Nick. I was sure she was kicking him under the table.

'You were the one who said Mr Bruno had gone to live in the sky,' Nick glared back.

'I want to live in the sky!' Finn sang, making Rory laugh before Mel shot him a look and shut him up.

'Oh, well, no.' Mel looked flustered. 'What I mean is that… er…'

'Do you remember watching the film *Up* with me?' Callum finally found his voice. Finn nodded. 'Well, in the film the old man –'

'Carl.'

'Yep, Carl. Well Carl was sad because his wife –'

'Ellie.'

'Yes, Ellie had died and the little boy –'

'Russell.'

I smiled.

'Yep. How do you remember that!? Anyway, Russell wanted to make the old man, I mean, Carl, happy again. Because when someone dies, like Aunty Abbie and Mr Bruno, it is very hard because they are never coming back so you feel sad. Like Uncle Callum does…'

He glanced at Mel and Nick who were nodding along.

'So, Aunty Abbie and Bruno are like Ellie?'

'Exactly!' He finished his beer.

'Oh, right…' Finley nodded. A long pause. I thought he'd grown bored of the conversation. 'They're all… dead?'

'Well, yes, but…'

'Can I have some birthday cake now, please?'

'In a minute,' Mel smiled gently.

I caught Callum press the base of his palm to his eyes when he thought no one was looking. The conversation moved on to Rory's new job and Abbie wasn't mentioned again.

*

'Right then!' Rory shouted, getting to his feet. 'Who's up for a game of footie?'

I'd been talking to Nick, feeling full, content and strangely comfortable amongst this new group of friends. Mel had put Noah down for a nap and ordered me not to move a muscle when I tried to help with the washing up. Everyone moved so easily around each other.

'Me, me, me!' Finn yelled.

'You sure you want to do that?' Callum asked Rory, then turned to me. 'Last time we had a kick about this one ended up in A&E with a sprained ankle.'

'Er, excuse me! It was broken!'

Callum threw his head back in laughter. 'It was not! You're such a liar. It was barely bruised. You just fancied the nurse and wanted to look manly in front of her.'

'Well, she was cute.' Rory tilted his head, lost in a memory. 'But it was definitely broken.'

Callum gave him a pointed look.

Rory held his hands up. 'OK, maybe just sprained then. Whatever, this time I'm going to own your ass.'

'Oh, is that true?'

'Will you two ever stop acting like kids?' Mel shook her head with laughter. She'd emerged wringing a tea towel between her hands. 'Grace, when we were growing up those two would always be betting each other stupid challenges. They're so competitive and it's still not changed.'

'Cal's just a sore loser,' Rory winked. 'He never could keep up.'

'Am not! Anyway, I think you're forgetting the Battle of Bottle Smash?' Callum raised a finger in the air. Mel groaned. 'I won that fair and square.'

'Fine,' grumbled Rory. 'But that was one time. Apart from that I always win. You can't deny it!'

'Probably because you still own his soul,' I blurted without thinking.

There was a second or two of silence.

'What?' Mel asked, confusion on her pink cheeks, at the same time as Rory slammed his palm on the table making the glass jump.

'Yes! Oh my god, thank you, Grace! I'd completely forgotten about that!'

'You what?' Mel repeated, louder.

'I'm so sorry! I wasn't meant to say!' I clasped my hands to my mouth.

Callum had his head in his hands, his shoulders juddering with laughter at Rory's outburst.

'Rory, keep it down! Noah's having a nap!' Mel chided before turning to her brother. 'Wait – Cal, you sold your soul?'

'Yeah, years and years ago. Thanks, Grace, for reminding him.'

He wasn't annoyed. In fact, he seemed to be enjoying it.

'It just slipped out,' I blushed, mouthing *sorry*, trying to ignore the evil laugh that Rory was attempting to perfect.

'Don't worry.' Callum pressed a warm hand on top of mine. 'It's fine.'

I smiled back at him then noticed Mel giving a knowing nudge to Nick, looking in our direction at our hands together. I pulled mine away and clasped them on my lap.

'Why on earth did you do that?' Nick asked. 'Hope you got something worthwhile out of it!'

'I'm still waiting for my Super Soaker.' Callum shook his head regretfully.

*

The night wore on. The boys flopped in the spare room. Everyone was a little merrier, especially Rory, who decided he wanted to get to the bottom of what I was doing there on his friend's birthday. It wasn't until after he'd asked me for tips on the best way to grow tomatoes, and gone on and on about the impressive trailing ferns that I'd planted, that I told him that I wasn't actually Callum's official gardener. We'd met in less happy circumstances.

'I think it's great, ya know!'

'What's great?'

He lazily dragged his hand between Callum and I. 'This, you two.'

It was hard to see Callum's face in the fading light. I fidgeted in my chair.

'What do you mean? Us two?' He gently scoffed. 'There is no *us two*.'

Rory acted like he hadn't heard him. 'I mean, you can never replace Abbie, you know that, right?'

'She sure was one of a kind,' I heard Mel mutter under her breath.

'You just gotta do what you want to do. I reckon it's a good thing.' He lowered his voice. 'I know you and Abbie weren't getting on so well...'

Her name hung in the air. I felt itchy and hot, despite the cool summer evening breeze.

'If that means hanging out and making new friends, a friend that happens to be female, then go for it. I'm sure as hell not going to judge you for it.'

'Er, when I'm dead there's no way I'm giving Nick permission to move on. I want him mourning for me for the rest of his life,' Mel butted in. 'I'll come and haunt you just to make sure.'

'Ach, what a load of bollocks.' Rory laughed, slamming a palm on the table. 'Grace, do you believe in this nonsense?'

'Well, I...'

'Cal, Abbie won't be haunting you. Wherever she is, she'll have much bigger things to be getting on with.'

'The only spirit I believe in is found in a bottle,' Callum tried to lighten the tone. 'Anyone for a top up?'

'She's not coming back. You know that, we know that. So, what else are you supposed to do? Stay celibate forever more?' Rory said, matter-of-factly. He was slurring his words now. Being the only sober one I wasn't sure the others had noticed.

Callum seemed to choke on his drink. 'This is not about sex!'

'Alright, calm down!'

'I'm so sorry about him, Grace, just ignore him. The drunkard Scot!' Mel placed a warm hand on mine.

'It's fine!' My voice was about three times higher than normal.

Nick passed a few squares of kitchen roll to Callum to clean up the beer he'd spilt. I focussed my eyes on the liquid bleeding into the paper towel, avoiding the looks I knew they were giving each other.

'You can't expect to stay isolated and cut off from the opposite sex forever. You can't live your life in the past. Whatever helps you to get up in the morning, to get dressed and face the day, well... no one can judge you for that.' Rory finished his drink and raised his empty glass in the air. 'Sure it's a little odd that it's the funeral arranger but, hey! I like the woman!'

'Me too!' Mel said, leaning over and pulling me into a hug.

'That's a first,' Nick snorted.

'I think you're both getting the wrong end of the stick. Grace has just been helping me out with some gardening, that's all.' Callum ignored their matching raised eyebrows. 'Seriously, she's an excellent gardener who just happens to be a woman. Nothing more than that.'

'Yep, what he said!' I laughed, but it sounded all wrong.

Mel smiled, getting to her feet. 'Now that's shut Rory up, I'll go and put the kettle on.'

I made my excuses to leave not long after that.

Chapter 24

'Are you awake? Stupid question. I woke you, didn't I?'

The sound of a phone ringing had pierced my dreams. It took me a second or two to realise my mobile was actually ringing in real life.

'Callum?' I yawned.

'Sorry, yeah. Listen, I'll let you go, I'm sorry for waking you.'

I heard a rustle of sheets. I tried to shake the picture of him in bed from my mind.

'No, it's fine.' I blinked rapidly. 'I'm up now. I'm guessing you can't sleep? Is everything OK?'

'Nah, I just wanted to go through my phone contacts list. I've made it all the way down the list to S for Salmon.'

'Oh.'

'That was a joke, Grace. Sorry, I clearly think I'm hilarious at four a.m.'

I could hear him smiling down the phone.

'Clearly. So, what's up?'

'I just wanted to apologise for my friend Rory,' he said deadpan. 'He's a real hoot.'

'Ah, yeah,' I winced. 'It's fine. I think he probably had a little too much to drink.'

'You can say that again. But either way I should have said something sooner, it wasn't fair him winding you up like that.'

'Honestly, it's fine.' I just wanted to move on. There was nothing between us and there never would be, despite what a drunk Scotsman wanted to intimate. 'Everything else OK?'

It seemed a bit drastic calling at this time, just to apologise for his best mate being a bit gobby.

He sighed deeply. 'I don't know…'

'Struggling to sleep?'

'Something like that.'

'Have you tried all the usual stuff? Warm milk, hot bath, lavender pillow spray, meditation…'

'You sound a bit like a sleep expert.'

'I sometimes struggle with insomnia. What you need is a pair of socks.'

'Socks?'

'I've read that the secret to a good night's sleep is to always keep your feet toasty warm. To be honest, I'd rate that above camomile tea, changing your mattress or installing blackout blinds. Thanks to the socks I've managed to get a solid, and pretty miraculous, five hours.'

'I'll keep that in mind. Mel wants me to get into meditating. It just sounds a bit wanky, if I'm honest. Apparently there's this thing called death meditation. The Buddhists are big on it. It makes you realise how lucky you are to be here, and worry less about trivial stuff. Or something like that.'

'I kind of get it. It might help? So, I think I know why you can't sleep – you've clearly got a lot on your mind.'

'Tell me about it!' He laughed.

'Do you want to talk about any of it?'

'It's four a.m. I've already taken up enough of your time…' He trailed off.

I suddenly didn't mind him interrupting my circadian rhythm. I realised I was enjoying lying in the dark, hearing his sleepy voice down the phone. Judging by his pause he wasn't desperate to get back to bed either.

'I'm awake now. Go on. What's up?'

'Where to start? OK, the newest thing is that I've been thinking about other people I know who've lost someone they loved, and realising I've been a properly shit mate to them in the past. It's like when someone dies you go into this club made up of people who've also been where you've been, and I just keep thinking how crap I was for others when they needed me. I'd try my best to cheer them up, then change the subject, not knowing what to say. I mean, I never realised how isolating grief was.'

'I'm sure they knew you cared.' I cleared my throat. 'Have you been struggling to sleep for a while, with things like this on your mind?'

'You could say that. Mel gave me some herbal sleeping tablets, but I'm such a groggy sod when I'm on them. I've got better as time has gone on, I guess. The first few weeks were the toughest. I couldn't settle into a deep sleep in case Abbie came back… telling myself that she might have forgotten her key or something daft.'

'I know of a few families I've helped who still, years later, sleep with the porch light on to light the way home for their loved ones. It's normal for something like this to affect your sleep. I guess the empty bed is another tough reminder?'

He paused. 'Between you and me and these four walls, I'd not shared a bed with my wife for the eight months before she died.'

'Oh…'

'Yep.' He let out a deep sigh. 'This perfect marriage wasn't so perfect after all.'

I remembered snooping in Abbie's wardrobe; no wonder I couldn't see any of Callum's things in that perfectly made-up bedroom. God knows when he had last slept in there. I hadn't expected them to live such separate lives. There was a long silence between us, long enough that I wondered if he'd fallen asleep.

'Grace, can I tell you something else that's been going around my head?'

'Of course.'

'This might just be me overthinking, but something's been bothering me about Abbie's death… Well… I keep thinking about it all.'

'That's perfectly normal. You've suffered a huge shock and trauma –'

'Yeah, I know *how* she died but not *why*.'

I stayed silent and focussed my eyes on the edge of my duvet. I wondered if he'd heard Mel's rumours after all.

'I don't know why she was on that road that night, or where she'd been after dropping Owen off.'

She had been with Owen on the night she died? I sat up straighter. I didn't know that.

He took a deep breath. 'We'd had a row over something

so small I can't even remember now. She'd stormed out. It wasn't an uncommon occurrence. I'd expected to wake up the next morning to face a stony silence, until one of us got over being so stubborn and attempted to make peace. I never expected to see a policeman at my door. He told me to sit down. Well, you know what that means…'

'I'm so sorry, Callum.'

'He'd asked me why my wife might have been on that side of town at that time in the morning. I told him I had no idea, that she probably wanted to drive to clear her head, but that wasn't the truth. Abbie hated driving.'

The pause stretched out between us.

'I knew that she'd been at a nightclub with Owen, gatecrashing a perfume launch together.' I wondered if Mel knew about this, if that was what had fuelled the rumours of Abbie being unfaithful? I'd tried not to think about what Mel had mentioned, about Abbie and Owen. It wasn't any of my business, and it made me uncomfortable to think that someone was spreading rumours about a woman who couldn't defend herself. I knew Mel and Abbie hadn't had the closest of relationships, so whoever had told her knew she would fall for it. But despite not wanting to believe it, my head and my heart said different things.

As fellow models at the same agency they could easily have turned their work friendship into something more. I still didn't know much about the man who was with Abbie the night she died, as his social media all seemed to be set to private.

'He told the police that she'd driven to the club, they

had stayed out until he'd got too drunk, and then she'd dropped him home about midnight or one o'clock, but he couldn't say for sure as he was so paralytic. Then she must have driven the long way home from his house, as she was found on the winding road that skimmed the edge of Ryebrook. But there's time unaccounted for, no matter how slow she was driving…'

'Maybe she wanted to go for a drive to clear her head?'

I could picture him shaking his head. 'No. She had never done that before. People change but not Abbie. Things just don't add up.'

'Have you told anyone else about this? How you're feeling, I mean?'

'No. For so long I blamed myself. But now, well, I don't know.' He sighed. 'Maybe I wasn't the whole reason for her death. Not coming home to face me wasn't enough for her to absently drive around town. There has to be something else I'm missing here. Something that I've tried to ignore but can't.'

In the dead of night, he had been able to summon up the words that he'd not told anyone else.

'I don't really know what to say, Callum.'

He let out a hollow laugh. 'I don't think there is anything to say.'

Another pause. I desperately wanted to lighten the tone. I could feel us heading into unfamiliar territory, and I wasn't sure how comfortable I felt. Suddenly this phone call in the dead of night felt very intimate.

'It's hard to find the right words sometimes, especially when it comes to death. Did you know that people are more likely to open up about their sex lives than their funeral plans?' I said.

He let out a sort of chuckle. 'I can believe it. What was it that Raj said at the end of last week's session?'

I tried to remember. 'Er?'

'Something about the only things you can say both during lovemaking and at a funeral?'

I groaned. Raj really did need to pick his audience better.

He laughed. 'He's great. A little out there, but great.'

'Don't tell me you'd go and see him at a comedy club?'

'What! Course I would.'

'Pfft.'

'And you'd come with me. I'd make you sit on the front row, we could be his groupies, it would be hilarious.'

'Never going to happen!'

'I'm serious, Abbie, it would be brilliant.'

I didn't move. His slip-up hung in the air between us. The brief laughter in his voice brought to an abrupt end.

'God, sorry. I don't know where that came from. I –'

'It's fine.'

'Grace, I wasn't thinking. I didn't mean –'

'It's fine. I mean, she's obviously on your mind. It's your birthday after all...'

'But, I really didn't –'

I held up a hand – not that he could see me. 'It's cool. Honestly. Speaking of your birthday, it's late and you probably need more beauty sleep now that you're a year older.' I tried to lighten the awkwardness.

There was a pause.

'OK, well, I'll let you get back to bed, but thanks for listening, it means a lot.'

'Anytime. I mean that.'

'Thanks, Grace.'

I hung up and rolled over, waiting for sleep but knowing I wouldn't find it.

Chapter 25

'So, Julie, how're you doing?'

It was Grief Club once more. The first time I'd seen Callum since his Abbie/Grace mix-up. I hadn't mentioned it and neither had he. We just carried on as normal, making small talk with the others.

'It's been a week of ups and downs,' Julie nodded at me. I'm sure she was wearing a little make-up this evening. 'I guess when someone suffers from a terminal illness, you think you'll know what to expect when they eventually pass away but it's not the case. I managed to hold it together for almost the entire day that my mum died until I went to her house. The silliest thing got to me: I caught sight of her slippers by the lounge door. Untouched since she had taken them off for what would be the last time ever, just sat waiting for her when she arrived home.'

The picture she was painting was so hauntingly sad. The room waited on her every word, heads nodding in sympathy, or understanding, or both.

'It was the normality of it all. Staring at these M&S dark pink slippers, ones I'd only bought her last Christmas, I realised she was really gone. The fact that they would never be worn by her again just ripped me apart. It has been so tough coping with these little empty spaces left behind. Spaces only she could fill.' She paused to dab the tears from her eyes with a tissue Ms Norris passed her. 'You feel sick at the loss of things you didn't even know you could miss.'

'It's the small things that get to you,' Raj nodded.

Others murmured in agreement.

'Exactly, like the trashy magazines that she adored, the half-empty bag of peppermint creams next to her favourite chair. The almost-finished tube of toothpaste, the knitting pattern she would never finish or the library book that she didn't get to the end of. These ordinary items made me yearn for her much more than the big striking memories. I craved for her to brew up – always milk first – in her tea-stained mugs. Trivial things we take for granted.'

'I know just what you mean,' Callum said quietly, his eyes low.

'I wish I could tell others to savour these moments with their loved ones,' Julie said. 'You can see them going about their ordinary business without a second thought about the small habits, but boy, those are the things you miss the most when they're gone.'

I saw Callum give a slight nod. He'd told the group that he and Mel were making a start on clearing Abbie's things at the weekend, a look of utter dread and resignation etched on his face as he'd said it.

'But, like so much in life, I guess, clearing their things is always a harder job in your mind than in reality.' Julie turned to face Callum. 'Along with all the sentimental heart-tugging items my mum had, there was a lot of old rubbish.' She let out a light tinkle of a laugh. I realised I hadn't heard her laugh before.

'I found myself rolling my eyes a lot and wondering why she'd bothered to keep hold of some stuff for so long. I can tell you, putting those two ugly china dogs that sat on the lounge window into the charity shop box was a good moment! I've always hated those dogs. Funny eyes.' Julie shook her head at the memory. 'Oh and don't get me started on the out of date food that had been lurking at the back of her cupboards since I don't know when. I'd been on at her for years to chuck them out but she was of that generation – waste not, want not.'

Her eyes misted over.

'I hope you're right,' said Callum. 'I expect I am building it up a little – the dread. It's just clothes and stuff, after all.'

I couldn't imagine how overwhelmed he must have been feeling at sorting through Abbie's many, many clothes, deciding which items to hold onto and cherish, and what could be chucked away. The surprising value he would place on innocent jumpers or pyjamas – now she would never wear them again, they'd turned into priceless artefacts. Her DNA woven into the threads. Her smell sewn in the seams. It was not a task to envy.

Ms Norris raised a hand to speak. 'As the oldest one here I feel it is my duty to add something.' Everyone turned to listen to her. 'With age comes experience, but it also means that I've survived when a lot of people I've loved have not. I've lost family, old colleagues, neighbours and friends, and the only thing I know is that the pain of losing someone you love never gets easier. It tears a hole through you, it leaves an indelible mark and will never not be painful.'

I really hoped she was going to add something to lighten the tone.

'But, being old, I've had a lot of time to think, and what I know is that despite how painful it is, you don't want it not to matter. You don't want to lose someone close to you and feel nothing. The more you break, the more you loved them, and that's something to be proud of and to embrace.'

A murmur passed around the group. I felt a funny ache in my chest.

'Nicely said, Ms N,' Deano nodded.

'Is this why you got into your job, Grace?' Julie's quiet voice caught my attention. I realised the whole group was looking at me, waiting for me to say something.

'Sorry?'

'I just wondered if you felt this way too? If it was what inspired you to become a funeral arranger?'

'Oh, well, erm…'

I fidgeted with my sleeve, wanting the conversation to move on but feeling like I owed them the truth. They had shared so much with me, after all, and I couldn't remain the neutral mediator forever. I'd allowed the group to evolve from Ask A Funeral Arranger into Grief Club, after all; we were all in it together. I thought of Callum, and how bereft he'd been, how hopeless, and how things seemed to have begun to turn around for him since he'd opened up and spoken about losing Abbie. I thought of him inviting me to his birthday, and calling me in the night, as if I were his friend. And then I realised, I *was* his friend, and he was mine. All these people were my friends. And if you can't talk to your friends about something, who can you talk to?

It was time.

'Did you lose someone close to you, Grace?' Raj asked quietly.

I nodded.

'Who was it, dear?' Ms Norris asked with trepidation. 'Who died, I mean?'

The eyes of those in the room were fixed on me. I felt hot and exposed. There was a pause as I summoned up the courage to finally reveal the truth. *Come on, you can do this. Be brave. Like they are every week.*

'This is a circle of trust, like you said, remember?' Marcus said quietly.

I nodded. He was right. They had shared their pain, it was time that I delved into my own personal wound, as much as it was going to hurt. I took a deep breath and stared at the floor. Feeling their eyes on me, willing me on, supporting me.

My voice seemed so very tiny in this large musty room.

'My son.'

Chapter 26

'You poor thing.' Julie's eyes had gone all misty.

I felt very vulnerable and exposed, as if I'd lost a layer of skin. I refused to look at the others but heard Ms Norris sighing and could sense her shaking her head in sympathy.

I jumped to my feet and closed the meeting. For the first time I was grateful to the line dancers for making a commotion outside, telling us our time was up. Saved by the bell. I packed up my things, with my back to everyone, reminding them to bring a friend next week, preferably someone who hadn't planned their funeral yet. Very aware of how hot I felt and how high-pitched my voice was.

When I turned around they had all left the room and let the sour-faced dancers in. I was still in shock that I'd opened up like that. No one knew about my baby, not even my mum, and here I was telling a group of near strangers. What had come over me? I took a deep breath and made my way outside.

'Oh deary.' I heard Ms Norris's gentle voice. She was waiting by the steps for me, Purdy's lead in one hand, her eyes translucent behind glassy, unshed tears. 'I'm so sorry. A petal fell before the flower bloomed.'

'Thanks,' I mumbled, looking at my feet. I would not break down. 'Er, do you need me to help you?' I glanced at her holding onto the railing.

'I think I've got something in my shoe. Will you please help me over to that bench so I can try and sort it out?'

'There's a nearer one just over there?' I nodded my head to a bench a short distance from the steps. The one she was pointing to was barely visible past a drooping apple tree, half hidden from the main path.

'I'd prefer that one.'

I didn't have the strength to argue so let her grip my arm for support, or maybe I was gripping hers, it was hard to say, and led her to the bench she adamantly wanted to sit on to rearrange her shoe. It was next to a pretty patch of pansies that someone had recently tended to in the neat flower beds. The paint was chipped but you could tell it had once been a royal blue colour, the scuffed wrought-iron legs and armrests looped and curled. It was slightly raised on a mound of earth; this elevation allowed you to see the park rolling out before you. I'd never realised it was even here before.

'Wow, that's quite a view,' I whispered, helping Ms Norris to sit down gingerly.

'My favourite spot of the town.' She nodded and eased off her right shoe, revealing a swollen foot wrapped in gossamer-thin stockings, blue veins visible through the sheer fabric. 'Don't you just hate it when you get something in your shoe?'

'Can I help?'

She was huffing, trying to lean forward and pick up the rogue shoe to give it a shake out. I didn't wait for her answer. I half crouched in front of her and picked up the beige low heel and tipped it upside down.

'I can't see anything stuck in here?'

'How strange…' She was looking over my head at the view beyond us.

I gave it another shake. 'Well if there was a stone in here then it's gone now.'

I put it on the ground for her to slide her foot back into it, and went to get to my feet. I wanted to get home. Despite the inviting light of the summer evening, and the warm breeze buffeting us, I just wanted to be on my own in the safety of my flat.

Something caught my eye as I stood up. Just past her shoulder was a shiny bronze plaque fixed to the middle slat of the bench.

'In memory of Donald Norris,' I read aloud.

Ms Norris let out a sniff. Her eyes still trained on the sprawling park behind me.

'Did you know him?'

She nodded sadly. 'He was my little brother.'

'Oh. I'm sorry…'

'It was a long time ago, lovey. Not that time completely takes away the pain but it certainly numbs it a little. Well, I'm sure you'll know about that.'

I gave half a nod.

'Do you want to talk about what happened to you?' she asked gently, placing a warm hand on mine. 'I'm here whenever you want to open that box. I'd like to tell you that, although it doesn't feel like it, there's a gift in the pain you're feeling.'

I took a deep breath, staring out over the park below. 'It's a really tough part of my life to dwell on. It was early days in the pregnancy and, well, things didn't work out.'

'With the pregnancy?'

I nodded. 'Then with my ex, Henry. He left me after I lost the baby.' I bit back the painful lump in my throat that had risen. My breath was all funny and wrong, as the painful memories from this time of my life rushed back from where I'd tried to bury them.

Her small mouth formed a perfect O-shape. 'How horrific for you. Tell me you didn't take that lying down!'

'I tried to…' I trailed out. The words refusing to form in my mouth. How could I explain that after so long of never wanting to speak to Henry, it was actually Henry that would never speak to me again.

'No one should have to go through such a tragic ordeal like that on their own. It's not right.'

She didn't know the half of it. 'Sometimes you have to leave the past in the past, I guess.' I had been doing OK, knowing this was buried so deeply away. I almost feared for the consequences that sharing this loss would have on me. I tried not to worry about that right now, instead I focussed on the slight drop in my shoulders from sharing just a tiny part of what had happened. It had been suffocating me, but in this instance, looking over the park, I felt able to take a deep breath.

'You carry the past around with you everywhere,

especially when love is involved.' She sighed. 'Can I ask what happened with your baby?'

'It was during the twelve-week scan.' I swallowed. 'They couldn't find a heartbeat, a missed miscarriage. I remember hearing a scream. A painful, deafening howl, then I realised that the sound was coming from me. I remember the doctor's words floating above me, or me floating above them, I couldn't tell. All I knew is that I was there but I wasn't really there. The most startling thing after leaving that hospital room was watching everyone else getting on with their lives. Car engines sounding so loud, drivers listening to the radio with their windows wound down, even the bird sound was deafening. Had it always been this noisy? How could people just be getting on living? Didn't they know the world had changed beyond belief? I felt like I needed to press pause, for everyone else to catch up with me.'

'I'm so sorry,' she whispered, clutching my hand in hers, as I let the tears slide down my cheeks. There was nothing else to say.

Chapter 27

Despite Ms Norris's best intentions to check I was OK, emotions bubbled inside that I didn't have the ability to acknowledge or properly deal with. Why was it still like a car crash every time he crossed my mind? I had been doing so well for so long, but now all I could see was his face swimming in front of my eyes, blurred from tears that refused to stop.

Whenever I thought about my son, Henry wasn't far behind. His name still caused a tidal wave of emotions inside me. I had tried, really I had, to move on. To deal with the fact that he was nothing to do with me anymore, that I would never see him again. The sadness I felt over losing my baby boy was displaced by the anger and hurt I still felt towards Henry. It was like an itch that I needed to scratch, and I'd been bitten badly. *You're going to regret it,* my subconscious warned, but it wasn't enough. I needed to dig my fingernails in and gouge at the incessant buzzing under my skin, like a parasite flitting around my body.

Henry, Henry, Henry.

Under the three shoe boxes, with the neatly written labels on, and the folded white fluffy towels that I saved for best, was what I was desperately searching for. An oblong shoe box that had once contained a pair of wellies. There was a time when this box was out on display, waiting for me to dip into it whenever I wanted. But I'd learnt the hard way that it wasn't healthy to keep him out on show as a constant reminder. The box had been hidden in the wardrobe ever since.

My ironed bedsheets sagged slightly under the weight of what it contained. I knew it was going to hurt, opening it again after all this time. I couldn't stop myself from tearing off the lid and diving into the past I kept in this one knackered cardboard box. My trembling hands rummaged through beer mats with stained, curled up edges from bars he'd taken me to. A broken Zippo lighter, slightly crumpled boarding passes – he'd gone so abruptly, there was no way I could have know that it was going to be our last journey together – my laminated work ID card. I'd often wondered if he'd ever kept a record of us, and if he did, where that was now. I flopped back, landing between my memory foam pillows. I'd bought them to help with my insomnia – because of him. Just like so much of what belonged in this flat, items he would never see with his own eyes, but which had been snapped up to deal with the after-effects of him. A broken heart, a broken body and a broken head.

*

I'd hardly slept. Henry's face looped in my exhausted mind, our story that had ended in ways I never thought possible. A burning insatiable rage had been lit in my stomach since seeing the horrified look on Ms Norris's face, and I was having trouble keeping the flames controlled. How dare he do that to me? How dare he leave me?

There was only one person who could help to calm me down. Maria. I called her and asked to see her, more insistent this time. I think she understood. As I pulled up to the pub where she'd told me to meet her, I took a deep breath, hoping I was doing the right thing.

The previous times I'd seen her had left me in a spin, after a lot of old issues were brought to light during our frank chats. I usually left feeling worse than when I'd arrived, but there was also something cathartic about having a good cry with someone who wouldn't judge me. I paused, one foot out of the car. Maybe I should head home and try to keep busy. I knew I shouldn't still be feeling this much anger towards Henry after so much time had passed. Time was supposed to be a healer, after all. It wasn't healthy, I knew that. I also knew that I needed to get a handle on this torrent of emotions, which propelled me from the seat of my car into the empty back room of the pub.

'Hi, Maria, how are you?'

'Hey, Grace. A little tired, but nothing new there!' She laughed and shrugged off her thin cardigan. She looked a little harassed. Her thick black hair fighting against being constrained in the high bun she'd put it in. Strands danced in the warm breeze as she sat down.

'Work been busy then?'

Maria rolled her hypnotic green-grey eyes. 'Like you wouldn't believe. I'm not complaining, though. What's that saying about idle hands?' She laughed again. Once she had relaxed it was as if tranquility seemed to exude from every pore in her olive skin, reminding me just how calming she was to be around. 'How about you? It's been so long since I saw you last!'

'Work is fine, same old. I just…' I sighed. What was I doing here? She wasn't really a friend; we were acquaintances at best. I had to keep a sort of distance between us, all because of him.

'Let me guess. Is it Henry?'

I nodded, hoping to hold back the tears of frustration that wanted to escape. I sniffed loudly, willing them to stay put. I don't know why I bothered Maria had seen me in all sorts of states. I just felt like I should be feeling better by now, I wanted her to think I had things under control, more than I actually did.

'I emailed him, demanding answers, like you said, but he hasn't replied, I've not heard a thing from him in so long.'

'Oh, Grace…' She tilted her head to the side. 'I told you that even if he doesn't read them it'll still be good for you to get your thoughts out. Put them down on paper and let them go. That was the reason I told you to write a letter, not an email,' she chided me.

'I know! But with a letter I need an address.' I threw her a loaded look.

She remained silent. She'd never tell me where he was, exactly. Always preferring to give vague answers. I didn't know who her loyalty lay with and that was the problem – the reason our catch-ups were so sporadic, why we would never be BFFs. Her vagueness irritated me. How difficult was it for her to give me what I wanted? She'd told me before how it didn't work like that; anything had to come from him, not her.

I should have cancelled meeting up with her. This wasn't a good idea; after every catch-up, I would leave clinging to any titbits of information she could give me about him, with the same reverence that Callum would grasp his dead wife's possessions. Never wanting to let them go but knowing that their existence would be more of a hindrance than a benefit in moving forward.

'Do you want me to get in touch with him for you again? Like I said, I've been pretty busy recently but I can try…'

I hated how she had a way to get through to him that I couldn't. *He doesn't want to talk to you.* I shook my head.

'Like you say, he'll get in touch with me when he's ready. I just have so much I want to ask him. I think it's time. I deserve to get some answers.' I clenched my fists to my sides.

'You have to be patient, Grace. I've told you this before. You have to keep smiling and keep busy. Laughter is a great healer. Do you laugh much?'

I thought of Raj and gave a slight shrug. 'My neighbour's a struggling comedian but his jokes are a little, er, out there.'

'Well, any form of laughter is a good thing! Why not

watch a funny movie? That might cheer you up and take your mind off Henry?'

'Next you'll be telling me to eat ice cream from the tub and sing along to awful power ballads.'

'Hey! You never know! It may work. And how about those tablets you mentioned you were taking the last time we met?'

She had a good memory. 'Well, I'm still taking them, not that I think they're doing very much.'

This wasn't entirely true. I'd been prescribed the anti-anxiety medication by Doctor Ahmed when I was at my lowest. He'd told me they would decrease the number of panic attacks; I was battling them on an almost daily basis back then. He'd been true to his word on that at least.

'They're probably just helping to balance you out a little.' The extent of her medical knowledge could rival mine. 'Seriously, Grace. You're doing OK. I know this is difficult. I've been through it, too, lots of people have. Just remember you're not alone.'

I wanted to shut my ears. I didn't want to hear what she had to say. This wasn't like what other people had been through, what she insisted she'd been through. How did she know what was for the best? Offering me ways to move on from him, when she could still talk to him and I couldn't?

'Grace?'

I smiled tightly. 'Thanks.'

It was a bad idea to come and see her. There was only one person who could give me the answers I needed and he refused to speak to me. The coward.

Chapter 28

I was grateful to take time out of my frantic headspace and focus on feeling soil between my fingers and the sun on my back. Gardening was giving me a break from the constant Henry loop that played in my mind. Hanging out with Callum was the strangest but most normal thing to have happened in the last few months. Our unconventional friendship, which blurred the boundaries of professional conduct, was left unspoken. We were just two people with a project. Two people who understood a situation that many others wouldn't be able to get their heads around.

Callum's garden had given me a sense of purpose. I think it had for him too. I went some evenings after work, noticing that he'd been busy weeding or tying plants to stakes in the ground. At the weekends I usually stayed until the last light. We'd then sit on his decking as the sun fell, eating a salad I'd rustled up from our home-grown vegetables. I imagined him in the evenings, once I'd gone, standing in his shorts and flip-flops, spraying the garden hose over the grass or checking on the chicken wire we'd put up to stop foxes snacking on the strawberries. I began to notice muscles in his upper arms and shoulders that had come to life from dragging the lawnmower around or tugging at stubborn weeds.

There were no difficult questions asked, no small talk to make, and any prickly topics were avoided at all costs. We both immersed ourselves in our respective tasks, feeling the solidity of the ground beneath our knees and the damp earth between our fingers. This reconnection with nature was bordering on healing, for both of us.

I was sure that I'd even heard him singing to the plants under his breath on more than one occasion, encouraging them to grow. He would be mortified if he knew. Freckles had popped out over my nose and my once-strong, pillar box-red hair had faded into a more of a strawberry blonde. I think I preferred this look.

Doctor Ahmed had once mentioned having a project to keep busy with and stop me overthinking, and coming up with ideas for Callum's garden may have helped. I'd been researching plants and trees and low-maintenance vegetable patches that I was excited about implementing. Whatever it was, my mood was a little brighter. Callum also seemed more together. He'd tamed his beard, had been wearing uncreased T-shirts, and I'm sure one day I'd caught the faint whiff of aftershave.

We worked in a comfortable silence alongside each other. Moving around with an ease I was growing used to. The only things unsaid were his dead wife sitting in the cupboard under the kitchen sink, and the baby I'd lost. We'd never spoken further about Abbie, or what had moved him to pick up the phone and admit his doubts over her death to me, that night after his party. We never discussed what I'd been through.

'Did you say we should get some climbing vines? To go up the trellis?' I couldn't help but smile at his furrowed brow, as he held up two identical plants.

'Yep, if you think so?'

This was the first time we'd been out in public together. We'd come to a garden centre in Hillside, a location I'd suggested, knowing it would minimise the chances of bumping into anyone he would know. Tongues would wag and eyebrows be raised if others saw us out together, especially doing something as mundane as plant shopping. I wondered if he was aware of this too.

'You know, I never gave you your birthday present,' I said, as we wandered down the narrow aisles, blooming bushes on either side, the heady scent of perfume in the air.

'You didn't need to get me a present.'

'Well, the truth is, I wasn't sure how you would feel about what I wanted to give you.'

He looked confused.

I'd purposefully led us through to the fledgling trees section, hoping this was the right thing to do.

'I thought maybe we could plant a tree in your garden… for Abbie?'

I paused, holding my breath for his reaction.

'Yeah…' He scratched his chin, looking as if he wanted to say something, but not finding the words.

'I thought cherry blossom might be nice? But, if you don't think…'

'No, I think it's a good idea.'

I let out the breath I'd been holding and watched him choose a suitable tree to put on the low trolley between us.

'It's already blossomed this year, but if we plant it now it'll have time to establish over the autumn and winter, and then next spring...'

'How about we get one for your son too?' he asked, his voice so quiet I thought I'd misheard him. 'I'm really sorry about what happened.'

I swallowed down the rock that had leapt up from nowhere, feeling that familiar clogging of my throat.

'Thank you, but this is about you, not me.'

'Grace?' A voice I knew interrupted whatever Callum was about to say. 'I thought it was you!'

I glanced up to see Linda walking towards us. The smile on her painted lips faltered as she saw who I was with.

Please don't remember him. Please don't remember him.

'Oh, hi, Linda. Wh-what are you doing here? I thought you were on holiday?'

I stepped away from Callum, as if by creating a distance she wouldn't place him. I sensed Callum shifting beside me, confused by my reaction. Saliva pooled in my mouth, my heart began to race.

She shook her head. 'I fly out tomorrow morning. Sun, sea and sangria, here I come!'

I nodded and tried to plaster a smile on my flushed face.

'You not going to introduce me? I'm Linda. I work with Grace,' Linda reached across me. My nostrils filled with her sickly-sweet perfume. She shook Callum's hand. I couldn't work out if she was doing this because she knew exactly who he was or if she genuinely couldn't remember meeting him before.

'Callum, I'm a... a friend of Grace's.'

'You look very familiar, Callum.' There was an ugly silence as she tilted her head to one side, trying to figure out the missing piece in the puzzle. I eventually met her eye and saw the challenge there.

She knew. Of course she knew.

'Well –'

Callum was about to speak but was cut off by a loud ringing sound coming from Linda's garish, diamanté handbag – the one she'd bought on a girls' holiday to Turkey, that I knew for a fact was a counterfeit, despite her protestations.

I tried to pass a look to Callum, but he was staring off into the distance. To the outside world we looked like a couple doing mundane weekend things like strolling around a garden centre, forgetting the fact that a tree, in tribute to his dead wife, was proudly standing between us.

'Hi, Denise. Yeah, I'm on my way. Alright, love, see you there!' she shrilled down the line, tapping the screen with one of her fake nails. Her phone was in a bejewelled case that also held her credit cards. I'd told her that I didn't think it was sensible, keeping all your valuable in one place, but she hadn't listened to my worries.

'Better go. I'm meeting my friend in the coffee shop here. They do a wonderful Victoria sponge. Nice to meet you, Callum. I'll see you when I'm back, Grace.' With another knowing look, laden with a warning, she spun on her heels and click-clacked away.

I felt like I needed to sit down. My legs had suddenly gone all wobbly; they couldn't possibly support my weight.

'Grace, are you OK?'

'Fine.'

I'm not fine. I could be in so much trouble if Linda decided to tell Frank who I'd been seeing out of work. In an instant, we weren't Callum and Grace, unlikely friends, but Callum, the grieving widower and Grace, the funeral arranger, overstepping the mark with a client's trust.

I decided right then and there that I would help unload the tree and other plants from his car and then head home. I needed to put some distance between us. If Linda thought there was something between me and Callum, then others surely would too. I hated that I felt the need to do this but I didn't have much choice. He would understand.

Despite the awkwardness with Callum, my mood lifted, thanks to seeing my phone buzz when I got home. I couldn't help but smile to myself when I saw Daniel's name on my screen. In his short text he asked to meet me next Friday for a drink. He had something he hoped I could help him with. I'd have to miss a Grief Club, but Ms Norris was more than capable of standing in for me. Speaking of whom, she would be very pleased that I was going for a drink with an eligible man, no matter how casual and confusing the offer was. She was right, after all: I wasn't getting any younger. Maybe this was the sign I needed. A sign that it was time to move on and leave the Andersons alone.

Chapter 29

'Grace, hi!'

A smiling, slightly sweating Daniel was calling my name. When he'd invited me there at seven o'clock, I'd figured it would be a meeting place before we found a nice cosy pub or relaxed wine bar, not that *this* was where we were going. The farmers' and local businesses' market took over two fields and a patch of woodland in Hillgate. It ran from Friday to Sunday and was a firm favourite in the social calendar for people who wanted to shop local at a premium, to ease their conscience or something. I'd never been keen on buying food from an exposed trestle table in a windy field. Nor would I be helping myself to the free samples, currently sweating on a tray covered in other people's bacteria, like the hungry couple in front of me were.

I found myself in a small marquee, and spotted Daniel's sign hanging on the back wall alongside five other creative businesses. A red-headed woman was polishing stained glass, an older couple were trying to pull people in to have a look at the wooden figurines they'd hand-carved, next to a lady with wiry glasses who was selling hand-made smelly candles.

'Hi', I said to Daniel. 'This is… er, different.'

'Yeah,' he smiled at the tourists milling past, clutching shopping bags. He scratched the back of his head. 'It's been pretty manic and it's only the first day! I thought I'd be able to get away early but, oh, excuse me –'

He was pulled away by a woman wearing a paisley headscarf, wanting to enquire about one of the smaller prints he had on display. I nodded my understanding but inside I felt confused. I stuck out like a sore thumb in my navy chiffon blouse with glittery stars and skinny jeans, and my new ankle boots were quickly covered in mud. Daniel was in a faded T-shirt, paint-splattered jeans and scuffed trainers. I stood aimlessly at the edge of his stall, waiting for him, feeling like a giant lemon.

'Sorry about that.' He rubbed my shoulder, the slight touch jolted me. 'I really didn't expect to be this busy, but I'm all yours now.'

'It's fine.' I smiled.

'Anyway, it's good to see you. I've asked the stall-holder next to us if he can keep an eye on things while we go for a quick drink.'

I nodded and tried to keep smiling as he jogged over to give instructions to a man dressed head-to-toe in khaki green. The rigid grin was still stuck to my cheeks when he came back. I was desperate to discover why he had asked me here.

'Right, you ready? There's a nice pop-up bar that's not too far.'

'After you.'

'So, do you go to many of these events?' I narrowly avoided stepping in a pile of dog poo, forcing myself not to think about the state of my new boots.

'Yeah, when I can. It's good to keep in with the organisers for a bit of free advertising, if nothing else. I tend to sell a few pieces, usually the ones that take no time at all, then encourage the buyer to come to the studio to see my other pieces. Oops, watch that puddle.' He steered my elbow. 'It's nice to be busy and have a change of location, I guess.'

I nodded, making way for a harassed mum who was pushing a double buggy over the uneven terrain. Smells of hot dogs, candy floss and fruity e-cigarette vape fumes wafted up my nose. It was manic with people. I tried to bite down the rising anxiety, as we tried to weave through the swelling crowds dawdling past stalls on their way to the large marquee further down the field. Daniel must have read my mind, or seen the sweat developing at my temple.

'There's a shortcut through here. Like I said, I didn't expect it to be this busy!'

'You sure you don't need to get back? I don't want to keep you from making some sales.'

He shook his head. 'I was due a break.'

He led me up an overgrown path, cutting through the woodland, holding back brambles for me.

'You look lovely by the way.' He smiled at my outfit, quickly pushing a low branch out of the way. The noise and hubbub of the crowd was muffled in here. My heart returned to its normal speed.

'Oh, thanks.' I could feel myself blushing. I had to file behind him down the snaking path because of the thick undergrowth around us. 'So, I've been meaning to ask you how well you know the Andersons?' I couldn't help myself. And I figured he must be a fairly close family friend to get an invite to the wake. He could surely shed some light on the Owen rumours.

Of course, it was normal for Abbie and Callum to have bickered, like any other married couple. Just because Abbie worked with Owen, it didn't mean there was anything more between the pair of them, and the missing note from the flowers could be a simple oversight that both Mel and I were reading too much into. But I also hadn't been able to drop Callum's concerns that the timings around Abbie's death didn't quite add up. A small voice kept telling me that something wasn't right.

'Oh, er, I wouldn't say we were that close.' I picked up on his hesitation. 'Why?'

'No reason,' I paused. 'I mean this is going to sound silly but I just have this feeling that things weren't quite right.'

'Right?' He stopped suddenly, I walked into the back of him.

'Whoops!'

'Sorry, there's, er, a big puddle here. Watch your step.'

We both side-stepped the puddle that was actually the size of a small, muddy lake.

'It's just up here. This is a bit of a mad route, sorry!' He laughed. I don't know if it was the quietness of the surrounding trees but it sounded hollow and forced.

We fell into silence, focussed on watching our feet along the muddy track. I was about to continue the conversation but was drowned out by the sound of laughter and music playing. The path rejoined a gravelled section and soon we were in a secluded area, away from the main crowds, where a cluster of trailers had been decked out as small bars and coffee carts. Fairy lights hung over rustic wooden picnic tables. A guy was playing a guitar, soft and gentle acoustic versions of popular songs.

'Worth the trek?' Daniel asked, his cheeks rosy red in the soft light. I nodded, taking it all in.

We sat down at one of the tables on the edge, far enough away from the musician that we could hear each other. I wrapped my hands around a homemade lemonade; Daniel had gulped down a quarter of his pint already.

'So,' he cleared his throat. 'You were saying something about the Andersons?'

'It's probably nothing.'

'Go on…'

'Well, you know they say you don't know what goes on behind closed doors?' He nodded and took another gulp of his drink. 'I just get a sense that something else was going on. Their life just seemed so perfect.'

Daniel scoffed. 'No one is perfect, Grace.'

'I know, I know.' I felt foolish for even bringing it up. It made me sound jealous, a trait I wasn't comfortable with. But the fact remained that Abbie Anderson had seemed, from the outside at least, to be close to perfection.

'Did you ever meet a guy called Owen Driscoll? He was one of Abbie's friends...'

Daniel tore his eyes away from the busker and on to me. He scrunched his face up in thought. 'The name doesn't ring a bell.'

'He's tall, dark, handsome.' I realised what a cliché this was. 'Welsh. I think he was a model with Abbie.'

'Oh, I wouldn't know about all of that. Not my sort of lifestyle!' He laughed, finished his glass and went to order another, without seeing if I wanted a top-up. While he was gone I pulled myself together. What was I doing delving into the possible inter-marital relations of the Andersons, when I should be getting to know Daniel and focussing on my own life? *Let it go, Grace.*

'So, how did you get into counselling?' he asked as he returned. I was pleased he'd changed the subject, but wished it had been a different topic. 'I'd been meaning to ask you.'

'Oh, well... it's a funny story actually.'

I needed to come clean and tell him what I actually did, the real reason I was at Abbie's wake that day. My mouth had gone very dry. I was cautious about how he might take the news.

'The reason I ask is, well...' He stopped and held a hand in the air. 'I know you're not on duty now, and I'm more than happy to book in for a proper session with you, but the thing is, I just really could do with talking to someone.'

I went to protest again but paused. The cheerful chap who'd been sat before me had left the building. *Get up and leave. Tell him that he should find someone else to open up to, a trained professional who can help him.* But my feet remained planted on the muddy ground. A small part of me was intrigued to hear what he had to say.

'Like you said, I'm... er... not on duty now.' I let out a laugh and took a large gulp of my drink. 'But I can tell you that if whatever's on your mind is to do with funerals, death or grief then you are more than welcome to come to Grief Club. If you want to talk about some stuff?'

'Grief Club?' he echoed, looking past me at a group of guys preparing to set up and take over from the solo musician.

'Yeah, it's this sort of weekly session that I set up for people to come and talk about whatever is bothering them. It's kind of evolved as the weeks have gone on, but the people that come are ever so friendly and very good listeners.'

'Mmm-hmm?'

'If that's the sort of thing you're into. Or even if it's not.' I let out a chirpy laugh. 'It's every Friday at seven o'clock, in the back room of St Augustine's. Oh, and there's cake. It's taking place right now actually.' My heart did a funny dip, thinking of them all there without me.

He nodded along, acting like he was listening.

'Yeah... maybe.'

'I mean, it's primarily just for people who have lost someone close to them.' I noticed a slight flicker of tension in his mouth as I said this. 'But if you feel like talking to others then it might help?'

I needed to change the subject. Something wasn't right, but I couldn't quite work out what.

Chapter 30

'Welcome home. You've got a lovely tan!'

Linda literally glowed at Frank's compliment. I, on the other hand, worried for her melatonin levels; she should know better at her age. I'd been dreading seeing her again. I'd had sleepless nights in anticipation of her return, ever since she'd bumped into Callum and I at the garden centre. I'd purposefully cut away from Callum, and coincidentally this 'break' from each other had timed with the temperature breaking too. The glorious Indian summer we'd been promised had been replaced with days and days of rain and wind that lashed the UK.

'So, the weather nice then?' I asked, once Frank had gone to his office. 'You chose the right time to go away. It's been non-stop showers here.'

'Oh, it was wonderful.'

She went on to tell me all about the karaoke competition she'd won and how friendly the locals were.

'Sounds great.' I got up to see to Mr Greenway who'd arrived early that morning; his sons were due in to see him later.

'Oh, Grace…' Linda said, as I pushed my chair back.
'Yes?'

'The funniest thing…' My stomach dropped and my heart began to beat faster at the strange look on her orange face. 'I've been thinking about when I bumped into you before I went away.'

I tensed my jaw. 'Oh?'

'It stayed in my head for my whole trip. I knew that man you were with had looked so familiar but I just couldn't put my finger on where I knew him from. I'm terrible with faces and names.' A short, sharp jolt of laughter.

'If I'm not mistaken…' She slowly wafted a biro in the air. 'Callum's wife had her funeral with us? I thought I'd seen him before! I just didn't know you two knew each other so well…' The accusation hung in the warm air.

I stayed silent. Beads of sweat tickled my hairline.

Just stay calm. Breathe, Grace.

'Well, we don't really…' I trailed off, wilting under her stern glare.

'I say this as a *friend*, Grace.' She lowered her voice. 'But you know it's against company policy to be having relations with a client –'

'We are not *having relations*!' I cried defensively, kicking myself for such an outburst.

She pursed her sticky, bright pink lips. 'Really? You looked ever so cosy when I saw you. All I want to say is that you need to be careful. If Frank ever found out it could seriously jeopardise your career.'

I felt like the blood had evaporated from my legs.

'Ah, here's Mr Greenway's sons now!' She rose from

her seat and adjusted her low-cut blouse. The spell broken.

'I'll go and prepare their father for the viewing,' I said in a whisper, leaving her to welcome the men in.

I closed the door and sank onto the chair opposite the closed coffin, glad to be alone with my racing thoughts. For a second I envied Mr Greenway, peacefully lying there. No drama, no gossip, and no suspicious colleagues to deal with. They say it's the living you need to be scared of, not the dead.

*

'You can't put a price on love, you know?' the woman with ridiculous gold hoops in her poor earlobes said for the third time since walking in. 'You've got to give them a good send-off. I mean, it's going to be the biggest day of my mum's life, just a shame it had to happen after her death.'

At this the lady swallowed loudly and flashed her eyes heavenwards to keep back the glossy tears threatening to spill out and dribble down her heavily made-up face. The man sitting next to her nodded his head firmly. He took this as a cue to speak for the first time.

'What Dawn is trying to say is that we've been to a few funerals in our time and for Mum, god rest her soul, it needs to be better.'

Funerals are not for the deceased, they're for the people left behind. Frank's words rang in my mind. Dawn and Nigel's mother, Vera, had passed away after a long bout of cancer, so they'd had time to come to terms with her death. They had also had a lot of time to think about arrangements for her final farewell, which would have made my job easier if only they could agree on something together.

'I understand. Is there anything else you can think of that we may be able to incorporate into the day?'

The siblings passed a look between each other.

'We want Mum to be buried with her Sky TV box and a remote control in her hand.'

'OK.' I wrote down the request.

'She loved watching telly. *Corrie* was her absolute favourite. That and *Crossroads*, when it was on,' Dawn said, dabbing her eyes with a tissue. 'She was heartbroken when Betty died. She always said she'd loved to have tasted one of her hotpots.'

'Maybe we could add a hotpot microwave ready meal in with her too?' Nigel piped up.

Dawn flashed him a look, her tissue crumpled in her hand. 'Are you mad!? That's the most ridiculous thing I've ever heard! You can't bury someone with a microwave dinner going mouldy next to them!'

'What? But you can put in a bloody remote control! What's next, the damn aerial dragged down from the roof? No doubt you'll be expecting me to climb up and pull it down to tuck in beside her?' he snapped.

'You selfish pr–'

'Selfish! I'm not the one getting all emotional over a sodding TV character!' Nigel shook his head and let out an incredulous laugh.

Dawn glared at him. I imagined them as children, squabbling over a toy. Back then their mum would have intervened, but who was going to step in to break up the childish bickering now? The atmosphere in this small room had just escalated to boiling point. I needed to try and get them both back down from the ceiling.

'How about we move on? We can come back to these ideas in a while?' I didn't let them answer before I turned my piece of paper over and passed them the brochure. 'Now, you said you'd like a burial? That's not a problem, we just need to –'

'You know what?' Nigel interrupted me.

'What?' Dawn spun to face him, soggy tissue intricately shredded between her long painted fingers.

'Mum never said she wanted a burial. *You* were the one who said it. I actually think we should do a cremation. Write this down, Grace!'

'Oh no! No, no, no. You're not changing this now. Grace, ignore him. He doesn't even know what Mum wanted. He was hardly waiting at her bedside every day like I was. How the hell do you expect to know what Mum would have wanted!?' she shrieked.

Nigel let out a vindictive laugh. 'Ha! Oh listen to Miss Nightingale over here.' He pointed a chubby finger at his sister. She glared at it as if she was about to bite it. 'I'm not the one who booked an all-inclusive fortnight in Lanzarote during the last stage of her chemo, am I!?'

Dawn slammed her hands on the table. 'That's it! I've had enough of you. I can't even bear to be in the same room as you. You know I deserved that holiday!'

'Alright, maybe we should take a break?'

Dawn stared at me as if she'd forgotten I was even there. Her heavily made up eyes narrowed at her brother. Tear stains streaked down her orange cheeks.

'Good idea. If he's going to waltz in here and think he can change everything then he can think again. Mum wanted a burial and that's that!' She roughly pulled her biker jacket from the back of her chair and stormed out, slamming the door behind her with such force the framed certificates bounced on the walls.

'OK…' I took a deep breath. The air felt stale with the tension. 'I understand this is a very emotional time for you, for both of you.'

Nigel looked up, muttering something under his breath. 'She's always been like this. Mum always let her get her way, for far too long. She's a spoilt brat.'

'It's a very tense time and emotions are bound to run high. What I would recommend is that we leave it there for today and you come back to see me when you've maybe managed to have a chat together about things?'

Nigel scoffed. 'You don't know her. She won't change her mind now she's made it up.'

'Then I advise that you perhaps ask someone you both know and trust to act as a mediator? You can let them know your wishes and come to some sort of compromise that your mum, Vera, would have wanted.'

At the sound of her name all the bravado puddled out. He swallowed hard and nodded. 'You're right. This isn't about me and that cow of a sister. This is about Mum.'

I smiled gently. 'Exactly. I think it's wonderful that you

both feel so passionately about giving her the send-off she deserves. It's just about trying to figure out a way to keep everyone happy.' He nodded firmly. 'Let's leave it there for today. Give me a call when you've had time to cool off and think about things?'

'OK, thanks.' He got to his feet. 'Sorry about…' he mumbled as he got to the door.

'It's what I'm here for.'

A wave of exhaustion rolled over me as I watched him leave. It had been a testing day.

Chapter 31

I waited for the microwave to ping. I promised myself I'd get back into the swing of eating healthy, nutritious dinners soon. My cleaning rota had also been somewhat neglected recently. I ignored the unsightly line of scum around the sink and the full-to-bursting kitchen bin. I was running late for Grief Club. After wolfing down my dinner I would have to rush out of the door and catch up on cleaning later.

As I peeled off the greasy film from my fish pie for one, I opened my laptop and impatiently waited for it to come to life. Deano had sent me a link to an article on Facebook that I'd promised him I'd read, but I'd forgotten all about it. He was bound to ask me about it later. I didn't know what was going on, but it felt like I was chasing my tail – even a few of my services at work had been less polished than I'd normally have liked. Thankfully Linda hadn't mentioned Callum again.

As I opened Facebook I saw Abbie's profile picture smiling back at me. There had been another article about her and the road safety campaign the local newspaper was pushing. Apparently they had now installed better street lighting in a few spots across town. Without thinking, my fingers moved to her profile page.

I clicked through to Abbie's photo albums, enlarging the images so Abbie's face filled my screen.

I paused on a photo. There was something about it that bothered me but I just couldn't put my finger on exactly what it was. Abbie wearing a fancy-looking beige rain mac on a soaked pier, a seagull swooping across dark ominous clouds in the background. She had pulled the wide lapels up, as if hiding from the wind that was whipping her hair. Her eyes were focussed on something in the distance. Hands clenched in her pockets. A Mona Lisa smile on her lips.

The doorbell rang, pulling me back into the real world.

Who can that be? I wasn't expecting anyone. I glanced at the time on my phone. I was running really late and didn't have time for unexpected visitors. I left my laptop, chucked the empty fish pie dish in the sink, and rushed downstairs. I could see a fractured silhouette through the glass. The height and build were difficult to make out, as whoever it was bobbing around outside.

Callum? My stomach flipped at seeing him again. I paused. Maybe he'd randomly decided to come here so we could walk to Grief Club together? He'd not texted or called to tell me of this unexpected plan, but then I had been ignoring his other messages asking how I was, hoping everything was OK, letting me know that he had a bumper load of onions and potatoes from the seeds we'd planted. He'd invited me over to help him get through them all, offering to cook, which according to his disaster culinary tales was a big deal. I'd deleted every message, needing to put some space between us. Linda's suspicious face loomed to the forefront of my mind.

I braced myself. I was going to have to face the music as whoever it was could clearly see me through the glass. I took a deep breath and fixed on a smile as I pulled the door open.

'Hi... D-daniel?'

'Hi, Grace. Sorry. Is this a bad time?'

Why was Daniel standing on my doorstep? How did he even know where I lived? He must have read my thoughts.

'Your mum gave me your address. She told me it would be a nice touch if I hand-delivered it myself...' He trailed out, taking in my confused expression.

'Hand-delivered what?'

He moved to the side. Behind him, resting against the tiled alcove was a large package wrapped in light brown paper. It came up to his knees.

'This...' His eyes flicked between my face and whatever he'd brought with him. 'I'm guessing you didn't know about it?'

I shook my head, waiting for him to explain.

'Ah. She commissioned a painting when you both came to my studio. Said it was for your flat, to add some colour or something. I was going to mention it when we met for a drink but, well, I hadn't realised how much longer it was going to take to finish,' he admitted sheepishly before trailing off. Clearly he wasn't used to this damp reaction when he handed one of his pieces over to clients. 'Do you want me to take it back?'

I was going to kill Mum. She was clearly trying to matchmake us. But after the awkwardness of our recent drink. It was a little too late for anything like that. I checked my watch. It looked like I'd have to miss another Grief Club. I couldn't just turn him away.

'No.' I shook my head and fixed on a smile. 'You're here now.'

I opened the door fully and led him upstairs, deciding that whatever it was should probably be hung in the lounge.

He dramatically tore off the paper packaging to reveal an abstract multi-coloured canvas, lime green cloud-like forms swirled into pops of indigo and pink. There must have been at least fourteen different colours. It certainly was striking, but nothing that I would have ever picked.

He was waiting for me to say something.

'It's very… bright.'

'Yeah,' he glanced around at the rest of the flat. The magnolia walls and cream furniture seemed to make the riot of colour pop even more. 'Do you like it?'

I nodded, not wanting to hurt his feelings. It wasn't bad, it just wasn't me.

'Your mum said she thought you'd love it.' *Course she did.* 'I can hang it up for you if you like? It's quite heavy?'

'Oh, er, I guess so. Thanks.'

Just then I noticed that he'd even brought a small tool kit with him.

'Here OK?'

I nodded at the bare wall above the sofa he was pointing to.

'I think I need to apologise for how I came across when we went out,' he said, rummaging for a suitable nail to hang it on. 'I may have invited you for a drink under false pretences.'

'Oh?' I felt a funny sort of flip in my tummy. That evening it had been abundantly clear that Daniel and I were not on the same page. He'd not been in touch since then, and neither had I. His face grew serious as he searched for a pencil to mark a spot on the wall. The smile in his voice faded.

'Yeah, there was a reason I asked to meet up with you, but I guess I kind of bottled it.' He cleared his throat. 'You said you were a counsellor –'

'Well, I…'

I suddenly felt wary of what confession he was going to make. I knew it was time to come clean. I shook my head.

'I'm not a counsellor, Daniel.'

'I know.'

'You know?'

What? I thought he just said…

'I googled you. Grace Salmon, Funeral Arranger. Why didn't you say?'

I winced, casting my eyes to the carpet. 'I shouldn't really have been at Abbie's wake. It's not very professional, and I didn't want to get into any trouble.'

His brow knotted. 'You looked after Abbie's funeral?'

I nodded.

There was a long pause. He looked as if he was about to say something but turned and hid his face from view as he rummaged for a hammer and nail. The banging noise competing with the growing headache I suddenly felt coming on.

'I'm just going to…' He was too focussed on the task in hand to hear me. I left him to it and went to look for a paracetamol to stop the tension in my head. I was sure I had some by my bed. Abbie's face caught my eye as I walked into my bedroom, staring up at me from my laptop screen. The photo on the windswept beach. Then it hit me. All thoughts of painkillers were forgotten as I quickly zoomed in on the image, my fingers trying to catch up with my brain as I moved the curser around the enlarged photo, feeling a wave of trepidation at what I saw. What my brain had registered when I'd first seen this photo.

Pinned to the lapel on her rain mac was a glinting badge. I just could make out the shape, a sort of infinity knot, the size of a pound coin. It was a dull gold colour. It had struck me as odd as Abbie only wore designer high-end pieces, a shabby brooch didn't fit right with her flawless style. The other strange thing was that I'd seen this unusual design before, but it wasn't in her jewellery box that I'd rummaged through. If only my brain would connect the pieces together.

'All done, Grace!'

Daniel's voice filtered through from the lounge at the exact moment it came back to me. I remembered where I'd seen this same badge before. It was at Daniel's studio; as I'd walked out of the toilet something had caught my eye. Hanging on a hook behind the toilet door was his jacket, and that's where I'd seen the same shabby pin badge – except it wasn't a badge, it was a tiny antique brooch.

'I'll be right there!' I called, quickly pulling open another tab in my browser. I typed into google: *infinity knot brooch*.

Maybe I was reading too much into this. Maybe it was some trend that I'd missed. The search engine brought up an exact image of the brooch Abbie had pinned to her. I was right, it was hardly a common accessory. There were a few for sale on eBay, ranging from £10 to £600, depending on wear and tear. It was a small gold enamel Victorian love knot.

'You and Abbie were a couple?' I breathed, rushing into the lounge.

His face dropped. For a second I thought I'd made a terrible mistake. He shut his eyes and slowly nodded. His cheeks were devoid of colour. My head went into overdrive at what this revelation meant.

'How did you know?' His voice was a tremble of a whisper. 'No one knew!'

'B-b-but, she was married! You know her husband. You did that work of art for her?' Too many questions forming before I could keep up with them.

I thought back to the impressive sculpture he was working on in his studio. It wasn't a figure of eight but a larger replica of the love knot. This twisted metal had been staring me in the face all along. It wasn't a new project; it was for a woman who would never get to see it.

'That's how we met. She'd seen my work in a magazine and got in touch to commission a piece for herself. I ask all my clients to come in for a chat and we just hit it off. I present at different art colleges across the country, attend art fairs quite regularly, and she travelled a lot with work…'

So it was easy for them to be together without anyone knowing. I had already heard too much. I should have asked him to leave. Callum's face swam in my mind, my loyalty to him far outweighing the pleading look Daniel was giving me. But I was also desperately curious to know more.

'Did no one ever get suspicious?' I breathed.

'You can get away with anything if no one is paying you any attention.'

'How long did it go on?'

'Two and a half years.'

So, for half of her marriage to Callum she'd been secretly seeing another man. So much for Mel's suspicions that something had been going on with Owen.

'She wasn't happy in her marriage, Grace. I didn't steal her from her husband if that's what you're thinking.' Her husband; he couldn't even bring himself to say Callum's name. 'I know what we did was wrong, but the more time we spent together the more we realised that we had found what we were looking for in one another.'

'So why didn't you just come clean? Why didn't she end her marriage if she was that unhappy?'

He sighed deeply, he looked exhausted. 'She couldn't just give it all up for a penniless artist –'

'Pfft!' I couldn't stop myself. I'd seen how much his pieces went for. How he clearly made enough money to gallivant around the country, sleeping with another man's wife. I doubted they stayed in cheap motels.

'OK, not penniless exactly.' He shifted on his feet. 'But it was more complicated than that. Abbie was part of that glam world, she needed to be for her work. It was only going to be for another year or so and then...'

'And then what?'

'Well, we were planning to be together officially.'

I wanted to thrust my hands over my ears and not hear another word.

'Grace, we weren't just having an affair. We were in love.'

The small room closed in on us. His body no longer had the strength to keep the bravado in place. He crumpled onto the sofa as he let out belly-shaking sobs. As if on autopilot I passed him some tissues to wipe his eyes and blow his nose.

'Thank you. God, that feels like such a release.' He tried to smile sadly, snot glistened at the tip of his red nose.

Something came to me. 'The flowers.'

He looked up from scrunching the damp tissue in his hands.

'The expensive bouquet. They were from you. You didn't leave a note on the flowers for her funeral.'

'I did. I wrote her a message, but I took it off and burnt it.'

I felt all wobbly and nauseous. 'That night... the night she died...'

'She was with me.'

Of course. That's why she was on the back roads not far from the Stables Studios. It was all making horrible sense.

'She came to my studio a lot. The space was our little hideaway. That night...' He swallowed and tried to catch his breath. 'That night she came over after dropping her mate off –'

Owen. The rumours were half true. Abbie had been with another man but it wasn't her colleague. Callum had also been right: she hadn't just gone straight home, she'd headed to her and Daniel's love-nest.

'She said she'd had a row with her husband. She didn't ever want to go back to him. But we had this plan. We just weren't ready to come out in public just yet. I needed to end the rent on my studio, build up enough work before we could suddenly change our lives so much. I told her to keep pretending like normal. She just had to wait a few more months...' He balled his fists to his eyes. 'If her husband had found out about us he could have divorced her and taken everything. We both needed to get enough saved and in place for our new life together. We'd even talked about moving abroad, so she could be closer to her parents. When the time came, we wanted them to help out with grandchildren.'

'Grandchildren! You planned to have a baby together?' My voice rose, the pounding in my head threatening to knock me out.

He simply nodded.

I thought of the way Callum doted on his nephews. How desperate Mel had said he'd been to become a dad, and how he had learnt to accept that fate had played a different hand. For better or worse.

'She was going to save up as much as she could. Leave him with the house and move in with me. We would finally become this family, but then…' He raised a clenched fist to his mouth. The tears flowing once more.

But then she died.

Leaving him the only one in the world who knew their sordid secret.

The woman I'd created in my mind, whose perfect life I'd pored over online, and whose grieving husband I'd comforted, had been one massive lie. She'd fooled everyone.

'But now it's all been snatched away from me.' He blew his nose noisily. 'And the worst part? I didn't get to say goodbye. I can't even grieve for the woman I loved. I don't have that right. I have to deal with how my world has been shattered, all the joy stolen from it, on my own.'

I felt lost for words.

'Can you imagine how that feels, Grace? What we did was wrong but we were committed to each other, it wasn't some one-night stand or dirty affair. I loved her more than anything, and now no one knows what I've lost, no one knows what's been wiped out in a split second with nothing but memories to keep me going to try and survive this.'

Apart from me. In more ways than one, I knew…

Chapter 32

Daniel had left me alone in my flat, which had somehow turned into a confessional booth, me promising that his secret was safe with me, for now. I couldn't process everything I'd learnt that evening, let alone make a decision on what I was going to do with his sordid information.

I needed time to think.

Callum had been grieving for someone he didn't really know. I felt a rage burning inside. How could Abbie have done that to him? Strung him along, like his affections and devotion meant nothing? How had I ever wanted to be like her?

I touched my hair, mortified at my own foolish stupidity in thinking that Andre would transform me into a version of Abbie, and that all my problems would melt away. Abbie had clearly been storing a cupboard full of skeletons but, as one of only two people on the planet who knew the extent of her betrayal, what was I going to do?

Daniel may have felt better after unloading, but I felt like I'd been in a boxing ring all night. My head was pounding. I'd barely slept. My tired eyes were itchy and full of grit. Every muscle ached in my weary body. I rolled over and pulled up the duvet, hiding the morning sun that streamed in through the curtains. I'd told Daniel to give me space. Little did he know just which memory vault this had wrenched open. My past taunted me. Painful memories that I'd boxed away, locked and hidden, were trying to spill open.

I couldn't let that happen, not after all this time.

*

I sank further into my chair, overwhelmed at the mess piling up on my desk, half listening to Linda telling me about what she'd got up to at the weekend.

It struck me that I should have let Linda look after the Andersons after all. Linda would have planned a traditional service, let Callum get on with his life, and not interfered in his grief. No one would be any wiser about the double life his perfect wife had been living.

How could I even begin to explain to Callum how I had learnt of Abbie's infidelity? I'd only discovered the truth because I'd been obsessing over the tiny details of Abbie's 'perfect' life. It was such a mess. I mean, who did that? Who got so consumed with a woman they would never properly meet, that they prowled her social media in a bid to be more like her? The laughable thing was that it was all so fake. The smiling couple's dinner parties, the loved-up selfies, the honeymoon albums and heartfelt posts. Whose benefit were they really for?

I felt humiliated. I'd wanted to steal some of Abbie's confidence for my own life. I'd tried to be braver and bolder because of her. I'd opened up about my son to the rest of Grief Club, thinking I had the capability to be a stronger version of myself. I shook my head. Who had I been trying to kid? Trying someone else's life on for size. It clearly didn't fit.

I needed to see a friendly face, someone whose advice I trusted. I wouldn't have to wait long to see Ms Norris at Grief Club, but until then I needed to keep busy with work and try not to think about the dilemma Daniel had placed me in.

'So, how are things with you and your new squeeze?' Linda asked, breaking my sorry thoughts.

I frowned at her.

She had this odd sort of smile on her face. 'Mr Anderson...'

I clenched my teeth. 'Like I've told you before, there's nothing going on with me and Mr Anderson.'

I sharply turned in my chair and forced myself not to rise to her bait.

'Grace?' Frank's deep voice rang out. 'Have you got a minute, please?'

Frank rarely called us into his office, apart from for team meetings. He preferred to lean against the back wall by our desks, giving himself a break from the many emails and legal documents he had to sift throught.

'Everything OK?' I hovered uncertainly in the doorway. There was something in the way he was looking at me that made me feel uneasy.

What if he'd overheard Linda's suggestion that there was something between me and Callum?

'Take a seat please.'

He cleared his throat as I perched on the edge of a chair.

'Is everything OK, Frank?'

He sighed sadly. 'Grace, I'm afraid I have some bad news.' He had gone really pale. 'Ms Norris has passed away.'

I felt like I'd been punched. My head shot up. 'What?'

'I know you two had built up a bit of a friendship in the time of her frequent visits here. I'm terribly sorry, Grace.'

'A-a-are you sure?'

I felt stupid as soon as I asked. Why would he lie to me? My brain scrabbling for this to be an awful prank. No. No, this can't be true. I was going to see her at the next Grief Club, she was going to help me fix this mess of tangled lies I'd found myself in.

He nodded solemnly. 'I'm sure.'

I swallowed and tried to let this news filter in. I didn't trust myself to speak.

Frank sighed deeply. 'She had a fall. She was out walking her dog when it happened. Hit her head quite badly. You know how fragile people get at that age...'

I bit my bottom lip to stop myself from showing how much it hurt. I nodded along, trying to take it in. Ms Norris had seemed like she was made of steel. Tears pricked my eyes, but I wasn't going to cry, I had to remain professional. I blinked them away and picked up a paperclip from the table, rolling it around between my finger and thumb, unable to look at Frank.

'… She didn't regain consciousness. Bleeding on the brain, apparently. I'm so sorry.' He sighed and pressed his fingers into steeples. 'It's now a case of bringing together everything that you two discussed and making sure we follow her wishes. I'm more than happy to ask Linda to step in, as it may be too difficult for you?'

'No! I mean, no, I would like to look after Ms Norris, thank you.'

Frank kept his eye on me. I realised he looked exhausted. 'There's no shame in letting others help, you know.'

'I know.' My voice was barely more than a whisper. *Don't take this away from me. This is what I do best.*

'I can do it, Frank. I'm OK, I promise.' I smiled as tightly and brightly as I could muster.

The tears would come later, but I was grateful that I could keep it together to prove to him that there was nothing to worry about. There was no way I was going to let Linda handle Ms Norris, no matter how tough it would be.

'I understand your admirable work ethic, but I also have a duty of care for my staff. I remember looking after my first prepaid funeral; she was actually a bit like Ms Norris,' he mused. 'Miss Archibald. Always popping in to make small amends. I think she was just terribly lonely.' He sighed, lost in the memory. 'I wanted to give her the send-off she deserved, but by that point she had become like a grandmotherly figure to me. So when it came to it, I had to let my colleagues step in. I don't want you to feel like you can't do the same. It's OK if you need help.'

We had a very strict policy that if anything was upsetting us then we had to air it. I'd never needed to use that before, and I wasn't about to start then.

'Thanks, Frank. But I really would like to do this for her.'

'Alright, but you know that we're both here to help if it does get a little too much.'

I shut his office door behind me, before hurrying to the bathroom. I turned on the taps to hide the noise of the unsightly sobs racking my chest.

I'd only seen her last week. I blew my nose on the scratchy toilet paper and tried to calm down. No, wait, it hadn't been last week. It slowly dawned on me as my breathing evened out: I'd missed a couple of Grief Clubs as I'd been busy with Callum's garden, and then I'd had that awkward drink with Daniel, then he'd turned up with that painting. The last time I saw her was over three weeks ago.

Three weeks since I had last spoken to her. I hadn't even noticed that she'd not come into the office like she'd said she was going to. A wave of sickening guilt rolled up my body. I blew my nose and swallowed the painful lump in my throat. How could I not have noticed her lack of visits?

I knew the answer. Abbie Anderson. This woman had been a thief of time, energy and emotion. I had uncovered things I wished I never knew. I'd forgotten about those close to me. All because of being so desperate to uncover a truth that was best left unknown. I shredded toilet paper between my trembling fingers. My circle of friends had just shrunk even smaller, and I was to blame.

I vowed that I would be in charge of giving Ms Norris the send-off she deserved, even if this meant trying to ignore the awful realisation that the perfect goodbye means nothing if we don't get to tell the person what they mean to us while they're still alive.

Chapter 33

I could do this. *Then why was it so difficult to let go of the handle and enter the room?*

The last few days since the upsetting news had been busy. I'd lost myself in the welcome whirlwind of tasks I needed to tick off, keeping my mind focussed on Ms Norris only. But I had been putting off one task for long enough. I got a grip of myself and walked in, closing the door gently behind me. The calming dove-grey walls and luxurious padded carpet, which your feet immediately sank into, made it feel like a little haven.

An exquisite stained-glass feature stood in the place of a window, letting warmth and light in. There was also always a side lamp switched on. It stood on a small driftwood table, which had religious texts tucked into its elegantly carved shelves. The only sound in this room was a fan, keeping the air at an exact temperature. The thick walls blocked out any sound from the outside. It felt like you were in a perfectly safe vacuum. Usually I enjoyed being in there, but that day I would have rather been anywhere else.

I padded to the coffin that stood in the centre of the room. It was raised on a metal bed, covered by a silky, deep purple sheet. I took a deep breath and gently lifted the heavy wooden lid. Lying inside was my friend.

She had been embalmed, as per her wishes, wanting to look like she was sleeping. Ms Norris's eyes were closed. A light powdered foundation added colour to her round cheeks, a wand of black mascara waved over her grey eyelashes. Her hair and make-up had been left to the expert team at the mortuary. There was the slightest stain of coral lipstick on her thin lips, and a flick of peachy blusher down her cheekbones. She looked magnificent. A bubble of emotion threatened to rise to the surface as I looked at her. She would be so relieved she hadn't been made up like a drag queen. She was wearing Dior, as she'd requested many months ago. A neat spotty blouse with extravagant necktie was tucked into an expertly tailored skirt that skimmed over her plump middle. I picked off a loose thread from her sleeve, noting that her short square nails had a lick of clear varnish on.

'You won't believe how wonderful you look,' I said to her. 'I promise to make sure everything you wanted is be achieved.' My voice sounded funny, slightly off-key, as I spoke. 'I'm really sorry I let you down. I should have checked on you sooner and noticed that you'd not been in to see me. I'm so angry at myself for that.'

I missed her so much more than I ever thought I would. A realisation that did little to comfort me, only to bring frustration that I couldn't ever tell her how much she'd meant to me.

'Anyway, I'll pop in and check on you again soon, in

case you feel a little lonely…' Tears were beginning to make themselves known.

I lowered the lid and walked out of the room. Knowing that she was there and counting on me spurred me on to get cracking with the workload. Ms Norris would get the send-off she deserved. If I couldn't make my failings up to her in life, then I would in death.

*

'Grace?' Frank boomed over the noise of the coffee machine. I'd left Ms Norris to it, and was about to get stuck in with the rest of my to-do list, after a cup of coffee. 'Can I have a word? In my office.'

'Is everything OK, Frank?' I asked, hesitantly pulling out a chair.

Frank rubbed his eyes behind his glasses. 'Grace, something has come to my attention that I'm struggling to piece together.'

'Oh?'

I didn't like the way he was looking at me. Cold tingles ran up my fingers. I clasped my hands together under the desk.

'Abbie Anderson.'

'Yes?' I swallowed loudly.

'Her ashes are missing from the store room. There's no record of anyone signing them out, or her family coming to take delivery…'

Linda. She must have told Frank about the missing ashes. There was no way he'd have discovered them otherwise. The store room was our domain. She must have been searching for clues, ways in which to reveal Callum and I had grown closer. I clenched my hands tighter together and willed my heart to stop racing.

'I've spoken to Linda who says she has no knowledge of the missing sign-out form for the ashes. So I'm hoping you can shed some light on it?'

I lowered my eyes to the carpet. It needed a hoover. How could I admit that there was no sign-out form, and that I wouldn't be able to get one as that would mean speaking to Callum again, and I was nowhere near ready to go there? How stupid had I been?! I'd got so preoccupied with the Andersons that I'd gone against company policy and risked my job. And for what?

'Well, I –'

My voice didn't sound like mine. Was I really going to confess? This could cost me everything. Thankfully, Frank cut me off.

'I also want to talk to you about your use of social media.'

Linda again. I thought I'd been discreet. Apparently not.

'In a way I use it for work.'

'Sorry?'

'What I mean is…'

What was I doing? No one knew about my secret of using social media for inspiration. Until now.

'… I use it to find out about the people we have in our care. I look at their social media pages to help give me some insight into their lives, so I can plan a personal send-off…'

Words were spilling out of my mouth. I felt hot and uncomfortable under the stare of utter confusion he was giving me. I realised I was telling him all of this because I knew I couldn't produce a form for Abbie's ashes. Distracting him with the lesser of two evils.

'You do what?' A fleck of spit flew out of his mouth as he tried to get his head around this. 'Wait – you stalk the deceased's private life, because you think you can glean some personal details in order to turn their service into some form of... entertainment?'

When he put it like that...

'No! I mean, yes, but not like that. I –'

'What if the families had found out that this is how we plan our funerals? It's beyond unethical, Grace. I don't know enough about how social media works, but surely there are consequences and risks involved in such an activity?'

Like discovering the deceased has been having a secret affair, I thought. Looking at his reddening face it dawned on me that what I'd been doing had been risky. It wouldn't haven't take much to accidentally 'like' a photo, or in some other way be caught out.

'Grace, what's happened to you?' He shook his head. I'd never seen such disappointment etched in his face.

'I'm sorry,' I squeaked. I didn't know what else to say.

'I think it's best if you take some time off. I will need to do a thorough investigation into these allegations. We clearly can't have you working at a time when you're showing such signs of stress.'

'Frank, I'm sorry.' I was forced to swallow the lump

in my throat. *Don't cry, don't cry.* 'Ms Norris's funeral is next Thursday, so once I've done that I –'

He held up a hand to silence me.

'Grace, you won't be organising any more funerals. I don't think you understand how serious this is. I'm going to have to ask you to leave, starting right now.'

I'd never seen him this way.

'Right now.'

I couldn't finish off any of my workload? Bring any of my final ideas together for Ms Norris?

I suddenly sprang to life. I shook my head dramatically. 'Frank. No, I –'

I had to be in charge of Ms Norris's funeral.

'Grace. That will be all.' He clasped his hands together and nodded to the door. 'I'll be in touch. Please take this time to look after yourself.'

'But!'

'Thank you. That will be all.' He clenched his jaw and turned away from me.

How can this be happening? The one funeral I desperately needed to be in charge of, and I couldn't be there? I got to my feet as if moving through treacle. It was all too bizarre to be real. All I'd ever wanted was to give the perfect goodbye, the goodbye that I'd never had the chance to experience, and look where it had got me.

'What's going on?' Linda asked, hanging up her phone. She'd returned from wherever she'd been hiding.

'I think you know what's going on!' I couldn't help but snap as I turned off my computer and pulled my raincoat on. I couldn't bear to be anywhere near her. I knew we had our differences, but how could she sink so low just to get into Frank's good books?

'G-Grace?' she stuttered. She had a pretty good poker face, I'd give her that.

For the first time in my life I wanted to punch another human being.

'Thank you for being so considerate,' I growled.

I left her open-mouthed as I stormed out. I wasn't sure where to go or what to do. I kept pacing with no purpose, running things over in my head. Had I lost my job? Frank hadn't said so, in as many words, but I knew there would have to be an investigation. Linda would surely tell him about seeing me and Callum out together. Two and two would make five. But the real victim in all of this was Ms Norris. How could I have let her down so spectacularly?

Chapter 34

The guilt I felt about not being in charge of giving Ms Norris the perfect goodbye was eating me up inside. I was desperate to do something that would honour this wonderful woman. 'All we have, at the end of the day, is the legacies that we leave behind,' I remembered her saying to me one time. I needed to make sure that Ms Norris was honoured, but to do that I needed a clear head and right now I felt like my brain was on a spin cycle.

This torrent of wretchedness was heightened by the mess I'd found myself in, uncovering Daniel's secret. I ricocheted from preparing to admit the truth to Callum – opening up about how I'd discovered Abbie was having an affair, and then dealing with the consequences – to ignoring what I knew. What he didn't know wouldn't hurt him. It wasn't my place to get involved. He'd said himself that they'd not shared a bed for a while before her death, and that they'd rowed on the night of her accident; maybe on some subconscious level he did know more than he cared to admit.

My gut and my heart refused to agree. He wouldn't be grieving for her, planting a tree in her honour, and being so full of remorse for the part he believed he played in her death, if he knew she had been with another man. *In love* with another man.

I picked up my phone and opened up my messages. I was going to fix this. I had to tell him. Hopefully this would relieve me of the burden and allow me to give Ms Norris the full attention she deserved. I was missing my best friend like crazy and needed to prepare myself for her funeral. Even if I wasn't the one in charge of pulling it together, I was still going to attend.

I opened up a new blank message and found Callum's name in my sparse contact list.

Hi Callum...

I typed then paused, my fingers hovering. Just how exactly did you tell someone that their marriage was a lie? I was only seconds away from releasing a bomb into his already damaged world.

I shook my head and pressed delete.

Callum. It's Grace, I have something to tell you.

I pressed delete. I couldn't tell him over text. We'd grown close, our unusual friendship was important to me, I owed him more than this.

Can we meet up soon? I could really do with talking to you.

I typed quickly and was about to press send, taking a few extra seconds to read it back. We could meet for a coffee, somewhere full of other people. It was the adult way. The grown-up thing to do.

No. I shook my head. I wouldn't be able to sit opposite him, acting like two friends simply catching up over a flat white, with this secret. I deleted the short message and dropped my phone onto the sofa. I wasn't strong enough to deal with this right now.

The one person I was directing a lot of my frustration towards was Linda. I still hadn't worked out why she would tell Frank about the misplaced sign-out form? And why drop me in it about using social media at work? She could have simply asked me about it all first. She was no saint herself. I knew that she sneaked extras into the stationery order, especially around Christmas time when she stocked up on Sellotape. I knew that she had once forgotten to set the alarm properly when it was her turn to lock up; I discovered this when I opened up the following morning, but I hadn't wanted to get her in trouble. Everyone makes mistakes. But clearly she didn't take this sympathetic view. From the very start of our working together she'd wanted to do better than me, to win Frank's favour, to be his favourite employee.

My phone buzzed. It was another text from Daniel, asking if I was free to meet up for a chat. Now he had found someone to talk to he was desperate to offload. I ignored him. I thought I'd made myself clear that I didn't want to be part of his sordid secret. I couldn't fix him. I couldn't fix anyone, not even myself.

*

It had taken all of my energy to stand in front of them. I'd called an emergency Grief Club to share the awful news about Ms Norris with the other members. Well, all the members except one. Our normal meeting space wasn't available, a local amateur dramatics group had booked it, so we'd assembled in Marcus's mum's shop; she'd kindly let us use the back room. If the others displayed any surprise at how casually I was dressed, and the bags under my eyes, they didn't let on. I shifted in my hoodie and picked at a stain on the cuff that may have been ketchup.

There weren't enough chairs so I awkwardly stood, leaning against the huge cardboard boxes and stacks of empty plastic crates. It smelt as musty as our usual meeting place, but then again that could have been me. I couldn't raise the energy to make small talk as I waited for Julie to arrive. As soon as they had all assembled I took a deep breath.

'Grace? We've not seen you in a while. Is everything OK?' Raj asked.

'There's no cakes. Something's defo wrong,' Marcus said, his wide eyes flitting around the room.

'Where's Callum and Ms Norris? Should we wait for them?' Julie asked softly.

I cleared my throat and shook my head. 'I'm so sorry to call you here so unexpectedly.' I glanced at their worried faces. 'But I needed to let you know that Ms Norris has passed away.' I swallowed the lump in my throat which that sentence brought with it. Words that didn't feel right to say, no matter how many times I'd forced myself to try and believe them.

'No!'

Raj and Deano shook their heads in disbelief. I spotted Marcus's shoulders tense up and his eyes shoot to the floor.

'She was out with Purdy and had a fall. Unfortunately, she didn't recover.' My voice didn't sound like my own. 'I'm so sorry to be the bearer of bad news. Marcus, are you OK?'

He suddenly looked much younger than his fifteen years of age. Maybe I should have spared him the news. He nodded and wiped a fist at his wet eyes.

'She was like my replacement Grandma.'

As his voice cracked so did my mask. I went and placed an arm around his thin, juddering shoulders and let the tears flow.

'I can't believe it,' Raj sniffed. 'She loved this group and believed so much in all of us and our own journeys.'

'It's just crap. Even being in a group that meets and talks about death every week doesn't make this seem real.' Deano shook his head angrily.

'I know.'

He was right. It didn't make any sense. I used the heel of my hand to wipe away the tears, checking that Marcus was OK. I really wished I'd had the energy to bake; sugar could have been vital in helping with his shock.

'Did you know that she once told me she woke every morning at five thirty a.m.?' Raj said, shaking his head at the memory. 'I asked her why she chose to get up so early, and she seemed confused as to why anyone wouldn't wake up and greet the day as soon as they possibly could.'

That was her all over, wanting to squeeze every moment out of life. Even now I expected her to waddle in with a bright smile on her face and a tricky cake recipe for me to try and master.

'She never dwelled on the fact she was getting older,' Julie said. 'I'd noticed that it took her longer to get through the door, or get up from her chair. She began to struggle to walk across the room unaided, but she refused to let that hold her back. She never focussed on what she'd lost.'

I nodded. She was right, Ms Norris refused to show any frailty despite the fact her body was beginning to be let down by the ageing process.

'Grief Club's not been the same without you either, Grace…' Marcus blinked rapidly.

'I'm sorry I've missed a few sessions. I've… got a few personal things going on that I need to deal with,' I said, unable able to look any of them in the eye.

If they'd noticed that I'd skated around Callum's absence, none of them had mentioned it. I should get in touch with him to tell him, too. But I couldn't bear the thought of trying to act normal around him, when I knew what I knew about Daniel and Abbie. I still had no idea what I was going to do about that. Ms Norris was taking up all of my brain space and energy, but I knew that it would have to be dealt with one day.

I cleared my throat. 'But that shouldn't stop you guys from meeting. Our slot at the church hall is open for us on a Friday night, so you're more than welcome to continue to meet up without me. But, if you don't mind, I need to hand over my facilitator badge and focus on other things for the time being.'

Julie flashed a watery smile.

Deano coughed. 'Course, we understand. We're going to miss you, Grace.'

I looked at the room of misfits and proudly realised how everyone had blossomed since we'd first met. As much as this was a shock and a loss to all of us, we had the strength to survive it. I hoped. Whether the club would continue to run without two of its founding members, I had no idea. Honestly? I was too exhausted to care.

Chapter 35

So far everything had pretty much gone to plan. The flowers were perfectly placed on the light oak-veneered coffin, raised on a velveteen plinth. A piece of classical music was set at the right volume as mourners plodded into the sun-dappled room. I wished I'd been able to triple-check that Frank Sinatra was ready to play at the end. I observed the handful of mourners, who barely filled three pews. I couldn't see Linda or Frank, but I did spot Raj, Julie and Deano huddled alongside one another near the front. This felt a world away from Abbie's funeral. There were no glory mourners or flashy outfits. Why hadn't more people turned up to mark their respect for this wonderful woman?

Leon handed me an order of service as I snuck in, once the service had started, desperate to pay my last respects but wanting to avoid any small talk. Taking in the sparse audience, we may have printed off too many.

'Grace?' He seemed surprised to see me. 'I wasn't expecting you here. It's good to see you.'

'Yeah, you too,' I mumbled, focussing on the order of service. The font was all wrong, it should have been centred and in a dark navy, not black. I felt my pulse quicken as I looked at the words that had been capped up for no apparent reason. I clenched my fist around the card and forced myself to breathe.

The photo, which was a little on the large side for my taste, was of Ms Norris as a young woman, probably no older than I was right now. She looked beautiful in the classic black and white shot. She'd said to me, when she had picked this photo to go into her file, that she didn't recognise herself as a younger lady, but I could see her.

As the celebrant, Charles, stood at the front, I tried to stop myself from running through what was coming next, and to focus on the moment. I had to accept that if I'd been in charge things would have been very different, but I wasn't in charge. At least the basics had been covered, as per Ms Norris's wishes in her prepaid plan. I just wished I'd been able to give it a personal touch; it was what she deserved after all.

Charles cleared his throat and slowly ran his eyes over the waiting crowd. The huddle of mostly older guests, wearing their well-worn funeral clothes, sat peacefully with hands clasped and faces drawn. It was one of many they'd attend that year. I wondered if we would see most of them sooner rather than later. I tried to push away that grim thought; I may not even have a job to go back to. I'd received an official-looking letter in the post from Frank, informing me that an investigation was ongoing and he would be in touch in due course. HR jargon for an utterly disheartening situation. I needed to concentrate on Ms Norris, and not on my own sad excuse for a life that was currently unravelling at an alarming speed.

Charles's wrinkled blue eyes peered through half-moon silver-rimmed glasses to read the notes in front of him.

'Edwina Gwyneth Norris was a lady who liked the simpler things in life,' he began. The gentleman next to me flicked on his hearing aid. 'She was a woman of routine and order, which is nothing to scoff at in this modern busy world we live in. We gather here in reflection of a long and fruitful life. It is only right that we are all guests at her last supper, as Jesus said to his disciples: "I now give you a new commandment: love one another. As I have loved you, so you must love one another." A sentiment I believe fitting for what Edwina would want us all to take away from the service today.'

I stopped worrying if the flowers had been laid correctly outside, or if the route had been checked for traffic for those heading to the wake, and instead I sat back. I would never get this chance again. I needed to be present, in the moment, however painful it was.

'If you'll permit me, I have some words that Edwina herself wanted me to read.' Charles picked up a smaller piece of paper. Lit up by the light from the stained glass behind, I could see it contained Ms Norris's neat, curled handwriting.

Some of the mourners shifted as he cleared his throat. I wasn't sure if it was discomfort from the hard wooden pews, or at preparing to hear a note from beyond the grave. I wondered when she had put pen to paper. I felt my lips curl into a small smile. The fact she had taken the time and effort to write her own eulogy shouldn't really have surprised me.

Charles cleared his throat.

'I know this is not the done thing,' he read, 'to take centre stage and speak like this at your own funeral, but, if you will grant me this small moment in the spotlight I would be grateful, as it will be one of the first in my lifetime. I never did live a life full of adventure. I never married, never had children, and never really left Ryebrook. A long life such as mine has been a happy one, for sure, and that is thanks in part to all of you sat here today. But it was still a life filled with things I didn't do, instead of things I did.'

Charles paused to rearrange his glasses.

'I also know it isn't commonplace to look back at the things I've regretted. But this is my moment, so I will say what I like, thank you. If I could do it all over again then I would do it so very differently. Obviously, I hope that we would all be friends, but I would be a different, braver version of myself. I think you'd have liked her just as much as me, or even more. The fear of doing or saying the wrong thing, for so many of my younger years, truly crippled me, more than I could ever admit.

'I don't feel upset about never marrying or having children. You don't know what either of those would be like if you've never had them. But I do feel awfully saddened by the chances that I did have, but threw away. Did you know that I was asked to be Miss Ryebrook 1958, but I was too painfully shy back then to go to the casting? Or that I won a pair of return flights to Iceland in a charity raffle, but I never boarded that plane as I was too scared? The older I got, the more I realised that in many ways I'd wasted this long and healthy life because of my insecurities, but by then it was too late to make up for opportunities lost. So I am urging that whatever time you have left, you use it wisely.'

I couldn't breathe. Charles had asked everyone to stand for the committal but it felt like the blood had set in my legs. My bottom was firmly stuck down and my feet planted flatly on the carpet. Her eulogy, her last words, were directed at me. As self-centred as that may seem, it felt like I *must* have been in her mind's eye when she picked up her pen and those neat little pages of notepaper. The gentleman next to me cleared his throat with a crusty-sounding gargle. He was peering down at me from the precarious perch of his carved walnut cane. I mumbled an apology and pressed my hands against the cold wood, forcing myself to my feet.

'We have been remembering with love and sadness the life of Edwina Norris that has ended. Let you all return to your homes feeling enriched by the joy she brought to your life, and how she will live on in our hearts and memories. Leave in peace.'

There was a bowing of heads and the rustle of tissues being pulled out of plastic packets. The door to the right opened, letting chilly sunlight into the room. Charles signalled with a subtle flick of a finger to the back of the room for Leon to turn the exit music on. Frank Sinatra began to warble as mourners slowly made their way into the fresh air. I sank back down on my seat, pretending to neatly tuck my order of service into my bag. Needing a moment to catch my breath. Not wanting to see anyone I knew. Tears were pulsating at the back of my eyes.

'I did it myyyyyy wayyyyy!'

Ol' Blue Eyes reached his near-final crescendo.

I glanced up and realised I was the only one left. Leon was making his way over to me with a sympathetic smile on his shaven face. No doubt he would pass on to Frank and Linda that I'd attended the service. For a split-second I wondered how they were all getting on without me.

'Grace?'

I swallowed the lump in my throat. I really wasn't in the mood to chat.

'I heard about what happened. I'm sure that the form will be found sooner or later and this whole mess will be resolved,' he said, brightly. If only he knew.

A gentle ringing sound filled the air. Leon patted his suit pocket.

'There's our five-minute warning,' he winked and turned off the phone alarm. 'What's that thing you say? *Organisation is –* '

'*Liberation,*' I half smiled.

'I've learnt a lot from you, Grace. I'm sure it'll all be sorted soon enough and you'll be back doing what you do best.'

He picked up the discarded orders of service, wanting me to hurry along. Ms Norris's smiling face quickly disappeared into the fold of his pocket.

I got to my feet, unsteadily. My movements felt clumpy. I didn't want to go and put on my professional mask. I didn't want to make small talk with her friends and neighbours. I didn't want to say goodbye. I felt Leon's steady gaze as I padded across the plush carpet to the coffin. The loudly ticking clock was the only sound in the room, now that Frank had bid his farewell.

'Goodbye, Ms Norris,' I whispered, letting the tears drip down my face. I kissed two fingers and pressed them against where her name was engraved, running my index finger across the gleaming brass.

A pointed cough from Leon forced me to compose myself.

'Grace?'

'Yep. Thanks.' I couldn't look at him. I went to walk away but at the last second remembered to use the sleeve of my cardigan to buff away the fingerprint smudge I'd left behind.

Chapter 36

'Grace? Excuse me, but are you Grace?' An older woman's voice was calling to me as I hurried to my car.

I should have said hello to the Grief Club members, thanked them for coming, and seen how they were all bearing up, but I felt so fragile. I desperately needed to be on my own. Whoever was coming up behind me clearly hadn't picked up on the antisocial signals I was giving off. I sighed and turned.

'Yes?' I squinted in the bright sunlight as a woman I didn't recognise waddled over to me. She was about Ms Norris's age, with thick, NHS-style plastic glasses making her watery brown eyes appear even larger.

'Ah, I'm glad I caught you. I'm Alma, an old friend of Edwina's,' she said, slightly breathless.

'Of course, hi.' I blinked and forced myself to stay composed just a moment longer. 'I hope you felt the service went alright?'

'Oh yes! In fact, I'd put it up there along with Derek Maynard's and Pearl Carruthers's.'

I guess funeral top trumps was a popular pastime at her age. I didn't know what to say to that, so waited patiently as she got her breath back.

'I'm going to be getting fit soon, now that I've got Purdy encouraging me to get out and about.'

'You're looking after Purdy?' I couldn't help but feel relieved that Ms Norris's prized pet pug was going to a good home.

'Yes, she's settled in nicely. Dogs are very good at handling change. Better than some humans, I say.' She laughed but it came out in a wheeze. 'So, Grace, I wanted to catch you. I've been going through Edie's things, you see. She was so organised it didn't actually take me that long.'

I'd never seen Ms Norris at home, but had imagined a small, neatly kept bungalow with a well-tended front garden, porcelain figurines on the mantelpiece, and biscuits kept in a faded Quality Street tin. She may even have had those plastic sofa coverings, the ones that went out of fashion but were extremely practical, especially with a dog around.

'I found something that Edie left for you. I was going to come and see you next week at work, but then I decided to pop it into my handbag on the off-chance I'd see you here.'

'Oh.'

She smiled at me expectantly. I waited.

'Sorry, what is it?'

'Oh, right, yes.' Alma rummaged in her handbag and pulled out a padded brown envelope with my name neatly written on the front in Ms Norris's handwriting.

'I don't know what it is exactly, but it was in a box along with other letters for friends.'

Friends. That word made my eyes well up. I took the heavy envelope and thanked her, before politely declining going back to her house for tea and cake. It felt almost fraudulent to feel this upset amongst those who knew Ms Norris so much better than I ever had.

Without work to occupy my time I headed straight home. Thankfully, Raj must have taken Alma up on her offer for refreshments as he wasn't back at his shop yet, and Rani looked like she was in the middle of a stocktake so didn't see me hurry past and into my flat.

I got changed into a faded tracksuit, and curled my bare feet under me on the sofa. I needed to go back to bed, to hide under my duvet and sleep for a million years, but the curiosity of what lay inside the package Alma had given me was more pressing. Taking a deep breath, I opened the envelope and pulled out the contents. It was a book, a heavy ring binder. I frowned at it, confused, then without realising I began to cry.

It was Ms Norris's recipe book. So it did exist! A priceless collection of culinary creations she'd collected over the years. The first few pages were mainly handwritten, with her own notes and observations jotted in the gaps. Smudges of food stains had crisped some of the rough pages together. Cuttings from magazines had been stuck in with glue, Post-it notes with shopping lists, and later on printouts from the internet were all wedged in.

There was no note to go with the magical heirloom, only small quips about cooking times, suggestions of alternative ingredients, and mini reviews in her own words squeezed into the margins. It was really quite something. I felt honoured to even be holding a lifetime's collection, let alone be the sole keeper of it. I imagined something I'd once heard Ms Norris say: '*I would love to think of my recipes finding their way into new hands.*' I just wished I had the energy to honour her wishes.

As I stroked a thumb over the pages I began to struggle to catch my breath. It was as if all this pent-up emotion had been released. Ms Norris dying, losing my job, Abbie's affair, Linda's stirring, Daniel's dishonour, Callum's obliviousness. It was all too much to bear.

*

My days passed in an endless monotony of sleeping and crying. My curtains remained closed. My fridge began to empty. I was envious of those who drank; the thought of being able to numb these emotions and pass out in a catatonic state had never appealed as much as it did now. I ignored the doorbell and pulled the duvet over my head when Raj's concerned voice rattled through the letterbox. My phone remained switched off. Everyone could just go away. Instead, I slept. Each time I woke it hit me again: Abbie had been unfaithful. Ms Norris was gone. I'd lost my job.

Henry.

It was as if this recent trauma had exposed the years-old wounds of love and loss too. I didn't know who I was grieving for, from one moment to the next.

Thoughts of orders of service and funeral corteges just seemed so meaningless now. Why put on such a show after the person has died? They would never see the effort you put in to remembering them. Abbie's funeral had been packed with glory mourners, all crying over a different version of this woman, a woman who had fooled them all into thinking she led this perfect life. Ms Norris had a handful of faithful friends, which seemed an insignificant amount considering the long life she'd led. And then there was Sam, my son. He never even had the chance to live before he died. No perfect goodbyes were going to change the course of events that had occurred.

Flowers had arrived from Callum. I'd only seen the expensive, hand-tied bouquet resting in the alcove to my flat when I'd meekly opened the door to the delivery guy for the second night in a row. I'd picked them up as I'd taken the margarita pizza from the young man. The note said how he had heard the news about Ms Norris from Raj. How sorry he was, and how he would leave me in peace but was thinking of me, and I knew where to find him when I was ready. He said he missed me and signed off with two small kisses. I wanted to call him, to hear his voice, but how was I supposed to act like everything was normal when I knew that his wife had spent half their marriage in love with another man? I needed to focus on myself and my own problems. I had spent almost five years avoiding my own truth, and I was unravelling at an alarming rate.

I thought about Callum and how brave he was in facing his utterly, devastatingly tragic situation head-on. He could have easily refused to accept the unacceptable. I wished I had some of the strength he possessed. I needed to make a start in picking up the pieces of my own life. If Callum could do it then I had no excuse. I took a deep breath before I chickened out. I knew exactly who I needed to speak to.

I turned on my phone. A message alerted me that I had two new voicemails. I didn't bother to listen to them. Instead I called Maria, but she didn't answer. I glanced at the time on my phone. I knew where she'd be anyway, she was a creature of habit after all; that was one of the reasons we had clicked. I pulled on the nearest clothes I could grab and hurried out of the door.

I'd driven there without a second thought, the journey a blur. It felt like my brain was still trying to catch up with my body. Daniel's confession had triggered something in me and it wasn't just heartache for Callum.

I could see myself in the way that he was broken, shattered with love for someone who had left him in the most horrific way, with no chance for reconciliation or even to say a goodbye.

'I need to speak to Henry. I need to speak to him right now!'

Maria glanced up from the cosy huddle in the corner of the room. The lights were dimmed. Joss sticks and tea lights were lit along the mantelpiece. My eyes tried to adjust to the darkness. It had been so long since I'd set foot in there, but it hadn't changed a bit.

'Grace?'

'I need to speak to Henry!' I repeated, louder. 'I have to get some answers. It's gone on too long now.'

Two older women, sitting opposite Maria, spun their

heads towards me, confused and irritated at the dramatic interruption. I'd sat in their seat once upon a time. I'd gone there to find the comfort they craved too. Kidding myself that I was different, Maria had made me feel special, but she was probably saying the same things to them right before I'd barged in there.

'Grace, it's OK.' She was passing a look between the two women. 'I'm just with these ladies at the moment. But if you want to wait outside, I'll –'

'No!' I screamed. 'I'm sick of you doing this. Just tell me how I can speak to him myself!'

My throat burnt, salty tears ran down my cheeks.

'She's not well. I've been trying to help her for a while.' I could hear Maria explaining in hushed tones. 'I've not seen her like this though. I promise I'll only be a second. I just need to calm her down, then I'll be right back.'

Maria got to her feet, mouthing an apology to the women as she walked over to me.

Gut-wrenching sobs had taken over my body. It was like I was looking down at myself, wondering why I was having such a visceral reaction. I'd never lost control of my body like this before. It was terrifying.

That was a lie. I had experienced this before. Just once.

'Grace, please come and sit down,' Maria said soothingly.

I was shaking my head, trembling all over. 'Maria, just tell me!'

She sighed, her narrowed eyes darting across the room.

'Do you want us to wait outside?' one of the women asked. The other looked like she'd much rather stay and enjoy this meltdown playing out in front of her.

'Please, if you don't mind. I won't be long,' Maria replied.

My breath was coming out in starts. I couldn't get enough air. They moved past me, throwing sympathetic glances that I ignored.

'Please sit down, Grace,' Maria said, more tersely than before.

I sank into the chair she pulled out. Grateful for something to support my weight.

'What's going on? What's happened?'

I tried to speak but my voice was too strangled in the gasps of breath. She handed me a bottle of water, the lid removed. I stared at it. I'd been in this situation before. It was as if the cloth had been pulled off, the repressed memories springing to life.

'I need to speak to Henry.'

'You know that you can't do that, Grace.'

I shook my head forcefully. 'Please. Please!'

'I can try and get in touch with him, if you'd like? Although the energy you're sending off may prohibit us.'

It was my fault, always my fault.

I noticed a deck of tarot cards laid out on the table the women had been sat around. A picture of a skeleton riding a white horse, about to go into battle, was lying face up. The death card. She'd told me death was invincible and unconquerable, but that this card represented a significant change in life, not the end of it. She'd told me many things. I'd soaked them all up, allowing her to use her talents to tell me what I *needed* to hear. What I *chose* to hear.

I felt like the room was tipping. My feet were struggling to keep me planted upright. Truths and lies blending before my eyes. She moved the tarot cards to one side, sighed and closed her eyes. I waited, my breathing slowly returning to normal.

'I'm sorry, Grace. I can't do this.' She shook her head and flashed open her eyes.

He doesn't want to talk to you.

'I have to speak to him! I have so much I need to ask him. How could he have done this to me? To us?'

'Grace,' her tone was sharper. 'Stop this.'

'But –'

'You know that Henry is dead.'

Her words stabbed me. The truth that I'd hid from for so long, thinking I could outsmart it, had slapped me in my face.

Maria was right.

The reality of my situation finally hit home with the heaviest of force. I had to admit to myself something I'd tried so hard to lock away. The repressed memories flooding back, threatening to drown me.

Chapter 37

Henry pervaded every waking thought, he took over my fractured dreams and sucked all the air from the stale flat. It was like I was grieving all over again.

Henry's box was back on the coffee table, a macabre comfort blanket. He was never coming back. I couldn't kid myself any longer. The loneliness that I'd felt for years, buried deep within me had rocketed to the surface. I missed him so much. I felt like my ribs would fracture with the grief held in my chest. I was wearing Henry's stained hoody, fooling myself that it still smelt of him, after all these years of sitting in his memory box.

As I breathed in the slightly musty scent I felt a funny clarity settle around me. I knew what I needed to do, to begin to make a dent in the emotions I was drowning in. If I was going to face my fears head-on, then I knew where I needed to go. It was going to hurt a hell of a lot, but I had little to lose. Ms Norris would be proud of me for taking control of my own destiny, stopping myself from wallowing, and getting out of my comfort zone. I just hoped I could use her belief in me to go ahead with it. Without wanting a second of this courage to fail, I opened my laptop, but was stopped from booking my train tickets by the trilling of my doorbell.

'I'm coming,' I called. Who on earth could this be? I debated letting it ring, but knew I had to start making changes.

'Callum?' I gasped.

Callum took a step back from my doorstep. He looked terrible.

'C-can I come in? I'm sorry, I know you're going through your own stuff at the moment. Did you get the flowers by the way?' He didn't pause for me to answer. Instantly I knew that he knew. 'It's just I… I could really do with talking to you. It's stupid, but I didn't know who else to turn to.'

I nodded and held the door open for him, following him into the lounge, wringing my hands.

'Do you want a drink?'

I could have laughed at how absurd it was. Me playing hostess. Him pacing the messy lounge. He shook his head.

'I think Abbie was having an affair.'

He stopped and looked at me, wide eyes brimming with pain. I almost forgot to breathe at the sight of his wounded expression.

'I've been going through her things. I'd put it off for as long as I could. There just seemed to be so much of her in the house that I didn't know where to start,' he babbled, not looking at me. 'I found a bank account in Abbie's name that I'd never known existed before…'

The new life baby fund, exactly like Daniel had said.

'Grace? I thought you'd tell me not to jump to silly conclusions, that I was being ridiculous…'

'Yes. I mean, yeah, you probably are.'

In an instant his body language changed. He stared me in the eye.

'Grace. Do you know something?'

It was all I could do to nod. What was the point of lying anymore?

'What?' His jaw tensed. 'What do you know?'

I felt the blood drain from my face. I wished I'd let that doorbell ring and ring until it broke, rather than be faced with this. I'd been a coward but there was no escaping now.

'I –'

'It's true, isn't it? She was having an affair.'

I nodded slowly.

'How do you… Wh-what do you know?' he stuttered. 'Wait –' He pressed his fingers tightly against his temples and paused. 'Do you know *who* he is?'

'Daniel.'

Confusion ran across Callum's face. He sat down with a thump, the air escaping from the sofa as he did. The irony that he was sat directly under Daniel's painting was not lost on me.

'Daniel?' I could see his brain speeding through some virtual memory address book, trying to locate a Daniel. 'I don't know anyone –'

He stopped.

'Daniel Sterling? The artist?' he clarified pointlessly. We both knew he'd worked it out.

I nodded slowly.

He smashed his fist on the coffee table. 'Fucker! Wait. *You* knew she was cheating on me with *him*?' He spat. 'How did you know? You don't even know me at all!'

I let that hurtful comment pass. Where to begin? I could hardly tell him that I'd been snooping through his dead wife's Facebook albums and had suspected something wasn't right. That Abbie's lover had confessed everything, sitting right where he was sitting. He glared at me, waiting for me to say something.

I let out a deep sigh. It was time to confess. 'In my job I use Facebook to help research ways to make the funerals I plan more personal.'

His brow knotted in confusion at my apparent change of subject.

'It's a bit of a secret weapon, that allows me to be creative in coming up with ideas for a unique service. I did this with Abbie but, well, I kind of got lost in her life for a little bit…'

His fingers pinched the bridge of his nose. 'What? You stalked my wife's Facebook page?'

'I do it to help the families. To try and bring some of the personality across of the person they've lost. I tried to be helpful…' I trailed off. It sounded wrong, stupid and inappropriate.

He scrunched his face up, trying to get his head around it. 'So you knew all about my life, about Abbie, before we even became friends?'

I tried not to feel a glimmer at hope at him calling what we had friendship.

'Like I said, I got a little lost in her life. It all just seemed so perfect and, well...' My cheeks flamed in embarrassment at what I was about to say. I hung my head low and stared at my socks. 'I wanted to be a bit more like her.'

He let out this hysterical sort of laugh. 'I've heard it all now.'

'It sounds weird, I know, but my heart was only ever in a good place. I just wanted to be more confident like her, and have more of a life than the one I had. I never told you that we share the same birthday. It's ridiculous, but it felt like we were connected somehow. However, the more I got to know Abbie, and you, I discovered that some things weren't what they seemed. I overheard rumours that she had been friendly with another man... I thought it was Owen, the guy she worked with.' How wrong I had been there. 'But it was Daniel, there was this love knot brooch, and, well...' It didn't matter how I knew. I knew.

He let out a hollow laugh that boomed across the silent room.

'This is unbelievable. Here I was worrying myself sick, thinking I'd done something to upset you as you'd gone silent on me. Racking my brain to think if I'd said something I shouldn't have, trying to work out the reason you would just go AWOL after the time we'd spent together. Finding out from Raj about Ms Norris, and worrying that you were doing OK, when all along you've known that my wife has been shagging some other bloke. Were you ignoring me out of pity, or laughing at me? Look at this loser who doesn't even know his wife's been playing away for god knows how long!' he yelled.

'No. It's not like that. I –'

'Save it.' He got to his feet. 'I can't believe this. I trusted you, Grace.'

I jumped to my bare feet. 'Where are you going? Wait, Callum, we need to discuss this!'

He threw his head back. The twisted look he flashed would haunt me forever. 'Discuss this? Are you fucking kidding me! I thought you cared –'

'I do!'

He scoffed. 'Funny way of showing it. I can't stand liars, especially not ones who go around pretending to be so fucking virtuous. Oh look at me, Grace Salmon, with my strange name, strange habits and strange job. Aren't I just wonderful doing such a selfless thing for everyone in the world?' He put on a high-pitched accent, trying to mimic my voice. 'Bullshit. You're just as fucked up as everyone else.'

He raced down the stairs and threw the door open. My heart was beating so hard I thought it would break out of my skin.

'Callum! Where are you going?' I shouted behind him, but it was too late.

I flung cushions around, trying to find my phone. My fingers trembled as I dialled his number. It rang once then went to voicemail. The next time I tried it went straight to voicemail. *Damn it!*

I paced the living room. My heartache was in the past, long dead and buried; Callum's was fresh and exposed.

How could I not have told him the moment I found out? For him to find out like this, and accuse me of siding with Daniel, made me feel physically sick.

Daniel and Abbie knew that what they were getting involved in would only end in sadness for Callum. No one could have predicted just how catastrophic their actions would be, or the path of devastation they would leave behind. However, I was part of their mess whether I liked it or not. I couldn't stick my head in the sand any longer. I needed to try and fix it.

Chapter 38

I shoved my feet into my trainers and ran to my car, slamming my key in, tyres screeching as I sped off. I knew exactly where to go to find Callum before he did something he regretted. Blood pulsed through my temples. My hands gripped the steering wheel so tight that my knuckles turned white. What were all these people doing on the road at this time!? I revved up, soaring past an old woman fastidiously sticking to the speed limit in her Honda Jazz. I narrowly managed to tuck back onto my side of the road just before a lorry on the other side blared its horn. I didn't even notice how close we were. I just needed to get there, to find Callum.

'Move it!' I yelled as a white transit van blocked the road with an amateur three-point turn.

My head throbbed. I clenched my eyes shut just to try and block the pain thumping in my temples.

The van driver gave me a dirty look as I pressed the heel of my palm firmly into the horn for the third time. He'd overegged the reverse, so was trying to compensate for it and perform a sixteen-point turn to unwedge himself. After what felt like an eternity, he rejoined the flow of traffic. Thankfully he took the next right, taking the corner extra slowly just for my benefit. I zoomed on ahead, gritting my teeth.

My suspicions proved correct when I saw Callum's car parked in the empty car park. The place had closed hours ago. I wondered how many times Abbie had been there at that time of night, her high heels clacking on the cobbles that I now flew up, as she followed her heart to be with her lover.

I'd called Daniel. His number was on the business card he'd given me. He didn't answer, so I'd left a garbled voicemail telling him that Callum knew and was probably on his way to him right now. I hoped he'd picked up the message. I had betrayed his confidence, so I should at least give him some warning of the Callum tornado spinning his way. Grief tangled with anger and betrayal was a recipe for disaster.

The place felt eerie without shoppers milling around. The door to Daniel's studio was open, but no lights shone out over the dark pavement. My stomach fizzed with nervous adrenalin at what I was about to be faced with.

I had to squint in the near gloom. The shape of a man was sitting upright on the sofa. I clumsily felt against the inside wall for a light switch. Soon the room was basking in the low orange glow from a trendy floor lamp. My eyes focussed on the figure. Callum. I let out a breath I hadn't realised I'd been holding and took in the state of the room, half expecting to see Daniel unconscious somewhere. His studio had been smashed up but there was no sign of him. Callum had clearly taken his fury out on this place after discovering Daniel wasn't here.

His rage was spent on the impressive sculpture that I'd admired, the love knot, the secret that had been staring me in the face from the moment I'd walked into Daniel's studio. Huge chunks of it were now carpeting the floor. An armchair lay on its side and light awkwardly pooled on the floor from another lamp that had been knocked over. Callum was hunched on the sofa, his head in his hands, shoulders slumped forward. He didn't make any effort to move or acknowledge me.

'Callum?' I tentatively stepped over shards of twisted polished metal and fragments of ceramic. He didn't move. I desperately wanted to fling my arms around him and tell him it was going to be OK. There was something in his hands, it looked like a colourful flyer, half scrunched in his clenched fists.

'Callum? Please talk to me.'

'I hadn't been confused about the Thai restaurant. She'd clearly been there with him,' he said, his voice low and shaky.

'Sorry?'

He sat back, eyes red and tear stains on his cheeks. He looked like he'd been in a boxing ring, dark marks under each swollen, puffy eye and a quivering bottom lip. He raised his hands in my direction. It was a postcard. *Wish you were here!* in cheerful retro-style font across a sun-drenched Brighton beach.

'I don't understand…'

'It seemed meaningless at the time.'

I nodded, wanting him to keep on talking. He stared past me, looking at nothing.

'Shona and Greg Fitz, friends of ours, had come round for dinner. It was St Patrick's night. Abbie had gone to loads of trouble preparing an Irish menu and decorating the room with four-leaf clover bunting, not caring that none of us had a drop of Irish blood in us – any excuse for a party. Chat turned to holidays. With Abbie travelling a lot with her job, and me working hard on the pitch for the Stratton Estate, we'd not taken a proper trip away for ages. We listened to Shona go on and on about some wonderful five-star resort in Cancun they'd just come back from. Greg pissed her off by shattering this picture-perfect trip by admitting that the only thing they couldn't control was the awful weather, that next time they'd stay in the UK.'

I tried to keep up with what he was saying.

'Abbie laughed, saying how there was nothing wrong with the UK. That smile had caught me off guard; the week before she'd been thumping around the house complaining about everything. I'd presumed it was her time of the month, her mood swings increasing over the years, all her anger directed at me. But she'd been on great form all evening, probably to do with the prosecco she was knocking back. She went on about how Brighton was a favourite place of ours, especially this Thai restaurant by the front.'

I blinked rapidly at the picture he was painting.

'I told her I'd never been to Brighton. Abbie kept repeating how she couldn't believe I didn't remember. How we'd sat by the window and I'd made a joke about how in Thailand they have this vegetable that's called

Morning Glory, or something stupid like that. Both Shona and Greg laughed along, but I could see Abbie growing more irritated by the fact I couldn't remember this trip. She gave my hand a tight squeeze and asked if I was losing my marbles already. For an easy life I said of course I remembered. I smiled along, but there was a complete blank where this memory Abbie was adamant we'd shared was. She must have confused me with him. She must have been there with him. She'd been too drunk to notice her slip up. I knew I hadn't been losing it!'

He rushed to the toilet and threw up.

I stepped over Daniel's business cards that were scattered to the floor and picked up the crumpled postcard. On the back was a short note written in black pen. No stamp, postmark or address.

Our special place. Forever, A and D x

I thought of the photo I'd seen of Abbie standing at the end of a pier. Brighton Pier. Both she and Daniel in their secretive love pins, the sign of their members-only club. I tried to block out the retching sounds Callum was making, and poured him a glass of water from a mug that I'd hurriedly washed out. He flushed the toilet and staggered back to slump on the sofa, every movement a Herculean effort.

'I'm so so sorry, Callum,' I said, gently pushing the water in his direction. He gulped it in one and slammed it back on the table, blocking out the scene on the postcard. 'I don't know what else to say.'

'It was all for nothing.'

'What?'

'My marriage. Our life. I feel so fucking humiliated. I've been wasting my tears on her. Grieving for a woman who I didn't know! For what? For nothing! Do you know what? I'm glad she's dead!'

He let out this painful sound, like an animal crying in agony. His shoulders juddering violently, unable to hold back the raw emotion any longer. Sobs wracked his body. He heaved and gulped at thin air. Something had broken inside him and I didn't know if it would ever be fixed.

I quickly moved next to him and placed a hand on his shuddering back, his chest expanding with each heaving sob. I felt tears drip down my cheeks too. I didn't know how to comfort him, to make it better. I couldn't bear to see his pain, knowing I was a part of the deceit too. He was a man broken by lies, betrayal and damaged pride. The man who'd stoically sat opposite me in my office all those months ago, holding back his shock and grief, had now been broken into a thousand pieces.

'What the hell am I supposed to do now?' he asked. He balled his fists into his eyes and rubbed them, trying to stop the flow of tears. 'She's fucked me over from beyond the grave.' He finally fixed his eyes on mine and angrily pulled away from my touch. 'You kept this from me. You knew and you kept this from me. I thought I could trust you.'

He got to his feet, disappointment palpable from every pore. The look he gave me wounded me more than any weapon could.

'Callum. You *can* trust me. Please let me explain!'

He began pacing around the room, crunching china shards underfoot.

'Go on then.' He dropped on the sofa opposite and glared at me.

I bit my lip.

'Grace?'

I nodded and took a deep breath. 'They got together because of a chance encounter when she was decorating your home.'

'But that was over two and a bit years ago...'

I nodded.

He didn't say a word. His mouth flickered with tension.

'They used to meet here or combine work trips when they went away.'

'And the money? Seeing as you know everything else, do you know about that too?'

He meant Abbie's large and secretive bank account.

'They were planning on starting a new life together. She was going to leave you and move away with him to live near her parents.' I couldn't tell him about their plans to have children. 'Daniel confessed all of this to me. I was going to tell you!'

He ignored my hollow insistence.

'Her parents knew? Was that why they didn't come to her funeral?!'

'I don't know. All I know is that they'd spoken about getting everything in place before she told you. She was going to leave you the house –'

'How fucking generous of her,' he snarled quietly.

'– and move away.'

'It wasn't just a bored wife looking for a cheap thrill

with a fucking tormented artist. I had no chance at resolving this! I'd lost her two and a half years ago without even realising it...' He rubbed his face as this sank in.

His gaze fixed on the bruised knuckles resting in his lap. Vomit stained his jeans.

'The night she died...'

'She was here, on her way home from seeing him.'

'For so long I believed that I'd killed Abbie, but it wasn't because of me that she avoided coming home that night...'

I shook my head vehemently. 'You did nothing wrong! She didn't come home after dropping Owen off because she came here to see Daniel.'

He blinked rapidly, letting the truth sink in.

'He was the last person to see her alive.'

This fact hung in the air like smoke from a party popper.

'Come on. We should leave.'

The past few hours had rolled into one long, painful open wound of emotion. He got to his feet, looking exhausted. Even if I was the last person he wanted to be near, he let me gently guide him out of there.

'How did you get in here anyway?' I asked softly.

'Picked the lock.' He nodded at the door then, without thinking, half-smiled at my shocked expression. 'Learnt it from my mum.'

I turned off the lamp and pulled the door behind us. Our footsteps were loud on the empty pavement. Whenever Daniel next turned up, he would see the state of his studio and know Callum had been there. The insurers would think a burglary had taken place, but he wouldn't pursue any further action.

'What now?'

'Now we go home.'

Callum kicked a stone, sending it skittering over the cobbles, and nodded. I wondered if he was picturing Abbie here. If he could see the ghost of her reflected in the dark windows. I thought about the trail of destruction she'd unwittingly left, how no secrets were ever truly buried. I thought of Henry. I thought how Callum and I both had a choice to move forward and leaving the ghosts where they belonged. Our feet fell in sync as we walked away from the past.

Chapter 39

We'd driven home in convoy. I drove cautiously, slowing down to check Callum was following me, my brake lights lighting his swollen face in my rearview mirror.

I'd helped his shaking hands fumble with the keys to his front door. From the pleading look he gave me I knew that he didn't want to be left alone with his thoughts, alone in this huge house. I'd offered to stay. He'd produced two tumblers and a bottle of whisky. For the first time in over five years I joined him in a glass; the burning heat of the amber liquid both smooth and difficult to swallow. We needed this. We both did. He sat on the floor with his back against the sofa, effortlessly draining his glass before pouring another. I was reminded of the last time we'd been sitting up at a similar hour of the morning, in similar positions in my flat. It felt a world away.

'You want a top-up?'

I shook my head. I was going to nurse the one I had.

'It's probably a good thing you're here.'

I glanced over from the sofa I was sitting on.

'Why's that?'

'Well, with you here I'm going to be a whole lot more restrained than I normally am with this stuff.'

'Happy to be of help.'

The silence curled between us once more.

'How are you feeling?' I bit my lip. What a stupid question – but I couldn't just ignore the elephant in the room.

'I thought I was doing OK…'

He probably felt like he'd swum from the shipwreck to the shore when, in fact, he was completely lost at sea.

'I dunno. I mean, I thought I'd handled it when she died. I thought I was doing pretty well at the whole grieving thing but, well, after tonight I feel like I've been grieving for a complete stranger. I'm furious with Abbie, but where's this anger for a dead woman going to go? It's not like I'll ever hear her side of the story. I still can't believe it. I mean, as much as we bickered, I can't honestly believe that Abbie would have done this to me. We'd taken our marriage vows seriously. I'd been a good husband, tried my very best to keep her happy. I'd have known if she had been having an affair for over two bloody years, surely?' He shook his head in utter disbelief. 'When I was driving to yours I told myself that Abbie was innocent; my suspicions were false, the evidence I'd found didn't add up. Another part of my brain was more insistent – of course she didn't love me. I hadn't been good enough to keep a woman like Abbie Anderson happy and content. In the last few years she'd become more distant, despite how much I tried to tell myself otherwise. I realised that the clues had been staring me in the face all along.'

'The Brighton thing?'

'And others... phone calls Abbie had never answered, insisting they were sales calls, PPI, and I'd believed her. I mean, Abbie cheating shouldn't have come as such a surprise. She thrived on male attention. No workman who set foot in our house was safe. Every young waiter who served her got a flash of her trademark flirty smile. She'd never change, though. That was what had pulled me towards her. I was a hypocrite to think that I could tame her. For a year or so into our marriage she played the role of dutiful wife. We'd go to parties, basking in the looks others gave us; the lovebird newlyweds. We'd hold hands in restaurants and kiss by the dishwasher. But then she'd got bored, the shine had faded on matrimonial life around the time when most couples try to keep the spark alive by having a baby. Every time people said "It'll be your turn next", whenever the topic of children came up, Abbie would laugh and make some light-hearted comment that we weren't ready just yet. Once we returned home from this act that we'd perfected, and closed the front door, it was a different story. She would go to the lounge and stick on some awful reality TV show, telling me she needed some alone time, or have a long bath, pointedly locking the door behind her. I started spending more time alone, keeping out of the way of Abbie and her erratic moods.'

'I'm so sorry, Callum. I don't know what else to say.' Maybe if I repeated it enough times it would sink in.

He was on a roll, letting it all out to the stillness of the semi-dark room.

'It all happened so gradually. I can't even pinpoint the exact moment we drifted apart. The time spent doing our own thing outweighing any time we spent as a couple. Before I knew it we were living separate lives under the same roof. Or maybe we both did realise it, but neither us had the energy to stop it. Our marriage was less than perfect, but I still never would have imagined she'd do this to me.'

'I won't say I know what you're going through because I don't, but I do have an idea...'

He tilted his head to me.

'I thought I knew my ex-boyfriend, Henry, but I didn't.'

'Sorry?'

'He died too.' I half whispered.

He frowned. 'Sorry. I thought you said you had lost your son...'

I nodded. 'I lost them both.'

Callum dared look at me. The hurt I'd caused him was still etched on his pale face but it had faded slightly.

'Shit. W-what happened?'

Was I really going to do this – spill my whole heart out? Perhaps it was the only way to move on. I took a breath.

'I had a missed miscarriage, where you go for a routine scan but they can't find a heartbeat.' I swallowed the lump in my throat. 'Henry became distant after I lost Sam – that's what we named our son. He shut himself off from me, from everyone, and focussed his energy at the bottom of whatever bottle he could get his hands on to drown his sorrows.' My eyes flickered to the half-empty glass in my hand. 'Two days after I had to have the medical procedure to remove my son from me, Henry was on a work night out. He was drunk, well wasted, and got separated from his friends and fell into a canal. He didn't make it out. In the space of forty-eight hours I'd lost the person I loved most in the world, and our future.'

Callum stayed silent.

'I hated him for leaving me, just as you probably hate Abbie for lying to you. In my mind, Henry changed from this man who I thought would always be there for me, to this coward who couldn't handle the same thing I was going through. That his stupidity had cost him his life. He didn't think about me at all. God knows, I wanted to get obscenely drunk as soon as we left the sonographer's room, I wanted to forget, but I couldn't. I had to stay strong. I didn't deal with losing either of them very well.' I bit my lip, hoping to stem the tears. 'What I can't ever escape from is the fact that although he refused to open up to me, I should have tried harder. Forced him to talk to someone about how he was coping, encouraged him not to hit the bottle so hard. He lost his baby too but it was all I could do to concentrate on myself and surviving.' I paused. 'The truth is that I could have saved him.'

'Grace! It wasn't your fault.' Callum sat up straighter.

'The hardest part was that I never even got to say goodbye.'

He looked confused.

'With Sam, I was in too much shock with everything else that was going on to take it all in. I remember the doctor giving me a pamphlet on cremations for tiny babies, a line about a shared service with other grieving parents at the local crematorium. It was too horrific to contemplate.'

Callum winced.

'I couldn't go to Henry's funeral. I was too upset, too lost in the grief for Sam. My own physical reaction to this miscarriage meant it took priority over dealing with the loss of Henry. My body sort of went into shock mode, to protect me in some way I guess. But because of *how* Henry died, and how angry I was at him for doing something so foolish, I didn't want to say goodbye to this version of him; I couldn't begin to comprehend how he had done this to me. My Henry would never have left me alone, he would never have put alcohol before me, before us. I was too consumed with rage to contemplate blending in with the other mourners. I wanted to ignore everyone and everything. Hoping it would go away. But it's something I regret more than anything. I wish I'd had a service, that last moment in time with him, with both of them. I didn't get to say a proper goodbye to my son or my boyfriend.'

'Is that why you really became a funeral arranger?'

I nodded, finally admitting the truth. 'I needed to get so close to death it wouldn't hurt me.'

Chapter 40

I'd woken up in the same position I'd fallen asleep, facing Callum on opposite sofas. Our breathing eventually fell into sync. I allowed myself a few seconds to take in his peaceful face. His eyelashes fanned shut, his hair tousled and lips ever so slightly parted. The need for the toilet forced me to break the intimate moment.

Abbie's toiletries were still dotted about the surfaces of the upstairs bathroom. He must have become skilled at ignoring them. Shiny glass bottles, expensive creams, and half-empty make-up remover glared at me from the tiled cabinet. How had he been able to look past them? How had he managed to spend these months in their home, when her presence appeared to radiate from every surface? It was assaulting my senses.

After freshening up a little, I slipped out of the house, wanting him to sleep for as long as possible. I nipped out to the nearest corner shop and bought every possible breakfast item available. I needed to start making amends.

'Hey. Someone's been busy...'

'You made me jump!' I spun to face Callum. He'd had a shower, his hair wet and skin pink. He was

344

wearing a pair of grey jogging bottoms and a faded band T-shirt.

'I thought you might be hungry.'

'Grace, you didn't have to do this.'

'I wanted to do this.' I pushed a mug and the cafetière in his direction as he pulled out a stool from the breakfast bar. 'Coffee's just brewed.'

We quickly fell into a comfortable silence, moving around the other as we had done over the summer. It felt nice, like nothing else had happened, that we hadn't changed since that version of Callum and Grace.

'You not cutting it a bit fine to get to the office?' He glanced at the clock.

It was almost nine.

'Ah, yeah, funny thing actually...' I tried to say as lightly as I could. 'I've been suspended. It's actually because of you.' I hurriedly waved my arms around. 'Not *you*. I mean, my actions with delivering Abbie's ashes. Let's just say it wasn't quite by the book.' I felt the flame of embarrassment burn on my cheeks.

'What?' He frowned. 'You've lost your job?'

I gave a half nod, half shake of the head.

'I, er, didn't get you to sign the right forms and, well, I should have asked you to come to the office to collect them...' I thought of the foolish reasons why I'd done it. Why I'd been snooping around Abbie's things. How stupid I'd been. How I should have stayed out of her life, both of their lives.

'Oh.' He rubbed his stubble. 'Er, sorry?'

'No! It's my fault. To be honest, I was letting other

things slip too. I'm sure it'll all be sorted soon enough. I'm on gardening leave so it's not like I've been properly sacked...'

An unspoken *yet* hung in the air.

'Grace, you're too good at your job to let it be taken away from you. What you do is... well, it helps a lot of people, probably more than you'll ever know.'

'Maybe.'

'You might want to think about staying off social media though.'

I sipped my coffee and blushed.

'The Balinese sarongs? The umbrellas? It makes sense now. I knew I'd never told you about us going to Bali.'

I cast my eyes to the floor, my cheeks warm. 'I learnt about it from Abbie's Facebook page. I know it's hard to get your head around, but I honestly had my heart in the right place.' I sighed. 'Truth be told it was exhausting. Wanting to deliver the perfect goodbye nearly broke me. Not that I expect any sympathy,' I added quickly.

'But Grace, who is this "*perfect goodbye*" really for?' He made quotation marks.

'The family.' I answered in a beat.

His eyes widened and he let out a sort of laugh. 'I don't want to be rude but fuck – I can't remember half of what happened at Abbie's funeral. I don't know what was said, what hymns we picked, or even what colour flowers we had.'

I tried not to let his words hurt me, but I was shocked. Was that how he really felt?

'I couldn't have even told you who was there on the

day – you're in such a state of shock. It's all about survival mode, time ceases to exist. Like the days between Christmas and New Year. I'm guessing most of the people you deal with at work are the same. Those days are just utter numbness; you're on autopilot, dealing with the unbelievable, waiting to wake up and for it all not to be true.'

I paused. 'But you'd remember if it all didn't go to plan. People remember the disasters.'

'Yeah, you've got a point there, but that doesn't mean you have to go to such extreme lengths. However you go about it, it's still a messed up process for people to get their heads around. There is no such thing as the perfect goodbye; the perfect goodbye is not having to say goodbye in the first place.'

I glanced out of the kitchen window, thinking about what he was saying, my eyes resting on the garden we had poured so much time and energy into.

He caught me looking. 'You think we'll win any awards for largest courgettes or anything like that?'

'Who were we kidding?'

'What do you mean?'

'I mean this, the summer, us hanging out and thinking that a spot of gardening would fix all our problems.' His voice rose and crackled slightly. His eyes remained fixed on the lawn. 'All this time I'd been desperate to keep busy so I wouldn't have to face up to the reality of a life without Abbie, when all along I hadn't had that anyway. I should have known. I should have spotted the signs.' He rubbed his face. 'I need to give Mel a call and fill her

347

in. She's going to be doing her *I told you so* face. They were never the best of friends.' He tried to flash a smile but didn't quite pull it off.

I nodded, lacing my fingers around my mug.

'Thanks for opening up to me about what you've been through.'

'We make quite the pair, don't we!'

'You could say that. But, you know, these things that happened to us didn't happen because we're bad people, Grace.' He sighed. 'I'm still getting my head around what the hell has gone on. The only thing that is clear to me is that I thought I'd lost control but really, I never had any control to begin with. No one does.'

He was right. I'd tried to claw back control in my life by making things as perfect for others as I could. It had been the only thing to keep me stable after it felt like everything was spinning away from me. Henry dying. Losing our baby. I had lost control and had been determined never to feel like that again. What I hadn't realised was that I'd become manic, almost, in my desire to feel in control again.

'I know.' I nodded, my voice barely a whisper. How could he be so observant so soon after the shock he'd received?

Callum cleared his throat. 'I think I'm going to go away for a while.'

I looked up at him.

'To clear my head, you know… The house, this place, it's all feeling a little claustrophobic…'

'Where will you go?'

'Maybe up to Rory's for a bit, then take it from there.'

'Will you go for long?' I picked at my thumbnail.

He shrugged. 'I don't really know, Grace.'

Silence fell between us again. What more was there to say?

'I should be heading home.' I desperately needed a shower and a change of clothes. 'Are you going to be OK?' I asked, shifting my weight from one foot to the other, waiting for him to say something. Waiting for him to say what we both wanted to hear.

'I'll be fine,' he nodded but his eyes said the opposite.

'Well, you know where I am if you need me...'

He pulled open the front door. Every fibre of me wanted to stay. To stay trapped in the bubble we'd created – gardening and laughing and being in denial at what the world had thrown at us. But that bubble had popped. We couldn't hide from the world any longer. We both needed to jump feet-first into our respective griefs, and deal with it all head-on, as traumatic as it may be.

'Take care, Callum.'

He would pack a bag, put the bins out and lock the door. I didn't know when he would set foot in this town again, or when I would see him again. The thought almost broke me in two. As I walked away I realised what I'd been putting off for long enough. I knew what I needed to do, as painful as it was going to be.

Chapter 41

Fear gripped my throat. *All you have to do is get to the other side of the road. That's it, easy peasy.* My brain coaxed me but my body remained frozen rigid. I couldn't get enough air in my lungs. My breath was coming out in strangled starts. I stood motionless between two lanes of traffic. Hovering on the concrete island as cars whizzed past. Horns beeping, people laughing, songs from radios blaring. Black spots appeared at the edges of my vision. I blinked once, twice, hoping to shift them. I was feeling light-headed, not helped by the rush of heat that throbbed up my catatonic body.

Why was everyone else acting so normal? Two school kids messing about to my right. An older woman on her phone bleating about Andy not calling, again. A skinny black lad shouting out something to someone over the road. The smell of cigarette smoke. They all effortlessly moved forward when the green man flashed up, but still I remained stuck in the middle.

Drivers sniggered as they waited for the light to change. I could feel their eyes on me. Red double deckers, white vans, Uber drivers, cyclists, taxi cabs, sleek Mercs revving pointlessly as they drove past. Another lot of pedestrians joined me. I swallowed the saliva pooled in my mouth, willing this terrifying sensation to end. I was going to collapse. I was going to have a heart attack and fall into the road, into the path of an oncoming car. More eyes on me. People jostling and two men in sportswear nipping between a lull in the traffic, ignoring angry horns beeping at their stupidity.

That was the reason I'd left this place. The people, the noise, the constant movement, all too much to take after what had happened. My foggy brain unable to cope with such never-ending stimulus. I gritted my teeth and tried to stay strong, not let myself be dragged under by another panic attack. There was a reason I'd come all this way. I had to pull myself together and focus on that. As the traffic slowed I used every ounce of energy to move my feet like those around me, who made it seem effortless.

I made it to the other side. My legs were pure jelly. I tumbled backwards, grazing my arms against a brick wall trying to support myself. I felt like I'd run a marathon, my hands were shaking and clammy with sweat. I stared at the pavement, focussing on the cluster of weeds poking out of the cracks. A cigarette stub was being climbed over by a woodlouse. My breathing was slowly returning to normal. I needed to pick up my pace and get it over with, so I could be on the next train out of there, back home to sleepy Ryebrook where I belonged.

*

My feet instinctively knew where to take me. I'd walked the route so many times before. I still wasn't entirely sure if going there was going to make any difference to the healing process that I needed to embark on, but it had to be worth a shot. I took a left and then a right, past the tiny deli on the corner, surprised it was still there. I stopped and craned my neck. Looming in front of me was my old place of work. Our office was on the sixth floor of the twelve-floor glass building. The co-working hub in reception still existed, bright pops of colour from trendy pods and curved sofas visible through the floor-to-ceiling windows.

I could close my eyes and smell the air freshener the cleaners used. Imagine my feet treading on the patterned carpets. Within seconds I was back there. The day I stepped out of the lift. I was probably going back much too soon after what had happened; the doctor had offered to give me a sick note but I needed to keep busy. I could always go home early if it got too much. It took me a while to pick up on the atmosphere. My senses heightened seeing Mitchell with his arm around a woman who was crying silently on his shoulder, his face pale. Something bad had happened. Another two employees had their heads low, shaking them sorrowfully. Henry's name flashed in my mind. It was as if I knew before I knew.

My breath quickened. *Stop being stupid*, I told myself. I hadn't spoken to him that morning as he'd been at an event which would have gone on till the early hours. I was pulling my phone out, about to message him, when

I overheard Tasha tearfully say how she didn't know all the details, that they were all in shock. Everything slowed down as I watched her mouth move.

'Mr Clarke, yes. It's just such an awful tragedy.'

Henry Clarke. I was right. Something had happened to Henry. Had there been an accident? Was he in hospital? I kept watching her mouth move.

'He passed away this morning. So sudden.'

Henry is dead, Henry is dead, Henry is dead.

The words were wrong, all wrong. Someone had made a mistake, a cruel and horrific mistake. I couldn't breathe. Panic gripped my throat, its sharp fingertips digging into the base of my neck. My lungs were constricted with terror. She rushed over and picked me up from the floor. I'd fallen without realising. The sound of my blood rushing in my ears drowned out everything else.

A tangle of arms and firm, cool hands moved me to a chair that had appeared. Concerned faces peering down at me. A bottle of lukewarm water with the lid off, thrust in my hand, someone ordering me to take a minute to catch my breath.

The next few days were a blur as I managed to piece together what had happened. After the event, Henry and some work mates had gone for a few drinks at a bar by the canal. He didn't want to share a taxi back to the hotel, said he would walk instead. His body was pulled from the water by two locals walking their dog. They tried to save him, one began CPR, but it was too late. The dog walkers were now in counselling and Henry was dead. Death by drowning. An accident, a horrific accident.

There should have been better lights along the canal, a bungling council cut no doubt. No lifebuoy to throw to him. Students probably nicked it on a night out, thinking they were having a laugh. Nothing anyone could do. Numbed by alcohol, he wouldn't have been able to reach the side of the dirty water, his body in shock from the cold waters. It was too deep, even for confident swimmers.

'Grace?' I had to do a double-take at the plump woman waving at me as she approached.

I had been crying without realising. I hurriedly wiped my cold cheeks and swallowed the lump in my throat. I hadn't even heard her call my name until she came close enough for me to realise who it was. Tasha Birtwell.

'Oh my god! I thought it was you!' she screeched, flashing a mouthful of crooked teeth. 'You haven't changed a bit. What are you doing here? Are you OK?'

I nodded numbly. I hadn't expected anyone to recognise me. I hadn't even imagined anyone would still be working there from the time when Henry and I had been. I thought people moved on; apparently not.

'I'm just popping out for some lunch.' She nodded to the deli. 'Old habits die hard, ain't that right? This is such a lovely surprise! Please tell me you have time for a coffee at least? For old times' sake?'

Before I knew what I was doing I nodded and she swept me up. Linking a meaty arm through mine and steering me away from the spot I'd been planted on, as if it hadn't been five years since I saw her last.

I sat down, banging my knee on the Formica table as I did. Was I really doing this? Was I really having coffee with Tasha as if this was the most normal thing ever?

'So, you just visiting? You moved away didn't you?'

I nodded. It was all just too weird.

'God, so how long's it been?'

I found my voice. 'Five years.'

She shook her head in disbelief. 'Where does the time go?'

'You still work there then?'

'For my sins.' She chuckled and tore open another sachet of brown sugar for her coffee. I couldn't stomach drinking any of mine just yet. 'Yeah, there's probably not many faces you'd recognise actually. The place has changed, you know? People come and go and well, life moves on, and obviously Henry wasn't there steering the ship...'

It hadn't taken us long to reach the elephant in the room. I took a deep breath.

'I need to apologise, Tasha. I know I owe you an explanation for why I went AWOL.'

She smiled but it didn't quite meet her eyes. 'I was wondering if you'd bring it up.' She let out a deep sigh. 'What happened, Grace? You know I tried to find you? Found your brother on Facebook but he wasn't very helpful.'

Freddie had never said.

'I figured I'd done something wrong. One minute everything was fine, the next... you'd shut yourself off from all of us. I didn't realise how Henry dying had affected you so much that you had to run away…' She paused. 'That's why you left, wasn't it? Because of him?'

I nodded.

'I thought so. I knew you had that silly crush on him, but I didn't think it would cause you to just up and leave everything you'd worked for. To leave me without saying goodbye. I thought I meant more to you than that…'

'You did! Tasha, I wasn't thinking straight.'

I thought of the many appointments I'd had with Doctor Ahmed, the tiny white pills he'd prescribed. The waves of depression, the panic attacks and the gripping anxiety that I'd tried my hardest to get some sort of control over. Leaving London had been the best thing. The second best was burying my own grief into helping others with theirs. Training to work as a funeral arranger, in a small town where no one knew me or my history, was the only way I could function after everything. The only problem with sticking a plaster over a wound is that sometimes it comes unstuck.

Her face twisted with worry. 'What are you really doing here, Grace?'

'I guess I felt the time was right to face my demons. It's taken a lot of courage to come back to the city after all this time, back to this place.' I took a deep breath. 'I was in a relationship with Henry.'

'What?' Tasha's mouth fell open and eyes were rapidly blinking.

'Henry and I were a couple. We were in love, planning to have a family together.'

'W-w-wait… but he –'

'Was my boss. Our boss.' I sipped my drink, hoping the tremble in my hand wasn't obvious.

'I thought it was a silly crush. I'd no idea you were serious together.'

No one would ever believe that someone like me would have been so bold as to date her boss. That we had been planning a whole new life together, that we had *created* a new life together. I wondered if, when his family cleared out his flat, they'd found anything of mine, anything to prove that what we had existed, or if the mementos had been swept up with everything else he owned, no questions asked.

'That's not all.' I cleared my throat. 'Before he died I was twelve weeks' pregnant with his child. A little boy.'

'You have a son?' she gasped.

I shook my head, digging my fingernails into the palm of my hand to keep the tears at bay.

'I had a miscarriage.'

'Oh, Grace.' She was biting her bottom lip. Her eyes glassy. 'I'm so sorry.'

I had a flashback of her pulling this exact same expression. Back then it was full of concern as she ordered me a taxi, waited with me until the driver pulled up. It was after the office had been briefed on Henry's sudden death. She'd consoled me, explaining how we were all in shock but how management had said to take time off if we felt it necessary. 'Thanks, I'm sure I'll feel better after a lie-down,' I'd said, my voice hoarse. I lasted two more days then I never went back to the office. My mum let me crash in a flat she was renting at the time in Ryebrook. I lied and told her that London wasn't for me. Putting on a brave face I told her that I was done with living in the capital and being so skint. She had been too busy dating a loser called Dwayne, who rode a battered Harley, at the time. Too lost in her own happiness to realise I was drowning in grief. Because no one in my new life knew about my past, I could easily kid myself that Henry had just gone away, that he'd dumped me. A person's absence can also become a presence. I never drank again, knowing just how much of a part alcohol had played in snatching Henry from me. I'd been living with trauma, not grief. The anger, disbelief and shock had nowhere to go so I forced it down and created a new reality.

'It was one of the reasons Henry drank so much that night. Why he went AWOL. He was dealing with things in his own way. He'd been so excited about becoming a dad. Tragically, he… well, you know the rest.'

She nodded.

'It cut him deeper than I ever realised.'

I wished more than anything I'd seen the signs, that I could have got him to speak to me, to open up and work through our pain together. I was so engrossed in my own fog of sadness that I didn't reach out to him in his. That was something I'd have to live with.

Tasha shook her head sorrowfully. 'You went through all of this alone? Why didn't you speak to me? I could have been there for you. I thought we were friends. But you just… you just left.'

'I needed a fresh start.'

'So why have you come here today? Why now?'

'Well,' I paused. 'It sounds mental but... I tried to convince myself that Henry was still alive, that we'd just broken up, that one day we would meet again and...' I shook my head at the absurdity of what I'd conceived in my head as a coping mechanism, '... perhaps we'd make another go of things. I just couldn't comprehend everything I'd lost in one go, so I only really allowed myself to mourn my son. I was angry at Henry for the way he died. Obviously he didn't choose it and it was a tragic accident, but I felt like he'd put himself in that vulnerable position.' It still felt very new and odd to be verbalising this tangle of messed up thoughts after all this time.

'I also realised that I kind of ran away from everything and everyone who knew me before. I guess I'm only now accepting what I didn't want to accept.'

'Jeez, well I'm glad I saw you today. I can't imagine what you went through.' She shook her head and gulped her coffee. 'Are you happy now? With your new life, I mean?'

I thought about this. The past few months had been a complete rollercoaster. I'd lost Ms Norris but gained a new group of friends in the Grief Club who, when I felt ready to open up to them, would be there for me, able to understand the pain and madness of loss. Callum's face swam into my mind, along with the familiar gnawing feeling inside at how badly I'd handled everything with him.

'Yes, I mean, I'm getting there,' I replied honestly.

'You never said what you're doing now? Still working in events?'

'I'm a funeral arranger.' I waited for the inevitable shocked reaction.

'Wow,' she giggled. 'I wasn't expecting that.'

We both finished our drinks and the conversation moved on slightly, but too much had gone on over the years for us ever to be Tasha and Grace, the old versions of us. I had wasted far too much time already on the past. It was time to look towards the uncertain future.

Chapter 42

Since getting back from London I'd been determined to keep my spirits up and not let myself wallow any more, even if that was easier said than done. Tasha had texted to say how lovely it was to see me, that we'd have to do it again sometime. A hollow offer but one that was nice to receive.

The trip to London had taken it out of me. I'd slept in a deep and dreamless sleep for longer than I could remember. I'd not heard anything from Callum. I guessed he was still away at Rory's place in Scotland. Either that or he was back and not wanting to speak to me. Maybe he had realised he had to move on too.

I still hadn't heard anything from Frank either. I didn't know if I should be using this time to search for another job, but it just felt too daunting to know where to begin. I attacked my flat with an intense cleaning regime, hoping it would give me the satisfaction that the smell of bleach and shiny surfaces once gave me. It didn't, but perhaps that was a good thing.

A revelation came to me as I lay in bed at 10.00 a.m., knowing I should get up but also secretly enjoying the laziness. As much as I cared for everyone who came into the funeral home, I'd given my all to each service because I'd been denied a perfect goodbye for Sam and Henry. It was my way of making things right, I guess. I thought that the perfect goodbye was helping others tiptoe into the start of their journey of grief and acceptance. I thought that by making sure everything went to plan, by going above what they asked for and by ensuring a personal send-off, I was softening the blow of what life without this special person would be like.

But I was only human.

I couldn't protect people from the throes of mourning and unbearable grief, just as I'd had to face up to this darkness myself. In helping others with their perfect goodbyes I had been unable to move on. I was amazed this thought hadn't occurred to me earlier. I had been so engrossed in Abbie's online life, and the reason wasn't just because she was glamorous and had nice hair; it was as if seeing the fully lived life of Abbie had made me realise just how small my own world was. My own grief had meant I'd barely lived, ironic given that I worked with death every single day, but it was true.

Death shapes you and by having a close experience with death it changes you – and this is OK. I should have understood that when it comes to loss there is no neutral experience. It changes the way you look at things; it refines things whether you like it or not.

Losing Henry and Sam had meant I'd become a funeral arranger and helped many families manage their pain. I mean, what an honour that had been! Loss had actually taught me more than I could ever realise. I am the person I am today *because* of what happened. If I deny what happened then I deny who I am. Would I have chosen not to have met Henry, not to have fallen wildly in love and enjoyed all those happy times together just because of the scars it caused when our story ended? Not a chance. Why would I want to forget the deep and unwavering love I felt for both my boys? I no longer wanted to deprive myself of the happy memories, as painful as they may have been. What happened happened, but by not letting my nostalgic brain take me back there every so often, it was like saying that those times had never existed, that *they* never existed.

I sprang out of bed. I should have done this a long time ago. My eyes fell on Henry's memory box. The relics of the past, of lost love and unfulfilled opportunity, of heartache, of hope and pain, in one battered cardboard box.

Henry was my first love, there was no doubt about that, but he didn't deserve to be my only love. I was ready to say goodbye to him, to us. I had to look to the future without clinging onto the memory of a dead boyfriend. It had been long enough.

'Right. Come on, Grace,' I said to the empty room. I felt calm and clear-headed as I tipped the box of faded ticket stubs, positive pregnancy tests, crinkled Valentine's cards, and all the old emails that I'd printed off, whose words I knew by heart, into the bin. These were just things, stuff that I didn't need to give such a holy reverence to. Holding on wasn't going to bring him back but it was going to slow me down from moving forward. I felt a release as the box lightened in my hands, watching the contents fall into the bin.

I then turned on my laptop and logged onto Facebook. I wasn't finished quite yet. Leon had sent me a friend request, which I was about to accept before I figured I was probably meant to keep my distance from anything work-related. I didn't want to get anyone else in trouble, and until I heard from Frank I wasn't entirely sure what the rules were. It didn't matter really because I wasn't on there to connect with people. I was looking for the link to delete my account. Even if Frank welcomed me back to work, I was going to change my working style. Helping others had helped me, but I still needed to make sure that I wasn't giving too much of me to the job.

A red notification in the corner caught me eye. I told myself I'd have a quick look – probably something Mum had tagged me in – and then get on with what I was planning to do. It took me to the Ask A Funeral Arranger Facebook page I'd set up, all those months ago, desperate to attract new members and, most importantly, sign-ups to prepaid plans. I hadn't updated it for so long, and had forgotten I'd even given Marcus admin access; he must have been carrying it on in my absence.

The page now had sixty-four likes – the last time I'd looked we had five – and not only that, there were now also reviews. All of them gave five stars. I swallowed the lump in my throat as I scrolled down the page, reading them.

Grief Club is the one place I can be myself. I'd recommend it to anyone looking for a safe haven and respite from the loneliness of their own grief, which is down to the lovely Grace and her hard work in bringing us together. Five stars – Julie Rivers

I was sick of feeling so low so went along hoping to do something proactive but not expecting much. What I didn't expect was to find a group of wonderful people I now call friends. Ugly crying is welcome! – Raj

Cheers Grace for creating Grief Club, it's the opposite of morbid and actually has offered so much light back into my life. Also – the free cake is epic! –Dean O'Callahan

Allow yourself to sit in the darkness, embracing how broken you feel. Stop saying I'm fine if you're not. Open up to others who understand. These are all things I've learnt since joining Grief Club. – Ms. E. Norris

There were more but my eyes had misted with tears, so I struggled to read them. My heart surged with happiness. I desperately wanted to show Ms Norris, to tell her that her idea to keep the meetings going despite my reluctance had paid off. It was because of her encouragement that I now had this wonderful bunch of new friends. She really had done more for me that I ever realised.

I took a deep breath and tried to stay positive. I couldn't tell her in person but I could honour her by making sure I didn't give up on my Griefsters. I would make sure I went to the next meeting with an extra large box of her favourite cakes. These battle-scarred survivors gave me hope that I would get through my pain too.

There was just one thing I needed to do. The Facebook page was clearly in the more than capable hands of Marcus. Other than that I was done with this site, done with social media. I clicked on my profile page and found what I was looking for. I pressed delete and felt lighter than I could remember for a very long time.

Chapter 43

The music in there was clearly set at a level that was best for those with dodgy hearing aids. The whining bass and screechy vocals of an overweight man murdering 'Sweet Caroline' was a sure-fire fast track to tinnitus. I glanced around the pub trying to spot her. The dark oak stain of the timber beams only made it feel even more claustrophobic.

This impromptu trip was inspired by Ms Norris. She wouldn't have just sat back, waiting for her fate to be delivered to her, she would be out getting the answers she deserved. It was about time I took some control back too.

I remembered her saying she went to karaoke there every week, but apart from the balding singer with an impressive beer belly, and a wiry woman tucking into a bag of peanuts at a nearby low table, it was empty. I frowned. Maybe I'd got the wrong pub.

Behind me was a noticeboard with the darts team's fixtures, a poster for an upcoming talent show, and details on the next ladies' night. This was definitely the right place. So where was Linda and her gaggle of girlfriends cackling in the corner over cheap Malibu and cokes? I turned to leave when I spotted a flash of leopard print out of the corner of my eye.

'Linda?'

She was sat in a booth all alone. She blinked back the look of complete shock at seeing me.

'Grace? What are you...' she paused and flicked her eyes to the singer who was still warbling on. 'Are you here for karaoke?'

I shook my head.

'I mean it's not usually as dead as this.' She let out a funny sort of laugh to hide her embarrassment. 'The girls will be here shortly... oh, hi Brian!'

She smiled a toothy grin at a middle-aged man who plodded past with an unlit cigarette in his mouth, heading for the smoking area. He blanked her. A flash of blush flamed up her bronzed cheeks. I realised that there was no group of girls, there was no crazy social life. She was as lonely as I had been. This caught me off guard.

'Sorry, Grace, do you want to sit down? I have to say this is a bit of a surprise...'

I tried not to let her fabricated social life distract me from why I was really there.

'I think we need to talk.'

She twirled the plastic straw around her glass. 'I agree.' She took a deep breath. 'Can I go first?'

I nodded and sat opposite her, my elbows sticking to the tacky table top.

'I didn't tell Frank about the missing sign-out form for the ashes, if that's what you've come here to talk about. It was Frank.'

'Frank?' *Why on earth would Frank get involved in paperwork?*

The singer had finished. The landlord had taken the whiny mic and was asking for the next wannabe pop star to come and pick a song. We both ignored him.

'He'd finally agreed to this new computer software that I'd been pestering him to get since seeing it at Coffin Club.'

I had a vague memory of him mentioning this during a team meeting.

'Anyway, it's this bit of kit that electronically scans and saves forms. He must have been using it himself and gone through the ashes paperwork, which flagged up a missing form.' She shrugged.

With no new takers, the overweight singer got back up to the stage and began an awful Elvis medley. I was finding it hard to concentrate on what Linda was saying. 'What Frank didn't anticipate was that you would tell him about your *unusual* ways of using the internet to make your funerals so unique.'

'But he brought it up. He knew that I'd been using social media in work time...'

She shook her head. 'He brought it up because he wanted to ask you to use the company social media pages more as a marketing tool or something. He'd heard that it can be a good, cost-effective way of getting what we do out in the community, and wanted to ask you if you could help.'

I sat back. I'd gotten into this mess myself. There was no one to blame but me. I'd gone against the rules, and Linda had been telling the truth.

'I'm sorry for immediately thinking it was you who spilled the beans to Frank.'

'It's fine. I know we've never really seen eye to eye on things, but I wouldn't have gone straight to Frank if I did find out the ashes form was missing. To be honest you're so diligent I would have just assumed you had a good reason. You know we've not had the best relationship but I wouldn't have wanted you to risk losing your job,' she said, letting that fact hang in the air. 'I only teased you about Mr Anderson because I was jealous … I guess.'

We sat in a funny sort of silence, listening to the god-awful singer who was now trying to thrust his podgy groin in time to the beat.

'I did always think it was odd how you managed to hit the nail on the head with every single funeral you planned. The lengths you went to in order to give them the perfect goodbye.' Linda shrugged. 'I mean, yeah, it's a little on the creepy side, scouring the web for details of dead people –'

'It was always done with the best intentions.'

'I know. Perfect Grace and her perfect funerals.'

'Perfect Grace?' I scoffed.

She rolled her eyes. 'Oh, come off it. You're clever, kind, hard-working, pretty and patient. I'm not going to list any more as you'll get a big head. Oh, and to make it even worse, you don't even realise how many people like you!' I was completely taken aback, too shocked to correct her. 'You remind me of my sister. She could never put a foot wrong either.'

I was about to say that she had no idea how many mistakes I'd made, but she was on a roll.

'I don't know if you have any siblings but we were as competitive as you could get. Whatever I did, she did it better. But then one day we had a massive falling out, and she emigrated to Australia with her kids. Like I said, she always had to go bigger and better than anyone else.' She rolled her eyes. 'The thing is, it broke my mum's heart. She was getting on a bit so never saw her or the grandkids again before she passed away. God bless her soul. I've had to live with the regret that it was my fault Mum lost out on their lives, just because the two of us couldn't get on.'

'I'm sorry to hear that.'

She shrugged lightly. 'You're Perfect Grace and I'm just Good Time Linda, the one who'll get the next round in or be first up on the karaoke machine.' She blinked rapidly. 'You were always getting the most praise from Frank, the most thank you cards and gifts; your funerals were even talked about at the Coffin Club conventions I went to. The only thing I knew I could do better than you was to use my thick skin to my advantage. I suggested to Frank about the prepaid sign-ups. It was a challenge I could easily win. I just didn't expect you to then start this bereavement club thing, that's obviously taken off!'

So her issues with me had been a bizarre case of sibling rivalry all along? With no sister to fight with, Linda had used me as a stand in, Frank being the parent.

She laughed, but it didn't sound genuine. 'You couldn't make it up really!'

'You always seem like you have everything together.'

'What's that saying about smoke and mirrors? If you

371

act a certain way then you'll eventually convince others that's who you are.' She shrugged.

Immediately I thought of Abbie and her less-than-perfect offline life.

'I think I'm going to take a leaf out of your book,' said Linda, 'and be a little more true to who I am. I may not be perfect but I'm me.'

It was all too much to take in. Linda wanted to be more like me? I almost wanted to pinch myself to make sure I wasn't in some bizarre dream.

'You'll probably hear from Frank soon when he calls to apologise and get you back to work.'

'Apologise?'

Frank had nothing to apologise for.

'Well, he's still unimpressed at you stalking our clients' personal lives online, but I'm sure he'll at least say sorry for thinking foul play had been involved in Abbie's missing ashes. I found the form Callum signed when he took the ashes. You know how messy my desk is, it wasn't hard to convince him it was just mislaid paperwork. He'll probably call you soon enough to get you back in work. Right, I need a top up.' She shook her empty glass. 'Can I get you one?'

'I'm good, thanks. I need to head home, actually.'

'You not going to stay for a song? We could do a duet?' Her eyes lit up.

'Maybe another time...'

OK, so Linda and I would never be BFFs, she needed to have her head tested for all the mismatching leopard print she insisted on wearing, but we had certainly cleared the air. I had reached the door when suddenly I realised something didn't add up.

'Wait. You said you found the form from Callum, but there was no form. Did you forge his signature?'

She shook her head. 'He came in to see me. He'd heard you'd got into trouble on his behalf, and wanted to fix it.'

My heart did this funny flip thing. He must have paid her a visit before he left.

'He's one of the good ones, Grace.'

She smiled sadly.

I know.

Chapter 44

'Hey, Grace, we've not seen you in a while! I have to say that Grief Club isn't the same without you' said Raj.

'Sorry, things have been a bit...' I trailed out. Where to begin? It didn't matter now anyway. I couldn't help but smile at the thought of them carrying on without me. I would go back, one day, when I was properly ready.

'You know we have a few more faces that have joined? Obviously none of them are such skilled facilitators as you, or bring such wonderful cakes. So, what's the first rule of Grief Club? That we talk about Grief Club! I made that up myself.' He beamed.

'Very good.'

'So, what can I get for you? The usual?'

I shook my head. It had been a while since I'd played my tinned food lucky dip game and I wasn't about to start again.

'I actually came to ask you something. What are you doing on Sunday the eighth of November at seven p.m.?'

'Nothing. Well, working. Why?'

I smiled and pulled out the confirmation email I'd printed off.

'Ryebrook and Hillgate Talent Show are looking for

contestants. Do you have what it takes?' He took it from me and read aloud.

I had spotted the poster tacked to the noticeboard when I was in the pub with Linda. There was a contest taking place and they wanted singers, jugglers or comedians to take part, and help put Ryebrook on the map. I'd decided to enter Raj – there was no way he would have entered himself. He stared at me as if I'd lost the plot.

'I've booked you a spot at the talent show. You're going to be on stage performing your best gags for Ryebrook's Got Talent!'

Judging by the way he was blinking so rapidly, I immediately regretted being so bold. When would I learn to stop getting involved in other people's business?

'Seriously? But, but, what about the shop? You know Rani can't run it on her own,' he stuttered, his large brown hands trembling slightly. 'I don't know Grace, I mean I'm really touched that you thought of me, that you think I will be good enough but...'

'I'll help her. Or you can shut up early for the evening. Most of your customers will be coming to watch you and support you there, instead of buying pints of milk or cigarettes here.' The colour drained from his face at the thought of actually getting up and making this dream a reality. 'Plus, you've got what no one else has...'

'And that is?'

'Peter Kay's endorsement!'

He thought for a moment then nodded firmly. 'You're right!' He placed the paper on the counter, by the reduced packs of Bakewell tarts, before wrapping me in a hug. He smelt of cheap aftershave. He also gave a really good hug.

'I do. Wow, oh wow. Rani isn't going to believe it. Do you think I have a chance of winning? What does it say here... £250 prize fund is up for grabs. That could get us a new fridge freezer or maybe I could invest in the latest smart scanner things that the Tesco Express has.' He wrinkled his nose. 'This could be the start of everything!'

I couldn't help but be swept away by his enthusiasm. This man who worked every day of his life and had never grumbled, apart from about Tesco, deserved to take a chance and follow his dreams.

'Maybe. So you'll do it?'

He clapped his hands. 'Yes! Of course. Right, gosh, I better get on. Need to practice my set. Now, do you think I open with the Bag for Life joke or the one about the grim reaper?'

Chapter 45

'Grace?' Frank called me in from watering the hanging baskets outside. The cold was setting in but the violas were putting up a good fight. I'd been lost in my own thoughts, as droplets beaded from thick leaves, splattering onto the tarmac below. 'Have you got a minute?'

I put the watering can down and went inside to take a seat at his desk. I smiled proudly at the pristine room, not a speck of dust anywhere to be seen. I'd decided to go back to work. It turned out Linda was right; Frank had called the next day asking if I could go and see him. I'd agreed to come back if I could dial down the workload and take it at my own pace. I could see just how much of myself I'd been pouring into the funerals of others, and it wasn't healthy.

He'd let me add cleaning to my list of daily jobs, preferring to give me a less client-focussed role at the moment. I was grateful to him for that. Working behind the scenes had been best for everyone.

It had been three weeks since I'd last seen Callum. I missed him more than I imagined I would. I missed what I thought we'd had, feeling like someone cared for me the way I cared for them. Friendship.

'How're you doing?' He smiled, leaning back in his chair. 'You've done a lovely job with this place. Some really nice touches.' He nodded to the change of pictures and brighter up-lighters on the walls.

'No problem.' I was keen to get back to the store cupboard. I was going to tackle that space today, give it a thorough clean and alphabetise the containers.

Frank cleared his throat. 'What it is, Grace… well… as you know you've not really been yourself, and I just wanted to say how nice it is having you back. I know you've gone through a tough time.' *He didn't know the half of it.* 'But we're really glad you're keeping busy and back where you belong.' He smiled at me kindly. 'And you know that you can pick up working with families once more, whenever you feel you're ready. But I do think it's best if, for the next few weeks at least, you continue to do your marvellous work behind the scenes.'

'That's fine by me.'

The truth was I wasn't ready to be sitting with families who were going through hell. I had empathy fatigue, compassion overload, or any other way of saying I was burnt out. I was grateful to Frank and Linda for stepping up so I could step down. I had relinquished my hold and control, my obsessions with making every funeral completely perfect. It was actually nice to take a breather.

'But we still want you to feel useful and valuable to the business, so I had hoped, if you don't think it's too much work, you might take on the Love of My Light service?' He paused, chewing his bottom lip. 'Only if you think you're ready?'

The Love of My Light service was an annual event we held to remember loved ones who'd been in our care. Whether they had passed away recently, or we had looked after them years ago, it was a chance for their families to come and light a candle in their honour and have a chat over tea and cake. It was also usually Linda's baby.

'Linda won't mind?'

Frank shook his head vigorously. 'No, she's more than happy to pass this over to you.'

I doubted Linda would have had much say in the matter.

'Plans have already started, so you don't need to feel overwhelmed. I just know you'll do an excellent job, Grace.' He smiled, then faltered. 'If you think you're ready?'

I smiled back. 'That sounds great, thank you.'

Chapter 46

I glanced at my watch. I was running late. Really late.

'I just need to make one more trip home,' I breathlessly called to Frank who was helping me unload the boxes of cakes from my car.

'What?' His eyes widened at the sheer number of baked goods, pies, cupcakes and tarts in front of him.

I'd offered to do some baking for the event. Frank had seemed surprised that I would want to go to that much effort when there was a pot of money to cover catering. I told him that it was no problem, secretly grateful to have something to fill my evenings and weekends with, and instantly knowing whose recipes to use. *I promised you I'd get your cakes into the mouths of as many people as I could*, I thought as I pulled on my coat. Although, looking at the impressive spread, maybe I had gone a little overboard.

'I won't be long! I forgot the napkins.'

As I drove I found myself singing along to the radio. 'Bohemian Rhapsody' was playing and, despite not knowing all the words, I was bobbing my head and tapping my fingers in time to the beat.

I scanned my kitchen for the napkins I'd ordered,

trying to ignore the mess I'd left in there from the last batch of cupcake icing I'd done. Blobs of white liquid congealed on the work surfaces. It was chaos, but for once it didn't bother me. I'd get round to cleaning it when I had a minute. Ms Norris had always wanted me to get a hobby and I'd realised how happy baking made me. The satisfaction in creating something from scratch, and then seeing how happy it made other people, was infectious.

My phone was ringing in my pocket. I ignored it, it was probably Frank telling me to forget it and come back to man the fort. *Where were the napkins?* I tore around the kitchen, flinging open cupboard doors to look for the box I clearly remembered putting in a safe space. I hurried into the lounge, my phone falling silent. I dropped to my knees and reached under the coffee table, trying to wiggle out the cardboard box that I'd squeezed into the tight space. My phone began to ring once more. I glanced at the screen, it was Mum. I quickly pressed answer, even though I really didn't really have time to chat.

'Gracie! How are you? I was just about to pop in to see you but I remembered that last time you didn't seem so keen on me just turning up.'

'Oh, er, well, now's not such a good time actually, Mum. I'm just going out.'

'Out? Out where? You never go out.'

I let that comment pass.

'I'm going to this work thing I've organised. You can come along if you'd like?' I offered, without thinking. *Where had I put those napkins?*

'It's not some evening funeral is it?' I could picture her shivering at the thought.

'No, it's actually quite uplifting. Well, I'm hoping it will be.' *If anyone turns up.* 'I've been put in charge of our annual remembrance service, but I'm running late myself.'

I hung up after giving her the directions, not expecting her to show up, but hoping that it wouldn't just be Frank, Linda and I, with a mountain of food and unlit candles. I'd been too busy planning the event, and I hadn't given much thought to whether people were going to make it or not. I suddenly felt overcome with nerves. I didn't have the best track record. I shuddered, thinking back to the painful solitary wait during the first Ask A Funeral Arranger event, then smiled at how that had actually ended up being the best thing I'd ever organised.

*

I pulled up at the church car park but could hardly get through the throngs of people milling around. There was another event taking place there at the same time! Frank would be furious. There would never be enough parking spaces for two functions. I took a deep breath. If I had learnt anything, it was that I had to let go of the frantic control I felt I needed to put on everything. So what if two events were taking place? The more the merrier. I hoped.

I got out of the car. The old Grace would have been exploding with anxiety at such a change in events. New

Grace was totally breezy about this… sort of. I cast my mind back to the chat I'd had with the venue organiser. No, I was *sure* it was just for us. Then what were all those people doing there?

'Grace!' Linda waved. She grinned manically from behind the food stall. Half of my cakes had gone already.

'Look at this place. I've never seen this service so busy before.' She beamed as I squeezed into a tight gap behind the trestle table. 'Here's the star baker herself!' she said loudly to the cluster of women in front of us.

'You made these?' a woman I didn't recognise asked, crumbs from Ms Norris's blueberry and avocado tart spraying in the air as she spoke.

I nodded.

'You're wasted working with dead people if this is what you can do!' A few people behind her murmured in agreement.

I felt my cheeks heat up.

'It's my friend's recipe. Ms Norris. She's the real star baker.' I could feel my throat clog with emotion but swallowed it down.

'You tell her she's a genius!'

'Thank you. Wow. Where did all these people come from?' I asked Linda, smiling at her rosy cheeks and the slight sheen on her forehead.

It felt like the whole town had turned out. With all these people chatting and laughing and eating, it felt like a celebration of some sort, a party for those who couldn't be there in person. Exactly the mood I'd hope to create.

'I know. Frank's beside himself. If you can get even half

of them to sign up to a prepaid plan then you'll easily have beaten my target!'

I couldn't tell if she was being serious or not.

'I think you're still way in the lead,' I said without a hint of bitterness.

'Hmm, well, you put up a good fight.' She gently nudged me then lowered her voice. 'Seriously though, Grace, I'm impressed. None of my events have ever been as packed as this. I mean, I have to admit that I was sceptical about the party games area…' I followed her gaze to a section I'd decorated in bunting and helium balloons. Large bubbles spraying out of hidden bubble machines filled the air. That was another reason I'd wanted to cater it myself, so I had the cash to spend on things like that.

'You don't think the music's too loud?' I winced as an uplifting pop song played from two speakers.

Linda shook her head. 'It's like a party, not a depressing ritual. Seriously, you've done a great job.'

That was high praise indeed, coming from her.

'I think the free cakes might have something to do with the number of people here,' I grinned.

She gave my arm a friendly pat then tried to stop two women from squabbling over the last Moroccan lamb and butternut squash filo pastry.

'There's another lot coming out soon, ladies!'

I gazed out at the crowd, smiling as people cooed over the food. My food. Ms Norris's food. I felt a prickle of pride watching it all play out. She'd wanted her recipes to get into as many people's hands as possible.

'*Grace*!' my mum shouted, pulling me close to her. She looked well, the best I'd seen her in a while. 'You organised this?'

I nodded. 'I didn't think you'd come, Mum. I know what I do isn't your cup of tea and –'

She shushed me. 'I'm so proud of you. Look at this place, it's absolutely packed. I've been telling everyone that I'm your mum, so many people have told me just how wonderful you are and how much you've helped them.' Were those tears appearing in her eyes? 'It's incredible what you do for others.'

Callum's face swam into my mind. He was the one person I desperately wanted to fix, and I couldn't. I had to stop myself from hoping that I might spot his face amongst the crowd. His broad shoulders in a sea of bodies. Of course he wasn't going to be here, despite him being one of the first people I invited.

'Thanks, Mum.'

'Grace. Have you got a minute?' Frank called, beckoning me over. He was holding a microphone in his hand, looking at it as if it might bite him.

'Better go, Mum. Thanks for coming. It means a lot.' I squeezed her, then zigzagged my way through the crowd of familiar faces.

I spotted Nigel standing by the coconut shy, cheering as Dawn effortlessly knocked one to the floor. A young girl – Dawn's, judging by the identical hair colour – raced to collect it and passed it to her uncle. Looking at them you would never have known that they had been at the point of violence, just a few months ago, over the colour of wood for their mum's coffin. Time heals all. Feuds are dealt with as family dynamics shift. I could imagine them saying to one another how their mum would have loved this. That just because she wasn't here, didn't mean they shouldn't continue to spend time together as a family. It just altered things. Death did that. You learnt to figure out a new normal. You were never able to fill the void left behind, but you could at least begin to patch up some of the empty edges. You would grieve for as long as you breathed, it just wouldn't be as all-consuming as when it had first smacked you. I knew that to be true.

A slim arm pulled at my sleeve. I turned to see. I was met with the grinning faces of Rachael and Tom, Daisy's parents. Rachael pulled me into a hug. I jolted backwards for a micro-second. There was something in the space between us. She laughed at the surprise on my face.

'Yep, we're expecting again.' She caressed her slightly swollen tummy and radiated a look of pure love down at the tight fabric holding new life and new beginnings.

Tears pricked my eyes. 'Congratulations!'

'It's still early days, and, well you never know what could happen…' Tom trailed off, following a loaded look from his wife.

'We're staying positive,' she said resolutely.

He nodded and flung a protective arm around her.

'I think he wants to wrap me in bubble wrap and hide me in a cave for the rest of the pregnancy. To be honest, I thought that would be how I'd feel too but,' she jutted her chin out, 'you can't live in fear that something will go wrong, can you? A day doesn't go by when we don't think of Daisy, and we wanted to thank you for all you did for her and for us. We will never forget your kindness.'

I tried to gulp a breath of air. My throat swollen with emotion. 'It was my honour.'

I caught Frank waving at me from the corner of my eye.

'Excuse me, I have to go.'

'Of course! Thank you for inviting us tonight. I hope it will be on every year so we can bring this little one to remember his or her big sister.' Her voice was breaking slightly as she caressed her stomach.

I gave her a gentle hug, careful not to squeeze too tight, and made my way over to Frank.

'Grace, am I OK to go on? Are you sure you don't want to say a few words first? It is your night, after all.' A few beads of sweat had appeared above his top lip.

I shook my head. It was his time to shine, Ryebrook Funeral Home's time, not mine. 'You'll be great. Do you need me to get you a glass of water?'

He nervously ran a finger under his shirt collar. 'No, no, I'd better get it over with.'

I'd never imagined Frank to be so scared of public speaking. The music was turned down, the chatter silenced by the tap-tapping on a microphone. Frank had taken to the small stage, still pulling at his collar as if he was being strangled.

'Er, excuse me, ladies and gentlemen. If I could have your attention for just a moment? My name is Frank Burns and I'm the owner of Ryebrook Funeral Home.'

He cleared his throat. I remembered, with a wry smile, thinking when I first met him how differently his company might have fared if he'd used his surname for the name of the business.

'I wanted to welcome you all to our annual Love of My Light service. This is a time for both reflection, and to give thanks to those who've been by your side through the hard times. We understand that no words will take away any of the pain of losing a loved one, but by coming together and marking this night with love and light, we hope to keep their memories alive. I'd like to say a huge thank you to my amazing colleagues Linda Bates and Grace Salmon, who we have to thank for this carnival-like atmosphere today.' My cheeks flamed as a few people turned and raised glasses in my direction. 'We should remember our loved ones as they were in life. Celebrating them and all they meant to us. Death isn't the end of the relationship we have with them. I can personally imagine my late wife Margaret having a go on the carousel.' In all these years working for him he'd never mentioned his wife. He smiled. 'She'd have to beat me to it!'

He'd almost balked when I'd told him of my plans for the entertainment but now, surrounded by joviality not sorrow, he seemed grateful that he'd given me the chance.

'What I would like you all to do now, before we get back to the celebrations and the buffet, is to invite you to come to the front and join us in lighting a candle in memory of a loved one. Perhaps take a moment to collect your thoughts and then place the candles on the row of shelves behind. Obviously these are real flames so please be responsible. I will stop wittering on now and let you all experience what we do at Ryebrook Funeral Home. Our aim is to bring light into a dark time, and here, this evening, I'm sure that this will be achieved.'

He took an awkward bow at the smattering of applause and shuffled from the stage, wiping the beads of sweat from his forehead and giving me a thumbs-up.

'How was I?'

'Great.' I smiled then paused. 'Actually, do you mind if I do say something?'

'Of course not. This is your event, Grace.' I saw a surprised look pass between him and Linda. Grace Salmon, the wallflower, wanted to get on stage and speak, but I did. I really did.

I willed my legs to walk the short distance into the spotlight and cleared my throat, blinking back the light and the blur of faces before me. Gosh, there were actually quite a lot of people here. *Come on, Grace.* I wanted to do this for Ms Norris, for Henry and Sam, for me.

'Excuse me.' The microphone buzzed as I banged it too close to my lips. I winced. 'Sorry, if I can just have your attention for a moment longer?'

The murmuring crowd died down and conversations ceased as people turned to face me.

'My name is Grace Salmon and I'd just like to add to what Frank has said.' I swallowed the saliva pooling in my mouth as the many pairs of inquisitive eyes fixed on me.

'One of the things we at Ryebrook Funeral Home are conscious about not saying to anyone who walks in through our door is "I know how you feel". People may have said this to you to try and be helpful, as we can all recognise just how helpless you can be at a time of loss, but it's such a meaningless phrase. No one apart from you knows how you feel. I know how *I* feel, but you don't, and vice versa.' I paused. 'Grief can feel so utterly alienating and lonely. It's like no one in the whole world understands what you're going through. Except, well, the thing is, we know more than we realise we do.

'Look around at those next to you. The thing that you, and the woman on your left or the man on your right, the thing everyone in this room has in common, is that you've all experienced loss. This room is full of others who are on this journey with you. We all know *a little* about how the person next to us is feeling: the hurt, the pain, the regrets and the emptiness. Those stood shoulder to shoulder with you, these perfect strangers know this too.

'It's taken me a while to realise this. In fact, it's taken me many years to understand that although I don't know *exactly* what you're going through, just as you don't know *exactly* what I'm going through, I do know that we have grief and loss in common. We're not in this alone. I learnt this thanks to a group of unlikely friends who met in a musty-smelling church hall every Friday evening. This collection of people, who have all loved and lost, are now very good friends, but new members are always welcome to join even if it is a club membership no one really wants.'

I paused to smile at Raj who gave me a big thumbs-up.

'On the far wall you'll see the names of those we hold in our hearts and minds this evening.' I pointed at the large projector that was gently sliding through name after name of clients. 'Please take the time you need to cry or sit silently with your grief, but also head outside and experience the light that life still offers. By living, having fun, smiling and moving forwards, we are proof that we can bear the scars we have been given and refuse to allow our pain to sink us. It's not easy but we're here for you and you're here for each other. We are all together on this journey, never forget that.'

I nodded at the sound engineer to play the calming track I'd picked for this moment, and stepped out of the spotlight. My heart was galloping in my chest and my palms were clammy from gripping the microphone, but I felt a lot lighter.

*

As the quiet classical music played, people lined up to add their flaming tea-light to the growing collection. I took my place. I had four candles that I wanted to light. I waved briefly to Raj and Rani who were lining up behind Deano and Julie. If I wasn't mistaken, those two seemed awfully close. I wondered if he'd persuaded her to join a Bowie fan club. I'd already seen Marcus and his mum having a go on the fairground rides, and spotted Alma and a much chubbier Purdy outside.

I took a spot on my own, away from a man and his

wife who nodded hello as I passed. They were there to remember her dad, Colin, a man who'd loved Manchester United and real ale, who'd passed away suddenly from a heart attack. I gingerly reached out to light the first tea light, hovering a flame over the sealed wick.

'For you, Ms Norris. Thank you for changing my world more than you will ever realise.' I picked up the one next to it. 'And for you, Henry, it's time to say goodbye. I'm not angry anymore, I just wish I could have helped you when you needed me. I'm sorry.'

I tried to keep a steady hand as I lit the third candle. Tears were gently falling down my cheeks.

'For you, Sam, our baby boy, thank you for keeping Daddy company. He wasn't perfect but neither am I.'

Since coming to terms with the truth that Maria had forced me to believe, I thought of Henry in pulses, in waves, the pain lessening, but still there in memories. It would always be there. I would just learn to grow around it. I thought back to how neurotic I had been in my desperation to give others the perfect goodbye but actually how, at the end of the day, you didn't only get one chance to say goodbye; they would never really leave you and you would never let them. With Henry and Sam and Ms Norris, I still wanted to have them in my heart and mind, despite the pain. I would never really say goodbye to them. I lit the fourth and final tea light, trying to steady my hand.

'Callum, wherever you are, I hope you're doing OK. I will be here for you whenever you need me again.'

I stared for a minute or two at the hypnotic flames.

The heat warmed my heart, which felt full and content for the first time in a long time. I used my sleeve to wipe my eyes and collect myself. There was a party I needed to get to.

Chapter 47

'I'm so glad I found you! I've been looking for you everywhere. Gosh, there's so many people here,' Mel sang. She was struggling to peel off a thick scarf as she came into the warmth, just as I was leaving. I wanted to have a go on the fairground rides. 'The boys are outside with Nick, high on sugar from the candy floss stall I imagine. We'll be peeling them off the ceiling later. I bet they won't want to go to bed but, oh well, a treat every so often doesn't kill you, does it!?' She was talking ten to the dozen. Barely pausing for air. *Wait, was she nervous?*

'So, I said to Nick –'

'Mel, are you OK?' I placed an arm on her coat sleeve, hoping she would take a breath.

She gave up on the tangled scarf and finally met my eyes.

'Grace, I'm so sorry I haven't been in touch. I feel awful. Cal told me everything and, well, I wasn't sure if I should intrude. And now I'm kicking myself because of course I should have seen how you were. You two had grown really close, and when something bad happens you need people to check in with you, not give you time and space to get over it, isn't that right? God, I'm babbling again, aren't I?'

I laughed gently and helped loop the chunky scarf over her frizzy hair.

'It's lovely to see you, too.'

'And you, you're looking well. You've dyed your hair. It suits you!'

I hadn't bothered going back to Andre, instead Chatty Claire had done a good job on stripping the red out and softening it, so it resembled more my natural colour.

'Oh, thanks. I fancied a change…'

'It looks lovely. You still doing that Grief Club thing?' she asked. 'I was so proud of Callum for going to that. I think it's a great idea.'

'Yep, it's still running. I've missed a few sessions as things have been, well, you know…'

She didn't know, but nodded politely. I desperately wanted to address the elephant in the room, but I didn't know how to bring him up.

'So –'

'So –'

We both awkwardly laughed.

'You first.'

'I just wanted to say thank you for everything. I'm sure you're sick of all the people coming up to you telling you that.'

I shook my head. 'How could anyone get sick of that? But it's just us doing our jobs.'

'No, you go above and beyond your job description.' She paused. 'The inquest date has finally been set, apparently there was a cockup and Abbie's slipped through the system, which is why it's taken them so long to sort it out.'

My heart clenched. To be reduced to a number in a long list of files and then to be misplaced, as if denying you existed in the first place.

'But…' She sighed deeply. 'They've finally got their act together and have set it for the end of December. It's ridiculous how long it has taken but at least it won't go into next year. We all need to start with a clean slate. Anyway, Callum will be coming back for that.'

'Back?'

She looked surprised. 'Yeah, didn't he tell you that he'd moved up north? Edinburgh to be precise. He's living with Rory. You met him at his birthday? Not that I thought that was the wisest move, but actually it hasn't been all parties and beer. He seems to be doing well.' She sighed in relief. I thought he'd just been to stay with Rory for a break, not that he'd moved there. No wonder he hadn't RSVP'd to tonight. 'Getting away from it all was clearly the best thing for him, in order to try and move on. Oh, and Daniel has left too. Did you know?'

I shook my head.

'Yeah, his studio is empty and no one has heard from him.' She pursed her lips. 'Probably for the best. I actually thought I'd come and light a candle for Abbie. To show there were no hard feelings. What she did was disgusting, but it has done my brother a favour. It has pushed him to live the life he wants, not the one she chose for them, so for that I'm grateful to her.'

'You must miss him. Callum, I mean.'

'Yeah, we all do. We went up to stay during the last half term, which was nice. The boys loved Edinburgh Zoo.'

I couldn't help myself. 'Do you think he'll ever come back to Ryebrook? For good, I mean?'

'Maybe. He's thinking of putting the house up for sale. Too many memories.' She fixed her eyes on mine as if searching for something. 'I know we're here... but I get the feeling he's not sure if there's anything else to keep him here...'

She rummaged in her bag, flinging out scrunched up tissues and Chocolate Buttons wrappers.

'Before I forget. He asked me to give you this.' She handed me a sealed envelope. 'Whoops, sorry about the sweet wrapper stuck to it.' I turned it over in my hands. 'I know, a letter. How retro. I told him about tonight but he couldn't make it all the way down in time. Right, well, I'd better go and light this then check on the boys.'

She gave me cheery wave and told me to call her soon. I held Callum's letter as gently as if it was a sparrow with a broken wing. Unsure if I wanted to know what it contained.

Chapter 48

I pulled my coat tight against the chilly night air. Everything had been packed up. Frank had thanked me about fifteen times for such a good event.

Apparently he had suggestions for a summer celebration too. He'd asked how I'd afforded the night. I told him I'd made the small budget stretch, not wanting to tell him that I'd used a large chunk of my rainy day fund. I'd wanted the money to go on something special. I had five years of birthday parties I'd never celebrated and holidays I'd never been on, so it seemed fitting to spend the cash I'd squirrelled away living so frugally on this.

A strange cocktail of emotions coursed through my veins. I thought of all the people I'd spoken to that evening, who'd told me that acceptance and moving forward were made possible thanks to the support of the people around them. Back at work on Monday would be a fresh start, a chance to help families say their goodbyes, but without giving everything I had. I needed to keep something back for me.

The streets were quiet. I walked slowly until I'd found the place I wanted to be. The bench that Ms Norris had taken me to. The twinkling lights of Ryebrook spread out before me. It really was the best secret spot in the town, one that I knew would become our place. A place to visit and reflect on everything. I rubbed a hand against the metal plaque and closed my eyes. It was as if I could get closer to Ms Norris in some way.

'*In memory of Donald Norris and his big sister Edwina, who never forgot about him.*'

I'd had the tribute amended. I really hoped she would approve. I leant forward and gently brushed a gloved hand over the text. *This is for you, Ms Norris.*

Winter had taken its toll and stolen the lush green leaves from the apple tree and the bushes that had once half hidden this spot. The trees had shut down for the cold snap, but would re-emerge in spring. Apples would grow and fall once more. Life carried on.

I remember the first autumn after Henry had gone, watching the leaves die and drop to the ground, turning a crisp golden brown. It had stopped me in my tracks. Those leaves had been barely buds, full of life, when he and our son had been alive. Going through the seasons had been the hardest. They would never see the air turn crisp, auburn leaves falling, the spring sun melting the hard frost, the pure yellow daffodils blooming on grass verges. All the things we took for granted took on such a deep significance because *they* would never be there to witness them with me. Watching nature live and die and live again, when they wouldn't, was something I hadn't been prepared to deal with.

I pulled the letter out and tugged off my mittens,

carefully placing them on my lap, my fingertips tingling in the frosty air. I took a deep breath and slid a finger under the envelope seal. I imagined his fingerprints under mine, invisible but connecting. It was a sheet of handwritten A4 notepaper. I wanted to devour the whole thing, skipping forward to the end and inhaling it in one. But I forced myself to read each word, in his small cursive writing, as slowly as I could. Who knew what it would contain, or if I would hear from him again.

Dear Grace,

I can't remember the last time I wrote a letter, so please excuse my awful handwriting. I needed this to come from the heart, not to be easily edited or add an emoji in place of my feelings. If you've got this, then Mel has done her part. I'm sure she said herself how shit she feels about not being in touch with you more. It's been a bit of a mental time for all of us. I guess people think they know how they'll act during the tough times, but when it comes to it you can't control how you'll deal with things.

I'm living in Edinburgh with Rory. You met him at my birthday party. He's away with work a lot so I spend my days going on runs around the city, eating too much shortbread (cliché, I know) and generally taking care of myself. I've also stopped drinking. Have you ever been here? There's this amazing spot at the top of Carlton Hill where you can see the whole city spread before you. You would love it.

I've even got a counsellor, or a therapist as the Yanks would say. Shane. He's this big, fat, balding Scotsman. He swears quite a bit and has a dodgy obsession with deep-fried haggis but he's a good guy. He encourages me to talk about everything and anything.

We talk about you a lot. I really hope you're OK and not beating yourself up over what happened with Henry. You did nothing wrong, please remember that.

I've also been busy with work. Remember the Stratton Estate, I told you about it before? Well I'm really enjoying putting the finishing touches in place. It's only an hour on the train from here, so I'm able to go there when I'm needed. I hope it will be finished in the spring. And that's thanks to you.

In fact, it's all down to you. Me being here, getting help from Shane, getting space and perspective to realise that what happened wasn't anyone's fault. Mel would still say that fate played a part, but I'm learning that fate isn't this plaster you can apply to every wound.

Shane is probably right when he tells me there's a lot of history, not just with Abbie, but with my own parents, that I need to figure out and come to peace with. It's for the best if I do this on my own and at my own pace. That's why I've not been in touch. It's not that I don't think about you, Grace, I do. You may not even want anything more from me. You might get this letter and wonder what I'm going on about but I hope that you feel the same. I believe you did. You wear your heart on your sleeve like that.

Take care Grace.
Amazing Grace.

Callum x

The sound of a siren echoing through the town brought me back to reality. I could no longer feel my backside. I was crying without realising. His words blurred under teardrops. My heart swelled with hope. We both needed time and time was a healer after all. The paper trembled between my shivering fingers. My breath curled from my chattering teeth. I felt like I was waking from a deep sleep.

I folded the letter and put it back in my pocket, my fingers clumsy from the cold. I stared at my trembling hands and realised it was the first time they weren't red raw from cleaning. I rubbed my upper arms to try and warm up, and put my mittens back on. My feet began to find feeling once more as I made my way back to my flat. I knew that I'd see him again. I would just have to be patient. If I could wait five years for a man who could never come back to me, then I could wait a little longer for one who would. I had enough to keep me busy until then. More time for fun and friendship and less for cleaning and worrying. I felt renewed and excited for the person I would be when he returned. Not trying to be like Abbie or anyone else, but to be me. A better, happier version of me.

I glanced at my watch. I'd told Raj that I would help him rehearse, early tomorrow morning, for the Talent Show taking place in the evening. All of the Grief Club members would be there supporting him too. He'd bought a new suit, a god-awful shiny deep purple thing that Rani had embellished with black felt coffins and a garish sequinned skull on the back. It was hideous and he loved it. Enough people avoided talking about death, so why shouldn't he try to bring some light humour to what was inevitably going to happen to all of us? Isn't that what all the best comedians did? Forced us to look at the tough things and see the funny side?

I reached the main road to cross. Despite it being late there were still a few cars, two taxis and a night bus trundling down the road. I paused, and looked only twice before crossing. Well, you've got to live a little, haven't you?

Acknowledgements

This novel may be all about Grace but it's also inspired by events and people I never imagined I would ever cross paths with in real life.

A special mention to Jackie at Cruse Bereavement, who taught me that grief doesn't have to be suffered in silence, and heartfelt thanks to Nicki Whitting at Co-op Funerals, who handled my father's service with dignity, respect and patience. What you and others in the funeral industry do is beyond selfless, bringing light to those in darkness.

I scrapped a whole novel in order to write *How to Say Goodbye* as I felt I had to share Grace's story. A daunting task when you're pregnant *and* looking after a toddler but, thanks to some awesome people, I was able to do it all and keep my sanity (just!). A huge thank you to Jo and Rob Huggins for being A-star stand-in parents as I escaped to writing retreats, picking me up when I felt overwhelmed and generally being incredible good souls. Also, thanks to the yummy mummies who inspire me to keep juggling those balls – Claire, Emma, Kirsty and superstar Jen.

Thanks as always to my supportive family, with a

special shout-out to my aunty Jennie for emergency childcare, the in-laws (including Emily - welcome to the fold!) and my incredible mum for being my rock during the darkest days.

I'm so incredibly lucky to have a fab bunch of writers to call on for support, inspiration and a good old moan when things aren't going to plan. The Book Camp crew are now like sisters from other misters – thanks especially to Kirsty and Cesca for being early readers, and Izzy for providing many Classic FM lols. Shout-out to Charlie Haynes at Urban Writers for knowing that being able to switch off and focus on writing, never far from a slab of cake, is my happy place.

Thanks to the most wonderful team who have worked hard to polish this novel so it shines – in particular, Juliet Mushens and Clio Cornish. Trust me, with these women on your side you can do anything. Also, a big thanks to the talented HQ crew for the gorgeous cover and tireless backstage support, and the CaskieMushens team for their expertise and book cheerleading skills.

I have the loveliest readers and social media supporters whose retweets, likes, comments and messages help make writing feel a whole lot less lonely. If you enjoy a book then please leave a review, tell a friend or shout about it, as it makes such a difference! A special shout-out to Sharon McGrath Vasser and Tabitha Thorn for their winning name suggestions via Facebook – Henry is here because of you.

Of course, none of this would be possible without the insane support from my own special tribe. John,

Everleigh and Auben. This is thanks to you and all for you. I love you more than you know.

Thank you for picking up this book. If you can identify with any part of the story, please don't think you have to cope with what you are going through on your own.

There are many organisations doing wonderful things for people suffering with grief and loss including:

Cruse Bereavement Care – Run by trained volunteers (most have had their own dealings with grief and loss) covers England, Wales and Northern Ireland. Phone: 0808 808 1677 (Mon - Fri 9.30am- 5pm) or Cruse Scotland helpline: 0845 600 2227

Samaritans – Confidential support for people experiencing feelings of distress or despair. Phone: 116 123 (free 24-hour helpline)

Mind – Promotes the views and needs of people with mental health problems. Phone: 0300 123 3393 (Mon-Fri, 9am-6pm)

Anxiety UK – Charity providing support if you've been diagnosed with an anxiety condition. Phone: 03444 775 774 (Mon-Fri, 9.30am-5.30pm)

ONE PLACE. MANY STORIES

Bold, innovative and
empowering publishing.

FOLLOW US ON:

@HQStories